THE SPARK

JULES WAKE

One More Chapter
a division of HarperCollins*Publishers* Ltd
1 London Bridge Street
London SE1 9GF

HarperCollins *Publishers*
1st Floor, Watermarque Building, Ringsend Road
Dublin 4, Ireland

www.harpercollins.co.uk

This paperback edition 2021

First published in Great Britain in ebook format
by HarperCollins*Publishers* 2020

A catalogue record of this book
is available from the British Library

ISBN: 978-0-00-844434-1

Printed and bound in Great Britain by
CPI Group (UK) Ltd, Croydon CR0 4YY

For Sarah Wright née Spark. It seems fitting that this one should be for you, with love and thanks for an enduring friendship x

Chapter One

When my phone binged at ten to twelve, five minutes before I was due to leave, I could have predicted that the text message would be from my cousin Shelley. What I couldn't have predicted was that her absence that day would change my life.

Sorry babe, I'm not going to make it.

Why was I even surprised? Spontaneous was her middle name, which made her possibly the most unreliable creature this side of the M25 but also possibly the most fun, which, when you had a childhood like mine, was a blessing of the mightiest order.

I could have been miffed. After all, she'd insisted I come with her because we'd be the only youngsters at her parents' annual barbecue bash. I glanced at my watch. Nope. Couldn't do it. She might be able to let Aunty Lynn down with no qualms – she was her daughter – but I had a few more scruples. Plus, it was a glorious sunny Sunday and I had no other plans, no garden, and no food in the fridge. Aunty Lynn was a bloody fabulous cook and believed in the feeding of the five thousand, which meant there'd be enough leftovers not only to see me through the week but also to take into work, where her interesting salads, incredible pavlova and chocolate cake would all be hugely appreciated, especially by the children. Lynn was nothing if not generous – well, apart from the fact that it seemed she'd hogged all of the giving and sharing genes and left none for my mum.

Giving myself a quick once-over in the mirror, I decided that my navy shorts and pale-pink vest top, both of which had seen better days, weren't going to offend Aunty Lynn or Uncle Richard. Where hospitality was concerned, they were of the laid-back, the more the merrier persuasion. Anything went, as long as you brought a bottle. Pulling on my tennis shoes, because I planned on having a few drinks and the short walk across town was rather pleasant, I grabbed a four-pack of Budweiser I'd bought especially for the occasion and set off.

It was the sort of sunny day that makes you think that the weather might actually last and that the rest of the summer will be like this. There were a few wispy, cotton-wool-ball puffs of white in the sky, and the sky itself was that vibrant blue that feels as if it has depth to it, and as you stare at it you can almost see that it stretches right to the edge of the universe, which I think it probably did. Or maybe it didn't. This set me off thinking about the sky and the sun, wishing perhaps I'd paid a bit more attention in physics... No, I didn't. I bloody hated physics at school. Was glad to give it up. But I felt good that I'd sort of been pondering important things as I'd walked along. My job had been busy over the week, demanding on an emotional level which I was always careful to pack away in a metaphorical box. It's the sort of job that can consume you and take over your headspace, which is why pseudo-physics and the contemplation of bigger things were especially good for my mental wellbeing. It's the sort of job which, if you let it, could really drag you under.

And all this pondering had taken me through town, along the High Street, across the park with its fenced-in playground of busy swings and slides, teeming with small people who looked like plastic Fisher Price toys in their brightly coloured clothing, and now up the slight incline of Pettyfeather Lane to my aunt and uncle's modest-looking semi. Modest-looking as in Tardis-like because the front is deceptive: once through a narrow, dark hall, it opens out into an enormous open-plan kitchen-diner-living-area with a whole wall of bi-fold doors leading onto a spacious, perfect-for-parties patio.

The front door was ajar, which immediately made me smile. It meant everyone was in the garden and as I walked up the short drive, I could hear that happy cacophony of a party in full swing. I stepped inside, skirting round a few discarded pairs of shoes, dumped handbags and jackets in the hallway. In this small market town, a forty-minute commute from London, people were pretty trusting and my aunt and uncle's contemporaries and neighbours, having reached suburban, reasonably well-heeled mid-life, took the local low crime-rate and all-round decency of people for granted. It was a world away from the experiences of the people I worked with but it gave me hope that there could be a better way of life for them one day.

'Jess, Jess!' hollered my uncle in greeting from his spot behind the breakfast bar where he was doing battle with a Prosecco bottle, carefully easing out the cork. In his excitement, he let go of the cork, which promptly shot out with the pop of a gunshot and effervescent liquid foamed out of the neck of the bottle, which he waggled in his hand. 'Quick, lovely, grab yourself a glass. Don't want it going to waste. This is the good stuff. At least eight quid from Tesco.' He waved the bottle at me enthusiastically which wasn't doing the wastage any good at all.

Luckily, my darling rellies, unlike their daughter Shelley with her spontaneous unreliability, are totally by-the-book, stick-in-the-mud reliable (except they're so not stick-in-the-mud personality-wise), and the flutes were exactly where they always were when they threw a party, just like the large plastic trug filled with ice and water and lager bottles, which I neatly sidestepped as I grabbed a glass and rushed to rescue Uncle Richard.

'Well held, that girl.' He filled my glass up. 'How are you? Do you remember Fiona? Fiona, you've met Jess, my niece, right? Sorry, love, you know your cousin's buggered off. Shame.' He turned to Fiona who lived next door and whom I had met a gazillion times. 'Of course, Jess is our favourite daughter. The daughter we wish we'd had instead of Shelley.'

4

Fiona laughed. 'I'm not sure you're allowed to say things like that.'

'You don't live with Shelley,' said Richard darkly.

'Hi, Uncle Rich,' I said, giving him a quick hug, holding out my Prosecco glass so it wouldn't spill as he gave me an effusive hug back. 'And yeah, I should be favourite daughter. She's bloody rubbish.' I grinned at him as Aunty Lynn bustled up. 'Dumping me for some bloke she met five minutes ago.'

Shelley was incapable of being without a man, whereas I was a bit – no, make that *a lot* pickier. It might have had something to do with my job.

'Jess.' My aunt gave me a big hug and then stood back with that typical, maternal cock of her head. 'Are you eating properly? I can feel ribs.'

I laughed. 'You said that last time I came, and that was after Christmas day when you force-fed me a ton of turkey and made me take the rest of the Christmas cake home.'

'I probably did. You're so lucky.' She prodded her own contented-with-life rolls around her middle. 'It would be lovely to get rid of these. I should join you on your parkruns.' She pulled such a mournful face that both Fiona and I burst out laughing.

Richard put his arm around her. 'Don't you dare. I love you just the way you are.'

She brightened, patting his face. 'I've trained you well. It's only taken me thirty years.' Suddenly she straightened as if remembering something. 'Now Jess, why don't you go outside. It's far too nice to be inside.'

Given that the glorious weather was one of the principle

reasons for coming, I did as I was told, although most people did when Aunty Lynn was around.

I spotted him the minute I stepped out onto the patio. Well, you couldn't really miss him. He was the only other person my age. OK, and he just happened to be big, golden and … just downright gorgeous. He had one foot propped on the small wall edging the patio and he was leaning forward on his knee, lifting a beer bottle to his lips as the sun glinted off the blond hairs on his arms, which were tanned and muscled in all the right places. He had almost white-blond hair, tied back before exploding in a bundle of scruffy curls, and matching eyebrows that made him look like a Thunderbirds puppet. He wore baggy shorts which came down to his knees and were so scruffy they made mine look as though they'd been tailored by Alexander McQueen, the most hideous brown sandals (think: a pair of dead turtles) that were so middle-agedly awful that they were almost trendy, and one of those wife-beater vests in white (although, to cut him a bit of slack, it was very clean) that revealed plenty of bare golden skin (highlighted by design? I wondered) and a well-defined body (definitely highlighted by design). Oh dear, someone fancied himself.

I took first, second and third surreptitious glances – he was so not my type – but for some bizarre reason my hormones had other ideas and were jumping up and down in a state of parlous excitement that made my legs a little wobbly and my pulse take off like a bolting horse zigzagging all over a race course. There was erratic and then there were A&E-bound levels. All of which was completely ridiculous because I did not do laid-back surfie types. Seriously, he looked like he'd stepped off an exotic beach and left his bikini babe and surfboard behind. And as for those wrap-around sunglasses ... did he think he was playing in a Test Match for Australia?

I think I was protesting a bit too much. I wasn't normally this judgemental about someone I hadn't even spoken to, and I definitely didn't have this type of reaction just from looking at someone. I mean, I've had crushes on good-looking, totally unattainable, never-going-to-meet-them film stars and singers over the years, but never this instant zing of attraction for a real-life flesh-(oh yes, gorgeous flesh)-and-blood person.

With all these thoughts flashing through my brain, I think I must have been giving out flares of static electricity or something, because the blond god suddenly looked up, a bit like one of those glorious antlered stags scenting something downwind that you see on wildlife programmes on the Scottish Highlands. He looked straight at me and a fizz of excitement like an out-of-control Catherine wheel burst in my stomach, frying every last butterfly leaping about in there.

His wide mouth curved in a generous smile and he pushed up his sunglasses onto the top of his head.

'Hi there,' he said with friendly ease, crinkles appearing around properly deep blue eyes. Yeah, he was a regular perfect Adonis. And there was something in his eyes that said whatever I was feeling (and I told myself that it was just lust at first sight), I wasn't on my own.

'Hi,' I replied, relieved to hear that my voice hadn't let me down.

'Nice to see someone of my own age.' The warmth of his smile wrapped itself around my heart. Well, if not that then something was going on. There were some very weird fluttery feelings in my chest cavity. And there was definitely a level of interest in his gaze.

'I've just had an in-depth conversation about lawn maintenance with a man who probably went to school with my grandpa and before that – don't get me wrong, she was a very nice lady, but she was asking me if I could recommend a good electrician or a builder. Random or what?'

I smiled at his slightly bewildered expression. 'It's probably the vest.'

'This?' He yanked it down, which exposed a pair of smooth, almost hairless, perfectly toned pecs and a little vee of dark-blond hair between.

I swallowed and nodded.

'It was the only clean T-shirt I had,' he said. 'Everything is on the line drying … or at least I hope it is, otherwise I'll have nothing to wear to work tomorrow. And that will not go down well.' He flashed me a killer smile full of laughter.

'No, I imagine not.' I smiled back, doing my best not to think of him naked. 'What do you do?' I paused. 'Oh God, did I really just say that? I think I've turned into my uncle and aunt.' I nodded back through the bi-fold doors behind us towards the adults in the kitchen.

'Their party?'

'Yes. My cousin asked me to come as moral youthful support … except she reneged about half an hour ago.'

'Ouch.'

'Oh, it's not so bad. Have you seen the food yet?'

'Actually, it seems like a very nice party. I'm rather glad I came now.' He gave me another smile, this one a little more considered as he took a pull on his beer. 'My parents moved here about six months ago.' He nodded to the end of the garden. 'They back on to your aunt and uncle's. I'm housesitting while my folks are away, looking after the dog, and Lynn insisted I pop in.' He shrugged, with a twinkle in his eye. 'I was at a loose end and food was promised.'

I laughed. 'You definitely came for the right reason. Although I have first dibs on leftovers.'

'Did you come packing Tupperware?' he asked.

'No.' I couldn't help smiling at his humorous expression.

'Well,' he said with mock seriousness, 'all bets are off then.' He chinked my glass with his beer bottle.

'I might have to pull the favourite-niece card.'

'How many nieces do they have?' His laughing frown made me smile. In fact, I don't think I could have stopped myself smiling back at him if my life had depended on it.

'Only me.'

'That doesn't count. And I think favourite neighbour probably trumps that.'

'Favourite neighbour?' I echoed.

'On account of I'm quiet, good at carrying heavy things, and excellent at plant-watering when people are away.'

'So what do you do when you're not housesitting for your folks?' I was guessing carpenter or gardener; he looked as if he spent a lot of time outdoors, or maybe he still lived with his parents and didn't have a job.

'I'm a primary school teacher. Over in Redlands.'

'What, St Bernard's?' I certainly hadn't pegged him for a primary school teacher and definitely not at one that was dedicated to special needs.

He nodded. 'You know it?'

'I've heard of it. I deal with a lot of local schools through my work. Gosh, that must be … interesting. How old are the kids you teach?'

'Interesting is one way of putting it,' he said, his smile broad and full of sunshine. 'But I love it. I have a class of nine. They're aged between nine and eleven. Key stage 2. Nearly all with some form of autism.'

'That must be difficult. Coping with all those different needs.'

He looked at me slightly surprised. 'Most people think it must be an easy gig.' The light in his eyes dimmed for a second. 'They assume kids with special needs don't need an education. Or are too difficult to teach, so I don't need to bother.' There was a fierceness in his eyes, and if I hadn't already been halfway to head-over-heels in *something* with him, that would have pushed me over the edge.

I beamed at him. I couldn't help myself. And I suddenly realised that I could be completely open with him, completely honest.

'And I bet you do bother. A lot.'

'I do. I love working with my kids. They're a real bunch of characters and every one of them deserves to have the best chance in life that they can get. It's my job to make sure I give them that. Some of them are incredibly bright, super talented, but they just don't have the mechanics to cope with life in the same way that you or I do.'

'I'm impressed.'

'Don't be. I'm lucky. I'm doing a job I love. So what do you do?'

I smiled broadly. 'I bet some people feel a bit insubstantial when you ask them after telling them what you do.'

He shrugged. 'I'm not a saint or anything. I have good days and bad. And sometimes,' he paused with another of those charming twinkles, 'I tell the children off.'

'Shame on you. Those poor little angels,' I added in a mockney accent.

'Angels my arse, not when the little devils decide to superglue my shoes to my socks while I'm wearing them.'

'I won't ask,' I said, giggling now. Honestly, I felt a bit drunk on this smiley warm-eyed exchange; it was going to my head. Although I didn't feel fuzzy or out of focus. No, I felt sharper and more in tune than I'd ever felt before.

'Well, if I could wash the shoes and socks together, it'd save a whole heap of time getting dressed in the mornings.' We both laughed at the ridiculous image, our eyes meeting and then holding for that fraction of a second too long, but then neither of us looked away.

'I'm Sam,' he said, holding out a hand, still meeting my gaze, those too-blue eyes dancing with amusement and other lovely things. He was sunshine and happiness and it all seemed to be brimming out of his eyes.

'I'm Jess. Nice to meet you, Sam.'

'So what do you do, Jess?'

'I work for a women's refuge,' I said, going on to name the nearest town just off the M1.

'Wow,' he echoed my earlier words, 'that must be difficult too.'

I lifted my shoulders. 'It has its moments. My job is to help the women – and often their children too – get back on their feet. Most of the time, they've fled with nothing. There's a lot of liaising with schools, social workers, doctors, hospitals and, sometimes,' the corners of my mouth turned down, 'the police.' Not many of the women I worked with ever went through with it and pressed charges; their self-esteem had been too eviscerated for that.

'Sounds like a tough job. Makes mine look easy.' The admiration in his eyes made me shrug.

'Makes me appreciate how easy I've had it,' I said. 'And how lucky most people are and they don't even realise it.'

'That's very true,' he chinked his beer bottle against my glass again.

I'm not sure where the next hour went. Sam was the easiest person to talk to and we just seemed to have so much in common. We both disliked *Fawlty Towers* with a passion (and agreed that, horribly dated or not, comedy in the 70s must have been woeful); we both loved *The Big Bang Theory*; we both thought David Tennant was the best Doctor Who ever, adored *Hitchhiker's Guide to the Galaxy*, and both believed that Imagine Dragons was simply the best band ever, although Sam insisted that Coldplay came a very close second.

Despite my stomach starting to make grumbling noises, I felt a distinct lurch of disappointment when my aunt yelled, 'Food is served,' through the open doorway, making me realise that there were plenty of people in the garden but

I'd been so intent on Sam that I'd been unaware of anyone else around us.

'Good. I'm starving.' He gave me a quick once-over, his gaze running down my legs and then back up. I saw his Adam's apple bob. 'Are you eating?'

'Hell, yes,' I said. 'Why do you think I'm here?'

'Phew. I thought for an awful moment, with a stunning figure like that, you might be one of those lettuce sniffers.' He winked.

With a giggle, I shook my head vehemently, although I'd taken the 'stunning figure' on board to pore over later. 'Uhnuh, I love my food.' We headed inside and fell into line together as we collected plates, napkins and cutlery.

Aunty Lynn had laid out a fine selection of salads and breads, while Uncle Richard had clearly done sterling service over hot coals as there were several plates of sausages, chicken and pepper kebabs, and home-made lamb burgers.

'Well, you'd never guess,' he said shooting my legs an approving look.

'Thanks. It makes the parkrun I did yesterday worthwhile.'

'What? Here in Tring?'

'Yes.'

'I did it yesterday! It's a bugger. That hill's a killer. I normally do one over at Rushmere Country Park in Leighton Buzzard.'

'Is that where you live when you're not housesitting?'

'Yes, although I should move here really. I spend so much time this way. I play for Meadows Way Cricket Club at the weekend and spend a couple of nights a week in the nets there.'

'Nice. Well, I think it is. I know nothing about cricket, but I've been to the clubhouse a few times.' The cricket club was on the edge of town and had two big pitches bounded by high, well-trimmed hedges, between which was a large two-storey clubhouse with balconies looking out over the grounds and rather beautiful views of the nearby Chiltern hills.

'You should come up sometime.' He paused and looked away at the food. 'Gosh, this looks amazing.'

We ended up sitting shoulder to shoulder on the small wall seat outside, eating in almost companionable silence. Something had slithered into that earlier easiness. I could sense it in Sam's fierce attention to his food.

I kept my head down and carried on eating, conscious of the warmth of his leg next to mine and the movement of his forearm occasionally brushing my skin as he ate.

His fork dropped with a clatter to his plate.

'Jess, there's something I need to tell you.'

He lifted his head, frown lines etched into his forehead. 'This is going to sound like a proper cliché but I really like you...'

The *but* might as well have been there in ten-foot-high shouty capitals.

'Don't worry. It was nice to meet you.' I went to stand up but he put a hand on my arm.

'No, I mean it. I really like you. I'd like to stay in touch but ... I've got a girlfriend.'

'Hey, it's fine,' I said brightly, because really it was. He was a lovely bloke and we'd spent a nice (Jess? Seriously? Nice?), OK, bloody lovely afternoon together but that was all it was. 'It was lovely to meet you.' I ignored the heavy lump that seemed to have taken up residence in the pit of my stomach and the sudden sense of the sun going in.

'Jess, wait. Don't go.'

He stood in front of me, so close that I could see the quick pulse in his neck and the rapid rise of his chest. I think seeing his flustered state was probably what made me acquiesce when he took my hand and led me down to the bottom of the garden. Gorgeous as he was, and wonderful as the spark between us was, having a girlfriend was a red line. I'd seen the bitterness seep into my mother's soul when my dad left her for another woman, warping her spirit and stealing her positivity. The consequent fallout had caused cataclysmic changes in my life. Stepping on another woman's toes was something I would never do.

'Jess,' he said urgently. 'I'm sorry. I didn't mean to lead you on.'

'You didn't,' I said gently, trying to smile.

'This isn't a line, but I've never met anyone I...' he lifted his shoulders looking delightfully bemused, 'I just clicked with.' His eyes met mine, radiating sincerity and sorrow. 'I'd like to be mates with you,' his mouth pursed in a self-deprecating line, 'but I think that would last about five minutes.'

'Don't worry about it.'

'The thing is, I've been going out with Vic for four years. I've never looked at anyone else. Not once.'

'And that's good,' I said brightly, feeling horribly jealous of her.

'Can we stay in touch?'

All my instincts were telling me to say no, but the thought of him walking out of my life for ever was suddenly terrifying and I found myself saying yes.

Chapter Two

'You've got a bit of bounce in your step this morning, girl,' announced Holly, stirring her coffee for all she was worth, as though it might whip up a bit more energy for her. 'Good weekend?'

'Not bad. I've got food.' I held up a bulging carrier bag.

'Good old Aunty Lynn?'

'The very same.'

'Please say there's some of her tabbouleh in there. Ooh and that pomegranate and feta salad. I love that.'

'Might be,' I said swerving the carrier bag away from her gimme-gimme grab and crossing the kitchen to unload a series of plastic takeaway cartons into one of the large communal fridges.

'How was it here?'

One weekend a month we were on call in case there was an urgent need to offer refuge to someone. Weekends tended to be pressure points.

'Quiet. No new residents. And I think the council have finally found a place for the Thorntons.'

'Oh, that's fantastic. When do you think they'll be moving out?'

The refuge could house up to six families at a time, seven at a pinch. The Thorntons were our longest serving members of the household at the moment – Mum, three young boys and a baby. They desperately needed their own place. Most of the women that arrived – with little more than the clothes on their backs, their children clutching, if they were lucky, one prized toy – were given one bedroom, which for both practical and emotional reasons they shared with their children, although without exception the kids couldn't be prised from their side. All five Thorntons had been sharing one bedroom for the last four weeks.

There was only one lounge area with a shared TV, which led to a lot of bickering among the children, and a communal kitchen which was set up so that the residents could help themselves to the basics we stocked in the fridge. They could cook for their own family unit or for others. No one family was ever the same; some loved to cook while others barely had the energy or the strength to think about food. Having food that someone else had prepared was always a treat and it was guaranteed that Aunty Lynn's offerings would be a hit.

'They'll be moving out as soon as I can persuade the council to put a new carpet in the place. And I've spoken to the local charitable trust and they've agreed to provide curtains and bedding.'

'Oh, my aunt's neighbour has some spare bedding which she's going to donate.'

We were the queens of begging, borrowing and stealing to keep our residents in home comforts.

With coffees in hand, we drifted through to the little admin office, a somewhat grand title for the cramped space with two desks facing each other. It was a good job we liked each other so much, as we pretty much lived in each other's personal space. We were very different: Holly was pure Essex with dyed raven-black hair piled up into an ornate bun on her head with a French plait feeding into it. She wore tons of make-up and favoured bold, bright colours. The surface of her desk – well, I think under all that paper there was a surface – mirrored her personality, but at any given time, she knew where absolutely everything was. She was a demon for detail and never forgot a thing, which was jolly handy. She was also doing an OU degree in psychology and liked to involve me in the theories she was learning about at any one time.

By contrast, my desk was super tidy, but I too could also lay my hand on anything within seconds.

My first task of the morning was to try and persuade a local headteacher to take on two new children that had recently arrived with us, although there was only one place at the school. It took umpteen phone calls and several emails liaising with the county admissions team, the head, and the social worker assigned to the case before I was finally able to push away my keyboard and put down the phone to pick up the black coffee that Holly had just brought me. As I took the first life-saving sip, the bing of my phone caught my attention, and my heart skidded to a halt before kicking off like a frolicking pony.

Hi Jess. Hope you haven't troughed all those leftovers yet. Lovely to meet you at the weekend. Sam.

I picked up my phone and stared at the message. Conflicting emotions showered like meteorites: pleasure, regret, hope, guilt, annoyance. Chiefly annoyance, I realised. He had no business texting me.

'Blimey. That's a complicated look,' said Holly. 'Bad news? Good news? Indifferent news?'

'The jury's out,' I said with a sigh, holding my phone in both hands. Why had he texted me? That said he wasn't the man I thought he was. I should be pleased that it proved the point. 'I met this guy. Sam.'

'And that's him. Don't tell me, he's given you the I-just-want-to-be-friends message.'

'Sort of.'

Holly rolled her heavily kohl-lined eyes. 'See, I should write the book.'

'You'll dislocate your eyeballs one of these days if you keep doing that.'

'Whatever, sweet cheeks,' she replied with irreverent disdain. 'Are you going to text him back to tell him you weren't interested in him anyway or just keep looking at your phone as if it's got all the answers to the universe and everything?'

'Forty-two,' I said automatically, immediately thinking of mine and Sam's silly conversation (if you haven't read

Douglas Adams' *Hitchhiker's Guide to the Galaxy*, which we both had, the answer is forty-two). I sighed and put my phone down. I should ignore it. He was out of bounds. And then two seconds later I picked it up again. The message was innocuous; he hadn't done anything wrong. I wasn't doing anything wrong.

'Want me to text him for you? "Bog off, you bastard, and don't darken my inbox again."' Holly waved her bright-blue-tipped hands at me, trying to get me to hand it over.

'It's not like that.'

'Oh Lord, you've gone all moony-eyed.' Holly shuddered. 'He's not worth it. He's a man, remember.'

I rubbed my hand over my face. 'I don't know what to do. The thing is, he's really nice.' And I was scared that if I responded to the text, we could end up having one of those text flirtations where things are said that shouldn't be, especially when he had a girlfriend. There was a girl code. You don't mess with another girl's man. Another woman's husband. The code was ingrained. I'd seen the damage done to my mother. It was unfair to cause that much pain to another person who was innocent and blameless. And that didn't even begin to cover the additional casualties of any children involved.

'Who? What? Where?' asked Holly.

How could I possibly put into words that perfect storm of recognition between Sam and me? Every time I thought about it, saying *we just clicked* didn't come anywhere close to covering it. *Clicked* sounded like a seatbelt slotting home, fingers snapping; it didn't describe the feeling of completeness, the accompanying soar-away feeling as though I was taking flight, the magical, serendipitous sensation of being so in tune with another person, or the exchange of a smile because you didn't need words.

Holly would laugh her cute little pop socks off.

Particularly as it's all so unlike me. Seriously. I'm Miss Practical, a sensible, problem-solving kind of gal. This was not my style. I didn't fall in love at the drop of a hat, or in this case the chink of a beer bottle against a Prosecco glass. In fact, I wasn't sure I'd ever really been in love.

I think, in the quiet moments, when I was completely honest with myself, I was a little bit scared of love. Perhaps frightened of what loving can do to someone when it all goes pear-shaped. My dad left my mum when I was eight; she took it extremely badly and never really got over it. I'm probably guilty of keeping a shield up to protect myself from what I see as the fallout, the collateral damage, and the eviscerating wounds that not being loved anymore can leave. I've seen it first-hand and it's not pretty. I think it put me off opening myself to the possibility of falling in love. I'd had a couple of boyfriends. Long-term, too. But no one who'd ever made me feel quite like I'd felt in the company of Sam.

Being of a pragmatic bent, I didn't believe in fairy tales and certainly not love at first sight but there was definitely something about him that had left an impression that was proving difficult to dislodge. I looked at my phone again. Ingrained politeness forbade me to ignore the text, which is really what I should have done, and I'll admit that that little bit of ego that said, *he likes you too*, pushed my better judgement aside.

Lovely to meet you too.

My finger hovered over the keyboard, tempted to say more. God, I really wanted to. I liked him. More than liked him. But he belonged to someone else. I had no business here. It was wrong to even be thinking about him. Should I even send this polite innocuous text? But it said nothing really. I pressed send.

Three hours later, when there'd been no return text, I sadly acknowledged that I liked Sam even more. He was abiding by the rules. A good man who hadn't strayed when temptation beckoned. Damn. It really did make me like him. Our text conversation was at an end and I knew it made sense. I wouldn't contact him again. It was the right thing to do.

Chapter Three

'I thought I recognised those pins,' said a voice coming alongside me as I puffed my way along the dirt track, my feet crunching on the impacted soil of the avenue leading up to Nell Gwynn's monument.

Flicking my glance sideways I almost stumbled at the sight of Sam easing alongside me with a delighted grin on his face.

'Oh, hi,' I said in a ridiculously girlish high-pitched voice, but it's not easy being surprised and breathing at the same time, as well as wondering just what shade of tomato you're approximating. I was guessing anywhere between overripe and sunburned-to-buggery. 'Fancy seeing you here. Still housesitting for your folks?' Except it came out more like 'Fan … cy see … ing you … heeeeere,' between pants. I sounded more like a rusty old swing.

He grinned at me. 'No, I've been relieved of dog-sitting duty and been awarded the *Légion d'Honneur* medal for services to plant watering and recycling. My dad had a bet on that I would forget to put out the right bins for collection.' He beamed again. 'He never needs to know that Mum texted me reminders both weeks.'

'What if I tell?' I teased, managing to get it out in one exhalation. My memory had failed me; it had forgotten Sam's golden glow of effervescent energy and that aura of glad-to-be-aliveness that seemed to envelop him. God, yes, I know I sound ridiculously fantastical. He was a mere man and not some immortal Greek god, but he certainly had some presence about him. And he was just so easy to talk to.

'You wouldn't, would you?' His eyes widened dramatically and he clutched his hands to his chest, which made me laugh.

'Remind me, what was it I was telling?' I asked, enjoying the silliness between us. I'd thought about him quite a few times over the week. A memory I took out and stroked, like a child with its comfort blanket. I knew nothing was ever going to come of it but meeting a nice guy had been a pleasant reminder that there were still some out there.

He laughed, and for the next few minutes we fell into a silent rhythm, the pad, pad of our trainer-clad feet and the extension of our legs in perfect sync with each other and our breaths coming out in short energy-conserving pants as we matched each other step for step. I'd never thought about it before but there was something quite personal about running so in sync with another person.

We ran on in silence, which was only broken when I slipped unexpectedly on some loose dirt on the path. Sam's arm shot out to grab me, otherwise I would have gone down. I stumbled but managed to stay upright.

'You all right?' he asked slowing his pace to wait for me.

'Yeah,' I panted, my heart pounding even harder with the sudden surge of adrenaline the near-fall had released. He jogged on the spot for a minute, his blue eyes completely focused on me, and for a moment it was as if everything else around us receded and we were only aware of each other.

That pesky adrenaline rocketed back into place and I could feel my heart dancing about all over my chest. I did that eyes-widening thing, which was probably what scared him off. That or licking my lips – completely inadvertently. I was running. They were dry.

There was no denying the electrical charge between us and he looked away, his mouth tightening, alarm skittering in his eyes.

It was as if I'd suddenly scalded him.

After that, he ran a pace ahead of me, as if he felt it would be rude to sprint off but he no longer wanted to run with me. I didn't blame him. Another fall like that and I could take him out.

Gradually, he stretched out ahead of me and there was no way I could keep up with him. He passed me with a jolly wave on his downward leg as I was panting up the final hill before the turn around to come back on ourselves.

When I finished the course and picked up my sweatshirt and keys from the tarpaulin near the finish funnel, I saw him up ahead leaving the course without a backward glance. With a sigh, I said goodbye to a couple of people and walked back across the bridge over the dual carriageway, stopping in the middle to watch the cars whizz past under the bridge. They were like me and the man called Sam. Cars that passed each other, both headed in completely opposite directions. It had been nice bumping into him again – a bit too nice. Like when you spot a fabulous dress and you hunger for it but don't buy it because you either really don't need it or can't afford it, so you're good … although you can't stop thinking about it. And yet you know that if you went back, it wouldn't be as nice as you remembered; it's not the dress for you. Well, unfortunately Sam was not that dress. He was still every bit as gorgeous as I'd remembered. And still as unavailable.

Later that day he invited me to be friends with him on Facebook.

'Well, I binned him after that. Seriously? The man wanted me to wax his back after the second date. He'd even brought along a pack of wax strips!' My cousin Shelley's shrill indignation rang out in a quiet moment in the courtyard of the King's Arms where we and my friend Bel, short for Annabel, were all nursing rather delicious gin and tonics on a school night, which felt horribly decadent.

'I'd have gone for it and pulled each one off really slowly,' said Bel, her eyes gleaming with mischievous malice.

'Where do you find these men?' I asked, laughing as

Shelley took her disgust out on her ice cubes, poking at them with her straw.

'There's a special store with my name on it, Shelley Hilton Louses R Us, and they run the production line just for little ole me.'

'Aw hon.' I laid a hand on hers and gave it a quick squeeze. 'That's not true.'

'You'll find someone nice, one day,' said Bel, with the comfortable conviction of someone who'd been shacked up with their man for eighteen months, three weeks and five days.

Shelley caught my eye and winked. 'Who says I want nice? That's my problem; I love a bad boy.'

Bel shook her head. Her boyfriend Dan had written the book on nice.

'And,' added Shelley, with a wry smile, 'apparently I'm too indiscriminate. That's what Mum says.'

I shook my head, loyalty coming to the fore rather than honesty.

Shelley laughed. 'Come on, you know she's right. You never have these problems.'

'I never have any dates,' I put in.

'Because you always say no to everyone.' Bel nudged me with her elbow.

'You're too *discriminating*,' said Shelley rather proud of her clever observation. 'A little bird told me that you got on rather well with a certain Mr Hottie from next door at Mum and Dad's barbecue.'

I schooled my face into complete equanimity and shrugged.

'Don't give me that butter-wouldn't-melt look.' Shelley pulled a face. 'Mum said Mr Hottie was taking a lot of interest. Sorry I ducked out on you. If I'd known what a complete and utter lard-arse of a bastarding bastard Sean would turn out to be, I'd have stayed home.'

'It wouldn't have done you any good. Mr Hottie is well and truly taken. Sadly.' I pulled a jokey face of disappointment, which hid the raw hit of regret that punched me. 'Although, funnily enough, I saw him yesterday.' Both Shelley and Bel perked up and sat up in their seats, like a pair of cartoon villains smelling the scent of prey.

'At the parkrun.'

'Oh, bad luck.' Shelley winced. Exercise was a dirty word where she was concerned. 'That sucks. I bet you were all sweaty, weren't you? Not a good look. That's a nightmare.'

I gave a half-laugh. 'Not really, when he has a girlfriend and he's not interested.' Despite all my good intentions, I couldn't help the slight droop to my mouth which of course my eagle-eyed cousin spotted.

'You like.'

I shrugged. 'He's very…' *utterly delicious*, 'nice, but like I said, he has a girlfriend.'

'Ah, that's a bloody shame.' Shelley waved her gin glass in the air before halting suddenly, 'Is it a serious, serious girlfriend? Do you know that? I mean, are they living together?'

'Shelley!' I warned.

'What? All's fair in love and war.' She shrugged with a mutinous roll of her eyes. 'Come on.'

Bel caught my eye. She understood. 'No, it isn't,' I said quietly.

'They're not married,' protested Shelley snatching up her drink. 'They got kids?'

'Neither, as far as I know, but it's nothing to do with me because I'm not going there. As far as I'm concerned, he's out of bounds.'

'But you like him.'

'It doesn't matter if I like him. It's wrong.'

Shelley scrutinised me in an over-obvious way before saying, 'I've never known you even to "like" someone.'

I tried to play nonchalant. 'He's a nice guy. And this is a long-term girlfriend. It is serious.' I knew that because I'd been doing a little investigation. 'They've been going out for years.'

'Aw, that's a shame,' said Bel in her soft voice, cottoning on straightaway 'But you don't want to get caught up with him. It's so easy to start a flirtation and get carried away.'

Bel's words stilled me, although I probably wouldn't have confessed what I'd been doing since Saturday. I nibbled at my lip. It wasn't as if I was doing any harm, was I? But I still felt a little grubby about it.

Facebook is the modern-day Pandora's box. I kind of regretted clicking that *Confirm Friends* button. I couldn't resist and it had done me no favours. I'd spent a good hour trawling through Sam's posts, like an intrusive truffle hound sniffing out everything I could find out about him, including his surname, Weaverham … and her.

Every picture of him made me feel slightly gooey in the middle, but at the same time, I felt a touch guilty and voyeuristic, especially now I knew his girlfriend's name and what she looked like. And then I'd made the fatal mistake of moving onto Instagram to check her out. Big mistake – to quote *Pretty Woman* – huge. Victoria Langley-Jones was an Instagram influencer with her own vlog and half a million followers. Eek! I'd half hoped she'd be sort of ordinary – not that I'm exactly anything in the looks stakes – but she was flipping gorgeous. Long, long dark hair with a slight curl in it, with a tall, shapely figure that went in and out according to enviable proportions and the sort of legs that looked perfect in the high ankle-strap sandals she seemed to favour.

Immaculately groomed, she had that slightly high-cheeked pouty expression reminiscent of a more approachable Victoria Beckham. I also discovered – from her many posts and a couple of sneaky peeps at her vlogs – that she came from quite a wealthy background; her pictures showed that she drove a Mercedes convertible, shopped at Harvey Nicks and Selfridges, loved oysters and champagne ... and Sam. *Really* loved Sam. On her vlog she had features on shopping, dining and general opinion pieces which included: this season's ten best little black dresses, tux shopping with your man (and yes, Sam looked exceptionally handsome in black tie at some fancy tailor's in Jermyn Street), Marks and Spencer bra fittings versus Rigby and Peller, a parade of fashion faux pas at Ascot and what the best-dressed wore to a county cricket match.

'Why is it all the good ones are taken?' asked Shelley

plaintively, bringing me back to the little pub terrace with a welcome bump. I knew Bel must have been shooting vicious behave-yourself looks at her while I'd been daydreaming.

All my Facebook spying had revealed was that Victoria wasn't the sort of person I'd be friends with in a million years. And why was I even thinking like that? She was Sam's sort of girl.

'I mean, it's not like…' Shelley was off and, much as I loved my cousin, dear Shels could pontificate on the tragedy that all her friends had snaffled the best blokes and there were none left. Not single ones anyway.

When she finally came to the end of her diatribe and lurched away to the toilet, taking Bel with her, I picked up my phone and took an illicit shufty at Facebook, knowing I really shouldn't. Sam had posted a picture of himself, looking particularly handsome in cricket clothes. Who knew? Even with the funny pads on his legs and leaning one-handed on his bat, the sight of him set a few butterflies fluttering low in my stomach. Above the picture the caption read, 'Another century today – looks like I'll be getting a jug in.'

Below it was a range of comments and of course I couldn't resist taking a tiny peek into Sam's world. His friends.

'Make it two, you tight git,' commented Mike, his circular photo revealing a big, dark, handsome man with his arm slung around a blonde woman.

'About bloody time,' commented Drew.

'Lightweight. Only the one century.'

'That cover drive is getting dull, old man.'

'Hogging the crease again, Sam.'

I had absolutely no idea what any of that meant – not that it mattered. I sighed.

And then, unable to help myself, I scrolled through more comments until I came to the one I was really looking for.

Victoria had posted. 'My batting hero. Love you so much.'

The butterflies turned to rocks. I resisted looking at her latest vlog; it probably had shots of Sam in action and her in the perfect outfit cheering him on.

I switched my phone off and tucked it into my back pocket. I needed to unfollow him and stop with the stalking.

Chapter Four

'Is that another new top you're wearing?' asked my mother as she returned to the lounge carrying the large tea-tray. I stood up to offer to take it, even though I knew she'd decline. Just like she declined every Sunday and I kept offering. It was one of the mother-daughter dance-steps it seemed we had to go through each weekend. Don't get me wrong, I do love my mum, but she's what's known as 'a difficult woman'.

'Yes,' I said. 'Do you like it?' I spread my arms out to show off the sleeves with their cute cut-outs over the shoulder and upper arm which exposed a glimpse of tanned skin, which I was mightily proud of. 'I got it in H&M, in the sale.'

'And it'll probably last five minutes. I wouldn't stand too near a gas fire; you'll probably go up in flames in that cheap material.'

She smoothed down her beige wool skirt to make the

point. It was a pencil skirt that she'd had so long, it was about to come back into fashion.

'I know, but it was so pretty I couldn't resist,' I said with a smile at her. She still managed to look elegant in whatever she wore, in a straight-laced, buttoned-up sort of way.

'Well, as long as you've not spent your whole pay packet. Mortgage payments come first. Although they'd be a lot smaller if you'd been sensible and bought here instead of that place.'

'Don't worry, Mum. I'm—'

'I'm not worried,' she snapped, quick to deny any sort of emotional involvement in my life. 'But don't expect me to bail you out if you run into difficulty. I don't know why you had to live over there.'

She *did* know, and I refused to feel guilty about living within walking distance of my aunt, uncle and cousin instead of her.

'That's not going to happen,' I reassured her with a smile. 'I'm careful with money. You taught me well.' The latter was said with calm, resigned equanimity. Debt was Satan's temptation and spending money was evil – I'd received that message with bells on it.

'Hmph. How's your cousin?' My mum's question was asked with an added sniff. 'More tea?'

She didn't really approve of Shelley but we'd clearly run out of conversation, so this was her fall-back option. Jeepers, I'd been there less than half an hour.

'She's good,' I said, lifting my teacup and saucer towards the outstretched teapot, giving the clock behind my mother's head a quick glance. I swear, time in her house is different to anywhere else in the universe. A bit like dog years but in reverse. Somehow, here, it felt as if there were one hundred and twenty minutes in an hour instead of only sixty.

'Is she still working at the beauty place?' The lines around her mouth tightened as she pushed the milk jug towards me.

'Mum, it's Champneys, and yes, she's still working there.' I poured a tiny amount of milk into the watery Lapsang Souchong that she insisted on serving. It was like piss and not my cup of tea at all, but I'd never say anything, nor would I tell her that I would rather have a huge mug of builders' tea, the type that fuelled Holly and me at work.

'I suppose when you don't have much in the way of qualifications, it's as good as anything. Not much point in getting a degree if you're not going to use it.' I ignored the pointed comment. 'Mind you, she's so spoiled, I should be impressed that she even works. Lynn and Richard have been far too…' It was tempting to tune out because I'd heard it all before.

'Jessica!' Oh, darn it! I had tuned out and now Mum was looking at me with her bulldog's-chewed-a-wasps'-nest face, her chin sinking into her skinny, elongated neck, surrounded by a ruff of well-tanned contours. 'At least pay attention when I'm talking to you.'

'Sorry, Mum. I've got a lot on my mind at the moment.'

She raised a disbelieving eyebrow. 'I asked if you had any more thoughts about going to your great aunt's wedding. We're going to have to go.' Her mouth pursed with walnut wrinkles.

I shut my eyes for a second. I really didn't want to go there.

'I still need to find out if I'll be on call that weekend. Holly hasn't booked her holidays yet.'

'Well, I don't see why you have to wait on her. I thought you were the manager.' My mother's voice was shrill.

Technically I was, but it wasn't the sort of place you pulled rank, or even thought about it. I might have the paper qualifications and the shiny degree to which my mother had made scathing reference, but Holly's ten years of experience made her a million times more savvy and street smart than me. We made a good team; I never thought of myself as her boss.

'I'll ask her this week,' I said with a sinking heart. Third time around, Great Aunt Gladys's wedding was going to be fun with a capital F; going along with my mother would be miserable with a capital M. At sixty-nine, Gladys had bagged herself an extremely wealthy toy boy, Alastair, and they were getting married in style, the details of which had yet to be revealed but the save-the-date card featured Gladys in a jumpsuit and goggles, just about to launch herself out of a plane, with her fiancé grinning behind her and miming pushing her, which gives you a clue as to the type of couple they are. If Gladys has spent her three score and nearly ten years cramming as much joy and happiness into her life as she can, my mother has spent almost the commensurate amount sucking the joy out of her own and those of the people around her.

I know, I know, this is my mother we're talking about and I should be a lot more charitable, more of a loving daughter. I am being a complete bitch and I shouldn't. She's not really that bad and she's had it tough. Really tough. And I should have a lot more sympathy. My dad walked out without any warning when I was eight. Apparently he met the love of his life and couldn't live without her. Giving up his well-paid job in London, he moved to Cornwall and never paid a penny of child maintenance. To give her her due, despite our desperate finances, Mum never borrowed a penny. Aside from one brief period when my childhood turned into a nightmare, I was always clothed, fed and taken on holiday every year. Although the delights of Filey do wear off after the fifth, sixth and seventh visit. When I was sixteen, I signed up to go to Christian Camp with the local Sunday school just to escape the week's enforced shivering on a Yorkshire beach and the utter tedium of sharing a B&B room with my mother and her best friend, Dawn. If that sounds ungrateful, then I'm afraid I am. As I said, no one does stored-up bitterness quite as well as Mum, even though she now owns her own house and is practice manager at a very large GP surgery in Aylesbury and could actually start enjoying herself. She refuses to even talk about my dad and I've given up trying now.

'Of course, I might have a plus one by then,' I said, unable to resist being a little bit mischievous. 'Or you might.'

'Don't be absurd, Jessica.'

'You could always take Dawn. I'm sure Gladys wouldn't mind.'

'And can you imagine what she'd say if I did?' My mother's lips quivered with indignation. 'She'd make some ridiculous insinuation that we were *special* friends or something.'

'I'm sure she wouldn't. She knows you and Dawn are good friends.' I lied; it was exactly the sort of thing that Gladys would assume, thinking that she was being terribly liberal. Before Mum knew it, Gladys would be trumpeting about her niece, 'you know, the *lesbian* one'.

'So who's the young man you're thinking of taking? You haven't mentioned anyone before. It is such a shame; you are a pretty girl.'

'Thanks, Mum.' I laughed at her cautious compliment.

'You're very pretty. Is that better? I just don't want you to get big-headed. It's not just about looks. I can tell you that. You favour your father. And look what happened to him.' Bitter lines fanned out around her eyes. Part of me was tempted to go for broke and say, 'What did happen to him? After he left, why didn't we see him again? Why did he abandon us?'

'No, Mum, I look like you,' I said firmly, smiling at her. 'And you look great. And if I've still got a figure like yours at your age, I'll be well chuffed. You know you're *a very attractive woman*,' I said rolling my r's in an appalling Scottish accent, mimicking Duncan, her next-door neighbour.

Mum let out a you're-being-ridiculous huff but at the same time she allowed herself a tiny smile and patted her hair. 'The man is deluded but a gentleman all the same. I still don't have to dye it. Poor Dawn is always at the Nice and Easy.'

She picked up her tea and took a thoughtful sip. 'Well, if

you do find yourself a plus one, you might not want to take him. If he meets Gladys he might run a mile. You don't want him thinking insanity runs in the family.'

'Gladys is deliciously bonkers, Mum. She's not going to frighten anyone off, and it's highly unlikely I'll have a plus one. It was just supposition.'

'Supposition. That's a good word.' Mum nodded approvingly, as if to say, *See, that English degree wasn't wasted after all.* 'So there's no one on the horizon then?'

For someone who'd been so royally shafted by a man and whose life had been utterly shattered by the experience, there was a terrible irony in Mum's continued desire for happy-ever-after for me. When Dad left she crumbled and things had got messy quickly.

'No,' I said with a shrug, wishing just this once that there could be.

I didn't tell her as I backed out of her drive, my window wound down to wave at her as I left, that my next stop was dinner with my cousin and my aunt and uncle. With a touch of guilt, I watched her become smaller and smaller in my rear-view mirror, a neat little figure in her cream blouse and smart skirt.

Touch of guilt? What sort of bullshit was that? I had so much guilt where my mum was concerned. Even eighteen years on, she didn't know how to be happy, or seem to want to be. It made her hard to be around and for that my guilt exceeded Catholic proportions. I didn't mention going to my aunt's because I didn't want her to feel left out, although she probably knew. My aunt regularly reminded her that she was always welcome, that there was an open invitation. In fact, the invitation was open to every waif and stray in Tring. My aunt had a big heart and couldn't bear the thought of anyone being lonely. Despite Aunt Lynn's weekly phone call and invite, Mum declined ten times out of eleven, preferring to stay home and get organised for work the next day. We all still treated Mum with kid gloves, even though she was so much stronger these days – not that she seemed to appreciate it.

There was no way I was declining the invitation. Roast chicken was roast chicken. And roast chicken easily trumped washing and ironing, even when I'd been out clubbing on a Friday night. Staying over at Bel's sister's in London meant that I'd only managed to do one load of washing. Tomorrow morning, Monday, I'd be the one wrestling with the ironing board and rushing around grabbing clean knickers from the drying rack tucked behind the sofa in my bijou lounge.

When I pulled up onto the spare space at no. 11 Pettyfeather Lane, behind Shelley's car, I was pleased to see that there were no other cars. Just the family today, which I was relieved about, given my unwashed hair scooped up in a scraggy bun and the bags under my eyes as a result of too much girl talk on Friday after clubbing.

I let myself in, calling, 'Hello, honey, I'm home,' as I walked into the kitchen.

'Hey, lovely,' said Aunty Lynn wiping her hands on her

pinny. 'Oh, my darling, you've got some excess luggage going on there. Was it a good night on Friday?'

'Yes.' I laughed and wiped at my eyes. 'It was a late one, not helped by Bel and the girls yakking until the wee small hours.'

Someone grabbed me around the waist, enveloping me in CK One. 'You're a fine one to talk, Jess. God, woman, why don't you ever put on any weight? I hate you! Why couldn't I have got Mum's side of the family's genes instead of Dad's sausage fingers and stocky man-thighs?'

I turned to return Shelley's hug before stepping back and nodding at her cleavage, tastefully displayed in a very pretty floral dress. Next to me she looked all shiny and polished. 'Don't complain. You got boobage. I'm still buying teen bras in M&S.'

There was an awkward silence and from the shocked amusement on both Shelley and Aunty Lynn's faces, I knew before I turned around that I'd made this announcement to some complete stranger.

If only. Broadcasting my bra size to just about anyone else would have been preferable.

When I turned around, I met Sam's laughing blue eyes, which to give him credit did not duck below my neckline but held my gaze.

'Hi, Sam,' I said, an octave higher than my usual register.

'Hey, Jess, how're you doing? I haven't seen you at the parkrun for a couple of weeks.'

'Oh, I've been busy,' I lied. Busy avoiding you. My Instagram habit had got a bit too much and I'd decided I needed to go cold turkey. So much for that strategy. All the attraction I felt for him roared back into life with rocket-propelled jets.

'Sam, would you like a beer? He's just been helping Richard move a couple of paving slabs in the garden. He's housesitting for his parents again.' Aunty Lynn's jaunty tone wasn't fooling anyone. 'Jess, would you get one for him from the outside fridge and help yourself to a drink?'

Sam's eyes danced as I stomped to the fridge, which was actually inside the pantry but for some historic reason was always referred to as the outside fridge to differentiate it from the fridge in the kitchen. I snatched up a beer and grabbed the Prosecco bottle, realising my hands were shaking. *Must be the adrenaline rush*, I told myself. Lynn was directing Shelley, who was helping make gravy, even though it was still nearly thirty degrees outside. We were experiencing a week of record-breaking temperatures, even though it was late May, but still the Hilton family had to have their Sunday roast. Food was food. I wasn't complaining, although I did feel a little Shanghaied by Sam's presence. And also cross that no one had warned me and given me a chance to prepare.

Although, if I'd known he was coming, would I have been able to help myself? And did he think that I knew he was coming?

Flipping the cap off the bottle with the opener attached to the door frame, I handed Sam his beer and turned my back on him as I poured myself a small glass of Prosecco before topping up Shelley and Lynn's glasses.

'Why don't you two go out in the garden?'

'Don't you need any help?' I asked, desperately semaphoring a message to her with my eyes.

'No, darling. I've got everything under control. Shelley, don't let the gravy burn.'

'Are you sure?'

'Yes,' said Lynn, bustling away with a steamer full of uncooked broccoli. 'We'll be eating in about ten minutes, when Richard gets out of the shower. That all right with you?'

Faced with no other option, I grumpily followed Sam outside to sit at the table on the patio under a big cream umbrella. Despite the parched brown grass, the rest of the garden was a riot of colour, with pots of flowers lining the edges of the curved patio steps. I studied the blousy petunias spilling over the sides of the glossy blue planters.

'I'm sorry, Jess,' said Sam, his blue eyes sorrowful. 'I can see you're mad at me but I'm not sure what I've done wrong. Would you like me to go?'

I swallowed. 'No,' I said quietly. 'I didn't know you'd be here. I thought you might think...' My words trailed away. If I said any more, I'd say too much.

'I had no idea you'd be here, honestly. Richard popped around fifteen minutes ago asking if I'd help with the paving slabs and then Lynn invited me to stay for dinner.' His mouth drooped, his eyes hooded. 'Roast chicken was a lot more appealing than last night's Domino's.'

'Don't give me those puppy-dog eyes, Sam Weaverham!'

'Too much?' Laughter lit his blue eyes.

'Far too much. I bet your mum stocked the fridge to the gunnels for you while she's away.'

His cheeks dimpled with a naughty smile. 'You know her.'

'No, but you give off those spoiled-rotten vibes,' I said, trying to be snotty and failing miserably, as my face creased into a smile. 'How long are you housesitting for?'

'Just the weekend. They've gone to some fancy wedding down on the Isle of Wight, so decided to stay a day either side. They're back tomorrow.'

'I've never been to the Isle of Wight. My school always went in Year 6, but the day before we were due to go, my appendix burst.'

'Ouch. I've never been either, if it's any consolation.' He suddenly grinned. 'I'll show you my scar if you show me yours.'

'You've had your appendix out?'

'Yup, two years ago, the scar's almost invisible now.' With that he whipped up his T-shirt and showed me his very tanned stomach, with dark-blond hair disappearing below his shorts. Jeez Louise, was the man trying to kill me?

I had an instant hot flush, and my pulse went into overdrive as he traced the tiny silvery scar with his index finger.

'They glued it together,' he said. 'It's amazing. In the olden days we'd probably have died.'

'That's a cheery thought,' I said, taking a cooling swig of Prosecco and holding the glass to my cheek. There was no way I was showing off my equally neat scar, although a little bit of me had fallen even more for his total lack of self-consciousness.

And we were off, the conversation running free as we

discussed childhood ailments and competed for the most broken bones. He won; he'd broken three ribs in one go during an unfortunate incident with a cricket bat.

'So, are you enjoying this weather?' asked Sam after a comfortable lull in the conversation. He leaned back in his chair, completely at ease, his tanned limbs sprawling comfortably as the sunlight danced over the reddish blonde hairs dusting his arms and legs. He looked like a sun god. 'Or are you getting fed up with it?'

'I love it. I just wish I had a garden to enjoy it. I'm lucky I do have a teeny tiny balcony that I can sit on, but it gets the sun in the morning rather than the evening.'

'Nice for breakfast,' he said with a nod.

I sniggered. 'In my head, when I first bought the place, I planned to sit there eating healthy yoghurt, sprinkled with fresh strawberries and nuts.'

'And?' Sam's eyebrows lifted in amused anticipation.

'I'm usually rushing around with a bowl of Weetabix, trying to find my car keys and pull on my only pair of hole-free tights, which I had to wash the night before and which have been drying on the boiler all night … and that's way too much information, but you get the picture.'

'Sounds like real life to me. I'm a toast-in-the-car man, with my coffee in the cup holder and more toast when I get to work. And then toast at breaktime with the kids.'

'A lot of toast,' I observed, swatting at a wasp that was getting a bit too close to my wine glass. The pesky thing – the first of the season – was sluggish and stupid and was now dancing around the rim of the glass. I stood up to bat it away again and managed to knock over Sam's beer. As we both lunged for it, I somehow managed to trip over his feet and … there he was, both hands on my upper arms, holding me up. Classic romantic-comedy territory … except it didn't feel funny; it felt bloody terrifying. My stomach had gone into freefall and I couldn't look anywhere but into his too-blue, too-perceptive, too-knowing eyes.

I was so conscious of his fingers touching my bare skin through the stupid gaps in my top (so that's what they were for!) and of his lips just inches from mine. Oh yeah, every cliché in the book and it was horrible. Horrible. Horrible. Because I so wanted to kiss him and I knew, without being anything but honest, that he wanted to kiss me.

And we couldn't. The knowledge pumped a great big fist right into my stomach.

I'm not sure who reared back first; it might have been simultaneous. I do know I felt sick. Properly I-might-throw-up-any-second sick. Which was a rather bizarre reaction. Was it shame? Regret? Disappointment?

Sam rubbed his hand over his forehead looking horrified and took another step back.

'Dinner's ready,' called Lynn, appearing at the door.

'Blimey, are you ill, Jess?' said Richard after I refused a second helping of roast potatoes. I was still pushing the first lot around my plate.

'No.' I summoned up a smile I was far from feeling. 'I think it must be the heat. I'm not that hungry.'

'I'll have yours,' said Shelley as she leaned over and

stabbed one with her fork. 'Sod the man-thighs. At least they're all bought and paid for.'

Everyone laughed and I sneaked a quick glance at Sam, unable to stop myself. He looked serious and had been carrying on a conversation with Aunty Lynn about his parents' dog. She'd been talking about getting a dog forever – Uncle Richard called it Project Puppy – but never having owned one before, she entertained a certain amount of trepidation about the prospect. He hadn't looked at me once since we'd come in from the garden.

'Talking of which,' he said, putting down his napkin with a show of great regret, 'I ought to go and check on Tiggy. Make sure she's got enough water. With all that fur, this heat is not good for her.'

'Oh, you should have brought her,' said Shelley. 'Then Mum could have got her dog fix.'

'You should get a dog, Lynn,' said Sam rising to his feet. 'I'm sure Mum would help you out with any questions. Thanks for dinner, and I'm sorry to cut and run. It was really nice of you to invite me.' He looked around the table. 'Nice to see you… Shelley. Jess.' He gave a nod towards both of us, not making eye contact, and followed Lynn, who insisted on escorting him to the front door, still peppering him with questions about Tiggy's daily routine.

'Well,' drawled Shelley. 'He is seriously hot.'

Richard covered his ears. 'I don't think this is an in-front-of-Dad conversation, is it?'

Shelley grinned at him.

I huffed out a sigh. 'And it's not a conversation I want to have.' I turned to her. 'Please leave it.'

Her eyes widened for a second and then awareness kicked in and her face softened. 'Sorry, babe.' She patted my arm.

'Dad, have another Yorkshire pud. You know you want to. Now that Wonder Boy's gone you can stop holding in your paunch.'

Richard laughed and helped himself to not one but two big fat Yorkshire puddings. 'Your mum loves me just the way I am.' He waved one of the Yorkshires on his fork at her.

'What's that?' asked Lynn as she slid back into her seat. 'He's such a lovely boy. Richard! Two! You said you were worried your trousers were getting a bit tight. That's not going to help.'

'Really, Dad!' said Shelley with a wicked grin.

I let the family banter wash over me and luckily none of them noticed how quiet I was, or if they did, they thankfully didn't mention it.

Chapter Five

I hit the ground running on Monday morning. Holly was already there when I arrived.

'Two new arrivals this weekend. They're still sleeping. Came in late last night,' she said, handing over a mug of tea. 'Little boy, he's ten. Mum is twenty-eight. They're not in great shape. I've got a meeting with the housing department about the Slater family.'

Some of our clients had already been in the system for a few weeks when they came to us and this was a halfway house while they were waiting to be housed. Once they left we provided ongoing support along with the social workers. Others arrived having fled literally hours before with nothing. 'Not in great shape' meant the latter.

'No problem. I haven't got anything on today. I've got a TAF meeting tomorrow.' We use a lot of acronyms at work. I was referring to a Team Around Family meeting, which involves lots of different agencies involved in supporting our families. 'I can settle them in.'

I often wondered about how the children felt about their fathers. Not having had one of my own for the key years of my life it was something that I spent a lot of time thinking about. Would the children ever see them again? Would they want to? How would the things they'd seen affect them in the future? Had Mum got away before psychological harm had been done?

I knew that my dad leaving had definitely influenced my job choice. Although he hadn't been violent or abusive he had definitely inflicted a terrible wound on my mother's life. When I was eight I hadn't been able to help her when things had spiralled out of control. There had been no safety net for my mother, no one to help. This job, although far from perfect, was about us picking up the pieces and it made me feel that, in a very small way, I was making up for not being able to help my own mother.

'Hi, I'm Jess,' I said, introducing myself to the tired-looking woman with grey shadows dappling her petite, fine-boned features. 'Would you like some coffee or tea?'

'Tea, but I don't want to be no bother.'

'Well, let me show you the kitchen and then you can help yourself any time you like. It's Cathy, isn't it?'

Nodding, she cast a fearful look over her shoulder at the little mound in the bed. 'I can't leave our Jakes.'

'Is he still sleeping?'

'No.' Her worry-filled eyes darkened with fear.

'Perhaps he'd like some juice and a biscuit,' I suggested. Many of the women that came here had been bullied, coerced and told what to do for so long that making choices was often difficult. They didn't like to upset anyone. Our job wasn't to rehabilitate them or make any judgements; it was to provide unconditional support and a safe haven. Holly and I were not counsellors or legal experts; we were there to provide the infrastructure of the refuge, to make sure that the place ran smoothly, help facilitate access to a new life and ensure that the women felt safe.

'I can ask him.' She padded in her battered slippers to lean over the huddled lump. 'Jakes love, you want something to eat?' I noticed the scratches around her ankles.

A muffled 'No' came from the pile of bedclothes.

'It'll do you good, love,' she coaxed, flashing me a desperate look.

'There's no hurry,' I said, giving her a gentle smile. 'Why don't I bring a tray up and you can come down to the kitchen when you're ready? There's a bathroom just through here.' I pointed down the corridor. 'Towels are in there. And there are some clothes and things you might need in the cupboard over here. Help yourself to whatever you need for the time being.'

The women in the house had to do their own cooking, buy their own food and keep the place clean and tidy, but we helped out with food and clothing when they first arrived, as sometimes, like Cathy, they arrived with absolutely nothing. I guessed from the state of her ankles her slippers were the footwear she'd left in.

By the time I left work, it was after six. My tiny flat felt hot and stuffy and I dragged myself around opening every window, trying to get a through-draught, yawning as I went.

Dear God, it had been a long day. I peered at the inside of the fridge and pulled out the last can of Coke. I didn't feel like eating and the fridge and cupboards held slim pickings. I went out onto the balcony where I sat at the little two-person bistro table, staring at the second empty chair and letting myself brood. I couldn't get little Jake's face and its black eye out of my head. How could someone do that to a child? Let alone a father? Parts of my childhood had been scary and chaotic but at least no one had ever intentionally hurt me.

The view is probably what sold the miniature apartment; it's a conversion at the top of an older building and the balcony is built into the eaves of the roof, looking out over trees and fields which slope up towards the Chiltern Hills. It's the perfect thinking spot, although I don't normally let the job or the past get to me. We've been trained to have resilience – the ability to bounce back – which, as Holly told me regularly, was why I was so good at my job. Don't get me wrong, I'm not so thick-skinned that I don't care, it's just I know that for me to help and make a difference, I have to be practical and pragmatic. The women that came to us had all too familiar stories. Although stories is the wrong word. They aren't stories; they're real. You never get used to the harrowing accounts, but you do learn to manage your own response.

Today I'd not managed very well. I lifted the can of Coke with a heavy sigh. I couldn't get Cathy and Jake out of my head. What they'd been through and what life now held for them.

So yeah, I was moping. Not something I do very often.

I pushed at the second chair with my foot. Sometimes it would be nice to have someone sitting there, a man who would listen to me have a mini rant, a quick weep, and then tell me I was doing OK and give me a cuddle.

Oh dear, I really was feeling sorry for myself this evening. Good job I had a Pilates class at eight with Shelley and Bel, a bit of a treat as Bel was rarely around during the week. As an auditor for a big accountancy firm, she often spent weeks at a time working away.

I pushed myself to my feet. Enough brooding. I would go and see Aunty Lynn and scrounge tea there. She was bound to feed me and just being at her house always comforted me.

'Mum.' I squeaked the word as I sauntered into Aunty Lynn's big kitchen-diner, having opened the front door with my own key and yelled, 'Hello, it's me.'

'Jess.' My mother's face was a cross between disapproval and hurt. I wouldn't have dreamed of letting myself into her house. I wasn't sure I still had a key.

What was she doing here? Usually she only deigned to visit on high days and holidays.

'Hello, Jess,' said Aunty Lynn, deliberately not commenting on what a nice surprise it was to see me, as she usually would.

'Hey cous, come to scrounge tea. You've timed it perfectly,' said Shelley with a smirk, relishing the awkwardness.

'I thought I'd call in on my way to Pilates,' I said, not daring to look at the clock, the hands of which would have mocked me. The class didn't start until eight o'clock, it was ten to seven.

'Have you eaten?' asked Lynn, already looking at the damn giveaway clock. 'You've got plenty of time, your class doesn't start until eight. I've made a lovely niçoise salad.' She was already laying an extra place at the table. 'Why don't you stay as well, Joan? There's plenty. Richard, my beloved salad dodger, won't want any, far too healthy.'

'I heard that,' called an indignant voice from the other room and we all grinned at each other. My mother's mouth tightened.

'I'm afraid I can't stay,' she said in that prissy tone, which we all knew meant, *I know when I'm not welcome.*

'Oh, do stay, Joan. You can spend some time with Jess.'

Inside I winced. Wrong thing to say, Aunty Lynn.

'I can spend time with Jess whenever I want without your permission, Lynn.' And with that my mother flounced towards the front door. I raced after her.

'Mum, don't be like that. Lynn's just being hospitable. I came to see Shelley really. Why don't you stay?' I pleaded, although I couldn't begin to imagine what the atmosphere would be like if she changed her mind.

'I'm not being like anything. I need to go home. I've got a perfectly good supper waiting for me at home.' There was no arguing with the straight, affronted back now presented to me. Mum had taken umbrage and I felt horribly guilty. Me marching in unannounced just underlined that this house had always been and still was my sanctuary. As a child it had offered the light and colour lacking at my mum's house.

'I'll see you soon,' I said desperately.

'I'm sure you're busy but when you can fit me in. You know where to find me.'

Ouch, I really had upset her.

Could my day get any worse?

———————

'Blimey, why did I let myself in for this?' asked Shelley. Pilates didn't count as proper exercise, she'd decreed, because, allegedly, it didn't involve sweat, which just went to prove she wasn't doing it properly.

'Because it's good for us,' I said, actually feeling a lot better than I had earlier. All that breathing, contorting myself into the right shape and using muscles that were usually left to their own devices meant that there was no space in my head to think of other things.

'It's good for you,' she groaned. 'With your taut, bendy body, and tiny boobs. Mine just get in the way.'

'Stop boasting,' said Bel. 'You know we'd both love to have a cleavage.'

Shelley cheered up and pushed up her double Es with both hands. 'I've got a body made for lurve, that's my problem.'

We both burst out laughing.

'Obviously, that's where I'm going wrong,' I said. 'My body's not even built for dating.'

'I know someone who was very interested and he's young, free and single, now.' Her eyes gleamed with sudden delight and a sly smile lit up her face.

I ignored her, I refused to take the bait. It wasn't the first time she'd attempted to fix me up with one of her random and completely unsuitable mates-of-mates.

She arched an eyebrow. 'Don't you want to know?'

'No.'

'Not even if it's someone you really, really like.'

I glared at her. What? We were thirteen? Did she mean Sam?

'You do know he's broken up with his girlfriend?'

I didn't need any more information. She did mean Sam. A rush of adrenaline crashed through me so unexpectedly that I dropped one of my trainers.

'H–he has?'

She nodded, gentle for once, as if she knew it mattered. 'Yes, sorry, I assumed you'd know.' She lifted her shoulders in mute apology. 'Mum was talking over the fence to his mum; she mentioned it.'

'Wow,' I said. For some reason I felt totally numb. Sam had finished with his girlfriend. I think I was too scared of what it might mean to dare to feel anything. 'Do you know when?'

Was it before the weekend? After Sunday?

Shelley shook her head. 'Mum didn't say. I can ask her if you like.'

I gave her the look.

57

'Uh, maybe not.' Her quick grin was sympathetic. Given ammunition like that, Aunty Lynn would be straight round to Sam's mum like a secret agent on a mission.

But now I was confused. Sam hadn't made deliberate contact since he'd sent the Facebook friend invite. There'd been no further texts. Maybe I was imagining the mutual attraction, wishing it to be so, like some sort of reverse denial. People did that sort of thing all the time, didn't they? Stalkers who were fixated on people, believing their victims returned their affection. Maybe I'd just read too much into those feelings? Maybe he was one of those guys who was incapable of *not* flirting? Maybe Sam was like that with any girl who gave him so much as the flutter of an eyelash and let slip a flash of attraction? A complete man-whore, who tested the waters but never went in deeper because he had a steady relationship that kept him safe. The more I thought about it, the more convinced I became.

Bel and Shelley both kept quiet, for which I was extremely grateful. There were too many questions and thoughts churning around my head to make sense of anything.

———

As the sky was still cloudless and the sun blazing brightly, even though it was after nine, we walked home in our T-shirts and leggings. The pretty High Street was quiet, as if everyone had stayed home to enjoy the rare evening warmth. We walked along in near silence and I could feel Shelley and Bels shooting me concerned glances.

As we walked up the slight hill to the mini roundabout where Shelley would peel off, I put out my arms, catching both of them on the forearm. 'Guys, can you stop worrying about me. Shels, I can almost feel you plotting. And Bels, you can stop fretting about me.'

'Well, it's just not like you to be...'

'Quiet.'

'So serious.'

I laughed as they spoke at the same time. 'Well, you can quit worrying. I'm fine. Sam hasn't even been in touch, so he's probably not interested.'

———

That thought didn't stop me going straight on to Instagram and Facebook as soon as I walked through the front door and my phone picked up the Wi-Fi signal.

Sam had posted nothing since Saturday on his Facebook newsfeed, where he'd shared a video which featured him hitting a cricket ball with an almighty thwack that seemed to reverberate around the pitch. In his uniform he looked official and business-like, and the determined, predatory stance as he faced the ball made him appear quite different to the laughing golden man I'd met several times. I watched the video a second time, taking in the slow, deliberate step out to strike and the flash of power unleashed when he hit the ball. I knew bugger all about cricket, but I knew damn sexy when I saw it. My mouth went dry.

His Instagram feed hadn't been touched for over a week.

Knowing I shouldn't, I tapped Victoria's name into the search box.

Her most recent post was last night; she looked gorgeous but there was a dangerous hint of black widow in her dressed-to-kill pose. A midnight-black lace dress skimmed the tops of her thighs, the endless legs accentuated by high, sexy sandals. The look was completed by the dress's magnificent slashed neckline that dipped virtually to the navel, showing off high, full breasts. The picture had femme-fatale-on-the-prowl written all over it, as did the fifty comments below.

'Show him what he's missing, girl.'

'He's a fool.'

'You go, girl.'

'Shit for brains, that man. You deserve better.'

'Can't believe it, babe. Hugs.'

'Aw hon, you look beautiful. Plenty of fish.'

I sat down with a thunk on my sofa. It was true. Sam had finished with Victoria.

Chapter Six

My phone rang as I was rushing for a train. I had exactly six minutes to run up the escalator and make a mad dash to the platform for the 17.34 to Tring after a rare midweek day's shopping and lunch with an old university friend in London. I picked up my pace, ignoring the strident ring and after dithering with my oyster card and cursing when it didn't seem to work, I managed to catch the train by the absolute skin of my teeth.

As I got into the nearest carriage with the beeping signalling the doors closing ringing in my ears, I slumped into the first available seat, breathing so hard I barely noticed my own feet, let alone who I was sitting next to, until someone laughed. So much for all those parkruns! They hadn't prepared me for a sprint.

'Jess Harper!'

'Michael!' A familiar face loomed into focus. Michael had been in my year at school and his girlfriend, Helen, had been in the same year as Shelley and one of her best friends. 'What are you doing here?'

'On my way back to Tring. I'm staying with the folks at the moment. I've been working down in Southampton since finishing uni, and then a job came up in London and I fancied a change … and Mum and Dad have downsized. And,' he looked a touch embarrassed, 'helped us out with a deposit to buy a place.' Then his eyes lit up. 'Me and Helen have just got engaged.'

'Oh wow! Congratulations! Shelley didn't tell me.'

'She doesn't know and Helen's going to kill me for telling you first. Please don't say anything. They're going out for a drink tomorrow.'

'I won't say a word.' I gave him a cheerful wince, easily able to imagine Shelley's excited shriek the minute she spotted the engagement ring. 'We should all get together sometime for a drink.'

The rest of the journey was spent catching up with news of old schoolfriends and passed so quickly that I completely forgot my missed call.

It was only as the train slid into the station that I pulled out my phone.

Sam's name on the screen left me suddenly dry-mouthed and I swear my heart stopped for a second.

'Bad news?' asked Michael, looking worried.

'No, just … an unexpected call.' It had been three weeks since I'd heard that he and Victoria had split up.

I'd spent a week and a half tormented by the ridiculous hope that I might hear from him. This was followed by a forlorn week and a half realising that he was obviously no longer interested, if he ever had been at all, and that I'd imagined that spark between us.

I must have looked shell-shocked. Even though stray thoughts of Sam managed to creep through every now and then, I'd filed him under O for 'out of bounds' and locked the filing cabinet as tight as a bank vault. I'd stopped peeking at his and Victoria's Instagram accounts and noticed that his Facebook posts had dwindled to virtually nothing. This was a complete bolt from the blue. Even though I wanted to call him straight back, the peculiar geography of Tring station being a mile and a half out of town and the constraints of politeness meant that I had to offer Michael a lift home.

———

As soon as I walked through the door I pulled out my phone. My hands were shaking as I pressed the bold black letters at the top of the recent calls list. He'd called twice but neither time left a message.

Wah! I'd pressed the screen too soon. What was I going to say? You were supposed to prepare for these things. Did I look too eager? Too desperate?

'Hey, Jess.'

'Hi, Sam.' I was shy? What the hell? I'm never shy. I walked into the flat and perched on the edge of the sofa.

There was a silence.

'Sorry, have I called at a bad time?' I asked, picking at a loose thread at the bottom of my shirt. I desperately didn't want it to be a bad time.

Sam laughed and all the silly trifling innate worries – like maybe he'd regretted calling me, or maybe it was an accident – vanished as I pictured his blue eyes crinkling, his face coming to mind as if I'd seen him yesterday.

'No, not at all. Any time is good.' I could almost hear him grinning. I mean, I just knew he was grinning from something in his speech. Is that crazy? 'It's just that earlier when I called, I had it all prepared. You know, exactly what I was going to say and now … I'm a bit thrown because I'd convinced myself that you wouldn't call me back and … would you like to come out for a drink with me?'

'Yes,' I said laughing, charmed afresh by his honesty.

'You would?'

'Do you want me to think about it?'

'No,' he said quickly before adding in a gabbled rush, 'Istomorrowtoosoon?'

Chapter Seven

A bad day in the refuge is when one of the women decides that going back to the life they know is preferable to living with the uncertainty of *if* the council will find them a suitable home, *if* their children will settle in their new schools, and *if* they can cut it on their own.

Holly and I know it's not our fault, we really do, but it doesn't help with the numbing sense of loss and failure. Today was a bad day. The Slater family, for whom I'd fought so hard to get the three children into the same school, had returned home. Mr Slater's texts promising to change, pleading with her to drop the charges, and photos of their spacious executive house in a nice part of Surrey had done the damage. You don't expect domestic abuse in nice, middle-class families. The stereotypical image of fraught, poverty-stricken lives affected by the issue is a long way from reality. There are no stereotypes. These are real people, real families, from every walk of life.

It was tempting to cancel Sam. I wanted him to meet the nice, shiny, happy version of me, not the sickened and heartbroken version who hated the powerlessness of days like these, when you wonder over and over if there was anything you'd missed. Anything you could have done. The truth was that the Slaters' immediate future was grim – a one-bedroomed council flat and living on benefits until the children were older. Mrs Slater used to drive an Audi four-by-four, shopped in John Lewis, and had lost a spleen.

I didn't cancel him. I rocked up at the pub twenty minutes early and went and sat in the garden at one of the benches, with my back to the table, under a shady tree with a large glass of Coke, the condensation dripping down the side, which I held against my neck. It was another heat-searing day with the temperature hitting the high twenties, which I didn't mind so much now that I was outside. I texted Sam to tell him where I was.

The pub was perfectly positioned, only a ten-minute journey from work for both of us, but I acknowledged, with a grim, unhappy smile, that wasn't why Sam had chosen it. I looked around the garden; it wasn't busy but even if it had been, I wouldn't have known a soul here. The pub was far enough away from Tring that it was unlikely anyone would spot us. I winced, hating the feeling that we were creeping around. I guessed that Sam was being considerate of Victoria's feelings; I got that, but it suggested things on too many other levels that I didn't want to examine. Was this a proper date? Did it mean something? I'd not been able to stop thinking about Sam since the moment I'd met him, even though I'd tried really hard. Was it possible that he could feel the same about me? The thought that he could thrilled me as much as it filled me with terrible guilt. I've got a pretty well-developed conscience. I'd seen my mum when Dad had gone; she'd tortured herself wondering what the other woman had that she didn't, what she'd done wrong, and whether there was anything she should have done differently.

I traced the condensation with my finger and tried hard not to think about how Victoria might be feeling. Even so, I couldn't help feeling a little bit sick at heart. No one should go through the pain my mother had suffered.

Knowing it was the dumbest move I could make, I picked up my phone and carried on looking at the Instagram feed I'd succumbed to peeking at earlier that afternoon. It was clear that she and Sam breaking up had not been a mutual decision. Her recent feed featured lots of pictures of happier times with her and Sam among the same group of friends. The numbers varied, but the same faces recurred in different groupings: lounging on the field at a cricket match, dressed up and posing for the camera at a wedding, a group selfie on a sun-drenched beach that looked somewhere exotic and well above my paygrade, in Barcelona at the Sagrada Familia. It was a gloriously technicolour, detailed documentary of their history together and an indelible testament to how intertwined their lives had been.

I snapped off my phone and pushed it away. Instead, I gazed up at the leafy canopy above and wondered how the leaves managed to stay so crisp and green when the grass had given up the ghost. The hillside view was probably normally rolling verdant field; today it was brown scrub.

'Jess!'

Sam appeared

'Hi.' I stood up. He smiled at me, his eyes dancing as they met mine, mischief and warmth brimming in them, and like magic, the dragging frustration of my day and the wearying feeling of guilt vanished.

Without a moment's hesitation, he walked right up to me and put his arms around me, his hands resting in the small of my back. He kissed me full on the lips, putting a marker in the sand straightaway. No messing about, but also no assumptions. No tongues and no lingering snog. It was a kiss that stated his intent, but he hadn't carried it through. It was an offer, but it gave me a choice. It was honest and straightforward. A man after my own heart.

'Hi,' he said, his voice husky and raspy. 'I've been wanting to do that for a long time.'

My heart banged in my chest and I must have looked like a right dorky idiot because all I could do was gaze breathlessly up at him like some dozy heroine in a black and white film. Luckily, I don't think he noticed or cared because he was grinning like an idiot back at me.

'Me too,' I admitted.

'Want a drink?' he asked.

I watched shamelessly as he walked back into the pub. He looked good in smart-casual gear, but I preferred him in shorts and a T-shirt. Like this, he looked slightly constrained and buttoned-up. It was a uniform – appropriate, but not really him.

When he came back with two Cokes, as soon as he sat down beside me, he ripped off his tie, a bland grey knitted affair that looked as if it belonged to a geography teacher circa 1950, and stuffed it in his pocket, undid a couple of buttons on his shirt, and rolled up his sleeves.

'Better?' I teased.

'Tie day. I bloody hate them. Had to meet some parents. The head likes us to look professional.' He shook his head as he took a long swallow.

With the avid attention of a lovesick puppy I stared at his Adam's apple and felt my hormones flicker like a light bulb in a bad horror film.

'You look lovely and cool and sort of floaty in that dress.' He grinned. 'I wonder what the head would say if I turned up in one. So much cooler than trousers.'

We slipped into a seamless and quite deep conversation about stereotypes, gender, sexism and #MeToo. It wasn't all serious; we laughed and joked as well.

Before I knew it, I'd drunk excessive amounts of Coke but had not wanted to waste a minute with him in order to get up to pee, so now my bladder was nearly the size of a Swiss ball.

'Don't make me laugh,' I said, getting to my feet. 'I really need to go to the loo.'

I hobbled inside and took a look at my face in the mirror. It was wreathed in a ridiculously broad smile. Nothing had been said about what today's meeting meant and I hadn't acknowledged that I knew he'd split up with his girlfriend. I was assuming he must know that I knew. But it wasn't as if there were any kind of elephant in the room. We hadn't spoken about anything personal, but it didn't feel contrived or deliberate, as if we were avoiding the subject; instead, we were so busy enjoying each other's company and had so much to say that we'd gone with the flow.

Giving myself a quick look in the mirror, my face flushed and my eyes brighter than normal, I shook my head. 'You've got it bad, girl.'

As I walked back to the table, I saw Sam frowning down at his phone, one hand playing with a block of blue and red plastic, but as I drew nearer he looked up, his face brightening with a smile. He put the phone face-down on the table. I glanced at his other hand.

'What's with the Lego?'

There was a wistful quality to his smile as he held it up, separating the two bricks.

'It was on the floor as I left work and I just shoved it in my pocket but there's something about Lego that's very satisfying.' He snapped the two pieces together. 'The pieces always fit together perfectly, never wonky or misaligned. They're perfect together.' His face was serious as he suddenly glanced up and held my gaze. 'That's how I felt when I first met you. We clicked.' His pause was filled with sudden shyness and a faint blush on his cheek and he fiddled with the two blocks again, pulling them apart. My heart melted just a little. I knew exactly what he meant; he couldn't have said it any better.

'Sorry, that sounds a bit … cheesy,' he apologised, putting the pieces down on the table.

I couldn't help myself. I laid a hand on his. 'No, it doesn't. I know exactly what you mean, but saying it out loud to anyone else would sound…' I lifted my shoulders. He'd expressed that instant sense of rightness I'd felt in the garden talking to him.

'Crazy?' He lifted those golden eyebrows, the lines around his eyes crinkling with sunshine and warmth.

'But it's not crazy,' I said, squeezing his hand before picking up the blue plastic block. 'It's Lego.' I palmed it and put it into my bag and he followed suit, putting the red piece in his pocket, both of us smiling idiotically at each other, oblivious to the rest of the world.

'Do you want another drink?' he asked.

I pulled a face. I really didn't but I didn't want the evening to end.

'Not just yet,' I said, pleased that I'd come up with the perfect compromise.

Right answer. His hand stilled.

'So … what happened with your girlfriend?' There, it was out, and I didn't feel the least bit pushy about it.

With a wry face he tugged at the cuff of his shirt. 'We broke up about a month ago.'

'You don't have to talk about it if you don't want to. I just wanted to clear things up. Let you know that I knew you'd split up. I wouldn't want you thinking I'm the sort of girl that goes after another girl's bloke.'

'I never thought that for a minute,' he said quickly.

I saw his Adam's apple dip furiously as he toyed again with the cotton fabric. 'The thing is, Jess, I … I couldn't stop thinking about you. That first time I met you … well, it…' He gave me a candid look. 'It bloody terrified me.'

'Oh,' I said, deflating inside. Not exactly what I wanted

to hear. *Fancied you straightaway* would have been nice. *Thought we clicked*, nicer still. *Terrified* made it sound as if I were some praying mantis-type who would chase him and gobble him up. It sounded too much like being the other woman.

He smiled, and then he only went and cupped my face with his hand. Cupped my face with his hand! Talk about romantic, tender and sweet. The gesture, totally natural and unexpected, set off a small explosion inside me.

'Hey.'

The gentle half-smile almost made me cry.

Then he dropped his hands to fiddle with the cuff of his shirt again. 'Terrified because I knew I wanted to be with you. It smashed through everything I thought I was sure about in my life. I'd been going out with Vic for four years. We were perfectly happy. At least I thought I was. There was nothing wrong ... but then, well, I tried to put you out of my mind. Told myself I'd imagined it. That it was ... I dunno, just instant attraction.' He swallowed hard, his fingers still playing with his cuff.

'But when I saw you at the parkrun, it was the same. No, it wasn't; it was worse, because I knew it wasn't fleeting. And I knew you felt the same way.' His eyes bored into me. There was no trace of arrogance there, just an honest statement of fact. I nodded.

'I did and, yeah, honestly, it scared me too. I had no business feeling anything for you. You had a girlfriend. You were completely out of bounds.'

Relief and understanding flashed across his face.

'I didn't know what to do. I sent you that Facebook

request. I wanted to stay in touch but ... I didn't want to do anything ... sleazy. I loved Victoria. Four years is a long time ... but the way...' his eyes met mine, slightly haunted and definitely guilt-ridden, '...the way I felt about you ... eclipsed that. Suddenly I just knew I didn't love her ... *enough* anymore. I could have kept going but it felt like lying. As if I were being unfaithful to her because I had feelings for someone else.'

The warmth of his hand enveloped mine where it lay on the table, like an anchor, as if reminding us both that this wasn't some crazy fantasy and that we weren't being blown off course by a tissue of myths and half-truths.

'I kept hoping it might wear off. That I could stop thinking about you. I hoped I'd imagined it all, but my feelings for you were like a tick burrowing. I did my best to ignore them. Pretended I'd imagined how lovely you were. I told myself you couldn't possibly be as nice as I remembered.'

I closed my eyes. There was such anguish on his face, it almost hurt.

'That doesn't sound very nice, does it?' he asked.

'Actually, it is. You were doing the honourable thing. The right thing by Victoria.'

'But it didn't wear off and when I saw you at Lynn and Richard's again, I ... I felt sick because I knew I was never going to get you out of my head. I knew I had to see you, but I couldn't until I finished with Victoria.'

I winced, guilt biting as my stomach clenched. So he had finished with her for me. I *was* the other woman. The weird mix of euphoria and nausea roared back. I felt like I was in the middle of a see-saw, balanced in between joy and pain.

'Then I wanted to wait because I didn't want you to be blamed for the break-up. I didn't want anything to…' He broke off with a mirthless laugh. 'Shit. This sounds so fucking cheesy. I didn't want anything to taint us.'

Then my heart wanted to burst. I'm Miss Practical; pink-hearts-and-red-roses romance is not my bag at all. I've seen too much of the reality of romance dressed up in fear, lies and loathing, but Sam's heartfelt words hit home like slugger punches. I knew he was being totally honest and for a minute I allowed myself to feel the glee, happiness and sheer joy. We were *so* on the same page, but he was right; it was freakishly terrifying.

I turned my hand over under his and opened my fingers so he could lace his through mine.

'Thank you,' I said. 'If it's any consolation, from the minute we met, I haven't been able to stop thinking about you. And I promise, I tried really hard not to. Women have enough trouble with men without having other women shit on them as well.'

'I left it as long as I could.' He squeezed my fingers. 'I've been shitting myself that you might hook up with someone else.'

With a laugh, I shook my head. 'I'm what's known as very picky.'

'So, Jessica Harper, will you go out with me?'

'Yes.'

'Can I take you out to dinner on Friday?'

'Next Friday?'

'No! Tomorrow, Friday.' He grinned. 'I didn't want to sound too needy.'

I nudged him with my shoulder. 'You idiot.'

He slung an arm around my shoulder. 'Who're you calling an idiot? I'll have you know my kids treat me with respect at school. They call me *Mr* Idiot.'

Chapter Eight

'So what're you going to wear?' asked Shelley, lolling across my bed, waving a glass of Prosecco towards my wardrobe. As soon as she heard I had a date with Sam, she'd hotfooted it over to my flat and insisted we crack open a bottle to celebrate the fact that I was *a hair's breadth away from getting a shag and all your dried-up inner workings might get lubricated*. Her words, not mine.

'I can't believe you didn't tell me before,' she moaned, taking a sip of fizz at the most awkward angle.

'If you spill that on my sheets, you can change them. I don't want Sam thinking I've wet the bed.' As soon as I said the words, I coloured bright red. Talk about the unconscious coming to the fore.

'Planning on bringing him back tonight, are we?' asked Shelley, immediately homing in on my slip of the tongue.

'No. Definitely not. Not at all.' I looked at the fresh duvet cover and undersheet which had been slipped on ten minutes before Shelley had arrived. I was not going to sleep with Sam. Not on a first date. I never did that sort of thing.

'Oooh, Jess is all flustered,' she teased. 'Aw, look at you, all pink and cute.'

'Just shut up,' I said, fighting a smile. 'You're such a bad influence.'

'Hardly, you're the goodest girl I know. Have you ever slept with anyone on a first date? Had a one-night stand?' She held up her hand before I could even shake my head. 'I rest my case. But I can tell you really like him. He's pretty phwoar. Bet he looks good naked.'

'Objectification, Shells.'

'Oh puhlease, girl. The man is sex on a stick. My hormones get in a tizz when I see him.'

'Your hormones are like over-anxious puppies. They get excited when they see anyone.'

'True,' sighed Shelley, not the least bit offended. 'What can I say? I'm the friendly type. I'm a people person. And this has all happened very fast. Spill, babes. Spill. What happened? And how come you kept so quiet about it?'

'Because there was nothing to tell until about seven o'clock last night. Now, what do you reckon? This dress?' I held up a silk dress that I'd only managed to wear once or twice. I'd bought it for a wedding a couple of years before and not had many occasions to drag it out again despite absolutely loving it. If I didn't work in a place where the women were lucky to have any clothes, let alone nice things, and had left all their favourite things behind, I would have been tempted to wear it for work just to get some use out of it.

Shelley rolled her eyes. 'I hate you. It's plain, plain, plain and you'll look flaming gorgeous in it. What size do they call that? Barbie?'

I ignored her and stripped off my towel. 'Oh God, I might need another shower before I go out.' I sniffed under my arms and Shelley tossed me the can of deodorant from my dressing table.

'It is sooooo hot,' she moaned flopping back on the pillows of my bed, making herself comfortable as I pulled on a strapless bra and my best knickers.

'Uh, shag me knickers. She's going in.'

'No, they're not,' I said perhaps a wee bit defensively. 'They're bus knickers.'

'Babe, no one is getting run over tonight. So where's Doctor Lurve taking you?'

'How old are you?'

'Twenty-nine and three-quarters, give or take a couple of days.' She grinned at me and lifted her Prosecco glass before taking a hefty, satisfied gulp.

I ignored her and pulled the dress over my head, loving the swish of the peacock-blue silk as it slithered into place.

'Yup, I really do hate you.'

I wrinkled my nose at her and smoothed the fabric over my hips, giving myself a quick glance in the mirror.

'And no, your frigging arse does not look big in that.'

'Neither do my boobs,' I pointed out, glancing at her magnificent cleavage displayed to full advantage in a fuchsia-pink playsuit, the fabric around her boobs only just containing the girls.

She patted them complacently. 'If you've got it, flaunt it.

Which is why you, pencil-stick-thin lady in the bias-cut number, look sensational.' She jumped up, her Prosecco shifting dangerously in her glass. 'You, cous, look flipping gorgeous. He's one lucky man and don't let him forget it.' She patted my cheek. 'Make him work for it, babe. You're far too nice to people. Although, give him brownie points for taking you to Olivio. It's well nice there.'

It was a smart restaurant over in the next town and she'd offered to give me a lift.

'I'm impressed. Good choice. You don't want to go out with a cheapskate no matter how manly or gorgeous he is. Sex doesn't put any meat on your bones.'

I ignored the latter comment. 'I'm not expecting him to pay for me. He's a teacher.' The restaurant was known for its relaxed, casual ambience and decidedly tasty food, which wasn't super expensive – but we weren't talking a quick Prezzo pizza either.

'You are so low maintenance.' She took a step back and pretended to study me. 'Are you sure you're related to me?'

I laughed. 'The jury's been out on that one for decades.'

'If a man takes me out for dinner, I expect him to dig deep.'

'And I prefer to pay my share. That way there's no expectation of any other sort of payment.'

'Again, are you related to me?'

'Shell, I'm not buying it. You're not that shallow. And you don't shag on a first date.'

She winked at me. 'Not always.'

'Sure you want me to drop you here?' asked Shelley with an exaggerated raise of her eyebrows as I directed her to the car park.

'Absolutely positive,' I said, gathering up my handbag from the footwell of her dinky Fiat 500.

'You spoil all my fun,' she said with a wicked grin, whipping the car into the smallest of spaces and ramming on the brakes, almost sending me through the windscreen.

'Yes,' I replied with a quick glance at my watch. I had ten minutes to walk to the restaurant, which was deliberate planning. 'You're not coming with me.' My repressive tone didn't have any effect. She grinned and I rolled my eyes. She would have waited with me like some kind of overbearing dad until Sam showed up.

'How are you getting home? Want me to pick you up later?'

'Sam said he'd give me a lift home,' I said, brushing an imaginary speck of fluff from the silk of my dress.

'And will you be inviting him in for coffee?' She shimmied her shoulders and lowered her voice.

'No!' I nudged her with my shoulder in protest at her pitiful attempt at being sultry and suggestive. 'Well, I might, but it will *only* be for coffee.' I opened the door, the heat of the afternoon hitting me as I started to slide out. It had been another scorching day with the temperatures soaring into the 30s.

'Have fun.' Once again, like a pair of naughty caterpillars, her eyebrows waggled. 'And make sure you text me all the deets as soon as you're home … unless of course he's with you.'

Ignoring her, I shut the car door, but I grinned as I walked away. Inside my stomach, a dozen drunken butterflies were lurching about, making me feel wayward and giddy ... and that anything could happen.

Maybe my senses were finely tuned to him or maybe I recognised his gait, but from the other end of the street I spotted him walking along ahead of me in the same direction and yeah, I almost stumbled. My hormones had some sort of early warning system and at the mere sight of him, my heart rate took off at a runaway gallop and my skin flushed with a rush of pleasure. In navy chinos and a white shirt with the sleeves rolled up to his tanned forearms, he looked yum. And no, I was not looking at his bum ... well, not especially. It was the first time I'd seen his hair loose, and although I'd didn't normally do men with long hair, the thick blond curls just added to the overall heart-socking package.

My pace slowed and for a moment I watched him, aware of the most ridiculous primitive urge to storm over, grab him and kiss the living daylights out of him. There was also a small matter of wanting to push my fingers through all that glorious hair. Yeah, my hormones had taken me hostage and were making crazy-girl demands. I needed to get a grip on them and on myself.

With a little involuntary sigh, I watched him for a few seconds more. OK, ogled might be more correct. I took in the long legs which my memory helpfully reminded me were nicely muscular and tanned. His phone was clamped to his ear and he was talking. He slowed and stopped, his head bobbing slightly. Even while admiring his perfect form, I could tell something wasn't right. He put a hand on his hip, then raised it to swap the phone to his other ear. It looked like a lengthy conversation. He started walking again. We were getting nearer to the restaurant. A few more paces and then he stopped again, waving his free hand in an expressive move that spoke of frustration and agitation. Then he stopped dead and as he turned so that I could see his profile, he threw his head back and looked upwards. It needed no lip-reading expert to discern the words 'God give me strength.' Whether he said them or just mouthed them I wasn't entirely sure, but it didn't take any kind of Poirot powers of deduction or little grey cells to figure out that he wasn't a happy camper.

I hesitated, loath to intrude while the selfish bit of me wanted to wade in, for him to stop the conversation. Today sizzled with so much promise and had been so long awaited. Pretty much since the first time I'd met Sam, he'd been there on the periphery of my thoughts. All day, anticipation had bubbled and fizzed, each hour marking another step closer towards basking in the fierce attraction between us.

He was now stationary and his hand movement was agitated, jabbing up and down in the air, so I took my time, giving the nearest shop windows a really thorough inspection. Five minutes later, I had price-checked every single holiday that the local travel agent were offering – I could fly to Malta for seven nights and stay in a four-star hotel for £599 from either Luton or Birmingham – and decided that the shoe-repair shop's less than inspiring display of shoe laces, insoles and polish didn't warrant any further interest but he was still on the phone, although he had now crossed the road and was outside the restaurant pacing up and down.

It was seven-thirty now. I glanced at my watch again, feeling uncomfortable. I could see Sam's face more clearly. Pain tinged the frustration. It was a conversation he really didn't want to be having and there was a sense of exaggerated patience in his words.

Every last butterfly in my stomach dropped dead mid-flight. This felt private but if he looked up now he would see me, so I couldn't retreat. I had to keep moving forward although I made my steps as small and slow as possible.

Chapter Nine

'No! I'm not lying to you, Vic... Yes, I'm seeing her tonight. Don't cry, please. I'm not trying to hurt you but we both have to move on. It's over.'

I stopped wishing I could retrace my steps. Any moment he was going to see me. A rush of guilt made me feel slightly sick. I'd caused this.

'It just...' He bit his lip and winced, listening intently with a pained frown on his face. 'Please don't do this, Vic. I'm sorry but...' I could see him searching for the right words and then backing away from them. 'It's over, we're just...'

'I've told you.' He sucked in a breath. 'I know. I know. I'm a dick. And a bastard. I'm sorry.'

From the way he flinched, I guessed another stream of invective had been launched. It was uncomfortable watching, voyeuristic and unpleasant, too much like seeing someone being beaten up. With each silence at his end, I could almost see the verbal assault coming down the phone, bringing blows that left his face an emotional landscape of wariness, frustration, guilt, shame and exasperation. With each of those gaps in the conversation, I felt something tugging at the tight, hard ball of guilt sitting in my gut.

'We've talked already,' Sam's weary voice belied his pain-filled face, 'there isn't anything... You didn't do anything wrong... I don't want you to change ... because *things* have changed ... not you.' He winced again. 'Yes! Yes, it's me. No! I don't mean it to be a cliché. I've tried to explain... You can't keep doing this.' He winced, his shoulders hunched, one hand rammed in his pocket and then he spotted me. For the briefest of moments, guilt tinged his eyes. 'I've got to go.'

I heard the wail.

'OK. OK. I'll call you later. I don't know what time. Tomorrow... No! I'm not sl—sleeping with her.' He looked up at me, horrified eyes catching mine. 'I'm going.'

Ramming his phone into his pocket, his face creased into another frown.

'Hi,' he said, 'I don't suppose there's any chance you didn't hear that?' Sadness and defeat filled his eyes as he tried to smile at me. Sam's usual kilowatt smile was nowhere in evidence. It was heartbreaking. Maybe I should make his life easier and stop this now.

I shook my head. 'Sounds like she's not in a good place.' I wanted to give him a big hug. He looked distraught. 'I'm sorry.' I reached out and squeezed his forearm as if that might help in some stupid pathetic way.

'Don't be.' He pulled a face. 'I... I made the mistake of telling her that I was seeing someone. She wanted to meet up tonight for a drink. She wants us to be friends. When I told her I was going out tonight, she asked who with. Of course she did.' He shook his head at his own stupidity.

'Oh.' I said in sympathy, because I could see exactly how that would have panned out, Sam too honest to lie and Victoria on it like a sniffer dog. Women always have a sixth sense about these things.

'I could kick myself. I might as well have issued a personal challenge. The minute I said, "No one you know," she immediately wanted to know who.' He rolled his eyes and I could see from his defeated demeanour that she'd worn him down. 'Eventually I had to tell her. That was this morning.' He rubbed a hand over his face.

I wondered how many times she'd phoned him today.

'I feel like a shit … but I've been trying to do the right thing. I deliberately waited for a month before I asked you out.'

'Do you want to take a raincheck?' I asked, all the happy anticipation vanishing, leaving my voice slightly flat. I looked down at my feet, not wanting him to see the unhappy disappointment I knew I couldn't hide. 'Maybe it's for the best.'

'Are you kidding me?' He clutched my arm, as if I might run off. 'No! It's over with Vic. I can't go back now and … I don't want to.' With a gentle hand he lifted my chin. 'Jess, I know this is all a bit crazy and sometimes it doesn't feel quite real until I see you again and then I know it's you I want to be with. Yesterday at the pub felt so right and easy.' With a hesitant smile he added, 'I've not stopped thinking about you. It's the only thing that's making all this bearable.'

Those butterflies made a miraculous recovery and took flight in one big surge, making me suck in a quick unexpected breath.

'Oh!' I whispered, smiling back at him before saying without thinking, 'Me too. Holly at work kept throwing things at me today.' Oops. Perhaps too much information, but because he smiled down at me, I added, 'I was a bit distracted.'

He stroked my lower lip, sending a sizzle rocketing through me, kick-starting a low hum of longing between my legs. Hello and welcome to Jess the slut. Where had this come from? Suddenly, I wanted to bite down on his index finger and hold onto it between my teeth and lick the pad of his finger. Down, Jess, down.

As if he'd read my mind, Sam gave me a low, lingering, warm smile.

'You look gorgeous.'

'You too.' I reached up and tugged at one of his blond curls, catching sight of a slightly drunken pink rose tucked in his pocket.

'Nice rose,' I teased. The blousy pink petals of the droopy flower were well past their best.

He pulled it out of his pocket, the thorn on the stem catching on the fabric and with a suddenly solemn expression handed it over, turning it so the sharp thorn didn't touch my hand. 'I'm supposed to give this to you. Sorry,' he pulled a face, 'it didn't like the heat. I did put it in water for a while but then I was worried I'd forget it. And then I'd be in big trouble.'

'Thank you.' From the serious expression on his face and the careful precision with which he gave it to me, the flower was clearly laden with some significance I had yet to divine.

'Esme in my class said I had to give it to you especially, if you looked pretty tonight. She's seven.'

My heart did a little bungy jump at his words and the considering tilt of his head, tipped to one side as he gazed down with a tender smile that had me turning to complete mush.

'Pretty girls get flowers apparently, and she was worried I didn't have any, because I don't have a garden and her mum has loads.' Hearing the little girl's words in his phrasing almost finished me off. Well, what the heck did a person say to that? This man was going to kill me.

With a slight croak to my voice, I said, 'Tell Esme that I loved it.' I lifted the droopy bloom to my nose, sniffing the distinctive floral fragrance – one of my favourites – as my eyes went a little blurry.

Sam leaned forward and with the pad of his thumb stroked the tell-tale dampness from beneath my eye as he said, quiet laughter in his voice, 'She also gave me some instructions for the evening.'

'She did?' I blinked.

'The whole class did.' He shook his head. 'They think I need the help.'

Studying his twitching lips, as if he could barely hold back his amusement, I bit back a smile.

'Must be bad if you're taking dating advice from, what, seven-year-olds?' I teased.

'Seven, eight, nine and ten,' he responded. 'My own fault. I never should have said what I was doing on a Friday night.'

'I did wonder how it came up.'

'Don't worry. I don't normally share my love life with my class. Or take relationship advice from them.' He cupped a hand under my elbow and we started walking towards the restaurant entrance.

'It's probably not a good habit to get into.'

'We were talking about weekend plans. I was asking them what they were all doing. And foolishly said that I was going out to dinner. At that age they're all desperate for me to be married and one of them asked me if I was going out with my girlfriend and…' he gave a sheepish shrug, 'it was easier to say yes. At that age, the boundaries are quite fixed. Adults have wives and husbands, boyfriends and girlfriends. Explaining the concept of a first date was beyond me.'

'I can imagine.' I bit my lip, smiling wryly. What would he say if I told him what Holly'd had to say about me going on a first date?

She'd thrown a stapler at me when I'd wondered aloud, admittedly for about the seventh time, what I should wear tonight, before saying with a long-suffering roll of her black-winged eyes, 'Just make sure, for my sake, you get yourself laid. Perhaps if you get it out of the way, you'll bloody calm down. You're like a cat on a hot tin roof on roller skates. You're going to break that chair with all your fidgeting.'

The restaurant was quiet and subdued and mercifully cool. Even though it was early evening, the pavements and buildings seemed to have soaked up the heat of the day and were now radiating it back into the air like the most efficient, ill-timed central heating on the planet.

Nearly every table was occupied and low chatter filled the air, but despite being quite busy, it was the sort of place where there was plenty of space around each table, offering a certain sense of privacy.

Sam pulled my chair out for me with a quick sidelong glance and I thanked him with a low murmur, both of us suddenly shy. Every sensible thought had vanished out of my head and all I could do was stare at Sam's white-cotton-covered biceps, my mouth as dry as the Sahara.

Luckily the waiter, oblivious to the anticipatory hush, scurried over offering menus and going into great detail about the specials.

'Would you like wine?' asked Sam, screwing his face up as he opened up the wine menu as the waiter stood in rigid anticipation.

'Can we have a minute?' I asked the waiter.

Sam's haunted look of relief as the waiter silently stepped away was palpable.

'What do you drink?' he asked not even looking at the open pages. 'Red. White. Pink stuff.' The gingerly hold he had on the menu, as if he'd be more comfortable handling explosives, made me pinch my lips so I didn't smile.

'You'd rather have a beer, wouldn't you?' I said with a pointed look at the menu, trying to hold back my amusement.

'I can drink wine.' Caution edged his words.

'Sam. Have a beer.' I hooked a finger over the edge of the menu, pushing it down towards the table.

'You sure?' he asked, relief already creeping into his eyes.

'Yes. Although it might have helped if you'd had the menu the right way up,' I added with a teasing grin.

A faint pink stained his cheeks. 'Ah, bollocks.' He laughed and dropped the menu on the table, his blue eyes dancing with mirth. 'This might as well be written in Swahili. I don't know anything about wine. Vic always… She knew about wine.' His uncomfortable smile had me reaching for his hand.

'You can mention her, you know. Four years is a long time.'

'I don't want to. This evening is supposed to be about you.' He reined in the quick flash of irritated anger I saw dart across his face. 'What would you like?'

'I'm actually not a big drinker. And … I've already had half a bottle of Prosecco with Shelley before I came out.'

'And how is your cousin?'

'She's good and sends her love.'

'And Aunty Lynn and Uncle Richard?' he asked, before adding quickly, 'I've told my parents about you.'

I laughed. It didn't take much to join the dots. 'Probably

a good idea. I love my aunt and uncle to bits but they wouldn't know discretion if it came up and slapped them round the face. I can't believe Aunty Lynn hasn't texted me; Shell is bound to have told her already. So, it's guaranteed your mother will know that we've been out by close of play tomorrow.' I hadn't mentioned a word to my mother and had absolutely no intention of doing so.

'Not a problem.' He reached over the table and took my hand. 'I've got nothing to hide. I told mum about you last week.' His eyes swept over my face and softened into gentle admiration which gave a kick to my pulse.

'W–what did she say?' Good job I didn't need to stand; my legs had turned to jelly. 'I mean, after four years, she must know Victoria quite well.' Not having met his mother, it was difficult to gauge whether Sam's mum would be wrapping a hat in newspaper and shoving it back in the loft or pleased that her son would be hers for a while longer. I knew Bel's boyfriend's mother had been dropping hints about weddings from the day she and Dan passed their six-month mark.

'Not much.' He lifted one shoulder and rotated it in a quick circle as if it were a physical manifestation of his sudden discomfort. 'I don't think she wants to know much at the moment, as Vic keeps in touch with her.'

'Probably easier,' I said, tracing the tines of the fork on my left. The enormity of navigating the family landscape and Sam's life as the new woman cast a shadow I hadn't really considered before. I had never met my father's new woman. Her hold on him had been such that he'd been withheld from me ever since. He belonged to her now and had done from the moment he'd gone. Not only had I lost a father, I'd also lost grandparents. Although Sam and Victoria weren't married, I wouldn't deny her the relationships she'd formed with Sam's family. It wasn't fair. After all, I was the usurper in this case.

'After all that time, she's part of your family. I wouldn't dream of coming between that. It must be hard enough for her as it is.' My heart ached for all that she'd lost, even while my pulse danced when Sam picked up my hand and squeezed it, his thumb stroking the sensitive skin on the inside of my wrist.

'I'm not planning on hiding anything, Jess.' The look in those deep blue eyes held unwavering determination and conviction. 'I didn't want to put Mum in a difficult position. Her knowing about you before Vic.'

'I understand that. It would be sad if they didn't stay in touch.' How would I feel? Turfed out of a family dynamic I was used to? It seemed unfair. And once again, my desire to be with Sam warred with the horrible feeling that I was the cuckoo in the nest. Poor Vic had lost more than a boyfriend.

Sam's phone, which he'd laid on the table next to his hand, beeped with a text alert, but he ignored it.

'So, what are you drinking?'

'I'll stick to Prosecco,' I said, having spotted they did it by the glass.

He grinned, his whole face lighting up and suddenly all my worries vanished. I felt that magic hit of sunshine as he lowered his voice and leaned forward across the table. 'That reminds me of the first time I met you. At Lynn and Richard's. Don't think I've ever seen quite so many empty bottles of Prosecco as in their recycling bin. Or a pair of legs quite so gorgeous.' He lifted his brows in over-the-top, lascivious admiration that made me burst out laughing, which handily hid the leap in my pulse and the warm burst of something between my thighs.

We studied the menus and although he was no longer holding my hand, his lay side by side with mine, our thumbs linked in a casual, easy touch.

'So what are you going to have?' he asked.

'I shouldn't, but I'm going to have Spaghetti Bolognese.'

'Why not?'

'Because I can make it any time at home and I ought to have something more … fancy.'

'Why? You should have exactly what you want.'

'What are you having?'

He grinned at me. 'Spaghetti Bolognese, because it's my absolutely favourite and if you can make it…' The mock swoon he did at the table made me giggle.

The waiter appeared and we placed our orders.

'Can you cook?' I asked, suddenly curious for details as the waiter disappeared, leaving us alone again. Despite feeling like I knew him, there was so much about him I actually didn't know. 'Where do you live? And did you live with…?'

'I cook a mean English breakfast, my poached eggs are to die for, and that's not a line, by the way.' He winked. By this stage I was comfortably sure that breakfast would be on the cards in the not too distant future. 'My BLT sandwiches are a lunchtime legend. And people have been known to rave about my Chicken Dansak, Prawn Pathia and Lamb Mogwai.'

'That's quite a particular repertoire.' I giggled. 'Although isn't a mogwai from *Gremlins*?'

Sam waved a blasé 'whatever' hand. 'Mogwai. Mogli. Muggli. Mrs Patel. Grandma at school. Her grandson Milan is in my class. At the end of term she always brings in a curry for us.' He grinned. 'She thinks it's shocking that I'm not married yet. So she gave me the recipes for the curries and came into the school kitchen to teach me how to cook them. That's my entire repertoire. You'll have to come over for dinner. As long as you like curry.

'And no, Vic and I didn't live together…' He paused, his look direct as if he too didn't want to give her any more of our evening. 'Thank God. It would have made breaking up even harder.' He frowned. 'I mean, getting away from her. She wanted to move in together. I was the one that didn't. She comes from quite a wealthy background. Her flat is … well, not what I could afford. Mine's housing association. Only twenty-five per cent is mine. It's a start.' He shrugged.

'Snap,' I said. 'You don't get paid much working for a charity.'

His phone beeped again. I glanced at it, catching sight of the text appearing on the screen, the three letters of Vic's name obvious even upside down and at a distance.

'Sorry.' He winced and put the phone on silent before turning it over.

'Cool cover,' I said, catching sight of the words on the case.

*Being a teacher is as easy as riding a bike … except the bike is on
fire, you are on fire, everything is on fire.*

'One of the kids' mums bought it for me at the end of
term last year.'

'That was thoughtful.'

'It was, and a welcome relief from the usual teacher
gifts.'

'Do you get many?'

'Tons. I never have to buy socks.' He grinned at me and
lifted a leg out from under the table, pulling up his trouser
leg to reveal a Homer Simpson sock. 'Or chocolate biscuits.
Or cake tins. I have to run every day in the holidays to work
off all the Quality Street. And I have boxes of Fox's Assorted
Biscuits stockpiled that will last until the Christmas after
next.'

'Poor you,' I teased. 'Must be tough.'

'I guess you don't get much in the way of leaving gifts.'

'No, but that's not why I do the job. When a family leaves
us, usually it's the start of a new chapter in their lives. And
no one's kidding anyone that it's going to be sunshine and
roses. But occasionally,' I pulled out my key ring which
sported a bright pink, purple and electric-blue wool pom-
pom, 'residents make us something. Lady called Nadya gave
this to me.' I stroked it. The pom-pom was huge and, to be
honest, a right pain. You couldn't just shove it in your back
pocket if you were popping out for milk or stuff it in a cute
clutch bag if you were out at night. But it was a wonderful
reminder of a success story and I wouldn't be parted from it.

'She came to the refuge three years ago. Her husband closed her hand in a car door one night,' I said, as matter-of-factly as I could, still able to recall her bruised, swollen and bent fingers. 'She'd disobeyed him by leaving the house when he was out, to get medicine for their youngest son who had terrible toothache. It was an arranged marriage. Her family refused to believe that her husband was being violent and abusive towards her.'

'He did it deliberately?' asked Sam, horrified.

I nodded. 'Nadya had to have several operations to fix her hand. She made this for me in one of her occupational therapy classes.' I shook my head. 'I … don't normally talk about this stuff but she's officially one of our success stories and features on our website. Although she still has problems with her hand. Two of her boys have been signed up to Watford's football youth academy and she's completing her second year in accounting and finance at the University of Hertfordshire.'

'That sounds like a good outcome.'

'Yeah, it is.' I stroked the pom-pom before putting it back in my bag.

'So how long have you worked for the refuge? And where do you work?'

'I've been there for five years. And the location is a closely guarded secret.'

Sam nodded. 'I get that.'

'You're one of the first, then. I've lost count of the number of people who say, "But you can tell me; I'm not going to tell anyone." And then they're quite offended when you refuse. Which is why I don't normally talk about my job.'

Sam rolled his eyes in understanding. 'I know exactly where you're coming from. I get a lot of "There weren't autistic children in my day" or "It's just parents wanting labels" and the best one, "They're just naughty children". Why are people so willing to comment on things they know absolutely nothing about? Drives me nuts.' He ran a hand through his hair, pulling at the curls.

I smiled. Who knew? Long man-hair was definitely growing on me.

As our food was served, we dropped into seamless conversation, gently mining each other's history, finding out about commonalities and differences. Both only-children. Both went to university. Neither had a burning urge to earn heaps of money.

'Just as well,' quipped Sam as we drained our coffee cups, one hand intertwined with mine as it had been since the waiters had taken away our dessert dishes, his index finger idly stroking mine, sending little runaway tremors of giddiness through me. Like a train in headlong flight, clickety-clacking over the lines, we seemed to be exchanging more and more loaded eye-meets, openly holding each other's gazes with twinkly private smiles that had my heart-rate skyrocketing.

Suddenly the waiter was presenting us with the bill and a pointed look towards the door where a queue had started to form. The last two hours had flown by and there still seemed to be so much more to say. We looked at each other with a small, loaded silence, Sam's finger freezing.

'Still early… Do you fancy going on somewhere?' he asked.

'I thought you'd never ask.' I grinned at him.

Sam paid, after a small argument which was quickly resolved when I said I would pay next time. His answering grin, so delighted at the quiet acceptance that there was going to be a next time, almost lit up the entire restaurant.

'So what are you doing tomorrow?' he asked.

'I … I haven't got any plans, as a matter of fact,' I said. There was no point even attempting to play it cool; Sam could see straight through me.

'I'd like to take you out somewhere.' His hand brushed my neck as he helped swathe the navy cashmere throw around my shoulders.

'I guess you could do that,' I replied, meeting his warm smile with one of my own. He leaned forward and brushed my lips.

'It's a date,' he murmured.

As we stepped out of the restaurant into the street, the daylight just starting to wane, he looked at his wrist. 'Do you fancy going to the Ferry Boat? Or somewhere else?'

An image of a crowded canalside, people packed onto the wooden picnic benches and strings of fairy lights illuminating the beer garden, popped into my head, quickly contrasting with the cool quiet picture of the four-pack of beer in the bottom shelf of my fridge, the bottle of white on the inside of the door and the two bistro chairs on my balcony.

And the grey and yellow Aztec print of the crisp, clean sheets on my bed.

'Would you...?' I paused, catching his eye with a shy smile. A tiny jolt of electricity sizzled for a bare second as he took my hand, nodding as if he knew exactly what I'd been about to say.

'Oh shit!' His grasp on my hand tightened involuntarily as his head whipped around.

Across the street, like some gothic heroine, in a flowing white lacy dress that emphasised her long, elegant limbs and golden tan, stood Victoria, her stance poignant with misery. Her head drooped to one side, her hands clasped together, and she looked as if a puff of wind might blow her away. I felt sick with apprehension and guilt.

Suddenly she darted across the road to the loud blare of a horn as a car narrowly missed her, and threw herself at Sam, wrenching him round. His hand popped out of mine like a cork pulled from a bottle.

'Sam, Sam.' She burst into tears and wilted into his arms. My stomach turned over, clenching as if someone had punched me.

'Please don't do this to me. Please, I can't bear it. We need to talk.' She wrapped herself around him, her beautiful face tilted up towards his, her eyes desperate and beseeching. All the pictures of them together that I'd seen on Instagram popped back into my head with Mary Poppins spell-like precision. Pop! Victoria's selfies of her and Sam on the beach. Pop! Queuing for a Ferris wheel. Pop! A candlelit dinner in a restaurant. In all of these images she was strong and determined, a glossy girl full of self-confidence and sure of her place in the world. Now she'd been reduced, somehow, become smaller and lost. She looked utterly distraught, almost mad with despair. It was a brutal reminder of how my father's departure had destroyed my mother.

'Vic.' Sam's hoarse voice dragged my attention back to him, and the sight of his face made my stomach clench even harder. He looked so torn. Shit, this was a mess. Stormy, in-your-face, raw emotion. My fingernails pricked the palms of my hands. At work I could deal with the bruised, defeated women who cried and wept because they were lost and displaced from everything they knew; but there, I was removed from their pain and hurt, and when I met them, they'd already taken the first step towards making their lives better.

Other people were responsible for their pain but this, this was right in my face and there was no escaping it. *I'd* done this. *I* caused this.

'I can't bear it, Sam.' Victoria buried her head in his chest and sobbed with gut-wrenching, shoulder-blade racking heaves. He closed his arms around her, his hand stroking the dark satin, shampoo-ad shiny, curtain of her loose hair, his eyes screwed tightly shut. I felt so desperately sorry for both of them. No one deserved to be hurt like this. I took a step backwards as Sam opened his eyes and looked at me, the expression in them so bleak I couldn't begin to dredge up a smile of sympathy.

Instead I waved my phone at him weakly and mouthed, 'I'll get an Uber.'

He started, and then gave a frown and a shake of his head, and then with a resigned look down at Victoria mouthed, 'I'm sorry. I'll call.'

I nodded and ducked my head, walking quickly away and rounding the very first corner I came to in order to get out of sight as soon as possible, and then I bent double at the physical ache of pain and guilt. How could I do that to another person? Strong as the feelings were that I had for Sam, I couldn't do this.

Chapter Ten

'You can take the day off,' I said to my mobile as I pushed it to the back of the messy make-up- and jewellery-strewn surface of the chest of drawers that served as my dressing table. Yes, I was being a coward but I didn't want to see what my text messages had to say.

I'd switched my phone off last night after Sam's apologetic text, which had coincided with the Uber dropping me off outside my flat. A brief one-line missive – so brief that I guessed it had been snatched in a moment of reprieve, perhaps at a urinal or at the bar buying a drink, and that he was still with Victoria. I predicted a long night there.

I hadn't bothered replying. Not last night and not this morning. I didn't want Sam's explanations, excuses or apologies. My feelings were too muddled and mixed up to get a grip on them. I wasn't sure what I did want, which was why the phone was staying mute. In one way I was Miffed – and yes, miffed with a capital M. The dictionary definition – annoyed by something someone has done to you – summed it up perfectly. I wasn't mad at Sam, but I was miffed at the situation. Miffed that despite all the feelings he'd professed, Victoria still came first, and yes, that was me being contrary, but despite my sympathy for her I still had a strong sense of my own self-worth. I wasn't prepared to be messed about. So, when I received his first text – *SORRY* – all-caps just wasn't going to cut it. I switched my phone off. Childishness, ten. Maturity, nil.

Ten minutes later, while in the shower, I realised I'd made a grave strategic error in switching my phone off. Shelley would have been expecting an update on the date and, given patience didn't feature in her DNA, she could batter down the door at any moment. And, right on cue, there was a heavy knock at the door.

Still tucking the towel in above my chest, I pulled open the front door. 'I knew you couldn't – Sam!'

My mouth really did drop open and my heart turned a couple of back flips in quick succession, making me light-headed and disorientated. He was absolutely the last person I was expecting. He didn't even know where I lived … except he patently did. For a minute I stared at all of that glowing good health and handsomeness standing on my doorstep, his still damp blond hair bundled in a ponytail as he gave me a hopeful smile.

'Hi. I wondered if you fancied coming canoeing?' He gestured over his shoulder to a car with a bright red canoe on a roof rack. 'I've got a picnic lunch. No phones. No interruptions. Just you, me and the ducks,' he paused. 'And abject apologies. I'm really sorry about last night. You haven't responded to any of my texts. And I don't blame you. What sort of bloke dumps his date for his ex? I just never expected her to do that. She's beside herself and it's so out of character; it scared the hell out of me. I was worried what she might do. Please give me a second chance.'

At the sight of his open face, his blue eyes brimming with sunshine, honesty and that earnest regret, all my good intentions wavered. My whole system had been poleaxed, and the sight of him stirred a yearning that I'd never felt before. I did want to spend time with him. There was a pull between us that hollowed out my heart. My brain leapt in with a stream of logic as if trying to cushion my emotional response and give it permission to move forward. He'd been hijacked last night; he deserved at least to be allowed to apologise. And wouldn't it be sad to deny that insane attraction shimmering between us that promised so much?

My brain kept bombarding me with reasons to say yes and, suddenly, being miffed seemed rather petty and really not my style. I don't normally sulk or brood and I don't like people who do. Sam deserved that second chance.

'I just need to put some clothes on.'

'If you must,' he sighed, his eyes crinkling with a naughty smile.

I raised a reproving eyebrow and watched as his face sobered as he realised he had a lot of work to do to earn my forgiveness. Leaving the door open, I turned tail and dashed up the stairs.

Tugging a brush through my hair, I yanked it into a high ponytail, sprayed a ton of deodorant under my arms – the weather forecast was for another scorcher – and pulled on some underwear. Everyday white cotton underwear this time. I'd wasted the good stuff on him last night; he wasn't getting a second chance on that front. But vanity made me dig out my Daisy Dukes, which did good things for my legs, and a skimpy vest top which did nothing for my uncontoured chest but did enhance my fine collarbones and smooth shoulders. All the while I felt the fizz of excitement and hope, and when I clattered back down the stairs, I couldn't help the big smile on my face.

'That was quick,' he said with a quick appreciative smile, still lurking in the doorway.

'No point wasting this glorious weather,' I said, looking up at the sky. I hoped my quick shrug looked nonchalant, when inside every cell was singing with happiness. 'You do realise it's the only reason I'm coming. It's a day to be outside and on water.' No point making things too easy for him.

He nodded gravely and I felt a bit mean. It wasn't like me to play games, but he needed to know how I felt about the situation.

'Look, I'm sorry I kept my phone off and didn't reply to your texts. This is uncharted territory for me, but I refuse to be the "other" woman. I'm just not playing that game. It's all or nothing.' I felt uncomfortable being cast in that role and it felt like a horrible irony. For years I despised my dad for running off with another woman and leaving a wife and child. But Sam hadn't run off with me and I needed to remember that. Even so, it made me wonder how Dad's partner had felt. Did she know how much damage she'd caused. Did she care?

'I understand.' He took my hand. Smooth move, Sam. Except, it didn't look *smooth*; it looked heartfelt. 'I'm sorry for abandoning you. It was an awkward situation that I didn't handle very well. We were out on a date; I should have taken you home.'

'Right.' I nodded, accepting his words, although part of me wondered what else he could have done without being a complete bastard. How would I have felt if he'd walked away and left Victoria? I wouldn't have thought much of him, for sure. He'd been in a no-win situation and I ought to cut him some slack. 'OK, shall we go?'

'That's it?' he asked warily.

'Yup. You messed up but you've admitted it. You've apologised. I've had my sulk. We're even.'

Uncertainty clouded his eyes, as if I still might have a tantrum or two up my sleeve.

'Sam,' I patted his arm, 'it's done. There's some famous saying, accept the past, don't let it affect the future, or something like that. Now, are you taking me out or not?'

'Have you ever been canoeing before?' he asked, taking my hand and leading the way to the car.

'Not recently. I used to go to a Christian camp when I was a kid – it was that or Filey with my mother and her best friend. We did all sorts of outdoor activities, but it's been a while. I'm assuming as you have your own canoe, you're an expert.'

'I borrowed it,' he said with a grin. 'But I'll try not to capsize us.'

The canoe glided through the water as Sam paddled – somewhat expertly to my mind – down the canal and away from the busy reservoir which today was teeming with people. We kept the conversation easy and impersonal, 'Oh, look, a heron' and 'Isn't it hot?' sort of stuff, which wasn't difficult to keep up given Sam, up front, had his back to me. After only a few minutes we had the shady towpath on this stretch of water to ourselves, with the rhythm of the splish-splosh of his paddle dipping in and out of the water the headline above the muted sound of bird calls and the whisper of a welcome breeze through the trees.

Despite the shadows of the trees dappling the sunlit water and the inquisitive ducks, their feathers gleaming with iridescence, my gaze kept straying to the muscles in Sam's back, the rise and fall of his shoulder blades and the strong forearms handling the paddle with smooth command. If I were the sort of girl looking for a hunter-gatherer type to take care of me, he'd just ticked every last box. I grinned. My thoughts were running on earthier lines, like what he'd say if I stripped off his T-shirt or licked the back of his neck just where the hairline stopped and his top reached up with each paddle stroke. Just watching him, dip and stroke, I was getting all hot and bothered, and it had nothing to do with the blazing sun.

Honest to God, when we stopped, I felt a little breathless. Making it look easy, he steered the canoe into the bank and hopped out, holding the boat with the paddle while leaning to grab my hand. Gingerly, I stood and clumsily stepped out with Sam's aid.

He hauled the canoe up onto the bank and picked up the wicker picnic basket that had been stowed in the bow. Get me, with the nautical terms.

'Nice spread,' I said looking at a number of Marks and Spencer packs of olives, sun-dried tomatoes and mozzarella, as well as a couple of packets of posh crisps and an assortment of sandwiches. 'Someone's been busy this morning.'

'I realised I needed to pull a few rabbits out of hats to make up for last night,' he said with a sheepish tilt of his head. 'I was hoping you'd be at the parkrun this morning, and when you weren't I knew I needed to move fast. I was worried you might be going out today. I got hold of Lynn's number from Mum and called her to get your address.'

I winced. 'I have a confession. I chickened out of going this morning. I'd decided that after last night, this...' I pointed between the two of us, 'probably wasn't worth the aggro.'

Sam's mouth crumpled momentarily but he rallied quickly to give me a reluctant smile. 'I guess I don't blame you. I'm really sorry about what happened last night. I just didn't know what to do. I never dreamed that Victoria would turn up. I've no idea how she even knew where we were.'

'Tracking your phone?' I asked. 'Shelley did that to me once; she thought it was hilarious. For weeks she was sending me what I thought were random texts when I just happened to be in Tesco. I'd get a shopping list by text and

JULES WAKE

a "don't suppose you're anywhere near a shop, you couldn't just pick a couple of things up for me" message. Once I was in Aylesbury and she asked me to pick up a delivery from Argos. It turned out she'd seen where I was and had gone online to order something knowing I was nearby. Cheeky minx. It took me ages to figure out what she'd been up to.'

Sam tried to bite back a wry smile. 'That is pretty funny.'

'Yeah, being my cousin's shopping bitch for two months was just hilarious.' I shook my head as he still diplomatically managed not to laugh out loud.

'And I think you're probably right about Vic tracking my phone.' He let out a long, noisy sigh. 'I don't know what got into her. She'd been fine about the break-up.'

Someone hadn't clocked the black-widow series on Instagram. I winced. 'Fine? Really?'

'OK, fine's not the right word. Sort of accepting. There's no good way of breaking up with someone. I did my best to be as kind as I could about it, but it was really difficult. How do you split up with someone without telling them that you've met someone else?' He pushed an impatient hand through his unruly hair. 'That's got to be a killer. So I didn't tell her that's why I was finishing things. Maybe I should have done.'

'What did you tell her?' I asked softly, conscious of the whiteness of his knuckles on his twisting fingers.

'The old, *it's not you, it's me.*' He scratched at his neck as he stared across the canal. 'There's a reason for clichés; they fit the situation. Now I realise I should have been honest at the outset. I guess I left her with some hope that if I'd changed my mind without any strong reason after four years, I might change it back.'

Unfortunately, I thought he'd made a very good point.

'I know it's not easy for her. I completely get that I'm the bastard here. I've been deliberately keeping a low profile. Not rocking the boat. I haven't been out with any of our group for a month, so I don't upset her. Mike, my best mate, is going out with Vic's best friend, Paige. Paige is refusing to speak to me and gives Mike a hard time if he sees me. And I get it; I'm the one who's messed everything up. All the girls think I'm a total wanker. And the lads are keeping their heads down.' His mouth twisted wryly. 'I'm about as popular as a fart in a spacesuit right now.'

Sam's patent disgust with himself made me put a hand on his knee which was jumping up and down, the sunlight glinting from the golden hairs on his legs. He looked so vital and full of life that the downbeat expression on his face seemed a terrible anomaly.

I had no idea what to say. Selfish Jess didn't want to hear any of this but Jess, the daughter of my mother, needed to ask as some sort of penance for being the person Sam had picked instead of Victoria.

I let the silence settle for a moment before asking the question quietly haunting me. 'Do you think you should go back to her? Wouldn't it be easier?'

There you go. One perfectly formed, Sam-shaped escape-hatch handed over on a platter. A nice, quick exit, fuss-free and no one's pride hurt – or even so much as dented.

Without hesitation, Sam looked straight into my eyes,

clear resolve in his expression. 'No. I want to be with you. I wouldn't have chucked away four years if I didn't feel sure. For me,' his eyes met mine, strong and steady, 'there's no going back. I want to be with you, whatever that looks like. I mean, in some ways we hardly know each other; in others I feel like I've always known you.'

His words made everything inside me soften. I knew exactly what he meant. That weird sensation of completeness which I couldn't find words to explain but I felt down to my fingertips.

I lifted a hand, palm forwards, fingers stretching up to the sky, needing to share it with him, and he placed his against mine, our fingers aligned. It was a silent acknowledgement between us as our eyes locked on each other's, while around us the air danced with insects dipping into the water, notes of birdsong sprinkling down from the trees, and the sun dappled through the overhead tracery of leaves.

'I've never felt like this before and … it scares me. The damage we could do.' I thought of my mother, hamstrung by bitterness.

'Don't be scared. We're in this together, Jess.' His fingers closed around mine. 'We have nothing to be ashamed of.'

He was right. We hadn't done anything wrong – but telling myself that was easier than truly believing it.

Chapter Eleven

S helley's scrawl in red Sharpie on a note pinned to my door greeted our return when we tumbled out of the car, sun-kissed, happy and ready for cold beers on my balcony.

*You are either walking around like John Wayne with an unseemly smile on your dirty little face or buried in a shallow grave somewhere. Either way, FFS turn your ****ing phone back on and call me.*

Sam laughed as I turned a colour which had nothing to do with the day's exposure to the sunshine and ripped the note from the door. One of these days I would overcome all my scruples and, favourite cousin or not, I would strangle her.

'Come on up.' I led the way up the narrow staircase to my first-floor flat, conscious of Sam still sniggering behind me.

'This is…' Sam did a quick three-sixty, taking in the high ceiling and big apex window of my lounge and the little balcony beyond.

'Why I bought the flat,' I finished. 'Beer?'

He followed me into the kitchen, which was just about big enough to swing a small hamster, its proportions best suited to a contortionist.

'Nice place,' he said as I wriggled between the old chimney breast and the fridge to pull out two bottles of Bud from the fridge.

'You mean, interesting,' I said wryly. I'd got used to the low sloping ceiling in the corner of the kitchen and the distinct lack of cupboard space. It wasn't the most practically shaped room, but the rest of the flat more than made up for it and, as I spent very little time in here, it didn't bother me. I am to cooking what John Sargent was to the Paso Doble. (Why is it always a surprise to everyone that I'm such a *Strictly* fan?)

'It suits you.'

'Hmm, I'll take that as a compliment,' I said, shooting him a grin as I dug out the bottle opener and a bag of Kettle chips.

'Cheers.' Sam chinked his bottle against mine. 'That noise,' he grinned and leaned forward, lifting his bottle against mine again, 'will always remind me of the first time I met you.' His foot nudged mine and like a pair of idiots we smiled at each other, holding each other's gaze for a ridiculously long time, until finally Sam lifted his head and took a long slow pull of his beer. Who knew that watching someone drink beer could be sexy? I felt as jumpy as a skittish cat all of a sudden, fidgety, impatient and far too hot. Without thinking, I rested the cold bottle between my cleavage – or what little of it there is. Sam's mouth quirked and I snatched the bottle up to my mouth, taking a hasty sip. The sudden movement sent beer frothing out of the neck of the bottle, down my chin and straight down the vee of my chest. Sam's eyes followed the line of liquid. Leaning forward, he lifted the hem of his T-shirt and dabbed the beer from my skin.

Don't look down, Jess. *Eyes to face. Eyes to face.* But it was no good; I'd already got an eyeful of Sam's bare torso which had tattooed itself onto my retinas, possibly for ever. Oh my, seriously! Abs like that existed in real life? And properly defined pecs? And the less said about the dusty blond trail of hair dipping from his navel down into the opening of his shorts, the better. All my hormones short-circuited, taking any ideas of being a good girl right off the table. His fingers grazed the sensitive skin in the vee of my chest which sent a few thousand volts racing straight down between my legs. I looked right into his eyes and stepped forward, sliding one hand across his chest to ease the T-shirt over his head. There was a brief flare of surprise in his eyes and then he took the beer bottle out of my other hand and settled it on the side.

This was the other side of instant attraction; I didn't feel the least bit shy. I wanted him and he wanted me. No games. No dancing around the subject. Just good, healthy appreciation of each other's bodies. An earthy acceptance.

The silence between us stretched out, a hum of anticipation before we stepped off the cliff edge. I could hear the birdsong outside, feel the warmth of the sun on my back and the thud of my heart as Sam's eyes held mine. I knew this moment would be imprinted for ever.

His fingers slid into the gap between my shorts and my vest, skimming the skin around my waist. The slow, deliberate strokes semaphored his intentions as they moved up and up and up, under my vest, tracing the side of my rib cage. His eyes never left my face and the moment simmered with erotic promise. His thumbs grazed the sides of my pathetically undersized boobs and I almost stumbled forward at the punch of desire. Then everything boiled over and we were kissing.

Kissing and kissing, a tangle of limbs, and it was like the proverbial floodgates opening with all the pent-up longing we'd both felt since the day we first met rushing out. His mouth on mine. Mine on his. Our bodies pressed against each other. Sam pulled my vest top off. I fumbled with the zipper of his shorts. I backed him out of the kitchen. His hand tugged at my shorts. I pushed at the denim of his. We stumbled, still kissing, into the hallway. Bump! I hit my elbow as we cannoned off the door jamb. He steadied me. Our mouths fused. A pause as he stepped out of his shorts. A shimmy of my hips as his hand slipped inside my shorts to work them down.

We hit my bed. His weight on me was heavy and delicious. Crisp cotton a soft chafe as he pressed me into the clean sheets. Our breath rasped in the warm, sweet air of the summer day. Hands exploring, touching and testing. I inhaled his sigh, drawing it in. His fingers flirted in butterfly-light touches on my inner thigh. Mine stroked his muscled back, pulling him closer. And still we kissed.

His fingers slid higher to the warm wetness and I moaned, lifting shamelessly to that sweet touch, desperate for him to ease the ache. One finger slipped inside. I gasped at the electric shock of pleasure. His mouth stilled and he lifted his head, his eyes languorous and heavy. I opened my legs, an incoherent mutter of pleasure escaping as that solitary wicked finger played me.

'Sam. Yes. Yes. Yes.'

I found the hot, hard length of him, another spark of desire firing with golden sparks at his groan and the lift of his hips. He dropped his forehead to mine. His breath was warm on my face. More groans and sighs as his mouth moved back over mine, our hips rising and pushing towards the goal.

With a stuttered breath I groped my way towards the bedside drawer.

We paused, staring into each other's eyes and a we-really-are-going-to-do-this message flashed between us as I fumbled for the box of condoms. Grasping it, I yanked it upwards and promptly dropped the bloody thing. Durex spilled out, some on the floor and one, thank you providence, landed on the bed near his hand. I groaned and closed my eyes.

'Smooth,' I managed to pant.

'Wouldn't … have it … any other way,' he managed to say as, with a grin, he snatched at it, tore it open and rolled it on, his fingers brushing my skin.

As he braced himself on his elbows, he held my gaze and gently slid home.

We spent the whole afternoon in bed, talking, having sex, talking some more. The second time we teased and tantalised, seeking the ticklish places, the instant turn-on spots, laughing and joking as we explored each other's bodies. The third time was raw and dirty. Blow jobs – his head between my legs (oh my God, he was seriously good at that and I might have shouted just that) – and serious orgasms, the delicious like of which I'd never experienced before. Sam found out that he could reduce me to mush by touching my inner thigh. I discovered that tracing the intriguing muscle from hip to groin brought an instant response.

At four we rolled out of bed and squeezed into my tiny shower, the intention to clean up and get dressed, although we took a diversion by way of soaping and stroking that had me pinned up against the cold tiles reaching yet another mind-numbing orgasm. Finally dressed, we sat out on the balcony, enjoying the balmy late-afternoon sunshine.

'Have you any plans for tomorrow?' asked Sam, tilting his beer bottle and taking a long slug as I watched his throat, already feeling a touch of possession, remembering the feel of the taut skin underneath his jawline where earlier I'd pressed kisses, my lips touching the sand grains of stubble bubbling under the surface.

I shook my head, content to stare at the gloriousness of him and savour the deliciously sated sensation buzzing around my lethargic, soft-as-marshmallow body.

'I'm housesitting at my folks. They've got a great

garden. I could fire up the barbecue and cook a couple of steaks.'

'You had me at garden. But steak seals the deal. If you're lucky I might even throw together a salad.'

He looked at his watch, a frown marring his face. 'Unfortunately, I've got a wedding thing tonight.'

'A wedding thing? I'm sure the bride would be thrilled with that description.'

He grinned. 'She's not thrilled with me, that's for sure. Thought I was very inconsiderate because I messed up her numbers, so my invitation was downgraded to evening only.'

'Ouch. Brutal.' As he shifted in his seat, his gaze holding mine, I twigged. 'You were supposed to be going with Victoria.'

''Fraid so. The bride and groom are both our friends.'

'And you're persona non grata, so you get the evening leftovers?'

'I'm a guy. You think I'm really that bothered about missing the formal, suit-and-tie bit? On a day like this I'd far rather be out on the canal with you than dressed up like a penguin.'

'No.' I laughed. 'I get the feeling you'd rather have been anywhere than in a suit at a wedding today.'

'Yeah,' he agreed, grinning back at me, and there was that little frisson in the air as we looked at each other for an extra second. 'You don't mind? I mean, Vic being there.'

'Sam, I don't own you and this has clearly been on the calendar for months. Don't be silly.' Jealousy wasn't part of my make-up. 'It just seems a bit unfair on you, being uninvited.'

He shrugged. 'It's their wedding. Their day. And more important for Victoria to save face. I'm quite happy to go in the evening. It'll be good to catch up with a few people; I've been keeping a low profile.' It wasn't difficult to read between the lines. I'd seen the pictures on Instagram. He and Victoria had been part of a big social circle together. A known couple. Stepping away from that, overnight he'd become a social pariah.

'I hope you … well, I hope it's OK.'

'It will be fine. I've got tomorrow to look forward to. Why don't you come over at lunchtime? You know where my folks live.'

Chapter Twelve

What the—!

After Sam left, following a prolonged departure during which neither of us seemed able to peel our lips from each other's, I switched my phone back on. It beeped back into life with all manner of alerts and chimes, channelling R2D2 at his most irate. I caught up with various messages and texts – a couple of gentle teasing ones from Bel asking for an update and a shedload from Shelley. It read like a complete timeline of her growing impatience which was pretty funny. I must remember to ignore her more often. Her last text, however, had not been funny at all.

Ouch. Facebook. What a bitch! Have you seen this? R U OK? I have vodka, gin, prosecco and access to mind-numbing drugs if you need them.

She'd helpfully supplied a link.

Seriously? Under an extremely unflattering picture of Sam and me coming out of Olivio, my eyes squinty and my mouth wide open, was the caption, *Anyone know who the skank is? The one who stole my boyfriend.*

Nice.

Under Victoria's post were fifty-three comments. None of them particularly pleasant.

Don't know the ugly bitch. That erudite comment came from a Naomi Kitchener.

Let's hope she gets what's coming to her. Genitail herpes and gonorrea. This from Janey McIlroy, the dyslexic would-be STD specialist.

Don't know the c**t and wouldn't want to. Paige White.

Ah, that would be the best friend then. Nice language, Paige.

Looks like Sam's had a brain fart. What a slag! What's he thinking? From Mary Weston-Hayes. No words, Mary.

I hope you bitch-slapped her and gave the slut a piece of your mind. Skank is the only word for her. Don't you hate women that do this. Whatever happened to sisterhood?

Clearly Teresa Whitehead was a muppet who had missed the not-so-delicious irony of her words.

My fists clenched as I stupidly carried on scrolling through the comments as compulsively as a moth to light.

Aw hun. Look at the size of her arse. You know you're worth ten of her. Isabel Merryweather's addled logic defeated me. And, Isabel Merryweather, I'd just like you to know that some people – OK, my cousin – coveted said arse.

I tried really hard, as I worked through them, not to let

the vicious words get to me and I was doing quite well until I reached the post where I was officially outed.

Looks like Jess Harper. Right stuck-up cow. Few years below me at school. What do you reckon **Flizzy Outhwaite**? Well, whoever Nicole Andrews was, I had no idea but she could fuck right off.

Yeah that's her. She's got form. Always nicking other people's blokes. And as for Flizzy Outhwaite, well, she was an outright liar. Talk about fake news! I'd never nicked anyone's bloke in my life. That was a red line.

I scrolled back to the picture at the top and sucked in a huge juddery breath at the unfairness of it all.

I was not going to cry. I don't cry. Never. Crying was weak, *is* weak. When the going gets tough, the tough get going. Crap, the massive lump in my throat was the size of a golf ball. I. Am. Not. Going. To. Cry. I swallowed again. Not good. I sat down on my bed with a thud and buried my head in my hands. Not going to cry. Not going to cry.

Where had all this hate and vitriol come from? I twisted the cotton duvet cover beneath my fingers as I held my phone in the other hand, unable to tear my gaze away. I didn't even know these people. They didn't know me. I'd been judged and vilified by other women using the worst kind of gender-based invective. It stung. It also appalled me. How could these women behave like this? And didn't they see the irony? Not one word of abuse was directed at Sam. Not that he deserved it any more than I did. But I was the innocent party here.

My phone rang, reminding me that there were thirteen

missed calls from Shelley. Boy, did I need to hear a friendly voice.

'Hey,' I said.

'Lovely, are you OK? Oh my God. I'm so sorry. There's no way I'd have sent that link if I'd known how nasty it was going to get. I can't believe it.'

'Read it and weep,' I drawled, trying to pretend that a moment ago I hadn't been crying into my pillow.

'What happened? I take it psycho ex-girlfriend took the picture. What was she doing there?'

'Stalking Sam. Datus interruptus.'

'What? She came up to you on your date?'

'Waiting outside when we came out of the restaurant.'

'Azerbaijan! Serious psycho, then.'

Already, talking to Shel, I felt so much better. Sticks and stones and all that. But I still felt a bit wobbly. Although my anger was starting to fire up. It takes a lot to make me mad but I'm like the Incredible Hulk – except without the green and the muscle: when I go, I go. Unfortunately, that usually does end in tears because when I blow, I end up saying a ton of stuff I regret later and then my ire evaporates, leaving me as limp and pathetic as a deflated balloon.

'Yesterday I would have described her as sad, cut-up, hurting and I'd even have erred on the sympathetic. Today I'm going with mental nutjob and I wouldn't trust myself around her with a large knife.'

'Let's go hunt her down. I'll bring Mum's Jamie Oliver butcher's knife.' Shelley sounded positively enthusiastic and then added in a gravelly, Ray Winston-esque gangster voice, 'Put the frighteners on her.' I did burst out laughing at that one.

'I do love you, Shel.'

'I love you too, Jess. I'm sick inside at this. Why are people so hideous? So you're not feeling shagtastic today? I had high hopes for your little vag.'

A little hicoughy sob escaped. My golden afternoon spoiled.

'Jess. Aw hon.' Shelley's voice vibrated with sympathy.

'I'm OK,' I said quickly. 'I'm fine.' But I wasn't. It was as if someone had swiped at my glossy, iridescent bubble of sex, smiles and sweetness, and popped all the bright, clear feelings. What had felt so right, so natural, so perfect now felt sordid and wrong. Whether he liked it or not, a big part of Sam still belonged to someone else. A part of his life that I had no claim on.

'Oh God. Have I made a terrible mistake?' The coldness in my chest made it hard to breathe. I'd stepped into two lives that had been a pair. I'd halved two parts of a whole and their shared history, their memories and their friendships. I didn't want to be the other woman. I knew the misery it caused. I'd seen how being left had withered my mother's soul.

'Oh Shell, I'm not sure I can do it.' There, I'd said it out loud.

'Jess! You're going to let her win?' Shelley's shriek of outrage spanned three octaves. 'You can't. Even Mum noticed you were all sparkly-eyed with Sam the other weekend and she hasn't spotted the tattoo I had done three weeks ago. Although it's a temporary one; I've reapplied it twice.'

'Shell, she noticed. She's ignoring it.' I rolled my eyes, glad my cousin couldn't see me. I didn't want to make a comment about the daisy chain of dark-eyed skulls encircling her right ankle.

'Gah! I thought that might be the case. But you and Sam… Dad was gushing about him. You know he's a nice guy. This isn't his fault.'

Hmm, it sort of was, although indirectly.

'He is a nice guy. A really nice guy but…'

'But crap! Don't you dare butt out just because … because of this ex-girlfriend. And this is harassment. And bullying. And what do we do to bullies? We stand up to them. We don't let them win. What does Bel say?'

'I haven't spoken to her.' And I wouldn't. Not yet. She'd be horrified by this and get all upset and tearful on my behalf and I was having enough trouble reining in my own waterworks.

'Promise me, you won't put the kibosh on things with Sam.'

'Can't do that, Shel,' I said, not prepared to lie to her.

'When are you supposed to be seeing him again?' she asked.

'Tomorrow.' All the rainbows, sunshine and promise of tomorrow had turned grey.

'Don't do anything hasty,' begged Shelley. 'Seriously, nice guys don't grow on trees. They're few and far between. Did I tell you what Sean did?'

'I thought you weren't seeing him again,' I grasped at the change of subject with single-minded focus.

'He caught me at a weak moment.'

At her pathetic whine, I rolled my eyes so hard it hurt. 'Shel!'

'I saw that.'

'Good. What did he do this time?'

'Took me out to dinner. Forgot his wallet, *again*. This is what I have to put up with.'

'The difference between us, Shel, is that I'd rather not be with anyone than with the wrong person.'

'But Sam is the right person. I'm sure he is. Honestly, the two of you go together like…'

'If you say ramalamadingdong, I will never watch *Grease* with you again,' I threatened.

'Harsh, cous. Harsh. I won't say another word.'

For which I was truly grateful, as I was torn enough as it was.

Chapter Thirteen

I t felt odd bypassing the house that was like a second home to me and somehow disloyal not calling in when I was so close. As I stood at the front door of Sam's parents' house, about to ring the bell, I glanced to my left, to the tall hedge, through which was my aunt and uncle's back garden. They might even be sitting out on the patio just a few hundred metres away. Yeah, it felt weird.

I looked up at the house. They'd not been here long but, judging from the overflowing hanging basket which had purple and white fist-sized petunias tumbling over the edge, and the assorted pots of impatiens around the doorstep, they were well settled. The cheery, welcoming façade confirmed what I already knew from Aunty Lynn: Sam's parents were a wholesale improvement on their wretched predecessors, the misery twins. They'd acquired this name, on account of them being miserable and unfriendly to the point of rudeness, which Aunty Lynn could not bear.

When I rang the bell there was a brief silence – call it the calm before the storm – and then came the sound of someone thundering pell-mell down the stairs to the accompaniment of a dog barking from the back of the house.

'Shh, Tiggy,' I heard Sam yell before he wrenched the door open, a towel wrapped around his neck, wet blond curls dripping down a bare chest with almost done-up shorts, his chest heaving slightly.

'Hey, Jess. Sorry. In the shower.' He rubbed at his hair with the towel, a huge welcoming grin on his face. All last night's doubts fried in a single laser blast of lust and sexual appreciation that left me tongue-tied and stupid.

'Hey,' I said, fixing my eyes on his face, as my nerve endings fired up like rockets about to blast into space. Dear God. I could die a happy woman. I was in danger of spontaneously combusting at any second and, dammit, Sam knew. 'Cocky, much?' I asked as his blue eyes gleamed with amusement, slightly cross with my weak-willed, sex-crazed self.

He laughed, reaching for me and pulling me over the threshold. 'The feeling's mutual, if it's any consolation. You're a gorgeous sight this morning.'

OK, I melted a bit more at the frank admiration and locked my knees. All my good intentions of keeping my distance and being measured and sensible went up in flames. I so wanted to jump his bones. I've no idea who moved first but that minty just-cleaned-teeth kiss turned my legs to noodles and my recently purchased contribution of salad and wine slipped out of my grasp and fell with a thud to the floor. Sam backed up and it was only when we knocked a picture off the wall that we stilled with chagrined expressions.

How the hell had I got myself into this position, with my legs wrapped around his hips and his hands cradling my bum?

Breathless and slightly embarrassed, I rested my forehead against his and slid down his body onto my feet. His hands slid up to cup my shoulder blades.

'Mmm. Hello, Jess. That's a great way to start the day.' He dropped a final kiss on the corner of my mouth.

'What would your mother say?' I picked up the picture and handed it to him.

He laughed and we spent the next few minutes trying to make sure the Jack Vettriano print was straight.

'There, she'll never know,' said Sam cheerfully. 'Come on through. Come and meet Tiggy.'

I ducked to pick up my abandoned tote bag. 'Here you go. I brought wine and salad.'

He took my hand and led me through the hallway, skirting a wooden staircase and opening the door into a large, stylish kitchen with French doors.

A golden retriever bounced around me, his tail wagging like a windscreen wiper on warp speed.

'This is Tiggy – completely harmless, daft as a brush and the stupidest dog on the planet.'

With a quick sniff at my crotch, Tiggy licked my hand and circled me several times, coating my legs in deposits of fine hair, before retreating towards the basket in the corner of the kitchen and flopping down with the doggy equivalent of an oof. If there was ever a clichéd dog that looked like its owner, this was it. Like Sam, Tiggy was blonde, bouncy and enthusiastic. I sniggered and Sam rolled his eyes.

'At least I didn't sniff your crotch,' he said, and I burst out laughing, realising he'd known exactly what I was thinking.

'You are going to feed me, aren't you?' I said, narrowing my eyes with suspicion, looking around at the pristine kitchen and putting my hands on my hips.

Sam laughed as he opened the fridge to stow the bag of mixed leaves, pack of cherry tomatoes and cucumber and the nice bottle of New Zealand white that the man in Marks had assured me was excellent.

'Yes, don't worry.' He waved his hand with a flourish towards the contents of the fridge. 'I've got it all under control. Two steaks.' He pointed to the dark-red meat on the bottom shelf. 'Corn on the cob.' Again, he indicated the neat foil-wrapped packages before dropping his voice, 'I had to call mum for advice on that and profiteroles for pudding. And no, I didn't make them; Mum suggested I dig them out of the freezer.'

'All sounds good. Although it has been said that I'm fairly low-maintenance. Feed me and I'm happy.'

Sam shook his head and came to stand in front of me, tucking a stray hair behind my ear. I'd shoved it up in a ponytail again because it was just too hot, and I had minimal make-up on, because a) it was the weekend and make-up is for work and b) in this heat it would just melt. And, stubbornly, I'd been determined not to look as if I was trying too hard. The whole Facebook thing had made me contrary. I wasn't into playing games. Sam was going to have to take me as I was, and I was never going to be the svelte, sleek, well-groomed Victoria.

'Describing someone as low-maintenance never sounds like a good thing to me. It's as if you're saying you're not worth the effort.' He paused, his blue eyes suddenly solemn, before delivering the killer line, 'I happen to think you are.'

Thunderbolts and lightning, my whole system went into silly mode. Fireworks, butterflies, the works.

'Oh shit, Sam.' *What did you go and say a thing like that for?* I sighed and the idiot just laughed at me.

His cool hand stroked my bare shoulder, tracing the collar bone to just below my throat, which from anyone else I would have thought was a smooth-bastard move, but Sam looked a little bit dazed and a little bit surprised.

'I know, it might seem all a bit quick,' his finger stroked my throat, 'but it's not a line,' he added quickly. 'Last night… It's crazy, but I missed you. At the wedding, I kept thinking of things I wanted to say to you. Things you'd laugh at. Wondering what we'd have danced to together if you'd been there.'

'That's easy. "Hi Ho Silver Lining" every time,' I said lightly, trying to cover up the fact that I felt like I was on a see-saw, trying to pretend I was perfectly balanced in the middle when inside I felt like I was flailing about like a flaming windmill. This was real, soul-matey, breath-caught-in-the-throat stuff like in films and books and songs. It was scary and my mother would disown me. I still needed to talk to him about the Facebook thing. Being here with him now had squashed all my earlier doubts, but they were still there, just conveniently compacted for the time being.

'Now why doesn't that surprise me?' Sam nudged me.

'Although to be honest, I haven't a clue who sings it. Did they play it?'

'Of course. It's in the wedding rules. Page ninety-five, paragraph fifteen.'

'I think you'll find it's page ninety-six,' I quipped and for no apparent reason other than utter silliness, we beamed at each other.

'Wine? Or beer?'

'I'd love a beer to start with. I walked here and it's already in the twenties. They say this weather's going to last all summer.'

'I'm not complaining. It's good for the cricket season. Fewer matches cancelled. And it's much nicer standing in the outfield in the sunshine than on a cold grey day freezing your knackers off.'

'I'll take your word for it,' I said. 'I know nothing about cricket. Except that,' I felt my cheeks dimple at the memory of the picture I'd seen of him, 'it could be said some people look quite cute in the uniform.'

Oops, had I just given away that I'd been spying on him on Facebook?

'That makes me sound like some kind of sporting boy

scout. Whites,' corrected Sam, poking my dimple and laughing before sobering. 'Jess, I ... cricket is quite a big thing to me. It's, well, it's important to me. And a pain in the arse, I've heard, if you're the girlfriend of a cricketer.'

Except Victoria had apparently managed.

'I play every Saturday during the summer and we often don't finish until seven or eight. Although there's usually a good crowd up at the club after a match.'

'That's OK. It's only a pain in the arse if you've got nothing better to do than hang around waiting for a boyfriend to call,' I replied cheerfully.

'And that puts me in my place.' Sam leaned back against the breakfast bar, crossing his legs at his ankles, not looking the least bit abashed by my comments.

'That wasn't my intention. I just meant that I'm not the sort of girl who's reliant on someone else. I have plenty going on in my life at the weekends. I don't need to sit around waiting for you.' I shrugged. 'It's been a while since I've been out with anyone.'

'That surprises me.'

I gave him a direct look. 'I think that's a compliment.'

'Of course it's a compliment. You're... Well, I just assumed you'd probably have a boyfriend.'

I shrugged. I wasn't about to lay the whole family history on him.

'And I'm on call every fourth Saturday; I don't go out then. It's easier to stay home where I can hear my phone ring and I can make calls in private.'

'I didn't mean it was impossible to see each other on a

weekend. You can always come up to the club and watch or meet me in the bar afterwards.'

'I'd like that. Although I might need a few lessons on cricket speak. I mean, how can you have a game that goes on for five days and no one wins?'

'It's a long story.' He winked. 'And I don't want to put you off just yet.'

He pulled out two bottles of beer, levered off the caps and handed me one before extending his bottle towards mine. We exchanged a quick smile.

'Come on.'

'Wow, someone's got green fingers,' I said, surveying the riot of colours in the beds surrounding a lush, wide lawn that stretched out to a little group of shrubs and trees at the end.

'Dad. Mum loves her flowers. That's why they bought the house, for the garden. She's got grand plans of her own and likes to direct Dad, but she also liked the fact that it was established.'

The patio was like something out of *Homes and Gardens* with oak sun-loungers, topped by Orla Kiely-style print cushions, a square wicker table-and-chair set and an enormous parasol.

'This is lovely,' I said, as Sam flopped down on one of the loungers. I took the one next to him. 'And very grown-up. That's some barbecue.' I nodded towards the black and wooden monster with its own gas cylinder. 'Do you have a licence to drive it?'

'Dad's pride and joy.' Sam rolled his eyes. 'It has hickory chips and everything.'

'Hickory chips, you say,' I murmured. 'Now I am impressed.'

He swatted my arm. 'They do something to the flavour, apparently.'

'I'll take your word for it. I take Aunty Lynn's lead on that one. Barbecuing is the man's department.'

We talked for an hour, lapping up the sunshine and sipping at our beers before Sam lit the barbecue.

'Do you need a hand?' I asked as he went off into the kitchen.

'You can keep me company and open that bag of salad. I think Mum's got some fancy dressing somewhere.'

'Can you tell me where I'll find a salad bowl?' I asked, reluctant to go rooting through his mother's kitchen cupboards; it seemed a little familiar when I hadn't even met the woman.

'Through there,' he pointed to a door, 'there's a sideboard in the dining room. There'll be one in one of the cupboards. Not sure which.'

The door opened to a dining room with a big table just off a much bigger open-plan lounge with more patio windows leading into the garden. Two vast sofas filled the room opposite each other. Crossing to the contemporary oak sideboard, I opened the cupboard and crouched down to take a small salad bowl from the top shelf, my eyeline level with the photos on top of the sideboard.

Sam throughout the ages had been captured, his blue eyes full of fun in nearly every picture, whether a young boy in cricket whites, holding his bat aloft, a toddler on a bright red trike or with his arm slung around a much younger and softer version of Victoria. There were a couple more of her, one at what looked like a family party, one of her and Sam in formal eveningwear, and another of her and a woman who was clearly Sam's mum laughing together holding up champagne flutes. I felt a twinge in my stomach. Victoria had been part of this family.

Casting my eyes back over the photos, I focused on the largest picture in a big silver frame taking pride of place on its own at the end of the sideboard: Sam and Victoria flanked by a woman in her mid-fifties with short blonde hair in a curly bob and a man with Sam's confident beaming smile and very twinkly blue eyes. Sam was the perfect combination of both of them.

What would Sam's mum and dad think of me? Suddenly I wished I wasn't in their house when they weren't. I felt like an interloper.

Snatching up the bowl, I turned and hurried back to the kitchen. I really shouldn't be here.

'When are your parents due back?' I asked, stopping quickly at the sight of Sam tying on an apron.

'Not until tomorrow,' he said and turned around to reveal the words on his apron, *Blow me, I'm hot*. 'What do you think?'

'I'll buy you a fan,' I said wryly, putting down the bowl and busying myself with making a very basic salad, thoroughly relieved that his parents wouldn't be turning up today. I could do without any awkward meetings. I was still feeling wobbly after yesterday's Facebook post.

'You OK?' asked Sam, with his usual mind-reading ability.

'Yeah, I'm fine,' I said, giving him a tight smile. 'Salad takes a great deal of concentration, you know.'

He glanced back through the open door. The gallery of pictures was in full view.

'It's going to be all right, Jess.'

'Is it?' I asked a little bleakly, backing away when he went to take me in his arms. 'I mean, really, how was last night?' The unspoken *'with all your friends and Victoria'* seemed to hover in the air and I felt sick. I did not want to come across as the jealous girlfriend.

Looking over at me, his eyes softened. 'It would have been better if you'd been there.'

'I'm not sure that would have gone down well.'

I'd noticed – OK, yes, I'd been on Instagram again – there'd been plenty of selfies of Victoria and chums in the morning. As always (except for when she adopted the victim look while hijacking dates; I hadn't missed that deliberate style statement) she looked immaculate, in her ice-cold mannequin sort of way, wearing a fabulous pale-pink dress – she did wear a shift dress exceptionally well. But the frequent pictures had stopped dead halfway through the evening, which I thought was odd. Her Instagram feed had always been resolutely defiant with Gloria Gaynor 'I Will Survive' tones. I'd have expected the evening to give her even greater opportunities to reinforce what Sam was missing and to show the world what she was doing.

'Possibly not.' Sam's jaw clenched and, for the first time, his easy-going expression darkened with a flicker of anger, which took me aback. He sat up and swung his legs over the side of the lounger.

'Something wrong?'

He raised an eyebrow and gave a self-deprecating sigh. 'I'm trying to work out if you saw the Facebook post and are being cool with it.'

'I saw it. And no, I'm not cool with it at all.' I leaned back against the kitchen counter.

'Fuck. I'm mean, that you've seen it. I'm sorry about that. Not that you're not cool, because I don't blame you.'

'Actually, I'm mighty pissed off about it. Your girlfriend really went to town.'

'She's not my girlfriend anymore.' Sam's jaw tightened, he folded his arms and casually crossed his legs at the ankle, except I could see there was nothing casual in his wired stance.

'Yeah, well, that message doesn't seem to be getting through. She's acting as if I'm the other woman, and I don't like it.' I slowly folded my arms, mirroring his stance. It was like a showdown at the OK Corral.

He snatched up his bottle and took a hasty swig and the angry pulse at his throat startled me. 'I'm fucking furious with her.' The growled words, reverberating with rage, made me straighten and study him with wary respect. Easy-going Sam wasn't as easy-going as I'd assumed.

'I made her take it down this morning.' The grudging words were ground out through tight lips.

'Made?' I asked. The word made me feel uncomfortable. I'd seen too many women *made* to do things. Coerced. Forced. Bullied. 'How?' I tried to sound neutral.

Sam shot me a furious look. 'I didn't force her, if that's what you're thinking.'

I lifted my shoulders. 'What *did* you do?' I asked, my voice a little shaky.

'I told her I'd never speak to her again if she didn't take it down immediately.' From the set of his jaw, I knew that when he said that to Victoria he'd meant every word.

I relaxed, my shoulders pinging down as if released from the talon-like grip of a griffin or some other Harry Potter creature letting go in mid-air.

'Do you think she'll stop now?' I asked, my imagination taking off with the magical imagery and presenting me with a vision of Victoria dressed as Maleficent, complete with the black horns. OK, that was a bit over the top; she wasn't evil, but I did feel that with her Facebook antics, she'd cast an unpleasant shadow over things. At the same time, her viciousness had given me emotional licence to carry on seeing Sam. She wasn't a victim anymore and for some reason it made me feel a lot easier about our blossoming relationship. Making the first strike absolved her of innocence. In that moment, I wondered if my mum had ever struck back at Dad. I remembered her despair and the awful time after he'd gone when she'd virtually stopped functioning, to the complete bewilderment of eight-year-old me.

'She'd better,' said Sam darkly. 'I'm not going to let her come between us, Jess.' As far as it was possible for one so blond, his face darkened, suddenly fierce and determined, like a knight in shining armour gripping his sword. (I really do need to stop with the Harry Potter DVD binges.)

And yeah, shoot me, I did the swoony thing, but it's rather nice for a change for someone to want to fight for me. Sam's quiet, determined declaration, sealed with a solemn kiss, made me feel that perhaps the two of us could be invincible.

Chapter Fourteen

'More Prosecco?' asked Uncle Richard, not even waiting for an answer as he topped up my glass.

It had been yet another balmy day and I was taking full advantage of my aunt and uncle's back garden to top up my tan, lying next to Shelley who was scrolling through her phone. The endless cloud-free days and soaring temperatures of the last few weeks had brought an almost festive atmosphere and a lightness of spirit to people. Even at work, smiles were readier and the assorted children played in the big garden, straying further from their mothers' sides than usual. The new little boy, Jake, now had a few freckles dotted across his bruised, haunted face and although his mother, Cathy, hovered in the doorway of the French doors by the patio, her tense face relaxed at the sight of him playing football with two other children. In the last week, I'd found a school place for him, but she was delaying his start. I wasn't sure which of them couldn't bear to be parted from the other. Letting him out into the garden had been a huge step forward and I was happy to give the long, sunny days all the credit.

'What time's lover boy picking you up?' asked Shelley, breaking into my thoughts.

'Not until the game's over,' I replied, checking the time on my phone. 'He reckoned about eight.'

'I don't think I could stand being a cricket widow. It was bad enough when I went out with that bloke Dave that played golf every weekend.'

'I see plenty of Sam during the week.'

'I bet you do,' said Shelley, grinning. 'Your legs have got a definite touch of the bandy about them. And I'm guessing there's a whole lot of him to see. He's got one hot bod.'

'Parents. Right here.' Uncle Richard clamped one hand over his ear. Aunty Lynn laughed.

'Is it all going well, dear? He's such a lovely young man.'

Hmm. I wondered how lovely she'd think he was if she had any idea how down and dirty he could get. Unable to help my slutty self, I squirmed on the sun lounger. Last night's champagne and chocolate-strawberry combo in celebration of our three-week anniversary had definitely got a bit fruity – quite literally. Who knew you could do so much with a strawberry? Sex with Sam was a constant uninhibited revelation. I'd never laughed so much or moaned quite so shamelessly. Not that we spent all of our time in bed.

'I saw that, Miss Lively Loins,' said Shelley.

I ignored her and turned to meet my aunt's hopeful gaze. 'He's lovely,' I said simply, because he was.

The amazing sex was a bonus, a big fat awesome bonus, but being with Sam was all the things that being with the right person was supposed to be. I couldn't put it into words without sounding ridiculously cheesy, the sense of completeness I felt when I was with him. We did mundane things. We did silly things. We did couple things. He'd bring his marking home, and yes, it felt like he was home, sitting at the round table in my lounge, his head bent over the pile of exercise books, and I'd glance at him and every time feel that buzz at the sight of him just being there.

In some ways, I felt like I'd known him for ever and in others, every day was like unlocking a special secret when I found out new things about him. He hated Marmite, which was wrong on every level, but still kissed me after I'd had my toast in the morning. He seemed to use three times as much loo roll as any normal human being. He was a terrible driver, absolutely rubbish at food shopping – he bought everything on offer and the last time he'd cooked for me, he'd served up pork chops and fresh tagliatelle – and he had a not-so-secret addiction to *Take Me Out* and Paddy McGuinness's dreadful puns. *No likey, no lighty* was now a regular refrain between us.

'Ah, I'm so pleased for you,' said Aunty Lynn. 'I really do like his parents. Sally's great fun. Have you met her yet?'

'No, not yet. There's not really been time.' And our time was still too precious to share with anyone else. In the last two weeks, we'd spent ten out of fourteen nights together, mainly at my flat, which was more convenient for both our jobs.

'You'll like her,' said Lynn with blithe confidence. 'And that dog – bonkers.'

'Oh, I've met Tiggy,' I said. 'When Sam was housesitting a few weeks ago. The garden is amazing. Someone has green fingers.'

'That's Miles. He's getting it ready for the party. Let's hope the weather stays like this,' said Richard. 'Although if we don't get a bit of rain, the grass is going to be dead. They're talking about a hosepipe ban.'

'Sally's been planning it for weeks,' added Lynn.

'What's the occasion?' asked Shelley.

'It's their thirty-fifth wedding anniversary. It's going to be quite a big do. We'll probably see you there,' said Lynn.

'Probably,' I said, tipping my glass, the bubbles of Prosecco hitting the back of my throat with a sharp bite.

'I really need to go shopping. If I get a nice dress, I can wear it for Gladys's wedding as well. And you do too, Richard,' continued Lynn, gabbling on. 'You are not wearing that manky brown jacket again.'

'What's wrong with it?' Richard grinned as his wife shook her head and groaned.

'Dad, you look like a redundant geography teacher. Elbow patches are not a thing.'

'Gladys won't mind,' said Richard, which was true given she favoured workmen's overalls, Doc Martens and silver lamé handbags. When I was a little girl, I'd liked to think she was some sort of space explorer.

'Besides, I always liked geography,' he protested, winking at me.

'What are you going to wear to Sally and Miles's wedding anniversary bash, Jess?' asked Lynn.

'I haven't thought about it,' I replied, and Shelley shot me a look. Wrong answer, Jess. I always knew what I'd wear. I'm a planner. I don't leave things like that to chance. She knew me so well; she immediately knew I hadn't been invited. Yet.

It was probably my new favourite sound in the whole world: Sam's soft-throated hum of pleasure filling my bedroom as I took him in my mouth and the heated pants of, 'Jess, Jess,' as I swirled my tongue around the head of his cock. Shelley, whom I'd left an hour before, had complained about her dull Saturday night and told me I'd better get some action in because, in her words, 'Seriously, babe, there's tumbleweed blowing about in my fanny.' Thankfully, this was of course out of earshot of Aunty Lynn and Uncle Richard. I'm not sure what either of them would make of my full-frontal attack on Sam as soon as we walked through the door of my flat, although I could guarantee Shelley would approve. She'd be cheering bad-girl Jess along from the side lines.

Spread out before me, his body was so male and larger-than-life with those toned muscles and long limbs. I wanted to lick every last bit of him, lap him up like the best ice cream you can imagine. Having him at my mercy, so desperate for me, turned me inside out. I was so turned on, I stopped and slid up his body, my tongue tracing from navel to nipple before I straddled his broad hips, lowering myself, then clenching around him as he groaned. I was lost for a few strokes, focused on the pleasure of feeling him inside me, until he flipped me over and thrust home, again and again, and suddenly we were both racing, hot and sticky with urgency. His blue eyes were cloudy, hazed with desire, but gazing down at me. My heart flipped and a sob slipped out. Then he pulled my head close and kissed me hard. There was a pause and then a heartfelt, 'I'm coming, I'm coming.' A beat behind him, I could feel him pulsing inside me. I clenched harder and then there was the whoosh, the cascading waves of pleasure, and I was there with him.

He collapsed on top of me, his weight heavy and all mine. I clutched his back, holding on to him, holding on to the moment. Just the two of us in the fading daylight of another perfect summer day, the rise and fall of our chests, rib cage to rib cage, our bones clashing with each other. Eventually, I had to relinquish the weight of him because I couldn't breathe properly. I didn't want to, but he was ahead of me. He levered himself up and kissed my mouth before saying, 'I'm too heavy for you.' He twisted, slipping his arm under me, so that we were face to face. Our favourite position. The one where we looked at each other. Sometimes we smiled and kissed. Sometimes he traced my body with his hands, his fingers outlining the underside of my breast, the curve of my hips or the line of my jaw, and it always seemed impossibly romantic. Other times we stared, almost in wonderment, as if neither of us could quite believe the feelings we had for each other.

I'd had boyfriends before. I'd slept with people before. But there'd never been this sense of awe and wonder, that implicit confidence that he felt as much for me as I felt for him. It was so romantic, and all the things I'd never believed in. Love – not that I'd voiced the word – was supposed to be practical, a good working relationship between two people that makes them feel happy and fulfilled. It's not supposed to be this ridiculously magical, soar-away sensation of bubbles and butterflies.

'I never even asked you how the cricket was today,' I finally murmured as he smiled down at me, still tinged with the glow of good sex and raging endorphins.

'Good,' he said, 'I got a century.' Even I, champion cricketing numpty, got that this was a big deal. The matter-of-fact delivery robbed the quietly stated words of any hint of a boast.

'Ah, I know that one. A hundred runs. That's really good, isn't it?'

He gave a small nod, but I could see a tiny touch of small-boy pride that crested beneath his inherent modesty. It was another thing I loved about Sam. He was so talented and capable, but it was all understated, never taken for granted.

'I've been mugging up on this cricket terminology. Although I still haven't a clue what a googly or a long arm silly mid-off is.'

Sam laughed. 'Long arm silly mid-off is a new one to me, too.'

'Did you win?' The whole game seemed impenetrable to me and although we've spent so much time together, it's the one area that I didn't feel part of. It wasn't that he wasn't letting me in, but there was an unspoken barrier there.

'Yes.' His eyes slid away from mine. 'Man of the match,' he added in a quiet voice.

A batting hero. The unsettling words floated into my head. I felt a tiny pinprick of something not right.

'We're top of the league.'

I remembered the banter on Facebook. The teasing comments. Sam's teammates. It dawned on me then, a sharp crystal thought that sliced through the moment, not quite coming between us but casting a dull shadow, that something wasn't quite right.

'Shouldn't you be celebrating?' I asked with a frown, my skin goosebumping with unwelcome awareness.

Without saying a word, almost as if he too could feel the tiny chill that wormed its way in, Sam pulled the duvet up over us.

It took him a moment to speak. 'I wanted to be with you.' Although his eyes softened as he said it, there was a sight strain about them. A shadow in his smile. A tightness at the edge of his mouth.

'It's still difficult?' I didn't want to say Victoria's name out loud. In the last two weeks we'd existed in a self-absorbed bubble, just the two of us, excluding the rest of the world. We'd talked about work; he knew all about Holly and her snarky observations that getting a regular shag was making me unbearably perky and could I stop glowing like a flaming lighthouse because it was bloody irritating. He knew about the Slater family, about Cathy and Jake, and the Townsends. He knew how we struggled for funds, scrounging everything from carpets, shampoo, dressing gowns and toys through to books and shoes. I knew the names of the children in his class, their foibles and their favourite lessons.

After the Facebook-skank episode and I'd checked – hell yes – I'd checked that Victoria had taken down the offending (and quite frankly libellous) post, I'd given social media a double-decker-sized wide berth.

He winced.

'It's difficult. The cricket club. It's—'

'It's Victoria's place,' I said calmly and reasonably, although inside my head a small insistent voice was saying that it wasn't fair. None of this was my fault. I wasn't the baddie here.

He winced. 'It's going to take some time. She's still … raw.'

I didn't want to sound like the jealous girlfriend. Besides, I wasn't jealous of Victoria. I had nothing to be jealous of; I had this gorgeous man in my bed, sharing my breakfast most mornings and texting me silly questions throughout the day. But I asked the question anyway.

'Was she there today?'

He nodded and the word glum summed up perfectly the downcast expression on his face, a dampening of the essential happy Sam-ness.

I squeezed his hand. 'I'm sorry.'

'What are you sorry for?' I flinched at the sharp bite of his words, even though the words absolved me. 'None of this is on you, Jess.'

'I'm sorry that she's so upset, and that you have to face her.'

'I hate that she's hurt. I hate that I did that. And I hate that I can't take you up there.'

Like picking at the scab, even though I knew I'd regret peeling it back to the raw wound underneath, I had to ask. 'Was she OK?'

I didn't have to ask him to be honest – another thing I loved about him. I wanted the bare-bones truth.

'She wanted to talk. We walked around the boundary. She still wants to know what she did wrong. Why after four years I don't love her anymore. What changed. We went round and round in circles. She cried. Wants me back.' The short staccato sentences hid a wealth of pain. 'She's asked me not to bring you to the club.'

'Oh,' I said.

'Jess.' His face crumpled. He wasn't used to being the villain; it didn't sit well. I wasn't exactly thrilled with it either.

'I'm stuck whatever I do. I'm letting you down if I give in to her, but she's ... so ... heartbroken. Says she can't handle it.' He eased away from me and threw his head back against the pillow. 'Why, why is it so bloody complicated?' His fingers worried at the frown lines on his forehead.

'What do your friends say?'

Again, that guilty look which told me so much.

'They ... well ... we all go back a long way.'

Those Instagram pictures of happier times floated back to the surface in my brain. Shared history. Intertwined friendships and loyalties. Of course his friends were predisposed to dislike me. They didn't know me. I'd rocked the boat, and snipped off a strand of the network. I understood it and I wasn't going to be that difficult girlfriend, demanding and shrewish. It wasn't my style – but a small, selfish part of me, of which I felt deeply ashamed, was cross.

'It will get better, Jess, when they meet you and see what a great person you are, but we have to give it some time.'

'I know.' A great big hand squeezed my heart gently but persistently.

'It's Jen's birthday this week, Jen from work, and she's having drinks after school. I'd really like you to come and meet everyone there.'

'OK,' I said, feeling a little like I'd been tossed a bone.

'Don't be sad, Jess. It's just a bit delicate at the cricket club.' With a careful kiss, he traced my mouth with his lips, softly and thoroughly, an apology and a promise. 'This is for keeps. I've never felt like this before.' He let out a mirthless laugh, 'If only I could just explain,' he clasped my hand to his heart, 'how you make me feel. The words aren't big enough without me sounding like some complete cheesy sap. Mike did ask me why, and whether it was it worth it. The aggro with Victoria. He can't understand. His girlfriend Paige is giving me the cold shoulder. Makes it difficult. They were all going out tonight. But,' he added, 'I'd rather be with you.'

'What do you want to do tomorrow?' asked Sam as we sat outside on the balcony, beer in hand, legs sprawled out in front of him, our feet touching as I sat opposite. Dressed in a T-shirt and his boxers, the sun-kissed skin turning brown already, it reminded me of the first time I met him. 'What?' he asked, catching my smile, which held a whole heap of smugness.

'The first time I saw you, I thought you were some kind of surfer dude.'

'The first time I saw you, I thought you had the sexiest legs on the planet. Still do.' He lifted his leg and with the arch of his foot stroked his way up my leg.

'Behave. We've only just got out of bed.'

He grinned at me, eyes crinkled, mischief dancing in a way that made my insides curl.

'Tomorrow, I really have to go and see Mum. I haven't seen her for a couple of weeks. Although she's going to be delighted to hear I've got a boyfriend.' I looked at his blond mop of curls which were now cascading down to his shoulders. 'And she'll be thrilled that you're a teacher and a star cricket player. She's partial to a test-match special.' Strange, I'd forgotten that about her.

'Sounds like the perfect woman.'

'Hmm, she's … well, let's put it like this: she and Aunty Lynn are opposite ends of the optimistic scale. Afternoon tea is more of a penance, which is why I often go to Aunty Lynn and Uncle Richard's for Sunday dinner to recover.'

'I ought to go home at some point. I've got a stack of planning to do for school and there's probably milk in my fridge about to crawl out unaided. I ought to pop into my folks', let them know I'm still alive. I'll probably scrounge dinner but,' he looked hopeful, 'I could come back in the evening.'

'I'll be at my aunt's for dinner; you can pick me up and bring me back here.'

'Sounds like a plan. I need to bring a decent razor with me.' He rubbed at the tiny nick on his chin where he'd had a falling out with one of my cheap, buy-in-bulk-from-Aldi disposable razors. We exchanged shy smiles. A toothbrush had already taken up residence in my dollhouse-sized bathroom. I liked that he was moving in, in tiny increments, and that each one felt like a natural progression without protracted negotiation.

'And as gorgeous as you smell, if I keep using your Jo Malone soap my masculinity is in serious danger of shrivelling up and surrendering.'

'My bank balance is in danger of shrivelling, the way you get through it,' I retorted. Showering together invariably took longer than it should.

'I like to make sure you've been thoroughly scrubbed. You've turned into one dirty girl.'

'You've corrupted me.'

'And I'm enjoying every minute of it.' He lifted his beer in toast, his outline silhouetted by the sun behind him, like a sunbeam-bordered Greek god. It was a perfect Instagram moment and if I'd been a smaller-minded person, I might have posted a picture of him and changed my privacy settings to public.

Chapter Fifteen

As soon as Sam left the next morning I raced around like a maniac to get all the unglamorous chores done and out of the way – cleaning the bathroom, changing the sheets and hoovering, as well as all the things that in the honeymoon phase you wanted to keep a bit of a mystery. Sam did not need to know that my eyebrows needed regular attention otherwise they looked like wayward caterpillars or that if I don't sort out the hard skin of my heels, they'll turn into something with which an armadillo would claim kinship.

I also made the mistake, while I sat and ate a quick sandwich, of looking at Victoria's Instagram and Facebook feeds – even though I'd promised myself I wouldn't. I immediately wished I hadn't. Despite the glorious sunshine outside, I might as well have invited a big black rain cloud to come in and hover over my head.

It was like taking a peek at another Sam.

Sam out on the pitch in the distance, wielding his bat. *Sam doing the biz for the cricket club...*

Sam striding towards the camera, having just peeled his navy helmet off, his face stern and the bat tucked under his arm. *Out for 103 but what an innings. Another century.*

Sam with a large jug of lager, surrounded by three grinning men – Mike and two others. *The lads celebrating. It's going to be a good night.*

A selfie with Victoria in the left corner, flanked by Paige, Mike, Drew, Izzy and Sam in the opposite corner, all holding up pints of lager. *The gang's all here. #Lovemylife #Lovemypals #bestfriends*

I knew all their names from the stalking I'd done on Facebook.

Of course that wasn't enough for me, was it? I had to go completely overboard and check Victoria's Facebook page. Big mistake. Huge. Her page came up with a memory from a year ago, the sort of shot that captured a private moment – Victoria in a scarlet evening dress and Sam in black tie, sitting at a table together, gazing at each other, completely oblivious to the camera and the rest of the world.

'You look well,' said Mum, with her usual thorough inspection of me. In a rare break with tradition we were sitting outside in the garden on the small patio under the shade of a large cream parasol.

'It's all the sunshine,' I said, waving my hand at the sky, deciding that it was best not to explain that in all likelihood my inner glow was down to a thorough sexual workout a few hours earlier.

'It has been lovely, but it's not very good for the older people. The surgery's been very busy. Lots of respiratory problems and people wanting appointments immediately.' Her lips pursed and she cast a look beyond the shadow of the parasol, as if the sunlight might be dangerous. 'Making complaints because they can't see a doctor immediately.'

Although Mum was practice manager, in her day she'd been one of those dragon receptionists determined to protect her doctors from annoying ill people.

'Honestly, people need to learn to have some patience these days.'

'Perhaps that's why they're called patients,' I quipped, unable to resist the gag, even though mum wasn't a jokey sort of person.

'Is that supposed to be funny, Jessica?'

'Yes, Mum. It's supposed to be funny.' I smiled at her.

She rolled her eyes but if you squinted very hard you might have seen the ghost of a smile on her lips.

'Did you get Gladys's wedding invitation in the post?' she asked, shaking her head with fresh disapproval.

'Yes.' I grinned. 'Typical Gladys.' The navy-blue postcard with a big white knot on the front had simply said on the back:

Getting hitched. Be there or be square. Gladys Wimpole is making an honest man of Alastair Tan. You're invited to the shindig. Bring your dancing shoes. Ceremony bit first followed by fun bit at Rose Bowl House. Champagne in lieu of presents.

'I swear she's getting worse. Talk about short notice.'

'We've had the save-the-date notice for a while.'

'Hmph. And what sort of wedding invitation is that? "Ceremony bit." What's that supposed to mean? I hope she's not going to have one of these New Age sorts of things. Although why she's bothering at her age, I don't know. And why Cornwall?' Mum's mouth pinched in disgust. Cornwall was associated with my father. 'For goodness' sake, she lives in Twickenham. We're going to have to travel down the day before and then stay over to travel back the next day. I don't know why she wants to make all this fuss.'

'Because she's happy and wants to share her special day,' I pointed out gently, leaning my elbows on the small patio table.

'Hmph,' said Mum. 'Well, I've found a nice-looking bed and breakfast which is just down the road, because I don't want to stay at this Rose Bowl House place. Knowing Gladys, it will be too noisy, and what sort of name is that for a house? It sounds most odd. Shall I book it for us?'

'Actually, Mum,' I paused, relieved that I had the perfect excuse to bag a room at the house where said shindig was taking place, because I had every intention of dancing until dawn, 'I'm thinking of taking someone with me.'

'Who?'

'A guy called Sam. We've been seeing each other. I'm going to ask him to come with me.'

'You've not mentioned him before. How long's this been going on?' Affront bristled from the top of her well-groomed head to her perfectly shod feet; even on a Sunday she wore neat little court shoes.

'Not long,' I said. 'I met him at Aunty Lynn's a while back, at a barbecue. He's the son of the people next door.'

'Oh.' There was a wealth of injury in the single syllable. 'And you don't think I'd like to meet him?'

Shit, what did I say that for? Of course Mum would take it personally that Lynn had met him before her.

'They haven't met him like that. They already knew him. Like I said, his parents live next door.'

'He still lives with his parents?'

Ergo a complete loser. It was such a Mum assumption.

'No,' I said keeping my voice light and pleasant. 'He was housesitting for them. We hit it off. And started seeing each other a couple of weeks ago.'

'And you want to take him to the wedding?' The subtext being that a couple of weeks wasn't long enough. How did I explain that Sam and I were … Sam and I?

'It's serious.'

She raised an elegant eyebrow. Seriously, those babies were her secret weapon; she could speak volumes with the damn things. With that one 'really?' lift, she managed at once to convey a wealth of disapproval and cynicism.

'You hardly know him.'

And she would know that … how?

'What does he do?' Her face had gone marvellously blank.

Because that was what really mattered. Not, does he make you happy? Does he look after you? Is he in love with you?

'He's a teacher.'

She straightened and her eyes sharpened. She dipped her head with a quick, sharp nod just slightly to one side.

'What does he teach?' At the sudden interest and warmth in her voice, my heart took a nosedive. She was in for a big disappointment. I bet she was envisioning a sports-jacketed man with neatly cropped mousy-brown hair, sensible shoes and pressed wool trousers, shaped by the ruler-straight crease down the front. Oh dear, even in his teacher get-up, Sam was not going to match her expectations.

'Children,' I said.

'I rather assumed that, Jessica.'

'He works in a primary school.' I kept my voice even, although the everything-about-Sam-is-amazing part of me was dying to jump to his defence.

'Oh, not a secondary school?'

'No, a primary school.' I reiterated, debating for a second whether to elaborate – and she would so love that piece of educated vocabulary – that it was a special school.

'So how long has this been going on? It sounds rather soon to be *serious*.'

'God, Mum,' I tempered my irritation with a tone of general question, the way I always did with her judgemental pronouncements, 'who defines how long something has to be before it's serious?' And what even *was* serious? Shagging each other's brains out on a regular basis, eating breakfast together every day, talking churches and vicars, or just knowing that this person with flaws and positives fitted perfectly into the gaps around your own personal jigsaw piece?

'I'm only asking. I worry about you. I don't want you to get hurt…'

I felt the weight of the unfinished sentence … *the way I did*. It hung in the air, portentous and ominous.

'What do you know about him?'

I know he's a good man. He cares that he's hurt his ex-girlfriend. He makes me smile.

'I know he's my Lego piece. We click.'

Mum looked startled. 'Now you're just being silly, Jess. I asked a perfectly normal question. You read about women who meet men online who pretend to be someone they're not. It often turns out they have wives and children tucked away and they're leading a double life.'

'I'm fairly sure Sam doesn't lead a double life.'

'I didn't mean to imply that he did, but you can't be too careful. How can you possibly know someone in a couple of weeks?'

Oh, but you can. Although six months ago, I'd probably have agreed with you.

'Look at poor Shelley. She gets through boyfriends faster than hot dinners. Didn't that last one steal money from her?'

Technically, Shelley had given it to him. She just hadn't expected him to pass it straight on to his wife to support his three children.

'No,' I lied, which was wasted effort as Mum always knew exactly what went on. 'And you can know someone for years and they turn out not to be the person you thought they were.'

Mum's face crumpled as if I'd punched her with an

Anthony Joshua left hook. 'If you're referring to your father, it was fine before he met *that* woman and threw away a wife and child on a whim.'

My father's new wife – although not that new, as they must have been married for nearly fifteen years – was still known as *that* woman. Her name, Alicia, was never spoken. She was the nemesis that had blighted our lives and changed things for ever.

Although I was only eight when it happened, the sense of bewilderment at the depth of my mother's grief still resonated. She'd been unable to get out of bed for months and I'd gone to live with Aunty Lynn and Uncle Richard, the company of my cousin and calm order of their house a blessed relief, although there'd been an overarching sense of guilt. At my aunt and uncle's house, things were normal again; dinner times were reinstated, adults were in charge and I no longer had a silent empty house to wander around at will, prying and poking into things, spilling the button box on the lounge floor, hearing the skitter-scatter as they bounced across the tiled floor of the hearth in front of the fire, eating illicit biscuits for breakfast and striking matches just because I could.

I looked down at the neat, unimaginative garden. The sparsely planted straight border dotted with aquilegia, bleeding heart and white alyssum which Mum weeded with a fierce sense of duty rather than any pleasure. Since those months of chaos, Mum had stamped order onto every facet of our lives, determined to ensure that the train never went off the rails again. I thought of Victoria and the recent pictures on Instagram; she seemed to be in control, but how did any of us know what was going on beneath the surface?

As I stared at the purple flowers an uncomfortable thought burrowed its way into my mind. I was Victoria's Alicia.

Alicia Harper. Married to my dad. We shared part of our name and yet I'd never thought of her as real person before. Alicia had always been a figure in the mist, a blurred outline, indeterminate and featureless. I had never troubled to know her. She was the enemy, so I had no idea if she was tall or short, blonde or dark, thin or fat? Did she make my father laugh? Did she work? Did she cook? Were they happy? What did their life together look like? I knew she must be younger than my father. A lot younger. There'd been a letter out of the blue, with a photograph, when I was sixteen and then another, this time containing two photographs, two years later. Addressed to me. The contents of the first one had turned Mum's lips blue. It was a terrifying moment when I'd thought I might have to call an ambulance. I burned both letters in a fit of adolescent aggrievement and self-righteous ceremony, although I hadn't quite been able to bring myself to burn the photographs, as if that were some kind of bad voodoo. Mum and I had never spoken about those pictures. Not once. I wasn't sure if she knew I still had them. They were tucked at the very back of the top drawer of my dressing table in a small brown envelope, which was sealed, so that no one could inadvertently open it. I'd never even told Shelley about the contents.

Mum stood up and even though we were in the garden,

bustled about clearing up the teacups, stacking them in each other on top of the saucers. Ever since that window of chaos, when my father had turned our life upside down, she'd become a bustler, always needing to do things – tidying up, wiping up, cleaning up. The house, now, was always spotless and clutter-free and the lounge the sort of room where you felt you should sit neatly, with your knees and ankles together. The minute a crumb was dropped, she'd whip out the handy cordless vacuum – mounted on the wall in the hall, so that it was equidistant to every room on the ground floor – and wield it like St George fending off a dragon.

'So when am I going to meet this boy?' she asked, standing under the edge of the parasol, the cups and saucers balanced in one hand as if this important question needed to be answered before she braved the sunshine en route to the back door of the kitchen.

After everything I'd said, I could hardly turn around now and say that it was early days.

'Er…'

The crockery quivered in her hand. 'He doesn't have a tattoo or something, does he?'

'Mum, everyone has tattoos now but no, Sam doesn't have a tattoo.' I lied because it was highly unlikely that she was ever going to see the lion on his left butt cheek. When I say lion, we're not talking roaring, fearsome king of the jungle; we're talking cute, cuddly soft-toy style that could have come straight from the pages of a children's storybook. He couldn't change the subject on that one for ever; I would get the story out of him one day.

'He plays cricket.'

Well, blow me. I wish I'd said that first. Mum actually smiled and put the cups back down on the patio table.

'Does he now? Batter or bowler?'

My batting hero.

'He's a batter,' I said, not having a clue.

'And where does he play?'

Oh God. Twenty questions, but at least I could answer that one. 'At Meadows Way in Tring.'

'For the firsts? They play to a very high standard there. Gosh, he must be good. What's his name?'

'Sam. Sam Weaverham. He got a century yesterday,' I said, lapping up this unexpected enthusiasm. I'd better encourage Sam to wear his cricket whites and pads when he came to visit. In that get up he could probably carry off a couple of tattoos and even a piercing or two.

'Did he now? Well, I look forward to meeting him.' With her free hand, she twisted her wrist to look at her watch, a tiny frown marring her forehead.

With the cups in her hand, she stood there waiting for a minute, looking at me expectantly.

Clearly, our sojourn in the garden was over and when I stood up she inclined her head with subtle sheepdog-herding signals, as if to head me towards the kitchen.

I followed her into the kitchen where she unloaded the crockery straight into the dishwasher, her head tilted my way as she said, 'I assume you're going to your aunt's for dinner.'

'I'm going to pop in to see Shelley. I haven't seen her this week and Bel's coming over. I haven't seen her for weeks.'

Playing the *my cousin is also my best friend* card sweetened the bitter pill that I was close to Aunty Lynn.

'Ah, Bel. How is she? How are the wedding plans coming along?' Mum's face softened. Bel had achieved approved status very early on. I think it was because she had hair that behaved itself and never messed about with her school uniform. Her skirt was always regulation length and she never rolled the sleeves of her shirt above the elbows – and when I came back to live with Mum, her friendship had been the anchor that kept me here through difficult teenager years when Mum had been fiercely overprotective at the same time as emotionally distant.

'Good, I think. I haven't seen her for a while. She's been away for the last month – an audit job in York.'

'Yes. Those professional jobs do give you opportunities to travel. Give her my best, won't you?' This was said with a saintly smile. I noted that nothing of the sort was directed Shelley's way. 'And look at the time.' She looked at her watch again. Come to think of it, she'd been looking at her watch a lot during my whole visit, and now she was doing the subliminal sheepdog thing again and somehow I was being shepherded out and down the hall. 'You'd better get moving. You don't want to get held up in traffic.'

Hello? It was Sunday. Four o'clock. I had a three-mile trip up the bypass. The trip would take me ten minutes at most.

For the first time during one of my visits, I wasn't desperate to get away. Contrarily, I felt a bit put out and unwanted. 'Got something planned?' I asked as we reached the front door, and to my astonishment she blushed.

'Douglas is popping round. Just for a gin and tonic. He bought some new gin. Thought I might like to try it.'

'That's nice,' I said, my tone deliberately as bland as bland could be. I might as well have saved my breath.

'It's just a gin and tonic, Jessica.'

Well, that told me, in no uncertain tones.

Chapter Sixteen

'She's got it baaad,' crowed Shelley when I bounced up from my chair at the sound of the doorbell. Sam was early – assuming it was him – but I'd committed now to answering the door. I wasn't expecting him for another hour.

'Look how fast she's moving that skinny little ass.' Shel turned to me and prodded my hip. 'Did I tell you I hate you?'

'Yes, numerous times.' I pulled a face at her, batting her hand away, much to the indulgent amusement of Lynn and Richard as I went to answer the front door.

'Shelley, you should be nicer to your cousin.' Aunty Lynn waved a cold sausage at Shelley before taking a big bite.

'You're right, Mum. It's you I should be abusing for passing on such crap genes.'

Their gentle bickering faded away as I jumped through the patio doors and dashed across the kitchen. Shelley was right; I did have it bad. Since I'd arrived from my mum's, I was aware that Sam was with his parents', a stone's throw away through the hedge at the bottom of the garden. A couple of times we'd heard laughter from neighbouring gardens; everyone seemed to be eating al fresco this evening.

I slowed my barefoot progress along the parquet floor in the hall. Maybe I shouldn't be so keen. But it was no good; my stomach felt as if it were chock full of excitable puppies rather than butterflies. Was it wrong that I was dying to see Sam again, after less than a day apart?

I threw open the door and grinned at him, only subliminally aware of the tightness around his eyes before they lit up as if I were the best thing on the planet.

'Fancy seeing you here.' I wrapped my arms around his neck and tilted my face up to his, unable to hide the sheer delight that just the sight of him made me feel.

'Hello, you,' he said, burying his face into the crook of my neck and shoulder and pulling me into a hug. He squeezed tight and held me for the sort of beat longer that sent up flags.

'Sam?' I asked.

'Are you OK to head straight off? I've still got some marking to do this evening.'

I paused for a minute. 'Yes, er … yes. Just let me say goodbye.'

I turned away, ignoring the quick duck-dive of disappointment. He was so early that I'd thought he might have been here to invite me back to meet his mum and dad.

When I came back, he was nudging at the doormat with the toe of his battered Converse as if it were annoying him.

'Everything OK?' I asked as we climbed into his car.

'Yeah, fine,' he said in that clipped, short way that invariably meant the exact opposite, as he turned on the ignition. His face was hidden behind his hair which, unusually, was down, almost as if he'd pulled it from his customary man bun to create a barrier. 'Have you eaten?'

'Hello? Aunty Lynn's house. Hell, yes, I've eaten.'

'Sorry, that was a stupid question.' He grinned at me.

'Have you eaten?' I asked.

'No … there wasn't…' His jaw tightened and as I looked at his profile, his eyes trained on the road ahead, I could see the tension in his neck. 'Wasn't time.'

The length of the car journey across town to my flat was not long enough for Sam's woefully inadequate air con to even attempt to limber up and attack the heat in the car, so we drove with the windows wound down, not quite hanging out like a pair of dogs but each of us clinging to our side of the car as if putting distance between us.

As soon as we walked into the flat I busied myself opening all the windows. The heat today had reached a point where it had gathered in our absence and sat heavy and humid in an oppressive fug, a little bit like the conversation that we weren't having.

Sam settled at the table with his exercise books, while I pottered about, tidying up and pulling our clean underwear from the drying rack out on the balcony. When I came back inside with the stack of pants and socks, Sam was staring miserably into space.

'Want to talk about it?' I asked, setting the pile down gently and standing next to him.

'I'm really pissed off with my mum.' His blue eyes met mine with a candid stare, as he poked at the pages of the book in front of him with his special green marking pen, leaving little streaks of colour on the white edge. He squeezed my hand.

'They're having a party. For their wedding anniversary.'

'I know,' I admitted. 'Lynn and Richard are invited. It's OK, you don't have to worry about me.' Saying the words out loud lessened the hurt that had been niggling since Sam had failed to mention it. I'd invited him to Gladys's wedding a week ago; it had been the perfect opening for him to bring it up and he hadn't.

'Mum's invited Victoria.'

'It is her party,' I said gently. 'She can invite whoever she wants.'

'That's what she said.' Sam's face furrowed in frustration, his thumb rubbing over my knuckles. 'It feels wrong that I can't bring you. She says it's too soon.'

'Ha! She's been listening to my mother, although I played the he's-a-cricketer card and it appears to be a get-out-of-jail-free card. Her eyes positively lit up when she heard you were a batter. You are a batter, aren't you?'

Sam laughed. 'I am.'

'And she seemed terribly impressed when I told her you were a centurion yesterday.'

'I scored a century.' He laughed and shook his head, pulling my hand up to his face and rubbing my knuckles against his smiling cheeks.

'I figure that makes you a centurion.'

'Never been called that before, but I'll take it.'

'In that case I don't suppose you'd like to come with me next weekend to see her? She's a bit miffed that Aunty Lynn has met you before her.'

He frowned, not understanding why that would be the case, and I didn't have the heart to explain the whole, sorry, complicated mess that was a hangover from my childhood.

'Sure.' He still seemed distracted. 'I'm sorry about my mum.'

'It's not your fault. She's never met me. You can't blame her.' I shrugged. I might not like it, but I did understand. 'She and Victoria are friends and have been for a long time.'

Sam's mouth pursed, making him resemble a mutinous turtle and I burst out laughing. Being grumpy really didn't suit him.

'Why are you so lovely?' he asked lifting a hand to cup my chin. 'You should be insulted. It's not on.'

I lifted my shoulders. 'There's not a lot I can do, and I certainly don't want to cause trouble between you and your parents.'

'It's going to be embarrassing with your aunt and uncle, if they see Vic's there and you aren't.'

'Don't worry about that.'

'I'm not. I'm just cross with Mum.'

'How did you leave it with her?'

He faltered. 'We're … erm, not speaking.'

'Oh, Sam, no.' From everything I'd heard about his mum and the pictures I'd seen, I had a rosy view of her. My mum might drive me distracted but I tried to avoid falling out with her, mainly because I knew that if I upset her, she was completely on her own. That desire to protect her had been there throughout my childhood. From the day she took to her bed, when my dad left, I'd been terrified of making things worse. For a couple of weeks, I'd attempted to fend for myself without telling anyone at school how bad things were. As soon as I was awake I'd dress in my uniform, dash between the kitchen and the lounge window to get my breakfast, so that I would see when other people started walking to school and I'd know it was the right time to leave. Some mornings that wait had felt like hours.

'Ring her. Say you're sorry. It doesn't matter. I don't mind about not being there.'

'But I do,' he looked fierce. 'Victoria should be the one to duck out. I feel like she's taking advantage of Mum by accepting the invitation.'

He definitely had a point there. 'It's still early days for her too, I guess. It's a lot to lose. Not just her boyfriend but everything else that goes with it.'

'Jess. You're too flipping nice. She's not doing badly. She's kept all of our friends and my name is mud.'

'Yes, but,' I gave him a deliberately winsome smile, 'you've got me.'

He snaked an arm around my waist and pulled me down on to his lap. 'I certainly do.'

'And I've got you,' I said, leaning into his solid chest. 'And I understand she's hurting.' I'd only been known Sam for a few weeks; Victoria had known him for four years. Losing that left a very big hole in someone's life. 'Call your mum. I can see it's troubling you.'

'Do you always try and fix people?' he asked, his fingers tracing the sensitive skin on the back of my neck.

'I wish I could,' I said, thinking of some of the women at the refuge, and of all the ones that hadn't made it to a refuge yet.

'You're a good person, Jess Harper.'

'And so are you. Don't fall out with your mum over me, please.'

'For the love of God, Jess, will you just leave.' Holly wrested the empty coffee cups from my hand. 'I'll wash these up.' It was Thursday evening and I was due to meet Sam and his work friends, and suddenly seemed to have acquired some kind of compulsive cleaning disorder.

'It's OK,' I said, snatching them back and skirting her desk to march into the kitchen with her trailing after me. I wasn't the least bit nervous about meeting Sam's friends. Not really. Not at all. OK, a little.

'Listen to Aunty Holly.' She knitted her dark brows together in what was supposed to be her serious face.

'Do I have a choice?' I teased, trying to keep things light.

With her dark-lined eyes and heavily highlighted brow bones, she looked more like an angry marmoset. Difficult to take too seriously.

'They will like you, Jess, because you're lovely.'

OK, busted. I'd never been more nervous about meeting new people in my life, and it really irked me because that's not the sort of the thing I usually worry about.

'But what if they don't?' I said in a small whiney voice, which is hardly ever let out of the box. Shelley would have been shocked and then smacked me around the head. Holly was a little subtler. 'It's the Facebook thing that's bothering me. What if … what if one of them is there tonight?' I said, squirting washing-up liquid into the sink and giving those coffee cups the most thorough clean they'd ever had, before reaching for a tea towel and drying them under Holly's impatient gaze, which was a dead giveaway because I always leave the mugs on the draining rack.

'Jess Harper, wash your mouth out with that very soap bottle. You have to forget that. You know what's it like on social media; people say things they'd never dream of saying in real life. And if they are, they'll be mortified that they let themselves get sucked in. Social media dehumanises people. Those people who made those comments don't think of you as a real person. You're just an avatar, an image; you don't really exist in their minds. You said yourself that you don't even know those two girls that said they knew you.'

'But even so, to say—' The post might have been deleted but the fact that all those women had piled in with so much gusto … it still grated.

'It's mob rule, lovely. Once one person starts and another agrees, it legitimises what they say and gives others permission to be as vile. If any of those people meet you in real life, they'll be mortified. I promise you.' She removed the tea towel from my hands, her face breaking into a teasing grin, 'They'll soon realise that you aren't anywhere close to being a skank.'

'Thanks, Dr Freud.' I straightened up. 'You're right.'

Holly clutched her throat in mock horror. 'You mean you ever doubted?'

'No,' I said, with a rueful smile. 'You're always right, Hol.'

'And don't you forget it, young lady. Now, go get that man. Have a good evening and don't spare a thought for me slaving over an essay on cognitive behavioural theories on eating disorders.'

'I won't,' I said cheerfully, giving her a quick hug. 'Thanks, Hols. See you tomorrow.'

'This is Jess.'

How could I not fall a little bit more for a man who in three simple words managed to imply to the small group in the pub that I was something really quite special? Especially when it was the first time I was meeting his colleagues, who, from the way he'd described them, had superhero tendencies and could have done a good job standing in for The Avengers.

As he pulled up a chair for me, squeezing it into a space next to the birthday girl and another woman with incredibly twinkly blue eyes, Sam's colleagues were already offering friendly nods and smiles before I'd even opened my mouth to utter a quick 'Hello.'

'Hi, Jess.' Twinkly eyes immediately squidged up to make more room. 'I'm Erin and this is Jen, the birthday girl, although you can probably tell from the outsize badges.'

As Sam disappeared to the bar, leaving me in the thick of it, Jen shimmied her shoulders making the two badges rattle together, one saying *I am two* and the other saying *I am nine*.

'They didn't have a twenty-nine badge,' explained Jen in a strong Scottish accent, tossing back her pure white Scandinavian-princess blonde hair and giving me an angelic smile. With her clear, glowing complexion she'd have been right at home in one of those old-fashioned soap adverts.

'They did have a thirty badge, though,' said Erin, winking at me with a wicked smirk.

'I refuse to be thirty in front of the children,' said Jen with a disdainful sniff. 'Thirty is ancient as far as they're concerned.'

'She's thirty-two,' Erin's stage whisper wasn't the least bit subtle, 'but in denial.'

At which Jen grinned, her cheeks dimpling, and shrugged her shoulders. 'If I can pass for late twenties, I'm going to milk it for as long as I can.'

'I bet you milk the "I'm so disappointed" line as well,' I said, looking at her pretty, angelic babyface.

'Too bloody right,' she said, lifting a large glass of wine and toasting me with it. 'Works a treat. Especially with my lot. I teach the reception class. It's like trying to manage meerkats. What, miss? Where? Oh look.' With her quick jerky head movements turning this way and that, she did a very passable impression of a distracted meerkat. 'Love 'em to bits but trying to keep them on task is a virtual impossibility. The I'm-very-disappointed look comes out at least once an hour; luckily they've got such short attention spans, it works every time.'

Erin and I laughed and then Jen lowered her voice. 'So Jess, what do you do and where've you appeared from?'

'And what did you do with Victoria?' asked Erin, looking around the pub as if she might pop up at any moment.

'That's Sam's story,' I said, without so much as a twitch. The ghost of girlfriend past was starting to irritate me.

'Erin. What have I told you about boundaries?' said Jen in what was clearly her teacher voice.

'Just askin',' said Erin, holding her hands up in surrender before going in again. 'So how long have you been seeing each other? And how did you meet?' she asked.

'Don't forget inside leg measurement,' Jen groaned, lightly tapping Erin's knuckles with her glittery nails. 'Give the poor girl a chance. If you interrogate her too much, she might not come back. And we like her … we think.' Jen cocked her head. 'You look nice. Nicer than…' She clapped a hand over her mouth. 'Pretend you didn't hear that, but we didn't warm to Victoria.'

Erin snorted. 'Since when did you swallow a diplomacy tablet, Jen Warren? I distinctly recall the words,' she held up her hands in cute speech marks, '"stick-insect strumpet with a snotty attitude", and wasn't it you that came up with the famous phrase, "her nose is so stuck up in the air she's probably sniffing St Peter's armpits"?'

Unable to help myself, I snorted out loud at that one, before quickly adding, 'I think I should probably be blocking my ears and not listening to this.'

'Have you met her?' asked Erin.

'Sort of?' I admitted cagily, shifting in my seat, not really wanting to get into the whole Victoria-crashing-our-first-date story.

'Was she a bitch?' asked Jen candidly, when I didn't elaborate.

Eek, I didn't want to be drawn into this, I slid a quick hunted glance over to the bar, but Sam didn't look as if he'd even been served yet.

Jen patted me on the arm. 'Don't fret, pet. You have to be nice. You're the new girlfriend and you've just met us. That's the law.' She turned to Erin. 'We, on the other hand, can tell it like it is. You probably think we're being unkind, but,' she paused and pulled a childish face, 'truth is, she never made much effort with us. Whenever she and Sam came out with us, which was not that often, she made it quite clear she was doing Sam a massive favour and the whole time made it obvious she couldn't wait to get away. She was so rolling her eyes under her breath.'

Erin rolled hers at the mangled images. 'Sorry to say, but Jen is right. It's Sam I felt sorry for. He always defended her. Said she was quite insecure really.'

'Insecure my arse! She was a spoiled princess.'

Erin glared at Jen. 'Whatever happened to the apple doesn't fall far from the tree?'

'They're children! She's a grown woman.'

'With wounds,' Erin insisted. 'My cousin was at school with her. By all accounts, her parents had a vile divorce when she was fifteen and both wanted custody. They competed big time for her – ski holidays, trips to the

Bahamas, designer handbags, open cheque book for Jack Wills, Hollister and Abercrombie and Fitch. Seriously, she got everything she wanted, and then after a couple of years, the court awarded joint custody, so she lived one week with her dad and the next with her mother. But the money splurging didn't stop; if anything, the stakes got even higher. They still tried to outdo each other. And then … one by one her parents remarried … and she became second fiddle. She's been desperate for approval ever since.'

Jen held a hand up. 'Yeah, yeah, poor Victoria, but it doesn't mean she has to act like the bitch queen of New Orleans.'

'Don't be mean, Jen. And that's not the lyric.'

I frowned. 'Isn't it witch queen?'

Jen grinned. 'I think you're going to fit right in.'

By the time Sam finally came back with drinks, I was deep in conversation with them. 'Here you go,' he said, squeezing in next to me and handing me half a lager.

I glanced up and caught his warm, intimate smile and there might as well have been no one else in the room but us. Sandy freckles dusted his nose and fine white lines bled out from the crinkles around his eyes into his tanned face. I focused on the little details, trying to work out what it was about him that drew me to him as surely as a compass to due north. Leaning forward, he dropped a quick kiss on the corner of my mouth.

'Thanks for coming tonight,' he whispered.

'They're all lovely.' And clearly a different crowd from Sam's other friends.

'They're a good bunch.' His curls bounced as he nodded.

'I haven't seen as much of them. You know, when you work with people all day, you don't always want to socialise with them as well.'

I gave him a sceptical glance. Holly and I could spend hours together in or out of work, and I got the impression that these people were no different.

'Happy Birthday, Jen.' He lifted his glass in a toast.

Everyone lifted their glasses in unison.

'Thanks Sam, and thanks for coming along. It's nice to see you,' said Jen. 'I meant to ask, how are your mum and dad settling into their new house?'

'Good,' said Sam, shooting a quick conspiratorial glance at me. 'Although they've been there for six months now.'

'Really? It's that long?' Erin pursed her lips. 'Just goes to show how long it is since you've been on a night out with us.'

'I'm here now.' He rolled his eyes.

'Yes, you are.' She patted his arm. 'And it's lovely to have you back.' Her twinkly eyes flashed my way and I knew I'd just got a tacit seal of approval, and that her words held a wealth of alternative meaning, but for now I'd take the approval.

'I think they like you,' he whispered so that she could hear.

'Your turn next week,' I teased. 'You have to face Bel, who is my oldest and bestest friend. She might not give you such an easy ride.'

I only felt a touch guilty when worry filled his face. Seeing Bel and Dan was going to be plain sailing. At least I was pretty sure it was.

Chapter Seventeen

B el looked up and waved across the pub, her face breaking into a sunny smile. It was Bel, for goodness' sake, my oldest friend, so the wobbles in my knees could just piss off. Sam, as ever attuned, picked up on my unexpected and ridiculous nerves.

'Worried I'll show you up?' he teased.

'No, I just really want her … *them* to like you.'

'Most people do, usually.' There was a shadow underlying his confident grin.

I tucked my arm through his and led him towards the table in the conservatory area where Bel and Dan sat. This was the first time I'd officially introduced him to anyone. He'd already met the other important people in my life; Bel had been away for a few weeks and I'd been putting mum off for as long as possible, more because I didn't want to put Sam off.

'Hey, Jess.' Bel bounced to her feet and beamed at me and threw her arms around me in a big hug, reminding me exactly why she was one of my favourite people. 'And you must be the famous Sam. We've heard lots about you, but don't worry, it was all good.'

'Phew, that's a relief then,' said Sam, holding out his hand to Dan. 'Sam Weaverham.'

'Dan Hamilton. Nice to meet you.' He shot a cheeky look my way. 'Bit of a relief. You look relatively normal. Bel and I thought Jess was going to turn into an old spinster. Her strike rate on dating hasn't been great.'

'Thanks, Dan, why don't you tell Sam that I'm a bit of a loser.'

'Dan!' said Bel, her voice pitching in mock outrage, before adding in a voice brimming with laughter, 'The party line is she's just a bit picky.'

Dan slapped his forehead, grinning with mischief. 'Aw, I forgot.'

'You two are awful. You're supposed to be my friends.' I shook my head at Sam. 'Ignore them. I've known Bel for ever, since pre-school, so she thinks she can say what she likes.'

'I can,' said Bel to Sam in a confiding manner. 'And I know all her worst secrets.'

My smile was brilliant as Bel and I laughed together, but when our eyes met, there was a promise in hers that she'd never reveal them. She, Lynn, Richard and Shelley were the only other people who knew about my darkest days as a child and my mother's mental breakdown.

'What're you drinking?' Sam flicked a thumb to their half-empty drinks.

'I'll get these,' I said laying a hand on his forearm.

Another thing I loved about him was his generous spirit. What he had, he shared, even though he probably earned a fraction of what accountants Bel and Dan did.

'Sure?' he asked.

I headed to the bar and as I was waiting to be served, I looked back to where he sat with Bel and Dan, catching him mid-laugh, his head thrown back, his mouth open. My heart stuttered just a little. What was it about him that had made me fall so fast and hard for him? Yes, it had been that punch of attraction, but there was so much more. Would I feel as desperate as Victoria if he left me? I blinked for a second, determined not to think like that, and when I turned back to watch them again, Dan was laughing too, and Bel was smiling with fond indulgence like a mother with two idiotic schoolboys. Looked like Sam had hit it off with them already.

By the time I returned, Dan and Sam were deep in conversation about some cricket match they'd seen, and I sat down next to Bel.

'Nice,' she murmured. 'Very nice.'

'Thank you,' I said. 'So, I have your permission to continue?'

'Absolutely.' Bel sounded positively wicked – well, as wicked as a good girl like her ever got. I studied Sam, trying to look at him with new eyes as if seeing him from her point of view. Tonight he was wearing faded navy cargo shorts and a navy T-shirt – nothing fancy but you couldn't help but notice the way the jersey fabric stretched over his broad chest. Animation danced over his face as he chatted to Dan, flashing smiles and nodding with enthusiasm, but in his usual relaxed, I'm-not-trying-to-impress-anyone sort of way. He looked up, caught my eye and his smile widened.

It got me every time. The brief flash of intimacy, the I-know-you're-there. It made my heart quiver, every damn time. I smiled back and then seamlessly we both tuned back into our respective conversations.

'Oooh, you've got it bad,' said Bel, nudging me with a quiet laugh.

I tried to shrug, but I couldn't hide the glow of happiness that just seemed to leak out of its own accord.

Bel stared at me, surprise narrowing her eyes. 'No! You really have got it bad.' Her arms clutched my shoulders. 'Oh my God.' I couldn't look away from her careful assessment of my face. 'You really are ... I've never seen you like this before.'

'He's lovely,' I whispered.

She threw her arms around me and hugged me hard, saying in a fierce whisper. 'I am so glad. You deserve to have someone lovely.' She pulled back and gave me another study. 'About bloody time too. I was worried you'd never give anyone a chance to get through.'

'What do you mean?' I asked, a little startled.

She sobered and raised a challenging eyebrow. 'Come on, Jess.'

I shrugged. 'In my job I see the unhappy endings. No wonder I'm a little cautious.'

'You were cautious way before you started work. I've always worried that your mother's... Well, you know, she's not exactly pro happy-ever-after.'

'You mean she personifies bitter and twisted,' I said, taking pity on her tiptoeing attempt at diplomacy.

'I was trying not to say that. Although it's a wonder you've turned out to be glass-half-full. You've always kept men at arm's length but,' she smiled, 'not this one apparently.' She squeezed my hand. 'I'm chuffed for you. You look all...' she waved jazz hands in a very unBel-like way, 'lit up. I'm glad. It's about time too.'

'Thanks, Bel. I'm taking him to meet her this weekend.'

Bel's eyes widened but she didn't say anything. Probably just as well. The thought of it already was giving me kittens and puppies.

As if sensing that the serious bit of girls catching up was done, Sam turned to us. 'Jess says you've been working in York for a month. I was there last year on a residential trip. Did you get to see much of the city or were you working?' His hand slid on my knee, warm and solid as he engaged Bel in easy conversation.

We were onto our second round of drinks when the door opened and a group of about six people came into the pub. I was vaguely aware of them because it was a biggish group, but they drifted our way to bag the big table next to ours when suddenly someone said, 'Sam!'

He looked up and he beamed in quick recognition. 'Mike!'

'Hey, buddy, how're you doing?' Mike clapped him on the back as they exchanged a man hug.

I watched curiously with a shimmer of nerves. This was Sam's best friend.

The rest of the group came into focus and my heart

stalled a little. Victoria. There she was smiling at Sam, looking demure and saintly in a white cotton dress, flanked by two friends who were already looking daggers at me.

Great. Of all the pubs in all of town, she and the gang had to come in here. I slipped Bel a quick agonised look but didn't say anything. Sam was suddenly surrounded by the group as two more guys hugged him, and then the two girls kissed him on the cheek, exclaiming how long it had been. All the while Victoria hung back a little, looking demure, lost and sweet, but clearly drinking in the sight of Sam. Her friends slipped her careful, worried sidelong glances and she gave them brave little smiles. One of them edged closer to her and put an arm round her.

Bel frowned and said in an undertone. 'Do you know them?'

Victoria was watching me, so I pushed away my irritation. 'No, but ... don't look and don't make a fuss, because she's watching us like a hawk: the girl in the white dress is Sam's ex.'

'What! Skankgate?' Bel's face darkened and she stiffened in her seat, as if about to turn around.

'Shh, don't.'

'But...'

'Just ignore her.'

Sam turned and held out his hand. 'Jess.' I took his hand and he tugged me to my feet. I pasted a friendly smile on my face wanting to make a good impression.

'Jess, this is Mike.'

'Hi,' I said, smiling up at the dark-haired handsome

man. God, he and Sam were a right pair of heartthrobs; they must have done serious damage in their schooldays.

'And this is Paige, Mike's girlfriend,' said Sam, a touch too eager, introducing me to the girl at Mike's side. Paige did not look at all happy to see me, and her mouth moved wordlessly for a second or two as if she were trying to decide how to handle this unwelcome introduction. Luckily, she was put out of her misery by the timely and surprising arrival of Victoria, who stepped into the circle to join us, linking her arm through Paige's. I thought the move was a bit controlling, as if she were some kind of enforcer who needed to remind Paige where her loyalties lay.

'Hello, Jasmine, isn't it?' Victoria took command with a smooth smile of utter condescension, like royalty greeting the pleb.

I forced a laugh, 'No, that's the princess in *Aladdin*. I'm afraid I'm just plain old Jess.'

There was a tiny flicker of something in Paige's eyes, which gave me hope.

Victoria blinked, assessing her options. I'd surprised her and it took a second or two for her to regroup. She was, I realised, a master tactician but the skirmish wasn't going her way. I got the distinct impression she'd planned her attack and I'd thrown that into disarray.

'No … you don't look like a Disney princess,' she agreed.

Paige's mouth twitched but she quickly hid her amusement as Victoria's eyes narrowed. I'd got her measure all right. Sam's ex didn't like to lose face. She wanted to win at all costs, and I was in danger of escalating her problem with me when I really didn't need to. We were never going to be friends, but I didn't need to make an enemy of her.

'Sam hasn't told us very much about you.' She gave my casual skirt an indifferent glance. 'What do you do?'

I shrugged. 'Admin.' There was no way I was dancing to her tune. I liked being patronised as much as the next person.

'Yes, but who for? What do you do?' Victoria pressed again. Jeepers, she was like a dog with a bone.

'It's really very dull.' I lifted my shoulders to emphasise my point while hiding my irritation. Nosy cow. 'I work in an office, answering the phone, making appointments and filing. What do you do?' I kept my tone conversational and friendly. I had a witness and I wanted to make sure nothing I said could be misconstrued. My question was designed for diversion in the hope that Victoria would want to brag about whatever she did, which was far superior to a lowly admin job. I remember Sam saying that she worked for her dad's company.

'Event management, social media influencer, that sort of thing,' said Victoria. 'I'm helping Sally for the anniversary party. I hear you're coming.' There was a not-so-subtle pause before she added, 'Now. It's taking so much planning but it's a really big deal for them. They want to celebrate with all their dearest friends and family. Sally really knows how to throw a party… We went to some brilliant parties at their old house, didn't we, Paige? Remember the barbecue when Sam almost set fire to the lawn?'

'Oh God, yes. And poor Tiggy was beside herself trying to eat the sausages.'

I just nodded as they began to reminisce and felt a lot better when Sam's hand brushed mine. He was engrossed in conversation with his mates on my right-hand side but still aware of me. My smile in response to his touch was involuntary, but unfortunately Victoria spotted the tiny gesture and her lip curled. Until that point, I'd felt I was doing OK in front of an audience that, while not quite hostile, was certainly full of prurient interest. I'd acquitted myself quite well. Paige had almost smiled a couple of times and Victoria clearly felt she'd established her superiority.

'It won't last, you know,' she hissed. 'No one is going to have anything to do with you. None of Sam's friends want to meet you. And Sam's friends are very important to him. They'll never accept you.' She pulled Paige away and the two of them went to sit down at the table behind us.

Schooling my face into a mask of polite serenity, I turned to Sam and listened into his conversation, smiling at the two guys talking to him.

Mike gave me a curt nod, but his eyes slid away quickly as he addressed his next comment to Sam.

'So, you playing this weekend? Tough match.'

Sam slipped his arm around my waist, pulling me closer.

'Yes. Their bowler is a bit handy.'

'Yeah, but erratic. You coming to the barbecue on Sunday?'

'Probably not,' said Sam.

'Not working, surely. Come on, man. You can take a day off marking books.'

'No. Jess and I are out.' We were? That was news to me. We hadn't even talked about the weekend, although I'd got used to him playing cricket most Saturdays, so that wasn't a surprise.

'Joined at the hip, are you?' Mike's laddish grin didn't take the slight sting out of his words. 'Got you well under the thumb.'

'We've got plans,' said Sam again, squeezing my waist. I swallowed down disappointment. He was making excuses and I could guess why.

'That's a shame, we haven't seen you for ages.'

'You see me every Saturday,' teased Sam.

'Yeah, but it's not the same. You bugger off after the match every week.' Mike's mouth tightened and he shot me a cold stare, although his tone when he spoke was decidedly matey. 'You ought to let him off the leash a bit, love. I'm sure you can spare him a few hours with his mates.' The jolly grin accompanying his words was not echoed in his flat-eyed stare of challenge.

Sam's fingers tightened around my waist and I felt him stiffen.

'I'm not the enemy here,' I said quietly, lifting my chin before Sam could say anything. 'Sam makes his own choices. This isn't a Brothers Grimm tale, you know. I'm not some enchantress who's ensnared him.' I brushed my hand down my denim shorts. 'I'm pretty ordinary, really.' I'd have loved to add that Victoria was doing a great job of channelling Maleficent vibes but I knew, without being paranoid, that every word I said would be taken down and used against me.

I couldn't see around Mike but I just knew the rest of the table were still watching with avid interest, so I kept my stance relaxed and friendly as if were having a friendly chat.

'Mike. You're being an arse,' said Sam quietly. 'Jess and I are just getting on with it. Why can't you do the same? If it's a problem for you, it's your problem, mate. Not mine.' He dropped a kiss on my temple. 'See you later.' Turning his back on his friend, he steered me back to sit down with Bel and Dan, keeping his arm around me. 'You OK? I'm sorry about that. He's not normally such a dick.'

He reached for my hand and interlaced his fingers through mine. My heart was beating a little too fast and I could feel the hint of colour running along my cheekbones.

'Don't worry. Divided loyalties. It's tough.'

'No, it's not. He was being a dick.' Sam's fist clenched on the table as his other hand rubbed along the top of my thumb. I felt the prickle of being watched but refused to give in and look over at the other table.

'Don't fall out with him about it. Why don't you try and fix up to go out with him, just the two of you?'

Sam shook his head, unclenched his fist and kissed me on the mouth. 'Why are you so bloody nice?'

'Because there are more important things to worry about? We're happy, aren't we?'

He ran a finger down my nose and kissed me again. 'We are…'

OK, I do have some inner bitchy genes and I just knew that someone on the table behind me must have seen that romantic gesture. I'd be a liar if I didn't say that gave me all the satisfaction I needed.

'Well, that was interesting,' said Bel. She and Dan had been watchful throughout the whole nervous exchange as if waiting for an explosion.

'Sorry. It's a bit awkward at the moment,' said Sam, screwing up his mouth.

I could see Bel bristling on my behalf. 'It's fine,' I said. 'It's still early days... It will blow over eventually. And Tring's a small place.'

'Early days?' Sam frowned as Bel raised her eyebrows in telling reproof. 'You two have been seeing each other, for what, over a month now?'

'Five weeks,' I corrected.

'I've never known Mike or the others to come in here,' said Sam, pushing his hand through his hair. The implication being that this had been a safe choice. 'They usually drink at The Akeman or the clubhouse.'

'Just bad luck,' said Dan lifting his glass and draining his pint.

Sam and I exchanged a glance. If Victoria had wanted to create trouble, it had been a very lucky guess indeed. She had a talent for interrupting.

'Shall we head off?' Dan looked at his watch. 'Table's booked for half-eight. We can have a drink there if it's not ready.'

'Do you think I should get her some chocolates as well?' asked Sam, his face already hidden behind the biggest bunch of flowers he could find. He looked quite pink in the face, thanks to the cricket sweater he wore over his best white Ralph Lauren Polo shirt, even though it was 24 degrees outside and only eleven in the morning.

'No, the flowers will be fine. And just a bunch of roses would have been OK.' Although the heady scented bouquet of roses, white lilies, gerbera and green stuff was quite impressive.

'I don't want her to think I'm a cheapskate. Red, white or Prosecco?'

'You probably don't want her to think you're sleeping with her daughter, but she's not stupid. Flowers are more than enough. Don't expect the fatted calf; she won't have pushed the boat out for us.' My mother was frugal with a capital F. 'In fact, she won't want us thinking she's made any effort, so she'll go the other way to prove the point.'

'Doesn't matter. I'd like to take a bottle of wine as well. It's good manners.'

I pushed the flowers out of the way and kissed him. 'You're a good man, Sam.'

'I know,' he said with that cocky, self-assured smile that got me every time. He put the flowers in the end of the trolley and began to push.

'And only ever-so-slightly big-headed.' As we walked down the next aisle, we grabbed what had become our usual grocery items: a pack of bacon for the weekend bacon butties which had become a routine, and cheese – two packs, because cheese on toast was quick and easy after a day at work. Hummus to go with cucumber, carrot, and peppers already in the trolley – our nod to healthy snacking, although several aisles down I could guarantee that a couple of packs of Kettle chips would find their way into the trolley.

'What can I say? If you've got it, flaunt it.'

'Is that what you're teaching those poor kids?' I stepped around him to grab a two-pint carton of milk as he snaffled a couple of packs of Magnums for the freezer.

'Poor kids, my arse. I had one of them tell me I was a loser this week because I couldn't name every member of the English test team for the last ten years.'

'And he could?' Even before I tried to reach for the jar of pesto, Sam had stepped in front of me to take it off the shelf.

'Of course he could. Asperger's. I'm going to put him up for the Test Match Special stats team. Honestly, this kid has a memory like a steel trap.'

Before long, our weekly shop was almost done and we were at the wine aisle.

'Prosecco?' asked Sam.

'OK then, I think Mum will be suitably impressed. Although if I were you I'd take off your sweater. You look like you might spontaneously combust.' I lifted the hem of his sweater and he gave in and peeled the rest off.

'Phew, that's better.'

'I appreciate the gesture.' I took the handle of the trolley. 'We need to get a wiggle on.'

'It was only going to be for first impressions.' Sam wiped at his forehead, the blond hair around his forehead springing into damp curls.

'You're crazy.'

'Crazy about you,' he said, putting his hands on either side of mine on the handle of the trolley and kissing the side of my neck. 'I—'

'Well, isn't this sweet,' drawled a sugary voice. 'Shopping together.'

My heart did a nosedive. Seriously? Victoria, again, here. Immediately self-conscious, I pushed a hand through my newly-washed loose hair, grateful that for once I was dressed up in visiting-Mum clothes.

Sam looked up, each hand sliding along the handle to top mine, closing into my body and hemming me in between him and the trolley. The protective move brought an involuntary smile to my lips which chased away the jittery nervousness. There was something unsettling about Victoria's sharp, glittering gaze that raked over me, taking in my flowered cotton dress, chewing it up and spitting it out with supercilious disdain.

'Victoria.' He nodded but didn't say anything else.

'This all looks very cosy,' she said, casting a desultory look over the contents of the trolley. 'And nutritionally delinquent.' I winced. The contents did look like a couple of five-year-olds had run amok.

'Don't you know the way to a man's heart is through his stomach? The only thing you're going to do with that lot is give Sam malnutrition. He's an athlete, you know; you should be cooking fresh vegetables, proteins and wholegrain carbs.' She sneered. 'Not looking after him very well, are you?'

After being so polite in the pub the previous week, I didn't feel like playing nice anymore. It was time she left us alone.

'Is that my job?' I clutched my throat in mock horror. 'Gosh, and here I was thinking I was living in the twenty-first century, an independent woman with a mind of her own and a boyfriend who is perfectly capable of making his own nutritional choices.'

Victoria turned a little pink, and in a lightning-fast change of tack, she softened. Hurt and sadness sugar-coated her face. 'Sam, are you going to let her speak to me like that?' Her mouth closed into a heartbroken quivering line. Behind me I felt Sam stiffen.

'I think the point, as Jess made clear, is that I'm not in charge of her. It's not up to me to "let" her do anything.' I turned in surprise, not at his words but at the tone. He sounded angry.

Normally he was Mr Nice Guy, his guilt making him be the better man. This was the first time his words had sounded so clipped and forced. 'I'm done trying to be nice. Leave us alone.'

Like Munch's scream, Victoria's face morphed into a harpy-like mask, her mouth a strangled O as her voice pitched and she screeched, 'You're done! You're. Done!'

People were starting to look at us with that avaricious mix of embarrassment and curiosity, some exchanging scared I-don't-want-to-get-too-close-to-this glances with each other and steering their children and trolleys in the opposite direction.

'Don't cause a scene, Vic,' warned Sam, his voice quiet and authoritative as he bumped his body against mine, urging me forward.

'Don't you tell me what to do,' screamed Victoria, her face burning with the sort of incandescent rage that made me imagine her burning up in a column of flames and glowing inhuman eyes like some Marvel superhero.

'That's it,' Sam murmured in my ear and he pushed me forward, walking past Victoria.

'Don't you walk away from me. You and that … that … skank.' She hissed the final word with defiant challenge, lobbing it into the air like an out-of-control grenade. The word hit me with a punch of humiliation and shame. I sucked in a sharp breath, conscious of the heavy silence around us, our bystanders rooted to the spot as if waiting for the explosion.

Sam stopped dead, and I turned to face him, my legs suddenly boneless. He let go of the trolley, his eyes darkening to almost navy blue. He stepped towards Victoria.

'Don't you ever, ever call Jess a name like that again. I'm done being nice. Stay away from me and Jess.' With that, he wheeled around, turning his back on her, came back to me and kissed me very publicly on the cheek as if making a declaration in front of the people all now trying to pretend to look elsewhere.

'I'm sorry, Jess.' His blue eyes softened. 'Sorry. Let's go.' We walked away down the aisle, a stunned silence in our wake. My shoulders were taut with the tension that filled the air, and it was a relief to get to the end of the aisle because I wasn't sure my legs were going to hold me up much longer. But before I could let out the much-needed sigh of relief, Victoria had to give one last parting shot.

'You're not done until I say so. This isn't over. You'll realise you've made the biggest mistake of your life and you'll come crawling back to me.' I flinched. I'd heard my mother, raging and demented, screaming similar words at my father. *You're making the biggest mistake of your life. If you leave, you'll never see Jessica again.*

Had my mother been like Victoria? It hadn't occurred to me before, but what if she'd been the one who was being unreasonable? Like Sam, my dad had the right to leave. Sam had tried to do the right thing. I knew nothing about my dad but my early memories had been of a kind man who'd read me stories, taken me to the park, taken me to the supermarket. It occurred to me now that before he'd left I'd spent a lot of time with him. With him, not Mum. And I couldn't recall time spent with both of them. What if her behaviour had driven Dad further away? What if he'd tried to do the right thing? What if he had wanted to see me? Would Mum have let him?

These were things I'd never even considered before.

Neither of us said anything until we got into the car, and for a moment both of us stared out of the windscreen. My legs were shaking and my heart banged so hard and fast, the beat thudded in every part of my body.

'God, I'm so sorry, Jess.' Sam put an arm round me and pulled me towards him, our bodies twisting awkwardly over the gear stick and handbrake. 'I'm so sorry.' He stroked my hair and I could feel his own thudding pulse and the tremor in his limbs. 'I … I don't know what's wrong with her.'

I let his fingers soothe away the tension and tried to relax into his chest, keeping my eyes tightly closed, trying to keep the seditious memory at bay. Shut it out. Keep out that knife-edged pain of not knowing what to do or how to help. Of being eight again, and powerless in the face of my mother's all-encompassing grief, her rage, her impotence and her disintegration.

'We can't even seem to avoid her. It's doing my head in.' Frustration seethed in his words before he added in a much softer way. 'I just want to get on with our life.'

Despite all the swirling crazy punch-you-in-the-head emotions bouncing around my mind, I calmed at those two little words and laid my hand over his and squeezed.

Our life.

I was so torn. Guilt and hope. But there was one puzzle I could solve. One practical thing that I could do.

'Your phone,' I said wearily. 'I think it's your phone.'

'What?'

At that moment I spotted Victoria and froze. She was stalking across the car park on her long stork legs, her high heels ringing out her pace. She passed us without even looking our way and I heaved a quiet sigh of relief and watched as she got into the convertible Mercedes three cars down and didn't say anything until I saw the personalised number plate VIC 29 disappear from view.

'She does well if she's driving a car like that,' I observed. Being an influencer obviously paid big time.

'Daddy – or it might have been Mummy. I lose track. They spoil her to death to make up for the fact that both of them have new lives now.' He winced. 'I think that's why she's being so difficult. I was hers and she was mine for four years. I guess that's why I've been trying to be gentle with her. Despite all her front, she's desperately insecure. She wants to be the centre of someone's universe.' He buried his head in his hands. 'God, Jess. I feel so guilty, but I'm so angry with her as well.'

I knew how he felt, but he didn't deserve to feel like that; he had tried to do the right thing.

'Sam, her insecurity is her problem. You can't be the solution.'

'You know she was never the centre of my universe. I thought I loved her but,' he paused and turned to me and lifted a hand to cup my cheek, 'it was nothing compared to how I feel about you.'

I swallowed and looked at his handsome face, my heart expanding in my chest at the tenderness softening those blue eyes.

'I love you, Jess, more than I thought was possible. And that makes me feel guilty, because if Vic feels about me one tenth of the way I feel about you, then she must be dying inside.'

'Oh, Sam.' I was too choked to speak. I laid my hand over his, blinking back tears. I had to work hard to get them out past the elephant-sized lump in my throat but finally I was able to say, through an unromantic sniffle, 'I love you too.'

'She's not going to come between us. I promise you.'

'No. We won't let her. I think I know how she keeps finding us. Your phone. Find My Friends. Remember we talked about it before.'

'And I forgot about it. Shit!' Sam's vehement curse startled me. 'Bugger.' He yanked his phone out of his pocket. 'Christ, I'm an idiot. I meant to check it before and forgot.' Head down, he pored over his screen. 'Shit! Still active.' With an impatient finger he jabbed at the screen, waiting for the icons to wobble before stabbing at the little cross to delete the app altogether. 'No wonder she kept "bumping" into us. I thought it was odd when we were in the Robin Hood with Bel and Dan. None of them ever go there. Never. God, I'm sorry, Jess. I should have thought of it before.'

'It's OK. It's not your fault.'

'Yes, it is. And I should have been tougher before. I've been too worried about her feelings. Well, that stops now.'

'You were feeling guilty.' And I had been as well, but I was starting to reassess things. The sliver of memory of my mum telling Dad he'd never see me again made me wonder if she'd been at fault in some ways, like Victoria making things difficult with Sam's mum, his friends, and deliberately causing trouble.

'I was, but this has pushed me into furious. She's obsessed and for the wrong reasons. I don't belong to her, but she has this warped view that I do.'

'Grief hits people in different ways,' I said gently, as one of so many images of my mother, with wide, unfocused eyes, blank-faced with despair, stole into my head. Those I remembered only too well, but the self-destructive, burning up, incandescent rage just like Victoria's had only surfaced today. I swallowed, pushing it away, not wanting to give it time or space.

How would Sam have described my mum when she'd descended into near madness for a while when my dad had left?

'Don't be too hard on her. She's obviously suffering at the moment. We can afford to be kind.'

Sam let out an angry huff.

'We can,' I insisted, even though inside I was finding it almost impossible to balance the scales – what I'd gained against the hurt caused.

'You're ... something else, Jess Harper. Kind, compassionate and strong. You are the best person I know. That's just one of a million reasons why I love you.'

203

I felt battered and bruised when we pulled up outside Mum's neat, tidy, and unimaginative home. The sight of the evenly spaced subdued Busy Lizzies in the dry soil on either side of the concrete path depressed me. They looked regulated and joyless. Like my mother's life had become after my father had left. Flowers were supposed to be abundant and blousy. I smiled. Like the ridiculous bouquet in Sam's hand.

'I'm the one who's supposed to be nervous,' he whispered in my ear, rustling the cellophane of the flowers. 'Not you.'

'Sorry. I'm fine. Just a bit shaken up.' For someone who did a job like mine, I ought to be used to confrontation. We were certainly trained to handle it. But that was different. It wasn't personal … even though some of the men tried to make it that way. After our supermarket drama I felt sick and liverish, as if I'd been on an all-night bender and woken up to the aftermath.

'I know.' Sam stopped, kissed my nose and gave me a lukewarm smile. 'I feel like I've got a monumental hangover with my very own black cloud hovering over my head.'

I stood on tiptoe. 'Snap. And that's why I love you, Sam Weaverham. Lego.' I dug in my handbag and pulled out the little piece I'd been carrying around with me since our first date in the pub. I held it between finger and thumb and he kissed both.

Then he dug in the pocket of his trousers and brought out the little red brick.

'Snap.' he said, taking my piece and clicking the two together and placing them in my palm. 'Stupid, but I carry it with me all the time.'

For a moment we smiled stupidly at each other and I felt that familiar bounce of pure joy in my chest.

'Hello, you must be Sam.' The door flew open as if Mum had been lying in wait for the last half-hour.

Smiling to myself, I stuffed the Lego pieces into the pocket of my dress.

'Hello, Jess's mum.' Sam held out the flowers. 'These are for you.'

'Thank you.' She took them and stood back like a guard at Buckingham Palace to let us in. 'You can call me Joan. I stopped being Jess's mum a long time ago.'

I frowned; it was an odd thing to say, although for a time she had. We never referred to that period in our lives. I'd come back from Aunty Lynn's to a spick-and-span house and a mother almost Stepford-wife in her perfection. Everything had been suddenly immaculately clean, tidy and ordered.

My eyes slid to the cobweb-free cornice in the hallway, but I think she caught the echo of my surprise. 'I mean, not since she was at school has anyone called me Jess's mum. Go on through to the lounge. I'll just put the kettle on.'

'And then I'll come and start the interrogation,' I muttered under my breath. Sam nudged me in the ribs.

Sam began to smirk as soon as he stepped into the small lounge.

'What?' I asked my lips twitching.

'You … erm … don't take after your mother.' He scanned the room. 'It's very tidy.'

'Sometimes I move the ornaments or tweak the pictures so they're not quite so straight. Bugs the hell out of her.' I darted to the mirror over the fireplace which housed a gas fire with fake coals and flames and pushed the corner ever so slightly so that it was a tiny bit offset. 'But she never says anything.' I'd wondered about that for a long time. Her reluctance to engage in any form of conflict. It occurred to me now that I'd been trying to provoke a reaction.

'Rebel,' teased Sam.

'And very childish,' I admitted.

'Yes.' He looked bemused.

I shrugged. 'She brings out the worst in me.' Now he frowned, confusion furrowing his forehead, as if this was something he couldn't quite fathom. 'We're not close, like you are with your mum and dad.'

'Hmm,' said Sam, suddenly intent on brushing a non-existent piece of something from his caramel-coloured chinos.

Before I could question him, Mum's arrival was announced by the chink of china and teaspoons and she appeared in the doorway carrying an overloaded tray, her arms braced as if she were a weightlifter who'd just racked up a record lift, reminding me rather bizarrely of Mrs Doyle from *Father Ted*.

'Joan, let me.' Sam rushed to her side and relieved her of her load.

'Oh, thank you, Sam. That's very kind.'

He put the tray down on the coffee table that was exactly mid-centre of the rug, right angled to both the sofa and the two armchairs on either side.

'Tea or coffee?' A silver cafetière and a china teapot sat on the tray and her hand hovered over them. Of course she'd made both. She couldn't ask us beforehand like a normal person and bring a mug through.

'Coffee, please.'

I watched as her eyes strayed to his man bun and then to his forearms. Hair nil, lack of tattoos, one.

'Do sit down.' She waved him to the sofa and I went and sat down next to him, both of us perched on the edge as if we were about to be interviewed, which in a way we were.

'Jess tells me you play cricket.'

I relaxed a little.

'Sam Weaverham, isn't it? I've heard of you.'

Hello? I turned to Sam, studying him as he gave a slight lift of his shoulders. Why didn't I know this?

'You've played for Essex a couple of times. I saw the game against Yorkshire. You batted well that day. Lovely cover drive.'

Sam actually blushed. 'Thank you.'

'Why haven't you played for them again? Don't you want to? What's your batting average this season?'

'Seventy-five.'

Even cricketing numpty that I was, I could tell from the shine of hero worship emanating from my mum that this was quite something.

'Well, that does surprise me. What's wrong with those selectors? Honestly, I sometimes think they've got cotton wool between their ears. I'm really surprised they haven't called you up again.'

Sam shifted in the seat next to me, his fingers twisting in his lap. He shrugged again. 'Just one of those things, I guess.'

I sneaked a glance at his profile, recognising the sudden tautness in his jaw belying the casual words. Something wasn't right, but I had no idea what.

'Very-short sighted of them. We went last Saturday and they could really do with a stronger batting order. I don't know why they... Douglas agreed. He thought—' She stopped, her mouth suddenly prim. 'Dear me, prattling on. Would you like a piece of cake? I made it this morning. It's lemon drizzle. Jess used to love this when she was younger. I'd quite often come home and she'd have picked off all the lemon sugar from the top. She's got a very sweet tooth.'

Sam laughed, oblivious to her uncharacteristic flood of prattle. 'I know. I have to hide the chocolate in the flat, otherwise I'll never get any.'

I saw from her brief bird-like nod that Mum had registered that little clue that we were practically living together. I'd get the inquisition about it later, although I had ammunition of my own. She seemed to be spending a lot of time with Douglas; I was dying to put her on the spot and ask more but I'd save it for my next visit.

Sam earned extra brownie points by having a second slice of cake and almost offering to cut the lawn.

The meeting was much more successful than I could have hoped for.

'He seems very nice,' said Mum as I helped her carry the

dirty cups back into the kitchen, and I knew there was a wealth of meaning in the deliberate choice of the word 'seems', as if she wasn't prepared to trust what she'd seen. 'So you're living together?'

I just knew she'd picked up on that and I closed my eyes behind her back, knowing what was coming next. And yes, there it was.

'Don't you think it's a bit soon?'

'I know,' I said lightly, 'But when you know, you know.' I patted my pocket, savouring an internal glow of happiness. Lego.

'That's a myth.' Mum was already reaching for the washing-up liquid and filling the sink with hot water; nothing was allowed to stay dirty or unwashed for very long in her kitchen. 'The sort of rubbish you read about in romance novels or the *Daily Mail*.' She gave a tut of displeasure before adding with sour-lipped disapproval, 'You work in a refuge. You of all people should know what men can do.'

'I know, Mum. But not all men are like that. Sam's a decent person.'

The corners of her mouth turned even further down as she dipped the cups into the foamy water and attacked them with a sponge as if cleaning them to the death. 'I'm just warning you. Your father was a decent man and look what happened there.'

'What did happen, Mum? We've never really talked about it.' My uncharacteristic challenge surprised her almost as much as it did me. For too long I'd been too scared to rake up the ashes, for fear of rousing a demon and bringing it all back.

'There's nothing to talk about.' Mum's voice was sharp and high. 'Your father decided, one day, that he didn't want me, or you, anymore. So he upped and left. End of story.' Her mouth snapped shut, stubborn and unyielding.

But there had to be more. Why had he gone? Why so suddenly? One day he was there, the next gone. That was all I remembered of him at the time. Had he moved out straightaway? Before I could ask any more questions, Mum had yanked a clean tea towel out of the kitchen drawers and was ruthlessly drying the mugs.

'All I'm saying is, don't become too reliant on him. Keep your own flat. Keep your own space so that when he leaves you, you have something left.'

'When he leaves? That's very pessimistic, Mum.'

'It's realistic. Nothing is for ever. You can only rely on yourself. I don't want you to go through what I went through.'

Our eyes met in a rare candid moment. Another thing we'd never talked about. Her complete mental disintegration. This was as close as she'd ever come to even admitting there had been a problem and that, for a while, she'd been lost. I looked past her at the garden and the row of three pots evenly spaced across the ugly paved terrace. It had taken her a long time to come back.

'Just take care and protect yourself. Now, I suppose you need to get off. Would you like to take some cake with you? I think your young man is partial to cake.' Her face softened and she almost allowed herself a smile, 'and heaven knows baking is not your forte. Which reminds me. Are you sure you want to take him to Gladys's wedding the week after next?'

'Yes.'

She huffed out a heavy sigh and shook her head. 'Let's hope it won't put him off. God only knows what she's got lined up. Did you see her latest note? Since when did anyone need to take wellington boots to a wedding ceremony?'

I was quiet in the car on the way home, thinking about things that I'd rather leave behind. I pulled out the Lego bricks and separated them, handing one back to Sam, feeling like it was a talisman between us.

He took it, kissing my fingers as he did and put it back in his pocket. 'Makes me think of you.'

I nodded and put my own piece back in my pocket.

'You OK? Did I pass?'

'Yes, with flying colours. You didn't tell me that you were that good at cricket. I thought Mum was going to have a full-blown fan-girl moment. She knew who you were. Why haven't you ever said anything? Like that you're famous or really, really good?'

Sam's gorgeous body shook with silent mirth. 'What was I supposed to say? By the way, as well as being God's gift to women, I've also played at division one county cricket level.'

'Don't get all technical on me. I don't know what that means.'

'I've played for one of the county teams in the top division. You know, what Premiership football is.'

'Well, duh! Yes. You must be really good.'

He shrugged but I could see the quiet, satisfied pride in the way he lifted his chin and the faint smile touching his lips.

'It's the equivalent except we don't get paid anywhere near the same whack as footballers. Unfortunately, I'm not contracted to the team, so I've only been called up occasionally. I was … well, I was hoping this might be the season.'

'So basically you're quite good.'

Sam lifted his shoulders in a modest shrug. 'Not bad, but I didn't think it was worth mentioning as I don't think it would have impressed you.'

'No, I was far too busy looking at your impressive deltoids and abundant locks, thinking you were a little too much in love with yourself and wondering what the hell was with the sunshades.'

Sam flashed me a delighted smile. 'Glad to know I wasn't the only shallow one. I was looking at your legs and wondering if your bum would be as cute if you turned around.'

We both laughed before I said, 'So when I've got old and fat, with flabby, cellulitey thighs, you'll leave me?' My words were light but Mum's negativity had weaselled its way into my head like woodworm hell bent on slow but sure destruction.

'Jess, what's the matter?' Sam laid a hand on my thigh, keeping his eyes on the road, a safe and steady Eddie. I was being ridiculous, I knew Sam would always look after me.

'Sorry. Just having a wobble. Mum being Mum.'

'She's quite uptight, isn't she?' Sam's astute observation made me wary. 'Not like you at all. Do you take after your dad?'

'I've no idea. He left when I was eight and I haven't seen him since. I don't really have many memories of him before then.' And the ones I did had been ruthlessly dismembered and refigured.

'You're not in touch at all?'

'No.'

Sam glanced across the car.

'That's quite unequivocal.'

'Unequivocal is such a teachery word.'

Sam ignored my pathetic attempt at deflection.

'An unequivocal "no" says there's more to it than that.'

'You're a mind reader, now?' I quirked a wasted eyebrow because his eyes were still on the road, both hands competently guiding the steering wheel, putting me in mind of a captain at the helm of his ship. Sam was good at steering through choppy seas.

'I know you, Jess.'

I sighed, part of me a little pleased at his insight and another part knowing that it was time to let some of this out. It had been bottled up inside me for so long.

'My dad left out of the blue – or at least it felt like that. I don't remember any rows or arguments. Just, one day he wasn't there.'

'Ouch, that's tough. Were you close to him?'

I lifted my head suddenly like a deer scenting danger.

'No.' I spat the word out so quickly that Sam whipped round to look at me, inquiry in his eyes. No one had ever asked that question before.

I gave him a quick, shifty glance before I added in a quiet voice, 'Maybe?'

There was silence. It took me a minute to sift through ancient images in my head before I could elaborate. 'I think I might have been. I've kind of shut it out but I remembered today, he used to take me to the park a lot. And he read stories.' Unbidden, a memory popped into my head, fully formed with no wispy elusive tails that I had to chase after. Me in the crook of Dad's arm, snuggled into the sofa as he read the first Harry Potter. He'd gone to town on the Dursleys' voices. A flood of happiness washed over me with the realisation that he'd taken as much pleasure from reading the book as I'd had listening. The memory crystallised with startling clarity. It could have been yesterday. Reading together had been our thing.

'He walked away and it was ... it was the worst thing.' Except had he walked away? What if Mum, like Victoria today, had driven him away? What if she'd been less emotional? Might he have come to see me?

'Things at home were ... Mum had, I suppose now you'd call it a complete mental breakdown, except then it was called "not coping".' I winced. 'Sure you want to hear this?'

'I think you need to talk about it,' said Sam as he

214

glanced at the slip road coming up. 'Why don't we pull off here, park up at the reservoir and take a walk?'

It gave me time to gather up the loose ends of all the memories and put them into a narrative order. They'd been so chaotic and jumbled in my head for so long, now it was like smoothing out a piece of rolled-up wallpaper.

The sun sparkled on the water as we walked along the parched brown grass of the retreating reservoir. It was ringed by a wide muddy band, illustrating just how much the unseasonably hot summer had shrunk the water's boundaries.

Sam took my hand. 'Your mum. You said she wasn't coping.'

'That's an understatement. At first, just after Dad had gone, she was angry, shouty and she cried a lot. I was at school then so it wasn't quite so bad. But then school broke up and suddenly we didn't have a routine. We didn't need to be anywhere or do anything and she just stopped. Stopped getting out of bed. Stopped talking. Stopped washing. Just stopped doing anything. We didn't leave the house. We didn't see anyone. She fell out with Aunty Lynn. I don't know what about, but it meant that if Aunty Lynn phoned, Mum just wouldn't answer the phone. I guess Aunty Lynn assumed she still wasn't talking to her. She and Mum have never got on well. Aunty Lynn had no idea how bad things had got.'

'What about you? What did you do?'

I pulled a face. 'Tried to fend for myself. I sort of went feral. Prowling around the house. Opening cupboards and drawers, looking at things I wasn't supposed to touch.

Watching television all the time. Going to bed when I felt like it. At first I ate whatever I could find and whatever I wanted. Biscuits, sweets. When those ran out, I ate cereal – dry because there was no milk. I worked my way through the cupboards. Then, when the readily accessible stuff ran out, I raided Mum's purse. Took her money and went to the corner shop. At first I bought sweets but after a week of that, I wised up and bought tins of beans and Heinz tomato soup. I'd learned how to use a tin opener by that stage.'

'Jeez, Jess.' Sam stopped and took me into his arms. 'That sounds horrendous. How long did that go on for?'

I winced and looked up at him. 'Until September. Into the third week of the new term. I couldn't quite carry it off at school.'

'Bloody hell. That long?'

'I guess I was quite a resourceful child. When September came, I saw the other children going to school, so quickly put my uniform on. Then after that I used to watch the street so I knew what time to leave.'

'When did the school realise? Surely they must have known?'

'Mum's money ran out. And she was getting thinner and thinner. I tried to feed her and I got caught stealing a tin of beans from the corner shop. I refused to tell the shopkeeper where I lived or even speak. He called the police. I had my school uniform on.'

'Rookie mistake.'

'Yup. They called the school and it all unravelled from there.'

'God, Jess. And then what happened? Social services?

Did you get put into care?'

'Social services paid a visit to Mum. Realised how ill she was…' I paused, still feeling the shame, even though it was irrational. 'She was sectioned.'

'And you?'

I laughed a mirthless laugh. 'I was the lucky one. I went to live with Lynn and Richard, and it was heaven. After living wild for a couple of months, having order, routine and regular food was such a relief. Not being responsible for Mum was like being given a reprieve. I felt so much lighter. I lived with them for nearly two years, which is why I'm so close to them.' I looked around as if someone might be listening. 'They're my real family. Lynn is more of a mum to me, Richard is like my dad, and Shelley's my sister. My younger annoying sister.'

'I can see that.' He took my hand and we carried on walking in the warm sunshine. It was another belter of a day and the birds were taking refuge in the water, ducks bobbing up and down and moorhens pootling this way and that with aimless manic speed.

'When Mum came home … she'd changed. Everything needed to be right. She needed to be in control. My untidiness is a bit of backlash against that. I think Mum felt that if she could impose order on everything, then she could stay in control. She also needed to show the social workers that she could cope. That she was up to the job of looking after me. And it's never stopped. She drove me mad as a teenager and, well, we don't have a brilliant relationship, I'm afraid.'

'God. After everything you've been through… It's a wonder you're so amazing.'

'I don't know about that.' I offered him a self-deprecating smile. 'I don't think I'm a particularly good daughter. We're not close at all.'

'I do. You're incredible. And don't you have a great relationship with Lynn?'

'Yes, but I know Mum's quite – jealous is probably harsh – but I always feel guilty that I'm closer to Lynn than her and Mum knows it.'

'And you've never heard from your dad since?'

I pinched my lips and stared out over the water, focusing on one particular duck chasing away another one with loud indignant quacks.

'A couple of times.'

Sam waited. He'd have made a good interrogator; he always seemed to know when I had more to say.

'I have two brothers. Half-brothers.'

He shot me a shocked look. 'Have you ever met them?'

I shook my head. 'He wrote to me when the first one was born, and sent me a photo. He married a woman called Alicia.'

'How long ago was that?'

'Ten years ago. Ben is his name. He's ten. Mum … Mum took it badly. I thought she was going to have some kind of stroke or something. She collapsed and I thought I was going to have to call an ambulance. I was so worried that she might relapse again, have another breakdown, that I burned the letter. I don't even remember what it said. Then, two years later, I got another letter and another picture.

Toby, another boy. The second time I didn't say anything to Mum, but I didn't reply either. Do you think I'm a bad person?'

'Bad? Why would I think that?'

'Ignoring my Dad's letters. I have two brothers.'

'You were protecting your mother, at the time. But, well, it's been eighteen years since your dad left. Have you not been tempted?'

My eyes slid back to the ducks fighting just below us. 'Now and then, but I think I might have left it too late.'

'It's never too late,' said Sam, kissing my temple.

Chapter Nineteen

'I'm just nipping out to Tesco to grab some last-minute bits for the journey.'

'Toothpaste. We need more toothpaste,' said Sam emerging from the bathroom with a towel wrapped around his hips and stepping right into the light flooding in through the overhead skylight.

'Mm,' I said, taking a moment to admire his glowing golden body. Even this many weeks in, the bolt of physical attraction still hit me every time.

'Don't look at me like that; I might get ideas,' he said in a gruff voice, snaking an arm around my waist and giving me a minty kiss that left me pathetically weak-kneed and clinging to his shoulders. I should be used to this by now but somehow my heart still did that magical ping at the mere sight of him. For someone who'd never believed in hearts-and-roses romance, I seemed to have been suckered right in.

Reluctantly I put some distance between us, feeling just

a tad distracted by the towel tenting in front of me. He grinned. He knew. He always knew.

'You're terrible,' I said. 'We haven't got time. We need to be on the road in an hour.'

'I'm terrible.' He put his hands on his hips and raised an eyebrow. 'You keep believing that, sweet cheeks. Now scram, you gorgeous temptress, otherwise we'll never get to Cornwall at a decent hour.'

I scrammed, grabbing my car keys and a shopping bag. Three whole days away. Just the two of us. Well, apart from the small matter of Gladys's wedding tomorrow, when I'd be surrounded by family. Lynn, Richard, Shelley and Mum were all travelling down by train later today. But the night after that I'd booked what looked like an utterly charming, wooden-beamed room over a pub in a small village not far from Bude. It had taken me a long time to press the book button as I'd stared at the picture. It was the only place to stay in Otterstow, so quite a relief that the room looked so nice and the pub so pretty and quaint. Still wondering if I'd done the right thing, I approached my car and zapped the key fob.

'Excuse me.' An older man I recognised gave me an apologetic smile from the pavement on the other side of my car. We were on 'good morning' terms as I often saw him and his wife gardening in their front garden. 'Sorry to have to tell you this, but you've got a flat tyre.' He inclined his head downwards and I hurried round to the driver's door.

'Oh.' I managed to curtail my expletive. 'That's annoying.'

'Your young man will be able to change it for you, I'm sure.'

'Yes, except we're about to drive to Cornwall.' And my replacement tyre was one of those you can only drive at fifty miles an hour for a short distance and we'd planned to take my car rather than Sam's, an ancient Nissan held together with elastic bands and string.

I nudged at the tyre with my toe.

'Take it to Kwik Fit; they'll be able to sort you out. Quite common in this hot weather.'

'Is it?'

'Oh yes,' said Number Ten, knowledgeably nodding his head. 'This hot weather makes the air expand inside and increase the pressure and they just go pop.'

I gave my sad flat tyre another look. It had chosen a very inconvenient moment to go pop. The reason we were leaving so early was so that we could pick the others up from the station later in the evening, although we'd have to do two runs. It was going to take a while to sort it out if we had to change it and then go and get a new tyre.

'Oh! That's odd.' The old man suddenly dropped to his knees by my car. 'Bloody kids. Someone stuck a screwdriver in this or something. There's a hole.'

Of course there was.

I felt slightly sick.

'Yeah, look.' He poked his finger into the black rubber. 'I don't know what the world's coming too. My nephew's car was done with an electric drill down Park Street. I ask you. Why do people do these things?'

The Spark

'I don't know,' I said dully. An odd sense of deflation, perhaps on a par with the tyre, had settled on me. I was pretty sure I knew who'd done it. Last week a mouldy bag of prawns had been pushed through the letter box while we were at work. Judging by the awful smell in the hallway it had happened sometime before the heat of the day had hit twenty-eight degrees and they'd sat there cooking at maximum temperature for a large part of the day. The week before, five unexpected pizzas had turned up. How much longer were Sam and I going to have to put up with this sort of thing? We weren't doing anyone any harm. Was I going to have to go to the police? It was my absolute last resort, as I was convinced it would stir up more trouble between Sam and his friends, because they'd all take Victoria's side. It was petty, mindless stuff on the surface but done with malicious intent to cause inconvenience and trouble. And there was no way of proving it was Victoria. I didn't even know for sure that it was her. Did she know we were going away to Cornwall this weekend? Was her timing deliberate?

I looked around the street, my skin prickling. Was she watching? Or was I imagining the whole thing and it was just bad luck?

Sitting high up in the comfort of Uncle Richard's Mazda CX5 I grinned as we sailed along the M5 on the second leg of our journey, already feeling slightly nauseous thanks to eating nearly a whole pack of Jelly Babies.

'You look pleased with yourself,' said Sam, offering me the last sweet in the bag.

'I'm just having a smug moment. If it was Victoria who did that to my car, her evil plan backfired spectacularly.'

'Karma,' said Sam, biting the head off the final jelly baby with a snap of his teeth. 'This is a very nice car.'

Upon hearing what had happened to my car, Richard had immediately suggested that we take his. I'd been insured on it earlier in the year when he'd twisted his ankle; because he worked not far from me, I'd chauffeured him to work every day as he'd refused to be seen in the Minnie Mouse Mobile, as he referred to my car. Like I was going to complain, when I got the chance to drive his big luxury car with its heated seats, warning beepers all around, and surround-sound entertainment system (actually, I might have made the last bit up, but the car had a jolly fancy console).

'But … that doesn't make up for what she did.'

'If it was her.' I sighed.

'I'm going to ask her.'

'But if it is her, she must know that we'll think it's her. She wants us to know.'

'Well, then I'll ask her to stop.'

'Like that's going to work.'

'When we get back I'll go and see her. Perhaps if I talk to her face to face.'

'Good luck with that one.' In frustration, I resorted to heavy sarcasm that Sam really didn't deserve. I knew he was as fed off with the situation as I was. Perhaps more so because he was being ostracised by his friends.

'Well, what do you suggest?' he asked with a distinct snap in his voice which made me feel doubly guilty.

'Hey.' I put my hand out and laid it on his thigh. 'Are we about to have our first row?'

He pushed his hand through his mop of hair. 'No. I refuse to row because of Vic. I'm sorry. I just never imagined it would get so complicated. It makes me so cross. I didn't fall in love with you on purpose and I tried to do the right thing. God, I did everything I could to put you out of my head.'

'Sorry. I'm a limpet.' I tried to make a joke of it.

'Don't apologise; that makes me cross.' And from the terse cut of his words, he sounded it. 'You haven't done anything wrong. Neither of us have. There's no reason for either of us to apologise.' His hands clenched on his thighs, the knuckles white on his tanned hands. 'It would have been wrong to carry on things with Victoria knowing that I felt something for someone else.'

I knew all that. 'But I feel like everything is still messed up. I thought by now things would have settled down. You don't see your friends anymore and you've fallen out with your mum.'

'We haven't fallen out,' said Sam a little too quickly.

'Hmm? When was the last time you saw her?'

'We've both been busy. She and Dad are away a lot at the moment, enjoying their retirement. I'll see her at the anniversary party.' He paused and then gave my hand a quick squeeze. 'She'll have to talk to me then.'

I let that one go; even Aunty Lynn had said that Sally was very busy at the moment. Although I wondered if that might have something to do with her connection to me. The ripple effect of Sam and me seemed never-ending.

'And I do see my friends.'

'As long as I'm not around,' I said, trying not to sound bitter. I'd had enough. The petty vandalism had really got my goat and the injustice of it all chafed at me.

We lapsed into an uncomfortable brooding silence as I concentrated on the road and Sam stared out of the passenger window. This wasn't how it was supposed to be. What had happened to those early euphoric weeks when we'd been invincible and being together had been all that mattered? I loved Sam and I knew he loved me but was that going to be enough to get us through? Oh God, I was being a complete drama queen, and it so wasn't my style.

'Would you mind stopping at this one?' asked Sam as we passed a mile marker to the next service station.

'Of course not,' I said, hating the politeness between us.

As soon as I pulled into a parking slot and before I'd even switched off the engine, Sam leapt out of the car and slammed the door. Butterflies shimmered in my stomach. I unclipped my seatbelt and watched him. Was he angry? Striding around the front of the car, he came to my door and wrenched it open. I stared down into his handsome, determined face, the butterflies taking flight at the focused expression in his eyes. Without a word, he reached into the car, put his arms around my waist and yanked me out. My breath whooshed out as he pulled me towards him, holding me tightly. Fierceness blazed in his blue eyes as he looked down at me. 'I'm not letting this come between us, Jess Harper. I love you and we will get through it.' With that he kissed me. Firm hard lips, possessive and greedy, claimed mine and OK, I admit it, I felt all girly and little woman-y, which normally I didn't approve of but on this occasion, boy, it was nice to feel that sense of being precious and cherished, as I stood in the circle of his arms.

I kissed him back. 'Yeah, we'll get through it. But in the meantime, we've got a wedding to get to, and you need to gird your loins to meet Great Aunt Gladys.'

It was with some trepidation that we wound up the lane to Rose Bowl House. We'd left the main road twenty minutes ago and had been travelling along a single-track road with leafy glades on either side. I almost expected to see fairies dancing in the beams of sunlight slanting through the trees, which was a bit fanciful for me. Knowing Gladys, I'd be less surprised if I spotted a sky-clad Wiccan priestess wading through the ferns of the undergrowth.

'I have warned you about Gladys, haven't I?' I said as the engine whined and I had to drop a gear to get up the steep slope.

Sam grinned. 'Several times. She's eccentric with a capital E.'

'Details on the actual wedding ceremony are sketchy and I haven't been able to find any details on this house. Apparently it belongs to good friends of her fiancé and he's as bonkers as she is.'

'Chill. It'll be an adventure. It's not going to put me off you, if that's what's worrying you.'

'Ha! It's worrying my mum. She was horrified that I was bringing you. Convinced that you'll think insanity runs in the family.' I bit my lip, thinking of what I'd told him about Mum. I'd worked hard to be pragmatic and sensible about things.

'Jess. You are the sanest person I know. And it's not like you to worry about stuff like this. Come on. Let's forget this week. Put it behind us and have a lovely time. I think I'm going to like Aunt Gladys a lot. And don't forget, I know half your family already. Lynn and Richard strike me as pretty sane people. And Shelley, although she scares me sometimes.' Sam's eyes twinkled as he said it.

'You big wuss.'

'She's a maneater.' His mouth quirked.

'She is, but underneath it all, she's just looking for the right man.'

'God help him when she finds him.' Sam gave a delicate shudder, laughing lightly.

We rounded the last final bend and the road widened into a large gravel turning circle.

'Oh!' we both said in unison as we caught sight of the view out over the sea. To the right, the house perched on the very top of the cliff, which fell away in rocky folds down to the shoreline below.

'Wow. That is one amazing view.' Unable to stop ourselves, we both got out of the car, barely taking time to stretch our stiff limbs as we crunched over the gravel like excited children to take in the view. Sunlight danced on the dark-blue sea, sparkling like showers of fireworks. Below us was a wide crescent of sand enclosed at either end by cliffs. Sam took my hand.

'This is magnificent. Do you think it's a private beach?' He stepped a little closer to the edge to take a better look, resting his foot on one of the small wooden posts of the fence a metre in from the drop. 'I think I can see a wooden staircase going down.'

'Looks like it might be. Smell that air. God, it's lovely.' The light breeze lifted my hair, carrying the tang of the sea, and I could taste the salt on the air.

'Yoo hoo! Jessica!'

I turned to see a tall scarecrow of a person in a bright pink tutu, fluorescent green leggings and a well-filled pink ballerina cardigan come hurtling out of a set of French doors on this side of the house and race over the lawn in bare feet before abruptly stopping to a teetering halt at the gravel's edge.

I tugged at Sam's hand. 'Come and meet my aunt... Looks like she's channelling ballet Barbie today.' I heard his low chuckle. 'There's still time to do a runner.'

'Wouldn't dream of it,' he murmured as we crunched our way over the gravel to meet my aunt.

'Darling, you made it.' She flung her long skinny arms around me. 'We're just having a ballet class. I say we, it's just me and the housekeeper. Do you want to join in?'

'We've been in the car for the last five hours, I think—'

'Perfect, it'll help stretch out all those kinks. You must be Sam.' Gladys gave him a full inspection. 'I bet you've got a fine pair of gluteus maximuses.'

'So I've been told,' said Sam. 'But I'm not sure I'm a ballet man.'

'Pfft, of course you are. But I'm guessing you young things want to get settled in your room. I've allocated you a lovely one at the top of the house, plenty of privacy. And I've put you at the opposite end of the house to your mother.'

'Thanks, Gladys.'

'If you go around to the front entrance, Hendricks will meet you. He's the butler. Sound man but doesn't say much.'

'Butler?'

'This is Dodie and Freddie's house. Old chums from my Oxford days. They Airbnb it these days. Far too big for them to rattle around in. They live in the coach house.' Gladys pointed to a set of barns further behind the house that looked pretty grand in their own right. 'Hendricks is Freddie's cousin and his wife is the housekeeper and general factotum. Scary woman but jolly good at ballet. And I must get back. We're all congregating for G&Ts on the side lawn at five. See you then.'

With that she ran off back across the lawn, executing a couple of quick grand jetés en route.

'She's a bit of a whirlwind.' Sam blinked and I laughed.

'Oh, yes, there's no one quite like Gladys. She is totally bonkers but harmless, and she just wants everyone to enjoy themselves around her.'

'And how is she related to your mother?' he asked in a dry voice that made me giggle.

'I know. Difficult to believe, isn't it? But you can see where Aunty Lynn gets it. Gladys is their dad's sister.'

'You have interesting genes.' He slipped an arm around my shoulder and kissed my neck. 'I think I'll stick around.'

'Let's hope you still think so by the end of the weekend,' I said. 'Come on, let's unload. In another hour I'll need to go and pick up the rellies from the train station.'

Hendricks, as delightfully stiff and snooty as a butler should be, invited us to leave our bags in the hall while he led us up a very grand staircase, along a corridor and up another flight of stairs to what were probably once the servants' quarters. It was clear they'd been considerably jazzed up since the last housemaid had vacated them. Our room was light and airy with a pair of dormer windows affording a glorious view of the sea which you could see from the big brass bed against the opposite wall. The nautical theme was continued with an abundance of blue and white striped cushions and pillows, and pictures of lighthouses in shades of blue around the walls.

We had time to unpack, make the most of the huge bucket-headed shower in the en suite bathroom, in which Sam had to duck his head when he cleaned his teeth because of the eaves, before I had to head off to pick up the train passengers.

They were already in high spirits when they rolled off the train at half past four. Lynn's idea of an in-carriage picnic had included a whole bottle of gin and not quite enough tonic to go around, and all of them, even Mum, had insisted on singing 'I'm Getting Married in the Morning' all the way to Rose Bowl House.

I abandoned them all in the hall to Hendricks and ran quickly up the stairs to collect Sam, conscious that the rest of the family might take a while to unpack and settle and I didn't want to leave Gladys and Alastair hanging. The wedding was going to be a relatively small affair and I had no idea how many guests were staying in the house.

'Everything OK?' asked Sam, looking up as I walked in shaking my head.

'They're all sozzled already, even my mother, and I can usually rely on her to be the sensible one.'

'Well your aunt and uncle are always good company.' He stood up and grabbed my hand. 'Come on, we'd better go down and start catching up.'

I'd worried unnecessarily because the little patio area outside the drawing room was already full of people and a rowdy croquet match was underway on the far side of the lawn. Gladys had changed and was holding court in a floaty pink number that wouldn't have looked out of place in a *Strictly Come Dancing* foxtrot. Next to her, Alastair, her fiancé, sported a very fine kilt with a froth of lace at his neck, and would have looked rather like a dashing Bonnie Prince Charlie if it weren't for his delicate Singaporean features. When he spotted Sam and me in the doorway, he immediately detached himself from the small group he was talking to and headed our way with small, neat, dapper steps, accentuated by the laced ghillie brogues he wore.

'Little Jess.' His deep brown eyes twinkled. It was an old

joke, given that I towered over his tiny five-foot-four frame. 'It's grand to see you. And this is yer young man, is it?'

I saw Sam start at his broad Yorkshire vowels. Alastair was somewhat of a hybrid, having been born in Singapore to a Singaporean mother and a Japanese father but raised in Doncaster.

'Hi, Alastair.' I gave him a kiss on his soft, clean-shaven cheeks. 'This is Sam.'

They did the pleased-to-meet-you handshakes.

'Nice kilt.' I nodded down at the yellow and black checked plaid. 'I didn't know you had Scottish blood.'

'Not a drop,' said Alistair with another one of his irrepressible twinkles. He always looked as if he were up to no good, which was probably what had attracted Gladys in the first place. 'But I liked t'outfit. Although I'm not so sure about going commando. Bit drafty, if you get my drift. Hardy fellas, them Scots.'

I swallowed down my laughter and nodded, pinching my lips together because he looked so much like an earnest robin. Beside me I could feel Sam's suppressed shake of mirth.

'Now what are you grand people drinking? Bitter, lad? Or these pink gins. Gladys had it mixed special to match her dress.'

'I'll have a beer, please,' said Sam.

'I'd better try a pink gin. The others have just arrived; they'll be down soon.' Although I didn't think they needed any more gin.

'Grand. Gladys is so pleased you were all able to come.' He lowered his voice. 'Between you and me, I think she was worried you might think making all this fuss is a bit daft at our age. But you only get married once. Well, at our time of life, anyroad.' He pulled a face and drew out a stopwatch from a hidden pocket in his waistcoat, reminding me of the white rabbit in *Alice in Wonderland*. 'Let's hope Gladys survives and gets through the ceremony in one piece.' And now I felt as if I'd fallen down a rabbit hole. Was he serious? I looked over at my Great Aunt who was in full flow, waving her glass about as she talked to three rather strapping young men with great animation.

'Oops. Mum's the word. You shan't get any more out of me.'

'I was going to ask about the wedding ceremony.'

'All will be revealed soon. Right, let's get you some drinks.'

Once we were furnished with drinks from a beautiful drinks trolley, we made our way over to say hello to Gladys.

'Darling.' She turned towards me and reached to pat my cheek. 'Don't you look gorgeous? Love agrees with you. Lots of sex too, I'm guessing.' Barely drawing breath, she turned to Sam and added, 'You're a rather fine specimen.' One of the three men backed away with a discreet coughing fit, while another one tossed back his drink in a single gulp before the three of them melted away.

'Filters, Gladys. What have we said about filters?' I said firmly, almost feeling the heat coming from poor Sam's cheeks.

'Oh God, darling. I'm far too long in the tooth for all that PC nonsense. I speak as I find. And I'm sure Sam doesn't mind, do you?'

'I've been called worse,' said Sam regaining his cool. 'I'm acquainted with quite a few cougars.'

Gladys loved that and she growled at him in delight. 'Oh, I like you. Found your match here, Jess. You'd better hang on to him. I give you my permission to have her hand in marriage.'

'Gladys!' Now it was my turn to go pink.

'What? It's not like your mother would. How is the miserable bat?'

I glared at her.

'Don't look at me like that, young lady. You know I'm not one to mince my words. She needs a damn good tickle. And a good roll in the hay. Loosen her up a little. Your father left eighteen years ago; it's about time she got over it.'

'Mum is fine, and the last time I saw her, about half an hour ago, she was extremely loose. Lynn opened the gin on the train.'

'Ah, that's more like it. And how's the slutty one, Shelley?'

I shook my head in despair.

'Still slutty then. I do like that girl. And here they are.' With a waft of pink chiffon, she abandoned us as Mum, Lynn, Richard and Shelley stepped out onto the patio.

'God, she's a hoot,' said Sam.

'She's a flaming liability,' I said darkly, as Gladys threw expansive arms around Lynn and Mum.

'Who wants boring relatives? We always rely on my Uncle Jeff to liven things up at Christmas. Every family should have a Gladys or a Jeff.'

'Hmm, I'm glad you think so.'

'I like her.' He lifted a hand to my face, his eyes softening as they looked at me. My heart did its usual misstep. 'And she's already given me permission to marry you, so she might just be my favourite one of your relatives.' A gentle, secretive smile flickered at his lips as his gaze held mine. 'It's not the done thing proposing at someone else's wedding. But maybe you could hold that thought.'

I opened and shut my mouth, too torpedoed by emotion to say anything. Amusement danced in his blue eyes and he brushed a thumb over my lips. I managed to regain control of my goldfish lips but before I could say anything – the words were all whizzing about in my head and I couldn't quite catch the right one – Gladys had moved off to greet some more new arrivals, leaving my family to come over to join us.

'Any idea who the three hotties are?' asked Shelley, pointing quite openly to the three men who'd been talking to Gladys when we arrived.

'None. Funnily enough she didn't introduce us.' Which I now realised had been a deliberate omission. Normally Gladys wanted everyone to be friends.

'Probably because she could see you were taken.'

'Down, girl,' I said at the characteristic feral gleam that lit her eyes.

'You're not going to spoil my fun, are you?'

'No, but wait until after the wedding. Just in case they're integral to the proceedings.'

'You don't need to worry.' Shelley's mouth turned down with uncharacteristic gloom. 'Let's face it, they are seriously way out of my league. They're probably decent blokes whereas I'm only fit for losers and bastards.'

I laid a sympathetic hand on her arm, surprised by her dejection, but before I could say anything my mother interjected with a 'Hmm,' and none of us missed the disapproving twist of her lips reserved specifically for Shelley. 'And do we have any idea of what is happening tomorrow? I do think it's most odd. You'd have thought Gladys might have grown up a bit by now. It's all so silly and infantile. I don't know why she couldn't have popped into a registry office and kept it civilised, instead of all this fuss. And expense. The train was nearly a hundred pounds.'

'Yes, but wasn't it nice travelling first class,' soothed Aunty Lynn. 'And the normal price would have been double, so we definitely got value for money.'

'Well, at least I didn't buy a new outfit. Wellington boots!'

'I bought new festival wellies. I was hoping it might be a mini Glasto,' said Shelley with a valiant attempt at being cheerful, but I could tell she wasn't right. 'I thought we might be glamping and she'd have Florence and the Machine belting out a few numbers.'

'I think Gladys is more of the Rolling Stones era.' Uncle Richard paused to take a sip of his beer. 'Didn't she say she'd once snogged Mick Jagger?'

'Hmph, her and everyone else. That's why his lips are that shape,' said Mum tartly.

Sam and I sniggered. It was a very unMum-like comment. She glared at us before adding, 'And Gladys does have a tendency to exaggerate.'

'I suspect it will be a ceremony on the beach,' said Aunty Lynn. 'This house is in such a fabulous location, why wouldn't you?'

'Yes, but what sort of ceremony?' asked Mum. 'I don't think your average vicar makes beach calls.'

'Knowing Gladys, her vicar wouldn't be very average,' replied Richard.

'Knowing Gladys, he's probably been defrocked.' Mum shuddered.

There was a tinkle as Alastair tapped at his beer glass. 'Ladies, gents and others.' Gladys stood next to him and they made an incongruous pair, especially as she topped him by several inches and in her frothy pink chiffon concoction looked rather like a strawberry ice cream sundae.

'Oh, dear God,' muttered Shelley.

'Thank you all for coming to our nuptials.' He linked arms with his bride-to-be and she beamed at everyone. 'It's grand to see you all here and we'd like to invite you to join us on the beach at o-nine-hundred tomorrow morning. Prompt start, and then we'll see how it goes. In the meantime, enjoy yourselves tonight and cheers.' He lifted his glass in toast.

'And you can't be late.' Gladys strident voice rang out imperiously. 'So if you've no head for booze, pack it in now. Dinner is served in the dining room.'

'Well, that's told us,' said Shelley. 'Why so bloody early?'

'It could have been worse. I was worried it was going to be some pagan ceremony and we'd all be up at dawn,' said Richard.

'God only knows what she's got planned,' said my mother. 'I'm relieved. Nine o'clock sounds quite civilised. So it can't be too outlandish.'

That depended on your definition of outlandish, I thought as we all filed into the dining room for a buffet dinner.

Chapter Twenty

Beach or not, everyone had made an effort, and as the sun burned brightly in a brilliantly blue Cornish sky, the assembled crowd epitomised gay and colourful. Sam's navy linen suit emphasised his lean hips and broad shoulders and contrasted nicely with my faithful peacock-blue silk dress, which flapped in this morning's sea breeze. I refused to let it hold onto the bad memories of the last time I wore it, on our first date; I wasn't able to afford a new frock and the ridiculous expense of this one meant it had to pay its way. I was a great believer in the principle of cost-per-wear, besides, I still felt good every time I put it on – and if we hadn't been under strict time constraints it might very well have come off again. Sam had been in a playful mood that morning. I think we both felt a sense of lightness being away and off Victoria's radar.

There was no sign of either Gladys or Alastair and everyone kept looking round.

'Do you think they're going to abseil down the cliff?' asked Sam.

'It wouldn't surprise me,' said Richard, eyeing the steep cliff face. 'Not going to do much for a wedding dress, though.'

'You think Gladys is going to be worried about something like that?' asked Shelley.

'Probably not. But I'd have thought Alastair would be here. Isn't it traditional for the groom to be waiting for his bride?'

Apart from a small gazebo with a sound system, there were no other signs that anything remarkable was going to happen on the beach, although a large area away to the left had been marked off and two ushers in wellingtons had done their job of ushering us to this end of the beach. I recognised them as part of the trio of handsome young men that had been at the party last night and wondered where the third one was.

At nine o'clock there was an undignified screech as the sound system was switched on and the unmistakable sound of the James Bond theme tune began to play.

Shelley and I giggled. 'Didn't I tell you it was going to be wild?' said Shelley. She seemed to be back to her usual perky self this morning, although I was surprised by her very decorous choice of outfit. Normally she liked figure-hugging numbers that made the most of her out-there cleavage; this was a round-necked floaty pale-lemon dress covered in daisies that was very pretty, but just not very Shelley.

Everyone fell silent as we all glanced back towards the

cliff path and the stairs down to the beach, looking for signs of the wedding couple. Gradually, I became aware of people turning around, and a few pointing out to sea. When we turned we saw a small speedboat from around the other side of the cove come bouncing across the waves. The two ushers began to wade into the sea as the boat neared. Standing upright in the stern of the boat, arms outstretched and doing his very own *Titanic* impersonation was Alastair, dressed in a black tuxedo with black bow tie. When the boat neared, the engine slowed to an idle and the two ushers caught the rope hurled towards them and pulled the boat into the shallows.

Then they carried Alastair, hands under each of his arms, in towards the shore before putting him down on the wet sand. He beamed as his best man, a grizzled old sailor by the name of John, went to his side. It was funny to see their heads together as some frantic pocket patting went on – John clearly reassuring Alastair that, yes, he did have the rings.

They moved up to the beach and took up a position just by a little outcrop of rocks. Alastair beamed from ear to ear, looking positively smug, as if he knew something that we didn't. Still, everyone looked up and down the beach and back at the cliff path, trying to guess from where Gladys would appear.

Overhead, there was the dull drone of a plane and I laughed to myself. I wondered what they thought up there, looking down at all of us on the beach. I bet we made quite a spectacle. Then Alastair looked up and one by one the wedding guests followed his gaze. The little plane circled again for its third fly past, and then a little black dot came hurtling out of the doors. The James Bond music started again but this time segued into the Duran Duran theme from *A View to a Kill*.

'Oh my God.' My mother's shrill tone rang out over the suddenly silent crowd. 'Please tell me that's not her.'

'I think it might be,' I said, craning my neck as a bright yellow and red parachute burst open and began to circle its way down.

'Well, that's one way to make an entrance.' Richard folded his arms and trained his gaze on the descending parachute. 'Got to hand it to the old girl, she knows how to make an entrance. Maybe we should think about renewing our vows, Lynn.'

'If you seriously think I'm jumping twenty thousand feet out of a plane, I'll be divorcing you,' retorted Lynn.

'Let's hope she doesn't break a leg or anything,' said Mum. 'It'll be hell to get an ambulance crew down here.'

'It's being so positive that keeps you going,' I said, hooking an arm through hers to take the sting out of my words.

'I'm just being practical.'

The parachute began to get bigger and its circles smaller as it came closer to the beach, and now I understood why the ushers had been so keen for us to be shunted to one end of the beach and why the wedding had had to be so early. The tide was at its lowest point, and that meant there was more room to land.

The tension began to rise as the parachute came nearer and nearer and I was relieved to see that Gladys was with someone else and he was pulling at the toggles to guide the 'chute this way and that as they came into land. Then suddenly both their legs were running along the ground, churning up the sand, the parachute collapsing behind them.

Spontaneous applause erupted and when I looked over at Alastair, he was just unpeeling his hands from his eyes.

From beneath the parachute, Gladys emerged, striding out like some Valkyrie, unzipping a white jump suit as she moved, peeling it off to reveal a froth of shimmering organza which was definitely an interesting juxtaposition paired with the black helmet and goggles. One of the men who had helped the boat went rushing towards her carrying a pair of sequin-spangled flip-flops, dropping at her feet like some errant Prince Charming to help her divest herself of her heavy boots before he stood to take her headgear. Behind her, I recognised the man gathering in the parachute silk as the last of the three young men from the previous evening. A brave man indeed. And from the speculative look in Shelley's eye, he was going to need to get a whole lot braver.

Gladys's matron of honour, Dodie, suddenly appeared, fussing around the bride, tugging at her dress and folding up the jumpsuit, which she handed over to the third young man before thrusting a simple hand-tied bouquet of pink and white roses into Gladys's hand. The bride straightened up, smoothed down her skirt and, clutching her posy, lifted her head to give everyone a beatific smile just as Handel's 'Queen of Sheba' rang out from the music system.

She and Dodie began to make their way up the beach

towards Alastair and the best man, and I noticed a woman in a smart navy dress had appeared and seemed to be in charge of proceedings.

Once Gladys reached her husband-to-be's side, the woman introduced herself as a humanist celebrant and invited everyone to gather round in a circle. As the light breeze teased at Gladys's slightly ruffled chignon, her eyes glistened with tears and happiness as the celebrant conducted the handfast ceremony. I don't think I'll ever forget the pure joy that lit up her and Alastair's faces when the celebrant pronounced them man and wife, or Sam stroking my shoulder and looking down at me with such a tender expression that I thought my heart might burst.

Everyone erupted into heartfelt applause and moved forward to congratulate the happy couple, but Sam caught my hand and held me back, capturing my face in both his hands, his thumbs grazing my cheekbones. The intensity of his gaze made me catch my breath and my chest tightened as I froze, unable to tear my eyes from his. We didn't need to say anything. Love filled the air – Gladys and Alistair's, ours, Lynn and Richard's and all the other couples that had exchanged those tiny glances of acknowledgement with one another. It was a moment in time. I could hear the rush of the waves in the background, the screech of gulls overhead, and feel the slight sting of the sand on my face.

'I love you,' whispered Sam.

'I love you, too.' I whispered back, feeling tears prick at my eyes.

With the pad of his thumb, he wiped one away and dropped a kiss on the very spot. It felt like a promise.

A noisy, triumphant party climbed the stairs back up to the house. On the lawn, the soft strains of Vivaldi's four seasons came from a string quartet of four beautiful girls, clad in matching floral dresses, playing with that quiet, soulful devotion that always seems to characterise classical musicians.

Alastair led Gladys to the centre of the lawn and took her into his arms and the music paused before changing into a haunting composition to which they began to waltz in a gentle rise and fall around the grass. I don't think there was a dry eye among the guests as he held her with delicate devotion as if she were a fragile piece of glass – quite a feat when he was inches shorter than her Amazonian frame, but somehow he managed to guide her round with such tenderness you could hear the sighs of all the women around.

'That is beautiful,' said Lynn. 'I'll renew our vows if you learn to dance like that.'

'Hmm,' said Richard. 'Small matter of two left feet, but if it will make you happy, my love…' He patted her on the shoulder and she laid her hand on top of his, and I caught the quick affectionate smile between them.

God, today was going to finish me off. All this soppiness was doing a number on me. I edged closer to Sam and put my arm through his, squeezing it and revelling in the delicious happiness that permeated every cell in my body. It was a glad-to-be-alive and of-the-moment sort of day that I was going to cherish for ever. The first dance came to an end, but the quartet immediately began to play a new piece and Gladys and Alastair danced on, Dodie and Freddie joining in.

'Want to dance?' asked Sam.

'I'd love to,' I sighed, enviously. 'It looks wonderful.'

He slipped an arm around my waist and took my hand, sweeping me into a traditional ballroom hold.

'You know how?' I squeaked.

'Private school. The only time we fraternised with the girls at the school next door. Don't worry, just hang on to me.' He grinned down with typical Sam self-confidence.

I knew the steps but I'd just never actually executed them with a partner. You don't watch fifteen seasons of *Strictly Come Dancing* without having a sneaky practice in the lounge on a Saturday night. Even so, I had to concentrate really hard on the one, two, three, one, two, three, and it was a struggle not to mouth the count as we danced.

'Relax, we've got this.' Sam's warm breath brushed my ear. 'I'm supposed to lead you.'

And suddenly it clicked, and I did relax against his warm, familiar body, enjoying the heady rush of delight at the two of us dancing as one. Just Sam and me, completely in sync, our eyes locked on each other, his big capable hand holding mine while his other at my waist steered me with gentle nudges. It was almost better than sex, being perfectly in tune with each other, and my heart soared as we glided around the lawn, conscious of the music and Sam's smiling regard. When the final notes died away, we stayed in each other's arms, a little stunned and reluctant to return to reality. A bit like when you've lost yourself in a really wonderful film at the cinema and then you step outside onto the crowded pavements to the intrusion of the noise and bustle of real life.

'You're quite a dancer, Mr Weaverham.'

'So are you. We must do it again sometime.'

I smiled up at him a little dreamily. A beautiful fantasy. Tea dances weren't exactly all the rage in Tring, or not that I knew of.

Trays of pink champagne were being circulated by rather youthful, fresh-faced staff who looked as if they'd been drafted in from the local sixth form, and people were starting to make their way to congratulate the happy couple. There were probably about a hundred and fifty people, which was far more than I'd been expecting. Everyone was starting to mingle, and I noticed that Shelley was talking to the tall, handsome parachutist who'd come down with Gladys and I smiled to myself. Good old Shelley, but when we drifted past, circulating, she reached out and grabbed my arm, almost spilling my champagne.

'Jess,' she said urgently. 'This is Fraser. This is my cousin, Jessica, and her boyfriend, Sam.'

She looked absolutely terrified and was still clinging to my arm as if she wanted to sidle behind me.

'You're a brave man,' I said. 'That was some entrance. Do you do many weddings?'

Fraser laughed. 'This was my first. Although I might branch out.' He had a faint American twang to his accent.

'He's a Falcon,' said Shelley. 'I mean, an RAF Falcon. Not a bird. A parachute … man. They fly out of Brize

Norton. Or I suppose drop out of. But not dropouts. Out of planes.' Poor Shelley's cheeks flamed. 'Excuse me. I need to go to the loo.' With that she dashed off.

'She OK?' asked Fraser.

'Mm, yes, er, I think so,' I said, staring rather bemusedly after my go-get-'em take-no-prisoners cousin. 'I'm not sure what's wrong with her.' Sam and I shared a quick frown.

Fraser grinned and looked quite pleased with himself. 'I think I mighta frightened her off.'

'Well, you'd be the first,' I said, still puzzled by Shelley's behaviour.

'Cool, that's good to hear.'

I was so surprised by his response I blurted out, 'Why?' and I felt Sam stiffen behind me.

A slow smile spread across his handsome American movie-star face. 'Means I'm having some effect on her. She's quite something.'

'She is,' I said, fixing him with a stern look. 'And she's had enough crap from men in her life. I'm sure you'll have the pick of the party here, if you want it.'

Even Sam blanched at my tart tone.

'Ma'am, I have nothing but good intentions and I think your cousin is old enough to look after herself and make up her own mind.'

'Hmm, you'd think.'

'So how do you know Gladys? She's one cool lady.'

'Sam, I'll just go and check on Shelley.' I left him to explain the family relationship to the rather smooth Fraser and headed to the ladies.

Shelley was in the little powder room sitting on a pink

velvet chaise longue with a glass of water pressed up against her cheek.

'Oh God, tell me I didn't make a complete dick of myself.'

'You want me to lie?'

She groaned.

'What's the matter?'

'He's flipping, flaming gorgeous.'

'And?'

'Jess. Look at me. He's way out of my league. He flipping drops out of planes for a living. I paint nails and do eyelash extensions.'

'So? When did you care about that sort of thing?'

'When it matters. Oh God, I looked across that beach, saw him gathering up that parachute and he looked up. Oh God, I'm an idiot. I have got the biggest hard-on crush. I suppose I should just go for it and shag his brains out. Make the most of it. 'Cos I'll never see him again.' She looked up at me. 'Oh God, this is how it was with you that time with Sam. Please tell me it wasn't. I don't believe in all that at-first-sight bollocks; I thought you were having me on. I mean, Sam's pretty shagtastic but I thought you just fancied him a lot.'

I sat down next to her and squidged up so we were thigh-to-thigh. 'No. It was the real deal and I didn't believe in at-first-sight either, but now look at us. I'm absolutely crazy, head-over-heels, in love with him. Sometimes when I wake up, I just look at him and I can hardly breathe because of the way I feel.'

'Aw crap. I don't need to hear that. You're OK, though.

Any idiot can see he's bonkers about you. A guy like Fraser isn't ever going to feel like that about me.'

'Why not?'

'Because look at the blokes I've been with before. I get what I deserve.'

Taking her shoulders in both hands I gave her a cross little shake. 'You need to love yourself more. Believe in yourself. You settle for second best too often because that's what you think you deserve. Well, that's bollocks. Now, you go out there and give Mr I'm-God's-Gift-and-I-know-it a run for his money. Be yourself. Love yourself. He's interested but he's a bit too sure of himself. Don't make me give you a slap.'

'Ha! You can try.'

'Exactly. That's more like it.'

'Thanks, Jess. You're the best. I'm glad you found Sam. You two fit. He's a good bloke.'

'Well, go and see if you can collar one for yourself.'

We sat down for lunch at three long tables in a vast dining room. Gladys and Alastair were on a table on a little dais, flanked by Dodie and Freddie. I'd been separated from Sam, who was sitting next to Aunty Lynn, although I noticed that Shelley had been positioned next to Fraser and I did wonder if Gladys had done it deliberately. Shelley was talking with great animation to her neighbour on the other side and pointedly ignoring Fraser which seemed to amuse rather than offend him. The speeches were short, heartfelt and Freddie's best man speech was completely random, but Gladys and Alastair beamed at each other throughout. All in all, it was a very jolly affair and surprisingly traditional in lots of ways, with the croquembouche wedding cake brought out at the end eliciting a round of impressed applause.

Towards the end of the meal I spotted Lynn and Sam deep in conversation, but I caught her shooting me a worried look. What had Sam been saying to her? We'd deliberately downplayed the flat tyre, blaming it on the heat. Lynn was good friends with Sally and I didn't want to cause any trouble there because Victoria was clearly still Sally's surrogate daughter. And there it was again, another one of Lynn's thoughtful, considered looks, as if she were weighing things up.

After lunch, the trestle tables were cleared away and the floor was cleared for dancing, which seemed a bit odd in the middle of the day, but when the lively jazz band struck up, there was no shortage of dancers on the floor, including the American, Fraser, who was quite a mover and twirled Shelley around in a series of spins and turns which seemed to end with her breathless in his arms.

Sam and Richard had sloped off to find more beer and I was taking a breather by the French windows – not that it was any cooler outside – when Aunty Lynn slipped out to join me.

'Enjoying it?' she asked.

'Yes. Gladys looks like she's having the time of her life.'

'She's waited a long time for this day. I guess she's had

plenty of time to think about what she wanted to do. Hiring a plane and befriending the RAF is no mean feat.'

'How do you even go about doing that?'

'I think she met the RAF guys through doing a couple of charity jumps, and when she said that was how she wanted to arrive on her wedding day, they offered to help.'

'Only Gladys.'

'She's a character. Wish my dad could have been here; he'd have loved it. Probably would have given her away. She was always his favourite and there were fifteen years between them.' She looked pensively out towards the sea. 'I still miss him.' I felt like there was something else coming as she gave me a shrewd study. 'Sam says you're going to stay in Ottershaw.'

I tensed.

'Yes.'

She raised an eyebrow but didn't press for any more information.

'I found a very nice pub that looked really good in the pictures.' I unfolded my arms which I hadn't realised I'd folded. I had no reason to be defensive. I could go and stay anywhere I wanted.

'You do know—'

'Jess darling, there you are.' My mother appeared by my side and I'd never been so grateful to see her in all my life.

Lynn gave me the sort of glance that said she wasn't done here but knew she was beaten for the time being. I prayed that Sam hadn't mentioned where we were staying to Mum, although it might not have any significance to her.

I couldn't be sure. Those long-ago letters with a return address had been sent to me, not her.

'I'm absolutely exhausted. This heat. It's like the summer of '76 all over again, isn't it, Lynn?'

'Yes. I can't remember another summer like it.'

They lapsed into reminiscing about their youth and the drought conditions they remembered and I took the chance to slip away, crossing the lawn over to the cliff path looking down onto the beach. I was still undecided as to what I would do when we got to the village tomorrow. We were only staying for one night. I glanced guiltily back towards the house. Sam had no idea why I'd chosen Ottershaw. I really ought to tell him why.

Chapter Twenty-One

'This looks great,' said Sam, bouncing with enthusiasm, his elbow propped on the open window and the breeze ruffling his hair, as the Black Bull came into view. 'A proper pub with proper beer. We should have asked your uncle Richard to come too.'

'What, for a romantic night away with him and Aunty Lynn? We could have invited Mum and Shelley too,' I teased.

'You know, this is our first night away together, not counting the wedding, which was nice but surrounded by people. It's quite nice to be here, just you and me. No one knows us.'

I liked the idea of anonymity. Everything in Tring had become a bit too public, and with the recent run-ins with Victoria, I didn't like the feeling of undeserved notoriety.

'We're just tourists. Daytrippers.' He burst into a loud and tuneless chorus of the Beatles song despite the open window, catching the amused attention of a couple just entering the beer garden.

We really had been tourists today. Following signposts to interesting-sounding places, meandering our way along the coast and stopping for ice-cream twice because we were 'on holiday'. We'd been enticed by the sunshine and a sense of having all the time in the world to take a snooze on one beach followed by a paddle that had turned into a splashing water fight and the two of us were still drying out, although it was so hot neither of us minded. I was starting to believe that this weather would last for ever and, according the forecast, there was to be no let-up for at least another ten days.

The village of Ottershaw delivered everything the pictures and Tripadvisor had promised: a village green with the pub on one side, the ancient twelfth-century church at the apex and a bow-fronted village shop with the tiniest of doorways. A large wooden sign, with a picture of a windmill, declared that the village was mentioned in the Domesday Book. We drove past this and turned left into the tiny pub car park and I just about manoeuvred Uncle Richard's big car into a space which had been designed in the days of much smaller cars.

We both sagged in our seats, with that journey's-end sort of flop, feeling hot and sticky because neither of us liked the fierce air conditioning of the car, and looked out of the window at the pub.

It was picture-perfect with its thatched roof and tiny eaves windows, although it did look as if it had just had an expensive makeover, with those fancy green wooden windows that seemed to be all the rustic rage of late, and the straw was still yellow-gold as if it had been done very recently. It looked newer and shinier than I'd expected. But it had rave reviews on Tripadvisor, so all boded well.

'First on the agenda, a very long, cold lager,' said Sam as we hopped down from the car. I unstuck my vest top from my back and wriggled my shorts down from where they'd ridden up.

'In the beer garden,' I said, nodding to the shaded area beyond the car park, which thankfully held a couple of spare tables.

'This looks very quaint. Excellent choice,' said Sam, taking my hand as we crossed the threshold into the low-ceilinged bar.

'Good old Tripadvisor,' I said with an inward wince at the lie. We'd have stayed in the Black Bull even if it had been a fully functioning brothel, because it was the only place to stay in Ottershaw.

Soft light glinted from the horse brasses on the walls, and hushed chatter came from the tables, which were full of older tourists and holidaymakers, the more sensible taking refuge from the sun. Sam and I were both outdoor babies and he, like me, wanted to make the most of every minute of the glorious weather. The balcony in my flat had never been so well used.

We took our drinks outside and savoured the cold liquid. Sam linked his fingers through mine and we sat there in contented silence.

'I was thinking,' said Sam and then didn't say anything else.

'Yes,' I prompted.

'About … about your flat. My flat.'

'The one you're hardly ever in.'

'That one, yes. Do you think it's…'

'Too soon? No.' As always with Sam, I knew exactly where the conversation was headed.

He grinned at me. 'I love it when you do that. So I was thinking we could sell both properties.'

I grinned back at him. 'Makes sense. Get a bigger one. Mine is a bit small for both of us.'

'We'd need to find a place with a balcony.'

'Or a place we can put one in.'

'You'd be up for a fixer-upper?'

'Yes, I think so. You're the practical one but I make a great labourer's assistant.'

And just like that it was all decided. By the time we checked in, we'd looked up respective estate agents on our phones, worked out what we could afford to pay in mortgage payments, and had a brief look at what was available in the local area. We celebrated the decision by having languorous, lazy sex in the slanting sunlight coming through the windows under the eaves.

I woke early and with a smile turned to watch Sam sleeping, an arm thrown above his head, the single sheet twisted around the waist of his leonine body. I loved him so much it almost hurt to look. I resisted the urge to trail a hand across his chest. If I went out now, I might not have to say anything. Last night, the excitement of our decision and all the plans we'd discussed had driven all thoughts of my father out of my head.

Now, in the quiet sunlit morning, they crowded in, and all the indecision bounced around like a demented moth drawn to light. My dad. He was less than a mile away. Was he asleep in his bed with his wife? Were his children, my half-brothers, awake? I didn't have to see him, them or her. I could just pass the house. Any old tourist out on an early morning walk.

That's what I would do. Resolve suddenly energised me. Not wanting to disturb Sam, I eased out of bed and slipped on my shorts and T-shirt. Just a quick peek, I told myself. An early morning stroll. With my heart thudding, I glanced guiltily back at Sam. I'd tell him later. Sending him a quick text message, I quietly pulled the bedroom door closed and slipped down the stairs to the deserted hallway of the pub. Kitchen noises from beyond the bar suggested that breakfast preparation was well under way and would be in full swing by the time I came back, which solved my worry about not being able to get back in again.

Already the sun was hot in another cloudless blue sky. In the quiet of the morning, birdsong rose and fell as sparrows dived and danced in and out of the hedgerows ahead. I listened to the musical lilt of a blackbird perched on the top of one of the thatched cottages lining the green, before it took sudden flight. Bees and other insects buzzed with industrious intent around my ankles in the long, parched grasses of the verges as I followed the road down along one side of the green, every now and then giving my phone map discreet glances. Shinfield Lane. The Paddocks. I kept a wary eye on the little blue dot and took the unmarked lane leading east away from the village. My target, because I did feel like a spy, was less than a mile's walk and I wished I'd brought my sunglasses because there wasn't another soul around, making me also feel horribly exposed and self-conscious.

I rounded a corner away from the houses, relaxing a little at being out of sight of the village, and took a few deep, even breaths, almost enjoying being outdoors so early. This was a gorgeous part of the country, so quiet and peaceful. Not a single car had passed me. I walked for ten minutes, passing a couple of cottages before a house on the distant bend came into view. According to my little blue dot, that was very likely The Paddocks. I slowed my steps as my stomach tied itself into a dozen hard, tight knots. Nerves warred with an unexpected fizz of excitement as I neared the house. *Act natural, Jess. Just a tourist out for a walk.* But I couldn't help pausing to take careful stock of the house, inventorying all its elements. The spring green leaves of a well-established wisteria climbed the whitewashed walls, long curling tendrils escaping to underline the pale-blue trim under the roof. The pretty blue paint was echoed on the windowsills underneath the leaded windows on either side of a squat, neat porch almost lost under another abundant climber with rosy-hued leaves.

In front of the house, a wide gravel drive bordered by colourful beds filled with lavender, alliums, geraniums and cornflowers offered plenty of turning room for the Range Rover and little Polo parked there. Away to the other side of the drive sat a separate whitewashed garage with blue-painted wooden doors.

An estate agent would have described it as a well-maintained, substantial property. It probably had at least five bedrooms and a very big garden. I refused to give in to the small kernel of bitterness that reared its ugly head and insisted on comparing this house to my mother's neat and dull 60s semi.

Instead, I studied the windows upstairs, where most of the curtains were still closed. The family was there. The fizz reasserted itself, pushing back at the nerves as it spread through my veins. My legs wobbled and I had to force myself to keep walking, trying to be surreptitious in my study of the house. Drawing attention to myself and looking like some weirdo was the last thing I wanted. Once past the house, I dragged in a much-needed breath and crossed to the fence just beyond to lean on the wooden fence rails. This must be the paddock the house was named for, and as I scanned the small field, I realised a pony was trotting directly towards me, a small boy on its back. Oh no. It was too late for me to move, even if I'd wanted to, and a part of me was committed now.

'He thinks you might have carrots,' said the boy, hauling on the reins. 'Naughty, Tiger. He's very greedy.'

'Tiger?' I leaned to pat the inquisitive pony's nose with a very shaky hand as I slowly raised my eyes to look at the boy. Familiar blue eyes stared back at me, before his face curved into a mischievous smile.

'After *The Tiger Who Came to Tea*. When he was a foal, he got into the pony nuts and nearly ate them all.'

'In that case, it's a very good name.'

'He's not a very good pony, but I love him anyway. My brother Toby has Jackson; he's much better behaved, but then Toby's only eight.'

'And how old are you?' I asked, shoving my hands in my pockets, crossing my fingers and fervently willing him not to say ten.

'I'm ten. Nearly eleven.'

Of course he was. Incontrovertible evidence that even now I was trying to deny.

This was my half-brother. The screwed-up monkey baby from the photo that my dad had sent all those years ago.

'You're up early,' I said, my arms resting on top of the fence.

'When I don't have to go to school, I don't mind. And if we want to take the ponies to the beach, we have to get up early, 'cos of the grockles. They don't like it.'

'Grockles?'

'Damn tourists,' confided the boy – who I knew was called Ben – with decided adult overtones.

I laughed and his eyes widened and he clapped a hand over his mouth, making me wonder which adult he'd picked it up from.

'Like me?' I said.

He nodded, mortification setting in.

'I quite like that word. I've not heard it before.' Trying not to look like some creepy weirdo, I focused on Ben's face, noting the similarities of his features, and with each one, a little bit of my heart fractured. His eyes were the same shape as mine and exactly the same shade of blue.

The arc of his eyebrows identical and his lightly freckled complexion all too familiar. Before I realised it, and too late to get away, because then I *would* look like some creepy weirdo, I noticed a woman was approaching, holding the reins of another pony with a younger boy atop.

Even if I'd wanted to escape, my feet had other ideas and wouldn't do as they were told; they had put down roots of their own.

'Good morning,' she said. 'Gorgeous day, isn't it?' Letting go of the reins, she climbed onto the fence a foot away from me, looping one leg over to perch on the top rail.

Oh God, was this her? Alicia Harper. My dad's wife. The woman he'd left us for.

No, she couldn't be. In my head she was an angular vicious-looking Morticia, with drawn, mean features. This woman was slightly plump, with a peaches-and-cream complexion and a sunny smile that stretched from the corners of her wide mouth to her crinkling eyes. She was far too pretty and wholesome to be Alicia Harper.

'Yes.' I nodded, itching to wipe my clammy hands down my shorts. 'Lovely day.'

'I think this is the best part of the day. Before everyone gets up and gets involved in everything they have to do.'

'Yes…' I wasn't going to make the mistake of saying his name, so I nodded towards Ben. 'He said you were going to the beach before it gets busy.'

'That's the plan. But we've got plenty of time.' Her eyes never left my face and a sudden flutter of unease unfurled at her words.

'Well, I ought to be getting back,' I said, backing away from the fence, ripples of panic dancing in my stomach.

'It's Jess, isn't it?' she said softly, her smile still warm and friendly.

I just stared at her, my stomach dropping away in freefall. How did she know?

'Erm ... I—'

'I recognised you from the photos. Lynn sends them.'

My aunt? She sent photos?

'It's lovely to meet you, at last. Sorry, that sounds complaining. It's not. Won't you come in for a cup of tea? Adrian would so love to see you.' Quiet empathy burned in her gentle smile. She was so unexpectedly like the good fairy, and so far from my evil stepmother imaginings.

Panic tied my stomach in knots and held my throat in a tight grip. I'd only come to look. This wasn't supposed to happen. This was supposed to be on my terms.

'I ... I can't.'

'You're always welcome. No pressure, but I think your brothers, Ben and Toby, they'd like to get to know you.'

I flapped my hands in the feeblest gesture, but I was too confused to say anything.

Instead, I backed away into the road.

'I've got to go.' I finally managed to spit the words out.

Despite my words, she still carried on smiling at me in a way that made me feel pathetic and totally stupid. She was being totally gracious and welcoming and I was acting like a churlish, flighty twit. I hated myself but I didn't know what else to do.

'You can come back later. We'll be here all day. You could

come for tea. I promised the boys I'd make scones today. We'll have clotted cream. Your dad's favourite, even though that's normally only for tourists.'

I was still backing away and now I turned and walked as quickly as I could back towards the village, feeling sick. My skin prickled with shame. She'd been so nice. She wasn't supposed to be nice. Or pretty. Or welcoming. Or talk about my dad with that soft-voiced love in her words.

My phone buzzed in my pocket and I took it out, grateful for the distraction.

'Hi, Sam, I'm just on my way back.' My voice sounded shaky and I wondered what on earth I was going to tell him.

My whole world had just been knocked off its axis. How was I going to face my mum? I'd met the enemy – except she wasn't. Alicia was me in the future. I deserved to be happy with Sam, in the way she so clearly was with my dad. Was my mum responsible in part for the acrimonious way things had ended with my dad? Maybe he wasn't the monster she'd always painted him to be, just like I wasn't the evil bitch that Victoria had made me out to be. Sam's friends were still ostracising him and me; perhaps it was time to show the other side of the story.

I needed to talk to Mum, which filled me with dread. Perhaps it would be easier to talk to Aunty Lynn first. In the meantime, I had some explaining to do to Sam, and it was only fair to tell him the truth.

Chapter Twenty-Two

'Are you sure you don't want me to come with you?'

I smiled at Sam, that bubble of love rising at his words. He had an uncanny ability to know when I needed his support. It was family history and hurt that needed to be unpicked alone. 'No, but thank you. I'm dreading it and I certainly don't want to drag you in.'

'But your mum likes me. I could charm her.'

'You probably could, but I need to do this on my own. Besides, you have to get that pile of marking done if we're going to go to your mum and dad's party tomorrow.'

He pulled a face and I wasn't sure if it was the marking or the party that was responsible.

'I'm not going to be long. Mum might do her usual and just refuse to talk to me about my dad.'

I picked up my car keys and Sam rose to give me a quick hug and a kiss on the forehead.

'I love you, Jess. You always do the right thing.'

'It doesn't feel like it right now, but I need to know what really happened.'

Ever since Victoria had started her campaign of harassment, which seemed to have died down since our return from Cornwall, my sympathies towards her and my mum had undergone a radical change.

When I'd returned to the pub after meeting Alicia and my brothers, I'd blurted the whole story out to Sam. I had brothers. Seeing them, their features so like mine, had kick-started an odd yearning somewhere in my sternum, but also a desire to understand more why Dad had left me behind. He'd had more children, so he wasn't averse to family. Why couldn't he have been a father to me?

While it would have been easier to ask Aunty Lynn, I needed to hear it from Mum.

I climbed out of the car, feeling woefully unprepared, despite all the words I'd prepared on the fifteen-minute journey and throughout most of the previous night.

'Jess!' Mum's surprise was touched with awkwardness. 'Is everything all right? You should have phoned and told me you were coming.' She glanced back over her shoulder. 'Douglas has just popped in for coffee. We were discussing bulbs for the spring. He has a lovely garden.'

Even in my own agitated state, I could tell she was rattled. Before I could say anything, she trotted off down the hall towards the kitchen, her sensible, ever-present courts clicking on the wooden floor. I followed her and found her neighbour sitting at the kitchen table with a large mug of coffee and in front of him a plate of cake. 'Look who's here. Jess.'

'Morning,' I said as he jumped to his feet. 'Sorry to interrupt.'

'No, no, not at all. I was just going. I'll pop back later, Joan, and give that lawn a mow for you.'

'Thank you. That would be very kind.'

'Please don't go on my account,' I said, feeling horribly guilty for causing the sudden awkwardness in the air and chasing him away. He seemed to be the only bright light in my mother's otherwise diminished life.

'No, Douglas was just going.' My mother's teeth were practically bared as she ushered him out.

'Coffee, Jess?'

'Yes, please.' It was the last thing I wanted but it gave her something to do as I tried to work up the courage to start. Luckily she made it easy for me with a tart 'So what brings you here for an unannounced visit? I thought Lynn was the only recipient.'

Combative as always, I thought. I was tempted to start with the opening line 'I saw Dad last week,' but instead I said, chickening out, 'I wanted to talk to you.'

'Oh.' She arched a perfect plucked, elegant eyebrow. 'You're not ill, are you? Oh God. You're pregnant.'

I laughed. 'And would that be so awful?'

'I suppose not,' she said grudgingly. 'Although it would be better to be married.' She pursed her lips, 'and preferably without the fuss Gladys insisted upon.'

'But it was fun.'

'It was a ridiculous waste of money, at her age.'

'Mum, you enjoyed yourself. I saw you dancing with one of the RAF boys.'

Her face softened. 'Who'd have thought he'd be so good at ballroom?'

'Did you know there are tea dances in Stone?' I named a village on the outskirts of Aylesbury. 'You should go.' I waited a beat before adding. 'Take Douglas.'

She stared at me, but I wasn't going to be cowed.

'You should. Live a little. He seems a nice man and he obviously likes you. You shouldn't shut out the possibility of...' Her impassive face almost made me stop but, bugger it, it was time for straight talking. My impatience with her sterile life and taboo subjects broke through. 'I don't know what happened between you and Dad, but you deserve to be happy. Let yourself be happy for a change. Why not take a chance? It feels like you're punishing yourself.' Oh God, I'd really done it now.

'I beg your pardon. How dare you speak to me like that?' Mum's face had turned white and I knew I had stepped into no man's land and might kick a landmine at any second, but I couldn't stop myself. Eighteen years of uncertainty, of tiptoeing around her feelings, too terrified to risk upsetting her, had come to an uncorked explosion and now I couldn't stop myself. It all just poured out.

'Because you won't ever talk about it. About what happened between you and Dad. About what happened afterwards, when you went to hospital. You just shut down. I've always been too scared to try and talk to you. You shut all your emotions away. The only one that ever comes out is your jealousy of Aunty Lynn and that's so unfair.'

'I'm not jealous of Lynn.'

'Yes, you are. You make me feel guilty that I feel

comfortable with her, that her home is more welcoming than yours.' Anger made me blunt. 'But why should I? You've made it like this. You shut me out. You shut life out. I don't think you even talk about things to Dawn, do you?'

Mum threw down the tea towel in a quick jerky movement and gripped the sink with one hand. Beady, bird bright eyes stared at me with unexpected malevolence.

'Talk,' she spat in uncharacteristic fury that immediately sparked a memory of her screaming at Dad. A painful tear in the status quo. Dad had been supplicant, pleading, soft-spoken, while she'd raged at him. Screaming abuse and threats. Her uncontrolled wildness at complete odds with the buttoned-up, repressed woman she'd become.

'That's all anyone wants these days.' She spoke in a vicious low-toned voice brimming with suppressed rage which made my heart pound. What had I started? 'What if I don't *want* to talk about things? What if it's too painful? Have you thought about that? You wait. When Sam swans off into the sunset with another woman, how will you feel then? Will you want to talk about how humiliating and shameful it is? Will you want to share how inadequate and stupid you feel? Will you want everyone to see that you're second best? That you weren't enough?'

'If that happens. Then I can look back on what we've had. The happy times. The joy we've shared. You must have been happy with Dad once.'

'He left me, and you, without a thought.'

'Is that true?'

'True!' she screeched. 'You're asking that?'

'I'm just asking what happened. Why he left, and why he didn't want to see me?'

'He left because he met that bitch who didn't care that he had a wife and a baby. So he walked out on us. Didn't want to know.'

'But it was eighteen years ago, Mum. Surely you've come to terms with it.'

'Come to terms? With having my world turned upside down?'

'But you've got over that. Why look back? It's not doing you any good. You've got a good job, a house, and you could have had other relationships if you'd wanted.'

'Your dad left without a backward look. He didn't want a family.'

'Is that true?' I thought of Ben and Toby.

She pinched her lips and suddenly all the bluster and fury disappeared and she sank into a chair, her hands covering her face. Part of me wanted to stay on my side of the table and keep my distance, emotional and physical, but another part, the stronger this-is-my-mother part, felt sadness, guilt and pity.

I walked around the table, pulled out the chair next to her, and sat and put my arm around her.

'What happened, Mum?'

She breathed out a tiny sob. 'It was my fault, he left you. I was so … so hurt. I wouldn't let him see you. I told him if he left, he'd never see you again. I would take you away and hide from him. I just wanted to hurt him as much as I could, and you were his Achilles heel. He loved you. More than me. I lost … I lost all sense of reason. I think, well, I *know,* I went mad. Nothing in my head made sense and all I could feel was terrible, terrible pain. It consumed me. I don't remember it, but apparently I threatened to kill myself if he came near you. Wicked now. I know that but I...'

I squeezed her shoulders. With her words came clarity of memory. I could remember the descent into madness. The crying, the wailing, the screaming rages. The inappropriate confidences to an eight-year-old. All the fear I'd felt rose back up and I shivered. It had been an awful time. Being allowed to do you as you pleased might sound like a childhood fantasy come true, but in reality it was anything but. I'd been so lost and frightened, especially once the school holidays had started and the days had turned into endless hours of nothing. Putting myself to bed at night had been the worst thing, not knowing when to go up to bed in the long, light evenings. Being terrified that my mum might be dead when I woke up. But it had been equally dreadful for her.

'I loved him and he didn't love me. He loved you. I thought he'd take you away and I couldn't bear the thought that I'd lose you both. It was a madness, and then finally they took me to hospital and all the noise in my head went away. And for those six months, it was peaceful, not feeling anything. The drugs soothed all the sharp edges away, and I didn't want to live. When I came out they said I had to show that I could cope before you were allowed to come back. It took another eighteen months. You came for visits. Do you remember?'

And suddenly I did. Painful sessions where I sat in the chair in the living room, anxiously picking at chocolate biscuits, too terrified to say or do anything that might upset my silent and watchful mum. They were an ordeal.

'Even when you finally came home, you belonged to Lynn, and that was almost worse. You didn't want to come back here. You cried a lot.'

'Sorry,' I said automatically, seeing her pain, old guilt resurrecting itself.

'Who can blame you? Good old Lynn, life and soul of the party, with her perfect husband.' Her mouth curled in faint bitterness. 'I had a perfect husband once, except he didn't love me. I was determined I wasn't going to lose you again, so I had to make sure everything was perfect, so that I wouldn't go back to hospital. So that the woman from social services wouldn't take you away again. I had to be in control of everything. But still you wanted to go back to Lynn's. Eventually she agreed to stop inviting you, so that I could have you back properly. And after a while you settled down. Bel helped. You remembered her once you went back to your old school. There's always been something special between you. The pair of you were so stubborn when you were little. Then you both got places at the grammar school. By the time you were fourteen, I felt I'd got you back. But Lynn kept insisting on family gatherings, and as you got older, I knew that you went round there.'

'Shelley's like a sister to me,' I said, feeling a little helpless realising that Mum's antipathy to Lynn ran much deeper than I'd ever realised.

'I don't blame you. Lynn's always been more fun.' Her mouth drooped.

It was hard to disagree with that, but a certain loyalty

forced me to speak. 'But you're *my* mum. And I know that I come first with you. Shelley will always be Lynn's first priority. Just like I'm yours.'

Unexpected gratitude shone in her eyes. 'I'm never sure that you realise that.'

'Of course, I do.' I lied because until that moment I hadn't been, but now I could see that her nagging, her desire for me to do better, her concern that I found the right man, all came from a good place.

'But maybe you need to start putting yourself first for a change.'

Her appalled expression almost made me laugh.

'Seriously, mum. Stop worrying about me. I'm happy. I've got everything I could wish for.'

'You're a good girl, Jess. I've not been the best. I'm sorry I fell apart when I should have been there for you. I've been trying to make up for it ever since, but it just seems to make me even more worried I'll get it wrong.'

In that moment I felt I'd crossed a threshold. I could see exactly what she'd been doing, and why she'd been they way she had. For the first time our roles were reversed, I the adult, and she the child, and I saw I needed to protect and her and look after her.

'Mum, why don't we do things differently from now on? Why don't we be honest with each other about our feelings?'

She looked at me a touch of suspicion darkening her at eyes at first, before they brightened with wonderment.

'You know, talk, really talk, about things in future. I've

been at fault for not always really telling you how I feel about things, for fear of offending or upsetting you.'

'That's very generous of you.' She took my hand. 'I'm not sure I deserve it. I've not been the best parent.'

'Yes, but you're mine,' I said squeezing her hand. We had a long way to go but today I felt we'd taken the first step in the right direction.

'Does this mean you're going to stop moving my ornaments around every time you visit?'

I burst out laughing and my mum's eyes actually twinkled with amusement. 'Yes, I promise.'

'Why don't you tell me more about Sam? I really liked him, you know. I had a lovely chat with him at Gladys's wedding. It's such a shame he's not been selected, I don't understand it. Douglas and I agree, he's one of the most talented young batsman either of us have seen. It doesn't make sense.'

'You know me, I know nothing about cricket. I know he practises a lot.' I sat up suddenly triumphant at my knowledge of a cricketing term. 'In the nets. Every Monday, Tuesday and Thursday. And I'm glad you like him. He's special.' My voice softened with love. He really was special, and mum liking him was just the added icing on the cake. I realised I'd been unconsciously looking for her approval for a long time.

'I am very proud of you, Jess. Just not very good at showing it. It's not everyone who can do the sort of job you do. It is extraordinary. I worry for your safety, but I think that those women are very lucky to have you on their side.'

'Wow, mum.' I swallowed down the lump.

She hugged me – a proper, impulsive full-on hug. 'I love you.'

It was the first time I could ever remember her saying it to me. There was time enough to ask her about Dad; now I was going to savour our tentative steps towards a proper relationship.

Chapter Twenty-Three

As we stepped over the threshold, immediately attuned to the low hum of a party in full swing, we both glanced left to the Jack Vettriano print on the wall.

'Looks straight to me,' said Sam with a wink, his face lighting up with sudden mischief. The moment of shared recognition chased away all the nerves that had been simmering in my system since the moment I'd woken up that morning. Although I felt much better for having been to see my mum.

The previous day's emotional showdown had left me shaky and worn when I returned home. Sam's answer when I'd returned to the flat, after I'd told him everything, had been to take me to bed and make love with tenderness and care, reinforcing his love for me with every kiss and touch, and then cook me pizza and open a bottle of Prosecco.

I skimmed a hand over the silk fabric which was filmy around my legs. It was my favourite peacock-blue dress.

When I'd worn it for Sam on our first date, it had been feminine and flattering. At Glady's wedding, bold and beautiful. Today it was armour. The vibrant colour said bold, brave and I am comfortable in my own skin. I'm me. I'd also made an extra special effort, layering on a little more make-up than I usually wore and curling my hair to give it extra volume before putting it into a loose bun with wispy tendrils trailing around my neck. I got a kick out of seeing Sam's eyes going big and wide when I emerged from the bathroom.

'Will I do?' I'd asked, and immediately hated that I'd asked the question. Even Sam's eyebrows had gone up at the rare neediness in my voice, before he'd taken my hand and laid it on his chest. Sounds cheesy but it wasn't; he understood things before I even said them.

'You're extra special gorgeous as Esme in my class would say. You're always gorgeous but today,' his eyes shone with warmth and kind reassurance, 'you'll definitely do.' He dipped his head and kissed my knuckles one by one. 'It'll be fine.' I realised then that we were both nervous.

And now, in the hallway of his parents' house, him clutching a present in one hand and me clutching a navy-blue glazed pot of purpley-blue delphiniums to my ribs with one hand, he grabbed my free hand and repeated the gesture.

'Right, let's brave the rellies.' He groaned. 'And there are going to be a ton of them. Mum has three sisters and two brothers. It's your job to stop me punching anyone that says, "Gosh, haven't you grown."'

'I think I can do that.' I laughed at his disgusted expression. 'Now you're making me grateful that our family is so small. Just Mum and Aunty Lynn.' But even as I said the words, images of a long-ago family party drifted through my head. Dad's family. Other cousins. Grandparents, possibly, although they might still be alive. Another aunt and uncle.

I despatched the ghosts of family past, and we rounded the staircase down the hallway and straight into the fray. There were a few people in the kitchen but we worked our way through them and out into the garden, Sam nodding here and there but striding forward in a way that deterred anyone from trying to engage him in conversation. It probably had a lot to do with the large, peculiarly-shaped parcel he carried, which looked as if it might escape from his arms at any moment.

'Happy Anniversary, Mum,' said Sam, handing over the gift with both hands into her surprised arms, as if filling them would ensure all the focus of the conversation went on the gift rather than awkward introductions. It had taken time and ingenuity to wrap up the beautiful life-size polished wood carving of a mallard duck about to take awkward flight – or maybe it had just come into land. Either way, as soon as Sam spotted it at the gallery in a small Devon town we'd stopped at on our way home, he'd not hesitated.

'Well, doesn't this look interesting? Thank you, darling.'

'And this is Jess.'

Sam's mum turned to me to me and I was grateful for

the gift-wrapped barrier that put paid to any social dosey-doeing around whether we should kiss on the cheek, once, twice or three times, or just shake hands. She gave me a smile – the polite, company sort of smile that tipped up her mouth and skirted her eyes. Not completely warm, but not completely cold.

'Hello, nice to meet you.'

'Hi, yes. Erm … these are for you.' At least I'd got the gift right because her eyes lit up with immediate pleasure – thank you Aunty Lynn – as she exclaimed, 'Oh, aren't they gorgeous?' She beamed. 'How did you know I love delphiniums? And what a pretty pot. Would you mind?' She nodded towards a table on the edge of the patio for me to put the pot. 'That's very kind of you.' With a charming laugh she followed me and turned to Sam as she put his gift on the table next to mine.

'Darling, did you want me to open this now?'

'No, it can wait until later,' said Sam. 'Then if you absolutely hate it, you don't have to pretend.'

'Sam, I'm sure it will be—'

'Blue smurf moneybox?' he teased.

'I'd forgotten about that,' her face fell momentarily before her eyes, so like Sam's, lit up with amusement, 'but you were only seven.' With a laugh, she turned to me. 'Of course, the horrid thing had to go in pride of place on the mantlepiece.'

I winced in sympathy. 'Hideous?'

'Oh, completely. I blame Miles. I wouldn't mind, but we'd only just had the lounge done – teal and elephant's breath. It was all supposed to be very tasteful.'

'This is tasteful, I promise. Isn't it, Jess?' He slung his arm around me.

'Don't bring me into this,' I said, tipping my head up, laughing into his face. 'I've only just met your mother. I want her to like me.'

'If it's hideous, I'll hide it in the spare bedroom,' said his mother, eying the parcel a little more warily now. 'Now, would you like a drink? There's plenty of Prosecco, or white wine, or rosé. And beer.'

'Prosecco?' asked Sam. I nodded as he disappeared towards the kitchen.

'Are Lynn and Richard here?' I asked, scanning the groups of people dotted around the immaculate lawn.

'Not yet. But then they do have a fair distance to travel.' Her eyes twinkled and inside I felt some of my nerves uncoil.

I laughed and glanced towards the hedge separating the two gardens. 'I expect they'll be the last to arrive.'

'Yes.' Sam's mum laughed. 'It's one of those laws that really needs to have a name, like Murphy's law or Sod's law. They are such lovely neighbours; since the day we moved in they've been so welcoming and friendly. We're so lucky. We lived in our last house for twenty years and barely spoke to the neighbours there.'

'Yes, I'm lucky to have them. I lived with them for quite a while when I was little.' Surprised by this admission, I added, 'My mum was quite ill. So Lynn's really like another mum.' I looked toward the upper storey of Richard and Lynn's house, which was clearly visible above the thick, leafy hedge. 'Their house is like my second home.'

'That's nice.' Her smile, although definitely a little warmer, still held a spine of cool reserve. I could see her looking around at her other guests.

'Thank you for inviting me today. I know it must have been awkward,' I blurted out.

'I just want Sam to be happy.' Her eyes, so like his, were candid and open, as she levelled a stare at me. 'That's all I want. I just hope he's done the right thing.'

Ouch. My heart thudded uncomfortably and I swallowed hard at the spiky lump of disappointment lodged in my throat. *Give her a chance. This is all new to her*, I told myself. Sam had upset the status quo, one that she'd been quite happy with. I should be grateful I'd been invited. I opened my mouth, wanting to defend myself, but it was too important a moment to mess up and I couldn't think of what to say, so I ended up saying nothing.

'I really ought to circulate, but it's nice to meet you, Jess.' Polite enough words, but I felt the dismissal resonate through them.

I winced as I watched her walk away. It wasn't an unconditional success, nor was it a complete disaster. I stood for a moment on my own, watching the other well-dressed guests, most of whom were in their fifties and sixties, talk and chat. They all clearly knew each other well; they had that easy camaraderie and confidence with each other. I smoothed the silk of my dress and studied the flowers in the nearest bed, recognising a few of the plants. I felt unusually lost. What had happened to Sam? Had he been ambushed by an elderly relative?

I tracked him down in the kitchen where he was talking to his dad, another man and … there she was, in all her glossy, gilded glory. A far cry from virago Victoria, the last time we'd seen her. Even so, my heart still clenched with an unwelcome sensation of anxiety and the thought of facing the enemy. But she wasn't really, was she? I thought of my mother and the depth of her pain and how she'd let it define her for too long.

Victoria was just the person who'd come before me in Sam's affections. Erin's revelations had also made me feel a little sorry for her. Although her supermarket snark and subsequent distress made me wary. Was it any wonder she was so possessive of Sam? Four years of constancy with Sam must have been a revelation after her upbringing, although I was sure she'd wouldn't welcome my sympathy. I realised that having an Aunty Lynn at such a crucial moment in my life had saved me.

I stood for a moment watching the four of them, a composite group laughing in unison. Victoria's hand was on Sam's arm, her fingers patting him as she talked animatedly to the two older men, her head flicking backwards and forwards between them. She looked supremely confident, sure of her place, and I didn't want or need to disrupt that balance; I had nothing to prove. I was totally sure of Sam's love.

'And then Sam did the most amazing cover drive,' Victoria said, turning her head and beaming at him, proudly and fondly.

OK, *proudly* and *fondly* irked me. Where was the line? Was there even a line? I'd never really thought about it before, but there had to be some sort of divide between being a girlfriend and not being a girlfriend anymore, didn't there? And if there was, was it the same for everyone? Or was it deeply personal? Did it depend on the couple, the break-up, the new relationship?

All I knew was that my hackles were up, and I'm mostly a hackle-free type of person. They were up with shouty, capital-letter, back-off-lady vibes that I wasn't the least bit proud of. It felt like she was straying near *a* line, in a deliberate, toe-in-the-water, let's-see-how-far-I-can-push-this tactic. *Proudly* and *fondly* twanged strings that I didn't feel comfortable with.

'Honest.' Her hand slipped up to his shoulder, her fingers straying to the skin on his neck with comfortable ease. An unconscious gesture born of habit and familiarity. I might have forgiven it but for the fact that Sam didn't so much as flinch. 'It went straight to the boundary. I don't think the fielders saw it coming.' He still felt comfortable with her. That hurt a little more than it should.

'Not lost any of your talent then, young Sam?' observed the other man. 'I expect we'll be seeing you playing for County again before too long.'

'That would be nice,' said Sam, 'but I haven't had the call yet.'

My stomach twisted. The two of them looked right together. Dance partners that had segued into the old choreography straightaway.

'You had a lot of injury problems last year, and the year

before,' said his dad, clapping his hand on Sam's other shoulder. 'Give it time. You're having a great season this year.'

'I'm sure it's only a matter of time. You're playing brilliantly.' Victoria gave him a suddenly intimate, knowing smile, her voice slightly lowered as if imparting some secret, which yes, I admit, made me want to slap her. A hitherto unrealised jealousy reared its ugly head and I felt the mean-spiritedness of it writhing like poison through my veins. Even so, I marshalled all my self-discipline to stop myself. 'I know the selectors are keeping a close eye on you.'

I bit my lip, loath to intrude. I was not going to make a scene, but neither was I going to slink away – and then Sam looked up. I caught the quick flash of guilt that shot across his face, as if he'd been caught doing something he shouldn't, which only made it worse.

'Jess. I bet you're gasping. Sorry. One Prosecco.' He turned and scooped up a glass from the kitchen bench behind him. 'This is Dad, Uncle Jeff and,' there was the briefest of pauses, 'Victoria.'

'Hello,' I said, forcing my mouth into a smile which was supposed to encompass them all. Had I practised for this moment? Hell yes. The bathroom mirror had done sterling work this morning with various versions of the oh-it's-you look of startled interest along with the more difficult indifferent, gracious, I'm-cool-with-you-even-if-you-did-hijack-my-first-date-and-call-me-a-skank–and–verbally–abuse–us–in–Tesco expression.

My foolish – duh, incredibly stupid – hope that Victoria

might have finally got used to the idea of Sam and me and was going to be civilised shrivelled and died at the sight of the flinty, you're-going-to-suffer-a-painful-death-one-day glare that she shot my way. I didn't hold out much hope for my chances if she got any closer to that butcher's knife block on her left.

'Jess, nice to meet you.' Sam's dad stepped forward, his forced cheer cutting through the sudden atmosphere. The diplomatic corps had been denied a star in the making. 'As well as *Dad*, I'm also known as Miles. You can call me Miles.' He had Sam's big friendly smile, and none of his wife's earlier reserve. I wanted to hug him.

'Nice to meet you too.' Nerves and Victoria's cool murderous gaze, which, although I avoided, I could feel down to every last goosebump, made me chatty. 'You've done an amazing job on the garden. Uncle Richard has severe lawn-envy. I'd watch him if he offers to cut the grass next time you go away.'

Miles laughed. 'Garden wars! I'll watch out for that.' And with that quick easy exchange, I knew I'd been accepted, and I breathed a tad easier.

'And I'm Miles's better-looking and younger brother,' said Uncle Jeff, holding out a wiry arm to shake my hand. 'Always nice to meet a beautiful young lady. And you're a friend of Sam's, are you?'

Miles closed his eyes briefly before lifting them heavenward. Victoria's mouth flattened.

'Yes,' I said, keeping it short and sweet. What else could I say without causing embarrassment to everyone? 'My aunt and uncle live next door.'

'That's nice,' said Jeff. 'And of course, you know this cracker, young Victoria.'

'Er...' OK, now we were straying into awkward territory. Did I acknowledge that we'd met once before? Probably best left.

Luckily, Jeff, Mr Avuncular, didn't need a response. Instead, he turned to Victoria, oblivious to his near brush with death. 'You and Sam have been going steady for a good few years now.' He prodded at Sam with his elbow, winking at me as if to include me in the gang. 'When are you going to make an honest woman of her? You youngsters, you don't half drag things out. You want to snap Victoria up, Sam. If I were forty years younger...'

Sam, Victoria, Miles and I all froze, not one of us daring to look at each other.

'I'll leave you to explain that one, Sam,' snapped Victoria, her whole body radiating incandescent fury as she grabbed her wine glass and marched away with an explosive toss of her glossy brown hair.

'Oh dear,' said Jeff, with the benign bumbling affability of the socially inept, looking at Sam with puzzlement. 'Had a bit of tiff, have we?'

'Victoria and I aren't together anymore,' said Sam, his jaw tight.

'Oh.' Poor Jeff's face went through a series of expressions as he tried to backtrack through everything he'd said and make sense of Sam's strained announcement. 'Ah, that's a bit of a shame. Lovely girl like that.' Then he clapped Sam on the back. 'Never mind. You'll soon patch things up. Play your cards right, I'm sure a sensible lad like you will work it out. Sometimes you have to do a bit of grovelling. She'll come back.'

'Jeff, why don't you come and see the garden,' suggested Miles, his mouth twisted with wry apology as he looked at me. If I liked him before, I liked him even more now. There was a quiet gentleness about him that made him feel like an ally.

'Garden? I've seen the garden.'

'You need to see it again,' said Miles firmly, taking his brother's arm and leading him away.

'OK,' said a rather bewildered Jeff.

There was a long-drawn-out silence as Sam and I stared at each other, unsure what to say while the tension took its time to settle, like dust motes gradually sinking back into place.

'Ouch, sorry, Jess. Bloody Uncle Jeff. I could have put money on it.' Sam shook his head.

My smile was tight. Something like this had been inevitable. 'I guess the worst is over now,' I said. 'Your poor dad… He was mortified.'

'Yeah, although he's used to Jeff putting his feet in things. You OK?'

'Sure. We always knew it was going to be awkward.'

'Not *that* awkward.' He leaned forward and lifted my chin to kiss me. 'But like you say, the worst is over.'

Was it? Somehow I doubted it very much. At least Jeff's faux pas had diverted us from his own. He'd been so busy chatting, he'd forgotten all about me waiting for him in the garden, and now wasn't the time to bring it up. We needed to put on a united front as there were quite a few people keeping a watchful eye on us.

We left the kitchen and joined a group of people on the lawn, friends of Miles and Sally who'd clearly known Sam for a very long time. When Sam introduced me to Gaynor, Mike, Felicity and Steven, I could feel their barely constrained curiosity, but everyone was pleasant enough. Throughout the conversation, Victoria never seemed to stray very far from my peripheral vision, flitting from group to group with charming hellos, greeting everyone with warm kisses and delighted smiles. Was I being paranoid? With every easy engagement and greeting, it felt as if she was deliberately making it very clear that, like some war correspondent, she was embedded in the Weaverham family. I fought to keep my spirits afloat, so it was a massive relief when Aunty Lynn and Uncle Richard arrived. They went straight over to Sally and Miles who were now standing a few feet away from Sam and me.

'Happy Anniversary, Sally,' said Aunty Lynn presenting her with a beautiful bouquet of white flowers that you could just tell had been specially selected down at the local florists. Aunty Lynn was one of the kindest and warmest people I knew, and she was particularly big on finding gifts for people that she knew they would love.

'Aren't they gorgeous? All my favourites.' Sally's eyes lit up. 'How absolutely beautiful, thank you, Lynn.' She stuck her nose straight into the extravagant display, her genuine pleasure apparent.

Victoria materialised by her elbow. 'Hello, Lynn.'

'Hello, how are you?' responded Lynn with a friendly smile. Lynn had met Victoria before? That was a bit of a shocker. Did she know who she was? Had Sam and I ever mentioned her behaviour in front of Lynn and Richard? Would Shelley have mentioned the Facebook episode? Lynn definitely wouldn't have approved of that.

'I'm very well, thank you. Gorgeous day for a party, isn't it?' Victoria was all smiles and completely comfortable in the situation. 'Would you like me to get a vase for those, Sally, and put them in water?'

'Oh, darling, would you?' said Sally turning to her, with a fond smile. 'That would be lovely.'

'The blue or the cut glass?' asked Victoria, being super helpful, and although she didn't look my way, I knew that she was completely aware that I was there. Did she know Lynn was my aunt?

'Mmm,' Sally considered for a second, 'The blue, I think. What do you reckon?'

'Definitely the blue.' Victoria beamed at her, shot me a triumphant little smirk, and disappeared through the French windows in the house.

'What can I get you to drink?' asked Miles as Lynn caught sight of me.

'Jess!' She moved to my side to give me a big hug. 'Hello, sweetheart, where's Sam? How's your week been? How's your mum?' As she asked the flurry of questions, she turned back to Miles and said, 'Thanks, Miles, I'd love a glass of Prosecco.'

'And you, Richard?'

'Beer, if you have it.'

A discussion about which beers ensued and the men gravitated back to the makeshift bar set up on the patio near the kitchen.

Sally looked at her watch. 'I ought to think about serving food.'

'Would you like some help?' I asked.

'Oh no, thank you. It's all under control.' And with that she disappeared back to the house and the minute she was out of earshot, the question spilled out, 'So how do you know Victoria?'

Lynn looked a little surprised. 'What's wrong with her?'

'Nothing,' I said.

Lynn wasn't stupid and she knew me far too well. She raised a motherly eyebrow that said she didn't believe a word of it and reminded me a little of my own mother's language skill with a facial twitch.

'That's Sam's ex. The one he went out with for four years.'

'Oh! That's her?' said Lynn. 'I didn't realise.' She wrinkled her face. 'She was here when I popped in for coffee the other day and she dropped in when Sally and I were going off to a flower arranging thing last week. I didn't realise she was Sam's ex but that makes sense now. I just assumed she was the daughter of a close friend or something.' She frowned. 'It must be difficult for Sally if they've been good friends.'

'Yes, of course it is, and there's no reason why Sally shouldn't see her.'

'Although...' Lynn gave me a worried look, 'she does

seem to drop in an awful lot. She still seems very at home here. Is everything all right?'

'Yes, it's fine.' I glanced across the garden at Sam's blond head and in the same moment he looked my way with a lazy smile, his mouth curving and his blue eyes crinkling as if remembering some secret between us. My heart expanded at the quiet intimacy of the smile. 'More than fine,' I added in a quiet voice.

Lynn gave me a sharp look, her grey eyes studying my face in a motherly, proprietary way, assessing and checking before she liked what she saw, and her expression relaxed into gentle pride.

'I'm happy for you.' She leaned forward and gave me a hug, squeezing me hard, and said with a tiny catch in her voice that probably only Shelley or I would have heard, 'You're such a good girl, Jess. You deserve to be happy. The more I see of him, the more I like him.'

I squeezed her back. 'He makes me happy.'

'Good, there's not been enough of that. I worry about you.' She gave me a kiss on my cheek. 'You look … happy.' Then she heaved in a large breath and with a naughty grin asked, 'I think Joan definitely approves?'

I laughed. 'She likes him because he spent an hour talking about Test Match Special at Gladys's wedding.'

Lynn sent Sam's long blond hair an unsubtle glance and smiled. 'That's good then.'

I laughed again. 'Before she met him she was worried about tattoos; the hair was a relief.'

Lynn shuddered. 'I wish Shelley hadn't got that horrible

one on her ankle. Honestly, when she's seventy, it's going to look ridiculous.'

Much as I love my cousin and do keep most of her confidences, the thing is, I love my aunt to bits and that little line of distress marking her face hurt me. 'Shall I let you into a secret?' I paused, not for one moment feeling the least bit guilty about revealing the truth. 'It's not a real tattoo; it's a temporary one that she keeps reapplying. They only last two weeks. She's winding you up.'

'Thank fuck for that.'

'Aunty Lynn!' Her heartfelt response almost made my eyes pop out of my head; she *never* used the F word.

'Well, it's been so hard not commenting, but it's hideous. And I do try to be fair-minded and not judgy but...' She shook her head and then scrunched up her mouth. 'And talking of which, just watch Victoria. I'm not sure she's the sort of girl that will give up without a fight.'

'I think I'd already got that.'

'Hungry? Mum's been cooking for days.' Sam came up behind me and put his arms around my waist, kissing my bare shoulder. 'Hey, Lynn, how're you doing?'

She beamed at Sam and held up her glass, the sun shining through the bubbles rising with satisfying continuity. 'I have Prosecco, I'm with my favourite niece, and I have a gorgeous garden to look at on a beautiful sunny day, and...' she paused before grinning at him, 'I don't have to do any cooking or tidying up.'

Sam joined in my snort of laughter. 'You love it, Aunty Lynn,' I said.

'I know but it's nice to be entertained by someone else for a change, and Sally really has gone to town.'

The table just inside the French doors was rapidly filling up with bowls and plates, which were being ferried from the kitchen by Sally, another lady who Sam told me was one of his aunts, and Victoria.

'I'm starving. Come on, someone has to start. Everyone's being polite,' said Sam taking my hand and leading me forward to the buffet.

Sally was surveying the table when we entered the room, Victoria at her side, a plate in each hand.

'If you can put one at each end of the table, that would be perfect. Then we need to get the cheese straws out of the oven.'

'I can do that. Which plate would you like me to serve them on?' asked Victoria.

'I'm thinking the one we bought in Portugal—'

'Oh yes,' Victoria shot me a quick look, triumphant with a touch of don't-forget-who's-Queen-Bee-here. 'Wasn't that man funny? I thought you were going to have to buy an entire place setting. He really wasn't happy about only selling one.'

Sally laughed. 'Obviously thought I was made of money, but it was a lovely shop. Have you still got those cute little egg cups you bought?'

'Yes, they're on the windowsill. They're far too nice to use and I'd hate to break one. That was such a wonderful holiday.' She lifted her head and gave Sally a smile tinged with poignant, brave sadness. Sally put an arm around her, unaware of Sam and me standing in the doorway, and they walked back into the kitchen. Just as they passed through the door, Victoria looked back, her eyes zeroing in on me, a delighted little smirk playing at her lips.

Pass me the sick-bucket. Seriously, how old was this woman? Any sympathy I'd had for her vanished in one fell swoop. What a bitch! I thought I'd been pretty patient with Victoria's I'm-the-indispensable-daughter-in-law routine throughout the afternoon and wasn't ignorant of the point she was making; she'd rather hammered it home. I got it: she and Sally were great friends; she belonged here and I didn't. Game, set and match to Victoria.

When she looked my way with another one of those victorious little smirks, I was through being polite and playing nice, I rolled my eyes and turned my back on her.

Obvious, much.

Everyone piled in for the food and the crush filling the room meant Victoria and her busy, busy, hostess act were subsumed by the crowd. With plates piled high, everyone then drifted back out into the garden to sit in small groups. Sam and I gravitated to Lynn and Richard, who'd bagged the end of the large wooden table and had been joined by Fiona, who lived next-door-but-one to them with her husband, Mitch. Cocooned by my family, with Sam's leg resting against mine under the table, I pushed Victoria's pettiness away and enjoyed the feel of his skin, the soft teasing of Uncle Richard, Aunty Lynn's gentle observations, and the general sense of happiness and contentment that hung in the air.

Puddings were brought out and glasses were refilled with more Prosecco, and then the tinkle of metal against glass brought everyone to a standstill as Miles called the guests to order.

'Thank you all for coming today.' His voice gained strength as he spoke, turning to encompass everyone in the garden now watching him, and Sally at his side. 'It is wonderful to see so many friends and family here today. I'm not going to waffle on—'

'Thank God for that,' yelled Uncle Jeff from the back of the garden.

'—but I did want to say a few words.' He looked at his wife standing by his side and took her hand.

'Thirty-five years… I was going to make a joke about it being a longer sentence than you get for murder…' Gentle laughter rippled through the guests. 'But,' his fingers tightened on Sally's hand, 'thirty-five years is half a lifetime, and what a lifetime it's been. I still think I'm the luckiest man in the world, and the very first time I saw Sally, there was something about her. Something special.'

Sally pulled a face and groaned.

He turned and laughed. 'We didn't actually speak for another month, but I still remember that very first glimpse of her, in Woolworths in Ramsgate.'

'God, that uniform was hideous – a nylon special,' said Sally, shaking her head but smiling all the while.

'It took me a while to summon up the courage to ask her out,' said Miles. 'I was a lowly stockroom boy, working during my university break, and she was a glamorous Saturday girl. But once I got to know her, we became the best of friends, and that friendship grew and grew, and one day, I realised she was the person I wanted to spend the rest of my life with. Sally's still my best friend, but she's also the woman I love with all my heart.'

There was a collective sigh and my pulse skipped a little at his quiet, earnest words. When Sam's fingers interlaced with mine, I risked a quick look at his face, my heart ballooning in my chest cavity. His eyes softened as they rested on my face, glowing with a confident, knowing smile as if he had all the answers and I was the only person he could possibly share them with.

'I'd like you to raise your glasses. If we have three score and ten, then Sally and I have enjoyed half a lifetime of marriage,' Miles lifted his champagne flute and turned to face his wife, 'and I'm hoping we'll spend the rest of our lifetime enjoying the rest.'

A quiet calm held while everyone raised their glasses, silenced by the emotion before, bit by bit, the hum of kind, good-natured chat began to pick up again, reflecting the general atmosphere of warmth that rippled through the smiling guests.

I really needed to pee, but the downstairs loo just off the utility room was already occupied by someone who, judging by the sound coming from the poorly soundproofed room, appeared to have a camel-sized bladder. I had no idea people could pee for that long. It was seriously impressive – or rather, it would have been if I hadn't been crossing my legs with such desperation.

When at last the woman emerged with an apologetic smile, I realised she'd clearly heard my shuffling and tapping as I'd waited.

I'd just parked myself down and enjoyed the merciful gush of relief when I heard a woman's voice as clearly as if she were standing next to me, which, plasterboard partition notwithstanding, she might well have been.

'Such a shame, Sally. It must be so hard for you. Do you want me to take that? Poor Victoria.'

I closed my eyes with dread, wondering whether I ought to cough loudly.

A cupboard door closed, there was the chink of china or glass and the thud of something on the melamine counter outside the loo.

'Yes, I really do feel for her. Thank you, if you could just grab the jug. She's been such a trooper today, insisted on coming to help me. I mean, the party's been planned for months, there was no way she wasn't invited, although I did say I'd understand if she didn't want to come. Bless her, she said she wouldn't miss it for the world and she'd be all right.' There was a pause and I squirmed on the loo seat. This was one conversation I could do without overhearing.

'I could strangle Sam, I really could.' There was a vehemence to Sally's voice that was at odds with the cool, calm woman who'd been serenity and grace embodied all day. I shrank down into the seat, as if making myself invisible in some way might also magic me away from the scene or render me deaf.

'I don't know what's got into him. He's far too young to be having a midlife crisis. Everything was fine with him and Victoria. That's what makes it so difficult to understand. It's also doubly difficult because this girl is the niece of Lynn and Richard, who are lovely. Great neighbours and Lynn is such good company.'

'Is she not very nice, the new girl?'

'I've no idea, she might be perfectly lovely, but it all seems so random. Why throw four years away? It's not as if he and Victoria weren't getting on or anything. They were fine. One minute they were booking a holiday to Turkey, the next Sam's ... well, when he called and said he had something to tell me, I honestly thought he was telling me he was going to ask Victoria to marry him. Instead he stands there and tells me he's met someone else and decided to finish with Victoria. I just don't understand it.'

'Perhaps it's just a passing fancy, you know – get it out of his system before he does settle.'

'God, I hope so. Poor Victoria is heartbroken. Absolutely devastated. She's putting on a brave face today, but I know the poor girl is desperate. I feel so sorry for her. She has no idea what made him change his mind so suddenly. That's what makes it so hard. There's just no rhyme or reason. She's still in love with him and she can't believe that he doesn't love her anymore. I mean, how do you go from loving someone one day to not the next? It doesn't make any sense.'

'Would she have him back?'

'Oh God, yes, in a shot. She knows Sam better than anyone. She says it's completely out of character. Like you said, all their friends are settling down, getting married, and she's convinced this is a bit of a panic, a knee-jerk thing.'

'What do you think?'

'I think he and Victoria will get back together once he's got this girl out of his system. I mean, I'm sure she's very nice but ... well, I don't know what's so special about her. From what Sam says, he seems to think it's love at first sight. I ask you. But you can't tell them, can you? Bless him. I love my son, but seriously, it's just an infatuation, but he's too ... infatuated to see it.' There was a heavy sigh from Sally. 'And I could kill him for throwing his cricketing career away. All over this girl. He's always wanted to play Test Match cricket. But this wretched creature has messed that up. No wonder the selectors are overlooking him this season. Apparently they are not impressed that he's missed so many matches, and I can't nag him about it because we've barely been speaking. Honestly, he was so diligent about practising. Always at nets. He'd never miss a match and now ... well, I get the impression he's not interested at all.'

My stomach turned over and over, as I bent over my knees, my face buried in the rich blue silk pooling around my thighs, waiting for the sick, light-headed sensation to pass.

'Oh, can you pass me that cake-stand in the corner? That should do it. I ordered a hundred cup-cakes and now I'm thinking we're going to be eating them for weeks.'

'Perhaps you could give people party bags as they leave,' suggested the other voice, growing fainter.

I straightened up, conscious of my knickers around my

ankles and the sheen of sweat across my forehead. I needed to get out of here quickly before they came back. As fast as I could, I washed my hands, pulled back the lock, and peered the through the gap in the door, just as my phone started to ring, giving me a minor heart attack. Thank God it hadn't rung a few seconds earlier.

Chapter Twenty-Four

'Houston, we have a problem,' drawled Holly's voice as I scuttled out of the front door to take the call on the doorstep away from earshot.

Holly was on call this weekend, and it was rare for her to phone me unless there was a real emergency.

'What's happened?' I sank onto the doorstep, crossing my fingers that nothing terrible had happened, feeling the kick of my pulse.

'Jake's school inadvertently posted a picture of him on Twitter.'

'Oh shit.' Social media was one of our biggest enemies. All it took was a picture of a child in a logoed sweatshirt online and it wasn't difficult to track down the school. To be fair, the schools all got it. They were pretty vigilant about photos and social media; the problem was often other parents.

'Dad spotted it. Stormed into the school on Friday demanding to see the kid.'

'And did we know?' Stupid question, because if we had, we'd have known about it on Friday afternoon before we'd knocked off for the weekend.

'Nope. The head was out. Deputy head out. Mum told the school she'd let us know. Of course she didn't because she's terrified. The school office arranged transport home for her, and they sneaked her and the kid out of the back entrance, so Dad couldn't follow.'

'And we're sure he didn't?'

'Well, no one's come pounding on the door all weekend, so that's as much as I can hope.' Holly's voice sounded resigned. 'I knew something wasn't right with Cathy, but you know how quiet she is.'

'Yes,' I said, my voice quiet and calm. There was no point getting cross; no one did these things deliberately and Holly and I were not there to judge. There were reasons we had protocols and policies, but every now and then someone slipped up. They were only human.

'She kept herself to herself all weekend and then about half an hour ago, Jake became hysterical. It all came out. He's terrified of going to school again.'

'Oh God, poor boy. Did he see his dad on Friday?'

'No, but he knew he'd been there.'

That was enough. School was supposed to be the safe place. The refuge was supposed to be a safe place. Beyond the reach of dads who were handy with their fists, loose of temper and purveyors of uncertain moods.

'Do you want me to come in?'

'Yes,' said Holly, no nonsense or prevarication. 'Everyone's very twitchy. Cathy's convinced her ex is going to turn up. I could do with you here to put on a united front and go over our lockdown procedure with everyone to reassure them all. How soon can you get here?'

I looked down at my dress. 'Give me forty-five minutes. I need to nip home.'

'Great. I'll see you then.'

I disconnected the call and sat for a minute, rubbing my face, aware of the odd peal of laughter as I thought about the little boy, Jake. Eight years old, with a black eye that had taken a week to fade. I felt disconnected and separate and had to focus on my blue silk dress, brilliant and bold, to anchor me. Beyond me, the sounds of the party vibrated in the air – amiable chatter and a contented, untroubled atmosphere.

It took me a while to rise to my feet, my knees stiff from crouching and my bottom numb from the stone step. As I made my way back into the dim interior after the blinding sunlight, I stumbled on a step, feeling disorientated and out of touch.

Unaware of anyone else, I headed back to the spot where I'd left Sam. He'd moved and was now in a corner deep in urgent conversation with Victoria. Really? I so was not in the mood to deal with this now. I needed to get out of here and fast.

She looked up with another of those – what I was coming to think of as her trademark – smirks.

'Jess.' Sam's relief was palpable and then, with unerring instinct, he honed in on my face and the phone in my hand. 'Is everything all right?' He knew Holly was on call this weekend.

We exchanged a private look and I shook my head very slightly. I didn't need to spell anything out.

'Do we need to leave?'

'Gosh, she's got you on a short leash,' said Victoria, her basilisk eyes cold and full of venom. 'But...'

'Vic—' Sam started but I interrupted him. I wasn't in the mood to play nice or to play games. My brief call with Holly had put things back into perspective.

I held up a hand, flat, no nonsense and gave her a steady, uncompromising look, as blank and unemotional as I could make it. I was through being pleasant or conciliatory. There were bigger things to worry about in life than whether she liked me or not.

'I'm not interested. There's no reason for me to dislike you, unless you give me one. I have nothing against you. I realise we can't be friends, but there's no reason for us to be enemies. I did not cause this situation.'

Her lip curled. 'Who the fuck do you think you are? Mother bloody Theresa?' She was almost popping on her toes, trying to hold in her indignant anger.

I shrugged. 'I have no argument with you.'

'Well, I bloody well do with you. You're not going to get away with this.' She turned to Sam. 'You do realise that none of our friends are going to have anything to do with her.'

'Vic, you're being ridiculous. None of this is Jess's fault. It's mine.'

'She should have left you alone. You were going out with someone.'

Sam sighed and shook his head. 'I'm trying to be nice

here and you're not listening. I didn't start seeing Jess until a month after we'd split up.'

'And we'd never have split up if it weren't for her. You're telling me she did nothing.'

Sam and I looked at each other.

'Don't make a scene at Mum's party,' said Sam in a low voice, rarely heard anger simmering in his tone. 'It's not fair on her. I know what you've been doing today. You shouldn't have come.'

'I shouldn't have come!' snapped Victoria. 'You don't know anything. This is your mother's party. She invited me. Not *her*.' She levelled a malevolent glare my way. 'You're breaking Sally's heart. Everything was fine until *she* turned up and couldn't keep her knickers on.'

Sam stepped forward, his blue eyes blazing, his arms ramrod-straight by his side. 'Don't you dare! This isn't on Jess. It's on me. I've told you. It's over, Vic. I'm sorry and I've said sorry a dozen times, I can't change how I feel, but you have no right to take it out on Jess. This is on me. You need to accept it's over and stay away from us and my family.'

'*Your* family,' she spat. 'You think you can just toss four years away without so much as a backward glance. I don't think so. You owe me. And don't try and tell me that Miss butter-wouldn't-melt is blameless.' She gave me another spiteful glance. 'I've met women like you before. You don't give a toss who gets hurts as long as you get what you want, and then once you've got it, you move on to the next poor sap. Sam will see through you eventually, even if he doesn't realise your game yet.'

With malice glowing in her eyes, she turned back to him. 'She'll get bored with you; she's got her prey now. When she spits you out, you'll come crawling back.'

Sam glanced at me and then back at Victoria. 'You've got it all wrong. There were no games,' he felt for my hand and took it, 'no chasing. I can't help how I feel.'

I saw the hit that Victoria took, a tiny flinch of pain that she hid well, but she slowed down and it took a moment for her to get back up to speed. 'Infatuation, more like.' She gave me a dismissive up and down look as if she couldn't begin to understand why he could possibly be interested, let alone infatuated. 'You're going to regret it. You'll soon realise what a mistake you've made. And you've made a huge one. Everyone thinks so. Your mum. Mike. Paige. My dad. Everyone at the club.' Her eyes narrowed in quick sly triumph.

My phone buzzed in my hand, a text from Holly. I glanced at it quickly. Confirmation that the social worker had managed to book an appointment at 9.30 with the headteacher at Jake's school, and a timely reminder that she needed my support. I needed to be elsewhere.

'Sorry, Sam,' my voice was husky with worry, 'but I need to go. I've got to get to work.' I held up my phone.

'OK.' He immediately put his hand out and slipped it into mine. 'Let's find Mum and Dad and say goodbye.' Ever the gentleman, he turned to her and said, 'Sorry, Victoria, but we've got to go.'

He didn't even wait for her response, just tugged me away, squeezing my fingers with his.

Chapter Twenty-Five

'**H**ow's everyone this morning?' I asked, tugging off my cardigan and chucking it on my desk on Monday morning. The lockdown briefing and practice had gone well the previous evening and between us we'd managed to reassure the collective anxiety, although Cathy was still very nervous.

The office was already stuffy and the windows, complete with bars, were as wide as they would open. 'They're wary and unsettled.' The lockdown had been a timely reminder of how easy it was for things to go wrong.

'Cathy's terrified.' I'd just travelled back from Jake's school with her in the car, her hand gripping the door handle the whole way. 'But I'm hoping we've reminded everyone that they're safe here and that we can look after them.'

Lockdown was the description for the alarm we raised if there was a possible intruder outside the house or someone was trying to get in. We had strict procedures with regard to opening the front door and there were high fences all around the property but there was still always the possibility that someone might try to get in. It had never happened at this particular refuge, but Holly had worked in one where an irate husband had managed to track his wife down and for an unnerving half-hour had tried to break down the door with an axe until the police arrived.

'Fair dos. How was the meeting this morning? The head suitably penitent?'

'It wasn't her fault. Some stupid parent. Posted Sports Day pictures. Didn't help that Jake had been on WhatsApp to an old school friend and told him he'd moved to this area. Narrowed down Dad's search.'

'Oh shit. So is he changing schools or sticking with that one?'

'The head's loath for him to leave; he's just started to settle and he's quite a bright spark. Loves his running. Doing well in class. Made a couple of friends. He'd really started to come out of his shell these last couple of weeks. The school are confident that they can keep him safe during school hours. It's a big site, and even if Dad is hanging around outside, he can't get close enough to the playground to identify his son.'

'Still, Dad knows he's there.'

'Yeah.' I sighed and slid into my chair. 'It's not ideal. The social work team are having an emergency meeting this afternoon, but they feel they can support Cathy. We just need to remind the cab company to be vigilant, let Cathy know she's safe here and make sure he doesn't get hold of this address.'

It wasn't until lunchtime that we managed to grab a break, taking our coffee and packed lunches out into the scrubby garden with its donated tables and chairs and a solitary umbrella.

'So, how was the party yesterday? Sorry I had to drag you away.'

'You couldn't have timed it better,' I replied, drooping a little.

'What?' Holly's kohl-black eyes narrowed.

'Sam's ex was there.'

'Tasteless.'

'She's one of the family.'

'Still tasteless.'

'And Sam's mum's hoping they'll get back together. They're quite close.' I thought of Victoria flitting about all afternoon being indispensable.

'No way. That's rude.' She paused. 'Hang on. She told you that? I got the impression she was all floral prints, clean fingernails and hair done at the salon.'

I snorted a laugh. 'That does sound remarkably like Sam's mum; most people would probably call her middle-class middle-England.'

Holly shrugged and slugged down her thick black coffee. 'Well-mannered too. Surely she didn't tell you that to your face?'

'No, an ill-advised conversation outside the downstairs loo, but I heard every word. She thinks Sam's infatuated with me, has had some kind of mid-life crisis, but that he'll see sense, get over me and go back to Victoria.'

Holly gave me a quick appraisal. 'That would be down

to your femme fatale wiles, traffic-stopping Jessica Rabbit figure and those intoxicating pheromones, I'm guessing.' She laughed. 'You should be flattered. After you told her to butt out and piss off.'

'It's Sam's mum. I can't do that.'

'Why the fuck not? A) it's got nothing to do with her, and B) it's still nothing to do with her. Sam, who I've yet to meet, I might add, is a grown man.'

'I know, but she and Sam are close. I don't want to come between them.'

'Too late for that. Seriously, Jess, stop being so bloody nice. You want to watch this Victoria.'

I gave a grim smile. 'By the time it came to Victoria, I lost patience. She's a complete bitch.'

Holly arched an eyebrow. 'That's more like it.'

'Apparently, according to her, everyone thinks Sam's making a huge mistake.'

'Well she would say that, wouldn't she?' said Holly with patent logic. 'Luckily, you know better. You're the best thing that's ever happened to him.'

I beamed at her unconditional support. 'I'd like to think so, although after yesterday I'm still licking my wounds. It feels like a skirmish and both Victoria and Sam's mum drew blood.'

Holly frowned. 'Jess, you're better than this. You know that. I hope you told her where to go.'

'Within the bounds of being at Sam's parents' wedding anniversary party, yes.'

'You're too nice.'

'Not anymore I'm not. I'm over feeling sorry for her,' I

growled, remembering her swanning about at the party as though she were hosting it alongside Sally. It had been deliberate posturing on her part, aided and abetted by Sam's mum but, do you know what? I could live with it. There was no reason for me to see either of them again – Victoria ever, and Sally not for a while.

'What did Sam say?' asked Holly, spot on the money as always.

That was harder to live with. I pressed my lips together before I could speak. 'Sam didn't say much.' At Holly's indignant huff, I explained. 'That's his default when he's upset.' Last night he'd internalised his anger and distress, withdrawing into silence as if he hadn't wanted to inflict it on me. 'He's furious with his mum. I thought I was just being over-sensitive about Victoria being there, but he was really angry about the way his mum treated her as if she were the favourite daughter all afternoon.'

'He's got a point.'

'Yes, but I don't want him to fall out with his mum about it.'

'I'd just lie low for a while. You've got the man. It'll all blow over soon. Just concentrate on you and Sam... And when do I get meet him?'

'Wasn't sure you'd want to...'

'Because I've got a dried-up old fanny?' she drawled with amusement. 'And I've got about as much time for love and romance as I have for a DIY vajazzling.' She shuddered. 'Did I tell you my sister's dyed her muff blue and decorated it with silver star sequins? Offered to come into the refuge and cheer our ladies up.'

'What, flashing her bits?' I asked horrified.

'No, you numpty, apparently vajazzle parties are all the rage. She's just bought into some franchise. Offered to come and demonstrate here for free.'

'Oh God, don't breathe a word in front of Shelley.' I groaned. 'It's the sort of thing she'd love. It's her thirtieth birthday soon. I can imagine her having it done and threatening to flash it at the party. Aunty Lynn has just rumbled her tattoo is fake, Shelley would love to wind her up with something like this.'

Holly snorted and then we both dissolved into giggles, and spent the rest of our lunch hour breaking into laughter periodically.

Holly had a great way of taking my mind off things, so that by the time I was ready to go home, the hideous party and meeting Victoria had faded into insignificance at the back of my mind where they belonged.

Chapter Twenty-Six

With a slice of toast in my mouth and clutching a coffee-to-go cup I hurtled out of the front door with Sam close behind me.

'See you later.' He took the toast out of my mouth, kissed me and then popped it back. I waved my cup at him as he crossed the road to his car and headed to mine. Just another manic Monday morning. We were both dreadful at getting out of bed, hence breakfast in the car.

I slid into the driver's seat already mentally running down my to-do list, as I arranged my bag on the seat next to me, putting my phone out of reach. We had a health and safety inspection today – also known as a right pain in the arse. I had an eighteen-page checklist that the local council representative would be running through. I hoped I could find the boiler inspection paperwork and that none of the children had moved/let off/played with any of the fire extinguishers. Managing the facilities, i.e. looking after the refuge building, was my least favourite bit of the job, but unfortunately it was part of my remit and as a result I was on first-name terms with Kevin the plumber, Josh the garden maintenance guy and Dev the odd-job man who was very good at fixing just about— What the?

My windscreen was smeared with a pattern of greasy finger swirls. Great. Local kids with nothing better to do with their time. Whoever had done it had really gone to town and really made a mess; they'd managed to coat pretty much the whole of the windscreen.

Turning on the engine, I pumped the windscreen wash and turned on the wiper blades. Yuck! It just spread whatever it was across the glass.

I got out of the car and examined the windscreen and put a finger out to touch the viscous mess. Bugger. Oil of some description. With a tissue from my pocket I wiped at a section of the screen and looked at the transferred oil. It was thick and had a dark greenish tinge. Engine oil? I sniffed the tissue. Seriously? I might not be much of a cook but I liked my food, especially Italian. This was high-grade, extra virgin olive oil. Obviously I was dealing with a better class of vandal. But who carried extra virgin olive oil around with them?

Someone who came prepared, that's who. I wrinkled my nose. Or maybe it was just a random act of vandalism – not. Was she ever going to stop this nonsense?

I trudged back to the flat to collect a bowl of hot soapy water, texting Holly as I went. I was going to be so bloody late. She was going to have to entertain James Martin, the health and safety man, who was due at nine o'clock.

Somehow I didn't expect him to have much in common with the gorgeous, famous chef James Martin.

Two bowls of hot water and a quarter of a bottle of Fairy liquid later, I had a windscreen through which I could see, although there were still a few suspect streaks. It was going to have to do. I was now running half an hour late.

I pulled out of the T-junction at the end of the street into the heavy flow of traffic – rush hour was now in full swing and it took me another fifteen minutes to reach the bypass. I was still brooding about my windscreen. Was I being paranoid? Was it Victoria or just some random prank? And then, as if I'd conjured her up, I spotted her car. I knew it was hers because of the number plate. All my spidey senses went on high alert. Since the meeting at the party a couple of weeks ago, everything had gone quiet. There'd been no posts on her Instagram account or Facebook account... I'd hoped it was the sign of a ceasefire. I looked again in my rear-view mirror. Yes, there she was.

Victoria's Mercedes sat three cars behind mine on the A41 heading towards Hemel Hempstead. It was a busy road; there was nothing suspicious about her being on the same road at the same time as me, but I still tensed. Now I was being ridiculous. It was probably purely coincidental, although with a sleek motor like that, why wasn't she steaming down the outside lane instead of pootling along at sixty in the inside lane, driving like an old lady – or like the owner of an old lady? My Ford Fiesta had seen better days, but I couldn't afford to replace it. Keeping an occasional eye on her in my rear-view mirror, I picked up a bit of speed although, as we were going uphill, I had my foot flat to the floor. I pulled out and overtook a couple of cars before sliding back into my rightful place in the slow lane. Behind me, I saw Victoria venture out into the outside lane and catch up before slotting back in behind me two cars back.

Was she following me? A trickle of sweat inched down my spine. It was a day that promised more record-breaking temperatures and my car did not have air conditioning.

When I turned off at my junction, I kept a wary eye on my mirror. Victoria followed, always keeping a few cars back. Why the hell would she follow me? Now the attack on my poor windscreen didn't seem quite so random. Or was I letting my imagination run away with itself?

I drove up through a residential area and Victoria's car was still visible several cars behind, but it was a reasonably popular rat run which lots of people used. What was she up to?

Darting frequent glances at my wing mirrors and rear-view mirror, I came to the final roundabout where I turned off towards the car park I always used. From there it was a short walk to the refuge, the location of which was top secret. Would she take the same exit as me or drive on up the hill? She was only two cars back now. I deliberately didn't indicate and then got a noisy horn blare when another car tried to pull out in front of me as I went round the roundabout.

She took the same exit. Now there were no cars between us. What was she playing at? Trying to get me on my own? She'd soon find out I wasn't easily intimidated if that was her intention. Staying behind me, she kept at a reasonable distance. With no other choice unless I wanted to spend the morning aimlessly driving around Hemel Hempstead, I pulled into the car park and sat there wondering what I was going to do. Would she confront me? To my relief, Victoria's car sailed past the car park entrance and carried on up the hill towards to the Old Town. I wiped my slightly sweaty forehead. So what had that all been about? Had she genuinely been following me? I really was starting to get paranoid where she was concerned. Like I said, it had been all quiet on the Western Front for the last week and I was hopeful that she'd finally given up on Sam. I still couldn't figure out what she'd hoped to achieve by stalking us, apart from causing us hassle. If I hadn't been convinced before, I was now a hundred per cent certain that the oil on my car was courtesy of Victoria or a friend of hers.

From the car park I took my usual ten-minute walk, rushing a little because I was running late, and when the house came into view I ran lightly up the steps and tapped in the security code, taking a quick look down the street. All clear. I was still feeling ridiculously paranoid. Why would Victoria follow me? Thanks to Find My Friends, she'd probably tracked Sam to my flat. Once through the steel reinforced door I closed it behind me and looked up at the red light of the security camera blinking at me before tapping in a second code on a new keypad to open the internal door.

I rushed into the kitchen to find Holly with two mugs of coffee in her hand.

'Slow down, girl. It's OK. Your man, Mr Health and Safety, phoned to say he was running late too.'

'Phew.'

'You're looking very perky this morning.'

'Am I?' I straightened up, pleased my stress wasn't showing.

'Please don't tell me it's the sex. You are becoming unbearably smug. I don't think I can stand sharing an office with you for much longer.'

'It's the sex,' I said, grinning at her, thinking of waking up beside Sam this morning.

She covered her ears and marched into our little office.

'But I'm not feeling perky really. Since I got out of bed, the morning has gone downhill fast.'

'Tell Aunty Holly what's been going on.' Once I'd finished, she said, 'Sounds like Bake Off Wars in your street.'

'I don't think so. I don't think it was random.'

Over coffee I told her about my suspicions that Victoria had been the one to vandalise my car and had been following me.

'Do you think I'm being paranoid?'

'You know those thrillers, where the coincidences start piling up and the heroine dismisses them as coincidences and you're screaming, "Wake up and smell the roses, you dozy cow" – that.'

'You don't think I'm paranoid, then?' I rubbed at my forehead.

Her heavily kohled eyes softened. 'We've heard too many stories here, haven't we?'

'I don't know what to do.'

'Exactly what we recommend our guests to do. Keep a record. Dates, times. It's a form of harassment. Certainly approaching you and Sam at the supermarket was. You need to report it to the police.'

'I can't report her to the police. That's going too far.'

'Why not? It's harassment.'

'But I can't prove the oil was her, or that she was following me this morning.'

'No, but if things escalate they'll take it seriously. Come on, Jess. You know how this works.'

'But this is different. She's not going to cause me any harm.'

'I still think you should go to the police.'

'I can't. It will make things so much worse. Sam's friends already hate me. It will give Victoria more fuel.'

Holly shook her head. 'Listen to yourself. Making excuses. Who do you sound like?'

I cringed. She was right. I sounded like so many of the women that came here. All the reasons why they couldn't go to the police. Why they couldn't report their abusive partners. Friends and relatives not believing them or supporting them was a common theme. But this was different, wasn't it?

'Please tell me you'll think about it.'

Chapter Twenty-Seven

'What do you think?' asked Sam, as the estate agent left us standing outside the dilapidated house.

'It's nice,' I said hesitantly. It was in our price bracket and had everything we wanted. We'd started our new house hunt and a board had gone up on my balcony. With two viewings already on my flat and a potential offer on the table, we needed to get a wiggle on.

'You don't like it.'

With a sigh I lifted my shoulders. 'I don't dislike it.'

'But?'

I shook my head.

'Jess, are you OK?'

'Yes, fine.' No, not really. 'Sorry, I don't think I'm in the mood. This is supposed to be a new start but...' I looked back at the house, which ticked all the boxes except one.

He put an arm around me. 'You want to live in Tring,' he said with flat finality.

I closed my eyes with part relief, that I didn't have to say it, and part guilt. This side of Hemel Hempstead was considerably cheaper, and we could get more for our money, and we'd both agreed that it was a fresh start – but it felt wrong.

There was a small tenacious part of me that wanted to refuse to let Victoria's harassment succeed. Tring was my home; I didn't want to move away but things weren't improving. Sam and his mum were barely talking. He felt Sally had encouraged Victoria by treating her like the incumbent daughter-in-law at the party and was still brooding about it, which wasn't helped by a third excuse from his best mate, Mike, who was too busy to meet up for a suggested double date with his girlfriend, Paige. I knew they'd had words but he hadn't talked about it. But then I hadn't told him what I'd overheard at the party. The only positive was that there'd been no sign or Victoria this week, but I had a horrible feeling she was biding her time.

He screwed up the details of the house. 'We might as well go home then.'

'I'm sorry, Sam.'

'Me too.' He pulled me into his arms and hugged me, dropping a kiss on my forehead. 'Why is it all such a bloody mess? We're not doing anyone any harm.'

I felt a little leap of fear at the despondency in his voice. Did he wonder if it was all worth it?

We drove home in silence back to the flat. As we were pulling up outside, Sam said, 'Do you mind if I go down the club and get a bit of practice in at the nets?' Which I was pretty sure was shorthand for 'have a quick pint with Mike'.

'No, you go ahead. I might go and see Mum.'

The flat felt stuffy as we stepped inside and Sam rummaged in his cricket bag for his bat, helmet and pads.

I managed to dredge up a smile as he tucked the pads under his arm.

Then he put down the pads, drew me into his arms. 'I love you, Jess. And if you want to stay in Tring, then we will. Things will be better one day.'

'I love you, too. I just never thought the aggro would go on for this long.' Although I'd seen the tenacity of some of the partners of the women at the refuge: they didn't give up easily on what they considered their property.

'Want me to stay, we could go out down to the canal?'

'No. Go play in the nets or whatever you do. And give Mike my best.' I smiled at him.

'Oh, Jess. Now I feel shit. I am going to the nets, but if I see him, I will have a drink with him.'

'And I don't mind. I get that it's difficult. Just don't hide it from me.'

He had the grace to look a little sheepish. 'I didn't want to hurt your feelings.'

'They're a bit tougher than that,' I lied and kissed him again.

Once he'd gone, I picked up the phone and called Mum.

'Jess. How are you?'

'I'm good, thanks. I wondered if you were around and I could pop over.' I was hoping that now we'd reset things I might be able to steer the conversation around to Dad and what had happened when he'd left.

'Oh. Is anything wrong?'

'No, I just...'

'The thing is … well, I've sort of … I'm going out with Douglas for lunch.' The latter was said in a rush of words as if she'd finally decided to confess.

'Oh, lovely.' I downplayed my delight, I didn't want my skittish mum getting defensive. This was a major step forward and inside I felt thrilled that she was finally making changes in her life. 'Are you going somewhere nice?'

'Yes. We are. He's taking me to a restaurant on the riverside in Wallingford.'

'Nice. Well, it's a lovely day for it.' I felt a touch of envy that she could enjoy the day without any of the complications Sam and I faced. 'Enjoy.'

After another minute of general chat, I hung up, deciding that I'd give Shelley a text and perhaps invite myself over to Pettyfeather Lane to sunbathe in the garden.

But as soon I finished the call my phone rang.

'Hi Holly,' I said. 'Everything OK?'

'No, it bloody isn't. That ex-girlfriend, she's only gone and posted pictures of the refuge on her flaming Instagram account, and posted a piece on her stupid bloody vlog-thing, and announced the sodding address online.'

'What?' My brain couldn't seem compute the information. 'Hang on. Victoria? Gimme a sec.' I put the phone on speaker and went into the Instagram app, needing to see it before my brain could process it.

'Holy shit!' I said when the picture came up, confirming

Holly's words. 'I don't believe it.' I stared at the pictures scarcely able to believe my eyes. Why would she do this? Did she even know what she'd done?

'You'd better believe it. All hell is breaking loose here. You need to get her to take it down. George wants to know how it happened. He's breathing smoke and fire like you wouldn't believe. Talking internal enquiries and God-knows-what.'

The trustees ran the charity that funded the refuge. George Renshaw was the head of the trustees and my boss.

'I'll get Sam to call her straightaway. What the…? How the hell did she get that picture?'

'No idea. I take it you didn't tell her.'

'God no!' I didn't feel quite so cocky now at thwarting her nosiness. This was retaliation for not telling her what I did. And suddenly I realised why she'd followed me to work that day.

'Oh shit! I know how she found it. She followed me. In the car. One morning. I thought I'd lost her. But she must have parked up and doubled back and followed me on foot.'

'I'm sorry, Jess, but it's bad. Shit is hitting the fan in major bloody gob-loads. Can you be here in two hours' time for a meeting? And for God's sake, whatever you do, don't tell George that you think she followed you.'

'Who lives here?' In the video, Victoria posed the question with an artful tilt of her head, tucking her thumbs in her stylish trench coat. Oh yes, she was rocking the chic lady-detective-circa-1940 look, along with the scarlet Veronica Lake lips, and I wanted to rip her stupid head off. 'Today I've turned detective and it's a mystery I'm asking you to help me solve. Our very own *Through The Keyhole*. This unassuming house, number...' Despite the fact this was the second time I'd watched the bloody vlog, I shuddered as she reeled off the address and held up her phone to focus on the unremarkable brown pebble-dashed house with bars at the window and the steps up to the porch with its heavy-duty front door.

I'd already phoned Sam and asked him to call her, and tell her to take it down. He'd come home from the cricket club immediately and was now sitting beside me as I watched the video again. I knew it wasn't his fault but I could barely bring myself to speak to him.

Who lives here? The damn video with her artfully posed question had already received over three hundred comments. Holly, bless her, had told me that she'd been trawling her way through every one of them, praying that no one revealed the truth about the house.

From her Instagram post, Victoria looked down at the camera with a smug, supercilious smirk in an arty shot that looked as if the photographer had taken it lying on the floor. It might have made *me* want to be sick but it had over a thousand likes.

Sam laid a hand on mine.

'I'll call her again and get her to take it down,' he said quietly. She hadn't answered previously and he'd left a message asking her to call urgently.

'How? How are you going to get her to take it down?' I asked, despair creeping into my voice. 'If you tell her why, she's vindictive enough to go ahead and reveal it anyway. Do you think that she'll suddenly see the light and do the right thing?'

'She's not a monster, Jess,' he said, being reasonable. 'She has no idea what she's inadvertently done.'

'Rubbish. She wanted to cause trouble. When she realises how serious it is, she's going to be delighted.'

'She's not that bad.'

I glared at him. How dared he defend her?

'I disagree, but it doesn't matter anyway, the damage is done. One of the women at the refuge has seen it. She's only been with us a little while and she's freaking out. Told the rest of the families. They're all terrified. There's nothing Victoria can do to fix that.' My stomach churned. Victoria had crossed a line, but she had no idea what she'd done. No idea that her idle curiosity had destroyed the peace of mind and security of half a dozen women reliant on the sanctity and sanctuary of the unassuming house she'd chosen to expose.

Sam dialled and held the phone up to his ear. Frustration simmered when I heard him leaving a message.

He called four more times in quick succession To. No. Fucking. Avail.

'Oh God, I think I'll go to work now.' I had no idea what I could do there before the meeting, but I couldn't stay at home. I needed to see that the refuge was still safe, that the women were safe.

'OK. Do you mind dropping me at Lynn and Richard's,

327

and I can get my car?' He'd left it there the night before when we'd been to a barbecue there and walked home.

'Sure, I can pick up my phone charger.' I'd left it plugged in by the toaster in the kitchen.

I'm surprised the steering wheel didn't crumble under my death-like grip or my knuckles implode with the pressure as I drove to my aunt and uncle's. Victoria still hadn't called Sam back and he seemed to know better than to speak to me; I'd never been so crazed with the strange combination of rage and despair before. I felt like I was being eaten from the inside out by it. When I looked in the rear-view mirror at one point, I saw that a blood vessel had burst in my eye.

As I pulled up outside the house, Sam began to wave, and I realised his parents were walking past the house with Tiggy. They slowed and waited for us to get out of the car.

'Hello Sam.'

''Lo,' said Sam with an uncommunicative shrug that made his mother dart a worried glance his way.

'Do you *both* want to pop in for a cup of tea?' she asked, including me in the invitation. I could see that she was anxious to mend fences.

Sam shook his head. 'Not now. Jess has got to get to work.'

Hurt flashed, sharply and briefly, on his mother's face, although she straightened her shoulders in stoic resignation.

'We've got some post for you,' said his dad with a touch of reproof.

'You go,' I said desperate for Sam to fix things with his

mum. 'I'll just grab my charger, and I could join you for a quick cup of tea.' Much as I didn't want to, I felt I ought to accept the half-hearted olive branch. There wasn't much I could do at the refuge before the meeting anyway.

His mother's wary glance my way was a mix of resentment and gratitude, as if I was the one keeping Sam from her and had just released him.

'Sure?' he asked with a brief featherlight touch to the inside my arm. One of our touches. A reminder of our closeness. Bugger, I was being a cow today. Holding him to account for something that wasn't his fault and still he put me first.

I caught his hand with mine and gave it a brief squeeze. 'I'm sure. I'll catch you up.'

The barely-there kiss he brushed across my temple almost made me cry.

'See you in a minute.'

I knocked on the front door and then opened it with my key.

'Hi love, excuse me.' Richard pointed to his dishevelled state and the water dripping down his forearms. 'Downstairs bog playing up.' Still talking, he turned and went into the tiny room which had been shoehorned in under the stairs at a much later date. 'Your aunt's out at the moment.'

'Oh.' Inside I shrivelled just a bit. If I was honest, I could have done with an Aunty Lynn hug and some of her down-to-earth, common sense advice. 'I just popped into grab my charger. Left it last night. And thanks again for the barbie, it was great.'

'Yeah, that new marinade worked a treat,' said his muffled voice as he knelt on the floor with his bottom sticking out of the room. 'Effing ballcock keeps sticking. I can't figure it out. Damn, why isn't this working? The water just keeps flushing. All plastic rubbish these days.'

'Right. I'd better go.'

'Aha, gotcha! What did you say, love? Oh, you little…'

Leaving Richard to his plumbing adventures, I left the house and walked around the corner to Sam's parents' house. They'd left the door ajar so I pushed it open, assuming that it had been left that way for me and followed the sound of voices towards the kitchen but stopped in my tracks feeling like an intruder when I heard Sally's aggrieved tone. Now I was stuck, did I creep back out and knock loudly on the door or did I stay here like an eavesdropper not wanting to get involved in a family discussion?

'You missed the Gledhill Cup, Sam.' Sally's voice rang with accusation. 'The county selectors were all there.'

'It's not a big deal,' said Sam but I knew him well enough to hear the strain he was feeling.

'Miles, tell him.'

'There'll be other games, son.'

'Miles! That's not what I meant. Sam, you should have played in that match. And now you've missed the chance.'

'Missed what chance, Mum?' Sam's angry snap made me freeze. I'd never heard him speak like that before. 'You seriously think I have a chance?' His disgust rang out. 'I don't have a cat in hell's chance at making the team and you know it.'

'No, I don't. What do you mean?' Sally sounded tearful.

'You're just encouraging her.'

A heavy silence followed and I caught my breath in my throat as my heart thudded with unease. What did Sam mean?

'As long as Victoria's dad is chairman of the selection committee, I won't be picked. Unless I go back to her. She's made that quite plain. And as long you continue to support her in that fantasy, she's going to believe it.'

Sally gasped and I heard her begin to cry.

'Sam. There's no need for that. Don't talk to your mother that way.'

'No.' Sam's voice exploded, and I heard the slam of something on one of the granite worktops. 'I'm sick of it. Sick of it all. You think I don't *want* to play county cricket?' There was another crash. I took a step backward. 'I'm desperate to play. This season could be my last chance. It's the first time I've not been selected for at least one game, but my batting average has never been higher. Even my fielding stats are better. But no. I've been passed over every time. I have worked my arse off, been to every net going. Done everything I can on the field to get a place. So no, I didn't play in the fucking Gledhill Cup because I knew it wouldn't make a blind bit of difference. I've wanted this all my life and Victoria is the one that has put the boot in. And don't bother denying it. She's pretty much admitted it to my face.'

I tensed, terrified he would come bursting through the door and catch me listening, but he must have gone out into the garden because I heard the slam of the patio doors.

'Oh, Miles,' said Sally. 'I didn't know.' She paused and then added with a horrified gasp. 'Oh God, that means … if he doesn't play this season, it could be all over for him. He might never get back onto the team.'

'I know, love. But that's sport for you. There's always someone waiting for your slot.'

'Oh, and he knows that, doesn't he? Oh, poor Sam. No wonder he's so angry.'

'Don't worry, love. It's not your fault.'

'But it is. I had no idea.'

'He'll be all right. You know Sam.'

'He's so upset. And he's never used that language before. Not in front of me.'

'That's because he's upset. And you don't blame him. He's worked hard. And knowing Sam it's the injustice of it all that's really got to him.'

'Miles, you don't believe it's anything to do with Victoria. It's not. It's because he's shown a lack of commitment this season. By spending time with that girl. Victoria told me that herself.'

'Are you sure that's true? I'm reasonably sure he's only missed a couple of matches.'

'Well, I assure you it's nothing to do with Victoria. That girl adores him. She's heartbroken and she'd never do that. She loves him. She wants what's best for him. She knows this other girl isn't right for him.'

'Sally.' Miles's tone held a warning. 'That's for Sam to decide, not us, and not Victoria, even if she does love him.'

'Oh, Miles, I'm so worried about him. It feels like he's making such a wrong turn. Everything was fine before.'

'Shh, we have to let him make his own decisions. His own mistakes.'

Pinching my lips together I blinked away the tears. Even Sam's dad, who I thought might be on my side, thought he was making a mistake. And now it appeared Sam was. Until he'd met my mum, I hadn't appreciated how important his cricket was to him. And now Victoria had put the refuge at risk. God, was any of this worth it?

Clutching my car keys, I turned on my heel and walked out, not caring if anyone heard me or not. I was done. Sam deserved a better outcome than this.

Chapter Twenty-Eight

'Jess!'

I ignored Sam's voice and kept walking even though I could barely see where I was going through blurry eyes.

'Jess. Wait.'

The car was just ahead of me. I could climb in and drive away. Just keep driving. Away from all this mess.

'Jess.' Sam's shout was right behind me now. I stopped.

He caught my arm and turned me round, the anger and confusion in his face softening when he saw my tears. 'Jess, what's wrong?'

'I can't do this anymore.' The words sliced into me as I managed to get them past the lump in my throat.

Sam just looked at me; he knew I meant it.

'Don't, Jess. Please don't.' He reached a hand out to wipe at the tear tracks on my cheeks.

I shook my head. 'It's too much. I can't do it.' The trail of chaos and hurt was too high a price to pay. 'I didn't understand about the cricket.'

'Hell, that's not important.'

'Yes, it is. But that's not just it,' I lied. I could put up with most things for him but I couldn't bear to see him lose something that had been such a big part of his life for so long and that could be cut off for ever. He only had so many more seasons to play at top level. I might not be a sports fan but I knew that much. My mum had said how brilliant he was. "He's one of the most talented young batsmen either of us have ever seen." How could I take that away from him?

'And I'm sick of it all too.' God, I sounded convincing. I had to. I loved Sam so much. This was my grand sacrifice. 'And now my job, my women... That's unforgivable. There's too much to lose.'

'But what about the gain?'

I lifted my eyes to his. He would gain. I'd bloody make sure Victoria and her unprincipled git of a father would do the right thing, if it was the last thing I ever did. 'I'm sorry. I don't think it's enough.'

'I'm not letting you do this.'

'You have to. It's hurting too many people.'

'I don't give a fuck about other people, I care about you, Jess.'

'Don't.' Tears were pouring down my face now. 'Don't make this so hard.'

He grabbed me and kissed me, his lips angry at first and, God help me, I couldn't resist. Last kiss. I deserved a last kiss. I screwed my eyes up tightly, shutting out reality and all the pain. And when the kiss ended, I breathed out a choked sob.

'Jess. I love you.'

I swallowed down hard. 'I know. I love you, but … it's just I don't think I can do this anymore.'

Grasping my elbows, he looked down into my eyes and my heart took a punch as I saw the tears welling up there. Oh God, Sam. I took in a sharp breath, tugging at my lip with my teeth.

'Give it some more time, please, Jess.' Sam's urgent plea almost tore my heart in two.

'I can't.' His time to play first-class cricket was running out. He was already in his mid-twenties.

'Please, Jess.'

I shook my head, not daring to speak. I didn't want this, but I couldn't see how else I could fix things. I'd had enough of fighting against Victoria, the guilt, messing up Sam's relationship with his mother, his friends and all the other problems that had arisen. Ruining his cricket career was the last straw.

I couldn't do that to him.

The mess at the refuge gave me the perfect excuse to finish things. To make them right for him. I was the one holding him back. This was something I could give him.

Chapter Twenty-Nine

'A ny luck?' Holly didn't look up from where she was
trawling through the latest batch of one-hundred-
odd responses to Victoria's blog.

Yesterday's meeting had been hideous, full of outrage
and bluster with the trustees wondering at length how the
secret had got out.

Today I was researching how to get a YouTube video
taken down and the trustees were due for another meeting.
I'd already reported the video, but the categories they
offered me in the list didn't fit.

'I've already reported it.'

'What about Sam?'

'What about him?' I asked, my heart doing a stupid
wobble just at the sound of his name.

'Can he go and see Victoria?'

'He phoned her four times yesterday. She didn't pick up
and she didn't call back.'

'Yes, but that was yesterday.'

I pursed my lips together, ducking my head.

'Jess?'

'Mmm,' I said, trying to sound busy, as I kept my gaze fixed on the computer screen as if it were about to impart the meaning of life to me.

'Is everything OK with you and Sam?'

'Why do you ask?'

'Because every time I've mentioned his name you have this kind of constipated-but-I might-have-crapped-in-my-pants look on your face. It's kind of weird and not you.'

'Sam and I...' Oh shit, my voice cracked. 'Sam and I...'

'Oh, Jess. Not over this.'

'Not just this, but it's bad enough,' I sniffed as those pesky tears leaked out. 'Other things. Too many other things.'

'You're not a quitter, Jess.' Holly left her desk and came to perch on mine. 'This isn't like you. I don't do the sappy stuff. I've been working here too many years. I'm a long-in-the-tooth cynical old harpy but you and Sam ... you're great together. Even I thought so, and I don't believe in all the till-death-us-do-part crap. Once this has blown over...'

'No, Holly. It's done. I could take all the stuff Victoria threw at me ... but this and what it does to Sam, that's the bit I can't do.'

'Oh, for crap's sake, Sam's a big boy.'

'Yes ... but she's blocking his cricket career.'

'So?' spat Holly. Wrong person to confide in. She so didn't do sport.

'It's a big deal to him.' Although he'd never made it into a big deal. My heart ached for how modest and uncomplaining he'd been about it. Last night I'd Googled him. He'd been a rising star for the last few years, until last year an injury had slowed him down. This season was supposed to be his big comeback. A couple of journalists had wondered why he hadn't reappeared on the scene, and there was one slightly spiteful column suggesting he'd taken his eye off the ball and had been seduced by a wild social life. Ha, if only they knew. Mine and Sam's idea of a wild night was a couple of beers on the balcony before he started marking and planning for the evening, while I planned rotas and reviewed current cases.

'Bigger than you.'

'That's not it. I realised that Victoria will keep on. It's like my mum all over again, and I'm doing that to her. And to Sam.'

'You are talking bollocks.'

I knew Holly wouldn't understand.

'I'm Victoria's nemesis. As long as I'm on the scene, she won't let up. It's damaging Sam. His relationship with his mother, his friends, the county selector people. The minute I'm off the scene, it solves all those problems.'

'And Victoria wins.'

'No, Sam wins,' I said quietly. 'And that's what counts.'

'Oh, for God's sake. You daft cow. You've done the big grand sacrifice, you stupid moo.'

I bristled. 'No, I haven't.'

'That's exactly what you've done. Dear God, Jess. I thought you had more sense.' She got up abruptly, almost knocking my coffee mug over. 'Well, you've made a right pig's ear of things.'

'Thanks for the support.'

'Sorry, Jess, but I think you're an idiot.'

'Message received. Loud and clear.' At my terse response, she came to stand next to me and I could see her trademark eyeliner was smudged. She put a hand on my shoulder.

'A lovely idiot. You've got a good heart. And as usual you're thinking of everyone but yourself. Don't you see? You deserve to be happy.'

I allowed myself a tiny sigh. 'I'll be OK. We'll both get over it,' I said, wondering just how long the awful sense of hollowness right in the centre of my chest would last, and whether Sam felt as bad as I did. 'In the meantime, we've got to get this bloody thing taken down before I lose my job.'

'It's not your fault some publicity-junkie social media slime decided to make a story out of nothing.' Even though Holly's indignation shone in her words, I could tell by her slight diffident shake of her head that she didn't entirely believe that.

'Isn't it? We're supposed to take reasonable precautions to make sure this place remains anonymous and secret. She must have followed me down the street and I didn't even see her. That's hardly taking reasonable precautions with security, is it? The irony is I saw her following me but I thought she'd gone.'

'No one's going to blame you, Jess.' She narrowed her black-lined eyes. 'You're just punishing yourself.'

The door buzzed.

'That'll be the Spanish Inquisition,' said Holly,

smoothing the papers on her desk. 'Try not to throw yourself under the bus.'

The meeting lasted an hour and it was duly agreed that a full enquiry would have to be conducted. In the meantime, by mutual agreement, I was to take a week's unpaid leave. The trustee's lawyers were in discussion and they were determining a strategy to contact Victoria and at this stage try to appeal to her better nature. When I explained that I had now ceased my relationship with Sam, this was greeted with approving nods. So maybe I had done the right thing, even though it didn't feel like it.

I left the building without saying goodbye to Holly, who was taking over from me and had to be briefed by the communications team who'd been charged with crisis management. They were terrified that the story might leak into the local paper. That really would mess things up. At the moment, what the building was still remained a secret; most people believed it was a brothel or an MI5 safe house. Unfortunately, there had been more than the usual amount of pedestrian traffic outside, with a couple of people taking their own photos. There was a real danger this could go viral. If only Victoria could be persuaded to take the vlog down, but she seemed to have disappeared off the face of the earth.

Being at home when you're supposed to be at work sucks, even after only one morning. You never quite know what to do with yourself, especially when it's pouring down with rain. Ironically, after days of unbroken sunshine, today the heavens had decided to open and the dull, grey sky felt horribly oppressive, as if it were pressing down on me. I stood on the balcony watching water trickle down from the eaves, the incessant rhythm of the drip, drip, drip feeding my misery. It was all very well being brave and no-nonsense in front of Holly but now, back in the flat, my eyes were constantly drawn to holes in places where Sam's things had been: the empty space on the dining table where he always did his marking, the round shaving-gel-shaped mark on the bathroom shelf, and the spot by the sofa where he kicked off his shoes. Even in the kitchen the solitary plate on the draining rack mocked me.

Below me, a passing car suddenly slowed in the middle of the road, its tyres hissing on the wet tarmac. Damn, I recognised the little blue hatchback. Almost immediately it pulled over and parked on the other side of the street and my aunt got out, waving up at me. No doubt wondering why I wasn't at work. With a sinking heart, I watched as she crossed the street and headed to my door.

'Hey, Aunty Lynn,' I said with forced cheer, opening up to her strident knock.

'I was just passing and I spotted you. Miserable day, isn't it?' Her kind eyes studied me carefully. 'Are you OK? I saw Sally this morning.'

'Oh,' I said, immediately wondering what she knew.

'She told me about you and Sam. I can't decide whether to be furious with her or sorry for her.' Lynn's mouth settled in a grim line. 'Sam isn't speaking to her.'

I shrugged. 'It's not my problem anymore. I suppose you want to come in. Tea?'

She nodded, ignoring my ungracious invitation, and followed me into the kitchen, slipping off her wet coat and hanging it over the back of one of the chairs.

'Why, Jess?' Her voice softened. 'I thought you two were so happy.' Again she studied my face and I had to turn my back on her. But it was too late, the punch of pain made me fold over, clutching my stomach as I bent double.

'Oh, love.' She enveloped me in one of her soft Eternity-scented hugs, a proper mum-hug, the sort that had picked me up after spills and falls over the years. The tears came quick and fast, along with gut-wrenching sobs. All the misery crept out of its little boxes in an avalanche, threatening to wipe me out. 'Oh, sweetheart.' She clutched me tighter as I sobbed into her shoulder, digging into her handbag to find me tissues.

At last I slowed to hiccoughing sniffs. 'I'm sorry.'

'Don't be. Come on. Let's have some tea and you can tell me all about it.' With her usual quick efficiency, so unlike my mother's bustle and fluster, she pulled down two mugs, shoved in teabags and made us each a tea, urging me to lead the way into the lounge. She sat down right next to me, thigh-to-thigh, and handed me a tea, watching as I cupped the mug between two hands. I was cold. Cold all the way through.

'So what happened? Has Victoria done something?'

'Something! I'll say. She posted a picture of the refuge on her vlog.'

'No!' Lynn sucked in a horrified breath. 'What a spiteful madam.'

'She doesn't know it's a refuge. But that's beside the point. The trustees who run the charity are understandably upset and because of my "alleged" link with Victoria, I've been suspended for a week, unpaid, while they get to the bottom of things. They're launching an investigation.'

'But it's not your fault. You barely know the girl.'

'Guilt by association.' My fingers clenched as I rubbed at a patch on my trousers with my knuckles.

'That's not fair.'

'My private life has impacted on the refuge. They're taking a dim view.'

'But why did you finish with Sam? It's not his fault. He told his mother it's hers.'

'Ouch, that doesn't sound like Sam.'

'He's hurting, love.'

My heart clenched in regret and pain. I'd done that to him. 'I couldn't carry on. Victoria will stop her campaign now. She has no reason to carry on if I'm not going out with Sam.'

'But what about you and Sam? That doesn't seem fair. To either of you.'

'It's not. But it's not meant to be. There have been so many conflicts and problems to overcome and then ... realising that Victoria is stopping Sam playing cricket, and then she revealed the location of the refuge ... they were just the final straws. Those women are supposed to feel safe. Victoria's ruined that.'

'You do realise that this is Victoria's problem. You and

Sam shouldn't have to pay for it. You both deserve to be happy.'

'It's not that easy at someone else's expense, is it?' I gave her a candid look. We both knew I was talking about my mother.

'No, but pandering to them isn't necessarily good for them or anyone else.'

I lifted my shoulders.

'Did you see your father?'

My head shot up at her sudden change of tack.

'Ottershaw. It didn't take a detective to figure out why you'd picked that particular village. Did you see him?'

I shook my head and closed my eyes at the prick of shame. 'I ran away. I saw his wife. She knew who I was. Immediately.'

Lynn looked away, fiddling with the tassels on the scarf that was looped around her neck.

'She said you sent photos. How did you know he was in Ottershaw?'

She smoothed the fabric of the scarf down her chest and then lifted her head. 'He's kept in touch with me, to keep in touch with you.' With a shake of her head, she raised her hands to her face. 'I never ... I never wanted to keep the secret, but your mum's my sister. She was in such a bad way and I was worried your dad might seek custody, and that would have finished her off. And then when she was better, I didn't want to risk her ever going back into that state again, so I didn't tell her I was in touch in with him. But over the years, I've sent him photos and news. You always seemed so disinterested in him; I didn't feel it was my place to rock the boat unless you asked about him. But he was desperate to hear about you. He never wanted to leave you, but your mum gave him no choice. I don't know all the ins and outs and she never spoke of it – and I didn't like to ask, not once she was better.'

'And I was too scared of what it might do to Mum if I asked about Dad.'

'The thing is ... she's been hiding behind that for a long time now. And now I wonder if I've done the right thing. What's happening with Victoria is like seeing history repeat itself. You deserve a life and to be happy with the person you chose. It's not for someone else to prevent that. I've been complicit in helping you lose out on knowing your dad.' Her mouth crumpled and she ran a shaky hand through her hair. 'I should have encouraged you earlier to seek him out.'

'I don't think it would have made a difference.' I slipped my hand into hers. 'I was protecting Mum too.'

'And I don't think protecting her was necessarily the right thing to do, for you.'

'I saw my brothers ... my half-brothers. I spoke to Alicia. It's weird knowing you have family out there that you know nothing about.'

'You have grandparents, too. Evelyn and David.'

I winced. 'Alicia seemed nice.'

'She is. I've only corresponded with her. Your half-brothers sound like quite a handful.'

'Toby and Ben,' I said picturing the two dark-haired boys, with eyes so like mine.

'Yes, she...' The pause couldn't have been more

pregnant as the seconds ticked by and I heard the steady drip, drip of the water outside. 'She called. She was worried about you.'

I buried my head in my hands at the sudden recollection of me backing down the lane, running away from a perfectly nice woman.

'Oh God. I made an idiot of myself. I was so shocked that she knew who I was. I panicked. I practically ran away.'

'You could go back. You've got the rest of this week off. Why don't you go and see them? Get away from here.'

My head shot up as I looked at my aunt.

'Bloody genius. That's a brilliant idea.' An escape from the overwhelming emotions that were threatening to derail me. Where was my pragmatism? My common sense? My eternal optimism?

'There are two sides to every story, you know. You know that you and Sam haven't done anything wrong.'

'Try telling Victoria that.'

'Exactly,' said Aunty Lynn looking exactly like a wise old owl, as she blinked very slowly. 'Perhaps it's time you heard your dad's side of the story.'

'I wouldn't have listened … before.'

'No, I don't think you would.' Lynn's voice was calm, and I was soothed by the complete lack of judgement.

Funny how things can suddenly turn on their head. I was mad as hell at Victoria for not letting go, and for making things so much harder, when Sam and I had tried to do the right thing. Suddenly, I was very keen to hear what my father had to say.

Chapter Thirty

'I s your young man not with you?' asked the owner of the Black Bull in her soft West Country accent when I checked in.

I shook my head. 'Not this time,' I said.

'Good journey? You came by train?'

'Not bad, I had to wait for the connection for Ottershaw, but the journey was so pretty I didn't really mind the last leg.' Funny to think that I'd only decided to come yesterday afternoon.

The long journey had been lifted by the news that Victoria's vlog post had been taken down, as well as her Instagram post, although I had no idea whether this was because Sam had got hold of her or the trustees' lawyers had served their letter on her. I'd had no word from Sam, not a single text or message. Part of me was grateful and another part was a tiny bit aggrieved that he had given in so easily – but then that was what I wanted, didn't I? I hated women who played games, who were ambiguous about they wanted. I told Sam I was done. I meant it. I should be pleased he respected it, and I desperately wanted things to be right for him again. I'd done the right thing.

I suddenly realised that the landlady was talking to me and I had to nod as if I'd heard every word.

'...although not many tourists use the train. Now, did you want to eat with us tonight? Or do you want me to send something up to your room on account of you being on your own?'

'I'm ... I'm meeting some people here. In the bar. At seven.'

'Ah, that'll be nice. Do you want me to book a table for you in the restaurant? We're quite busy.'

'I'm not sure. I don't know what our plans are yet.' I swallowed with the sudden realisation that by agreeing to meet in a neutral place, I'd also made it rather public. As it was the only pub in the village, she probably knew my father and stepmother already.

'No problem. I'm sure we'll be able to squeeze you in.'

I nodded, again. She must think I was a bit simple with all the nodding.

Unfortunately, she put me back in the same room, which did nothing to help ease the ache inside me. The sight of the bed brought back memories of that morning, sneaking out before Sam was awake. I regretted that now. I wished I'd told him where I was going, and why I'd picked the village, before we'd broken up. Now I probably never would, and it felt wrong. After a shower to wash away the careworn feeling after several hours on trains, I sat down on the edge of the bed, picking at the loose frill on the edge of the summery blouse that I'd changed into. It was half past six and I'd left myself far too much time to wait. Should I go down to the bar? Or sit up here on my own and brood?

Brooding was far too much the easiest option. I snatched up my handbag and phone and went downstairs into the quiet bar.

'Hello,' said the very friendly barman, with a mass of black curls, a golden hooped earring in one ear and a wide perfect smile, looking like a rather well-bred pirate. 'You're the lady staying here.' He added as an afterthought, 'On your own.'

'Yes,' I said scanning the empty bar and opting for a seat at the bar for the time being. His company was better than none, although even if I hadn't been grieving for Sam, I wouldn't have been interested in his very overt try-me-out vibes.

He followed my gaze. 'We do lunchtime trade for the tourists. But locals in the evening. Unless folk are staying here. We're quiet during the week. Booked out at the weekend. You here for a couple of days?'

'Yes,' I said, ignoring the obvious opening. I wondered if this was the sort of village where everyone would know my business by the end of the night. Had Dad and Alicia shared with anyone that his long-lost daughter had blown into town?

'What can I get for you?'

'Gin and tonic?'

'We have all the trendy gins you could wish for. What do you fancy?' He stepped back and with a flourish indicated a glass shelf full of an amazing array of different-shaped and -coloured bottles, as if they were vying for the best in show.

The familiar Edinburgh Gin logo beckoned. 'I'll have a rhubarb and ginger, single.'

'What kind of tonic, Elderflower, Light, Mediterranean, standard?'

When did ordering a drink become as complicated as coffee now has to be? 'Standard, thank you.' I half turned on my stool, pretending to study the bar as if I'd not been here before. Unable to help myself, my gaze slid to the table in the corner that Sam and I had shared for dinner barely a few weeks ago. Pain twisted my gut and I stiffened at the memory of our knees touching under the table and our casually linked fingers across the wooden top while we waited for Cornish pasties and chips. We'd been euphoric, buzzing with excitement at our decision to sell up and combine forces. I closed my eyes. It had all seemed so simple then.

'Here you go. Do you want me to set up a tab? Are you eating?'

'No, I'll pay now,' I said, now suddenly anxious to escape from his chummy interest. Taking my drink, I slid off the stool and sought out a table by the window where I could watch anyone coming up the path to the pub. With time on my hands, inevitably I picked up my phone, tempted to text Shelley for a random conversation. Lynn probably hadn't seen her yet. Bel was away again. Newcastle this time, but I knew that she'd be hard at work. They worked long hours on an audit to cram in as much as possible so they were away for less time. So neither of them knew about me and Sam yet? I knew them both so well that I could predict their responses. Bel would be warm and sympathetic and come around armed with Prosecco and crispage. Shelley would no doubt tell me I was an idiot to kiss goodbye to a regular sex life and that there were plenty of fish in the sea.

And, as if drawn to it, with a life of their own, my fingers had scrolled onto Instagram and there was Victoria's latest story. Looking fabulous, she posed in front of a florist with a large bunch of pink roses in her hand which co-ordinated perfectly with her floaty dress. *Life's good*, said the rolling animation. The next had her posing as if pulling a bow and arrow, *Going to bag my man*. The final picture was a close-up of her beaming face *Always knew it was only a matter of time* with a link to her vlog – and of course I had to follow the link.

Surreptitiously, I looked over my shoulder and turned the sound down on my phone before pressing play.

'So, ladies, what's a girl to do when that man comes crawling back? Make him eat dirt for a while and forgive him? The jury's out here at Victoria's towers. But in the meantime, I'm surely going to let him know exactly what he's been missing.'

She looked directly at the camera and raised her eyebrows in a gleeful come-hither look that quite frankly made me want to throw up. Seriously, how could anyone love themselves so much?

This vomitfest was followed by Victoria prancing about with that slinky hip-rolling walk that models do, in a series of outfits that that left nothing to the imagination, more cleavage than coverage. I could probably size her up for a bra fitting.

One would have hoped she might have some humility in her triumph but no, Victorious Victoria.

Tears pricked at my eyes. No. Sam wouldn't have. I couldn't believe that. He wouldn't have gone back to her. I knew it gut-deep. He couldn't. I blinked back stupid tears. That would break my heart. I'd set him loose to free him up from Victoria's focus on me.

If he went back to her, it would nullify all the good memories that I was clinging on to. The bright happiness of those shiny memories was all that was keeping me going. The precious months together that had been the highlight of my summer. A time to treasure. I couldn't bear to think that they'd be wiped out.

I wanted our time together to be a stepping-stone for him to move on to be happy with someone else, someone who deserved him. And that wasn't Victoria. That wasn't part of my plan.

'Jess.' I jumped as someone laid a gentle hand on my shoulder and I looked up into a more crinkled version of my eyes and my immediate thought was that these eyes had smiled a lot.

I rose to my feet. 'Hi.'

For a moment there was a strained silence as we measured each other up like wary dogs circling each other. My heart thudded as I took in the long clean-shaven face. He was taller than I'd expected, having grown up with Uncle Richard, who's quite a short-arse. It threw me for a moment.

'Shall I get some drinks?' asked my dad with a longing look at the bar.

Alicia's eyes twinkled. 'Very good.'

'I'm OK, thanks.' I indicated my still untouched gin.

'Shall we sit down?' suggested Alicia, her dark eyes warmed by a smile. 'I love your top. Shows off your tan nicely.'

I glanced at the printed fabric and the cutaway sleeves on the shoulders, remembering what Mum had said the first time she'd seen it.

'Thank you. It wasn't expensive.'

'Looks nice though. I wish I could wear things like that, I've got short, lardy, white arms.' She held them out with a mournful droop to her mouth that was quickly belied with another of her quick, bright smiles as she confided, 'I think I must come from Michelin-man stock. Thank goodness your side of the family has good genes, otherwise I'd have given birth to a pair of pumpkins.'

It was impossible not to smile back at her engaging grin.

Dad came back with drinks, a pint for him and her G & T, which looked a similar hue to mine.

'Rhubarb and ginger?' I asked, lifting my glass in toast.

'Yes, my favourite. Who knew that I'd like gin, let alone have a preferred flavour? When I was younger it was Gordon's and Schweppes. That was the sum total of your choice.'

'I only started drinking gin last year. My cousin, Shelley, introduced me to it.'

'Lynn's daughter,' said my dad. 'She's a couple of years younger than you.'

'Yes. We're very close. More like sisters. Well, Aunty Lynn treats me like that, and Shel's never seemed to mind.'

'Lynn's a very good sort,' he said, nodding as he took a sip of his beer and I noticed that under the table Alicia laid a reassuring hand on his knee. She was wearing a navy dress with bright red sprigged flowers and red flip-flops. I got the impression her personality matched. Bright and animated, she carried on smiling.

'It's good to meet you, Jess.' My dad tucked his hands under the table as if he wasn't sure what to do with them.

Alicia rolled her eyes. 'Adrian, you are hopeless.' She shook her head and gave me another of her bird-bright smiles. 'I know this is awkward, Jess, but we really wanted to get the chance to get to know you. There's no expectation. This must be difficult for you. Rome wasn't built in a day.'

My dad wrinkled his nose and relaxed a little. I could see now that there'd been stiffness in his shoulder. This was as difficult for him as for me. 'She's very bossy.'

'I have to be; I'm the only female in the house. If I wasn't, I'd be awash with dirty socks and tripping over sports kit every five minutes.'

I laughed immediately, thinking of Sam and his cricket kit, which was invariably dumped in the hall on a Saturday night. 'I know that feeling.'

'Exactly. It's lovely that you came back. I'm sorry if I startled you last week. I'm what they call impulsive. Act before I think. Drives Adrian mad.'

'Only when you bring another rescue dog home.' Now his mouth widened into a natural grin and I saw his shoulders drop another notch. 'We have three. Heinz varieties.'

'Hugo is almost all Labrador,' Alicia protested.

He shook his head. 'Hugo the hooligan. I think he has a passing acquaintance with Labrador DNA, but he is most definitely not almost all Labrador.'

This was obviously an old argument, but I couldn't help smiling because they were both looking at each other with such fondness.

'That was what the rescue people told me.'

'They could have told you he was part-elephant, part-hyena and you'd still have brought him home.' He leaned closer to her and I could see the affection between them.

'Do you have a dog?' asked Alicia.

'No, I live in a...' My throat tightened up at the quick stab of memory, Sam and I talking about getting a dog when we bought a house. 'I live in a flat.'

'Whereabouts?' asked my Dad.

'I live in Tring.' I didn't know how well he knew the town. When he'd lived with us we'd been in Aylesbury.

'Nice. I used to work there. Before I ... before I moved down here.'

Silence fell again.

'Look,' said Alicia. 'There are going to be these awkward pauses while we get to know each other ... and there's one already. I'd really like to get to know you, and I know you want to get to know your dad, otherwise you wouldn't be here. But ... we're a package and you might not want to know me ... the other woman and all that, although ... I wasn't. And I'm rushing on. Wanting you to like us. I'm probably pushing too soon. But if you want me to butt out so you can spend time with your dad, that would be OK.'

How could I not like her? Open, honest and vivacious, wearing her heart on her sleeve, she was the sort of person I was naturally drawn to. And her plain speaking definitely made things a lot easier.

'It's OK. To be honest, I didn't know what to expect. I thought you might be cross that I've ... that I've resisted getting in touch all these years.'

'It had to be when you were ready,' said my dad in a gentle voice. It was quite weird suddenly seeing him in the flesh and realising that he was a quiet, self-effacing man and nothing like the cold-hearted villain who had turned his back on his wife and child that had lived in my head for so many years.

Now I felt ashamed. Thoroughly ashamed. It had taken me far too long to grow up about this.

'I'm sorry. I...' How did I apologise for being blinkered and immature when I didn't even know it myself? I'd always prided myself on being open and honest, like Alicia, but I hadn't been. Not on this one. I'd been lying to myself. A self-righteous cow who had preferred to believe (and actually enjoyed believing) that my dad had abandoned me and I was tough enough not to care. When he'd contacted me in my teens it hadn't fitted with my burgeoning feminist construct of being the daughter of an abandoned woman left by a selfish, heartless, controlling man. Of being part of a self-sufficient matriarchal unit that didn't need male influence. So, instead, with a heightened and misguided sense of moral superiority, I'd refused to even consider responding to the contact. That point of principle had insulated me against any sense of guilt or curiosity, even though I'd kept the pictures of the two babies for all these years.

'You don't need to apologise,' he said.

But suddenly I realised I did. There were two sides to every story. I'd never even acknowledged that he had a side, let alone been prepared to listen to it.

I threw my head back and looked at the ceiling before sucking in another breath. 'I don't know much about what happened with you and Mum. Just that it was pretty horrible at my end. You know she had a breakdown? And I ended up living with my aunt and uncle for a while.'

I saw him wince and Alicia reached for his hand.

She nodded and looked at my father. His mouth twisted and he put both hands on the table.

'We wanted you to come and stay with us but … Lynn was so worried about Joan. She thought it might push her over the edge. We agreed to keep our distance so as not to upset her. We thought it would be temporary.'

'It had been before,' explained Alicia with a quick glance at her husband.

'Before?'

Alicia laid a hand on mine and her other on my dad's and squeezed both of our hands. 'Adrian, I think it's long past time to explain.'

With a heavy sigh, he turned to me. 'Your mother and I weren't together very long before she got pregnant with you. We got married very quickly and a year in, we knew it wasn't working. We argued, we had different views and …

we actually separated, but then your mum became very depressed and I moved back in to help look after you because she couldn't cope. So we tried again. This time we managed another couple of years, over which time she had several bouts of depression. By this time, I knew that whatever I did, it wasn't going to stop her suffering the depression but I stuck it out, even though we both knew our marriage was over – but your mother wouldn't have it. I stayed until you were nearly seven but then … I met Alicia. We worked together. She made me realise just how miserable I was at home. We were friends and I can tell you that nothing happened for a year. You don't have to believe me and, to be honest, I don't actually care whether you do or not, because Alicia saved me.'

It was a bold statement but I saw the exchange between them, the bright dart of love, the tenderness of her smile, and it hit me with a punch straight to the heart. That was what Sam and I had.

And I'd thrown it away. My stomach twisted and I shifted in my seat.

'I can spout all those platitudes, that life is short and every other justification under the sun. The truth was, I didn't love your mother and I fell in love with Alicia. I had to make a decision, so that one of us would be happy. I've never regretted the decision to leave your mother but I do regret that it meant I had to leave you too. I'd hoped that we'd work out some amicable custody arrangement.'

He gave me a level, candid look.

'But Mum wouldn't,' I said, immediately filling in the blanks. Stubborn, recalcitrant, I knew my mother well.

'Not at first and then…'

We both knew how things had panned out. I'd lived with Aunty Lynn for two years. It had taken Mum a long time to get back to even a semblance of normal.

'I sent cards and birthday presents, Christmas gifts, but they always came back unopened.'

Alicia's fingers tightened around her glass. I followed her fixed stare out of the window.

Dad scrunched up his mouth.

'There's more,' I said.

Dad shrugged but Alicia lifted her chin. I recognised the signs of someone wanting to defend another. I'd seen it with the mothers and their children at the refuge.

'Your mother wouldn't take a penny from me in child maintenance. She even insisted on paying the mortgage herself. There's a pot of money for you. I kept putting it aside. The money you should have had.'

Alicia nodded, her shiny dark hair bouncing with vehemence and as he stopped, she nudged him, prompting him to add more.

'She said you didn't want anything to do with me and that I was upsetting you and it would be fairer on you if I left you both alone.' His voice was filled with apology and kindness. Unlike my mother, he was sad rather than bitter.

Sorrow swamped me. That must have been so hurtful. And to my shame, there was a grain of truth in there. I hadn't wanted anything to do with him.

'I don't remember that, but in my teens I was quite outspoken and I didn't have the best view of you.'

'Hardly surprising,' said my dad with a rueful grimace.

'Well, you're here now,' said Alicia with a welcome injection of positivity. 'There's no point dwelling on what can't be changed.'

'That's very true, love.' He picked up her hand and laced his fingers through it, dropping a quick kiss on the top of her wrist in a rather old-fashioned courtly gesture at odds with his youthful appearance. It suddenly dawned on me that when he and Mum had split up, they hadn't been that much older than me. Mum had had her whole life ahead of her. She could have remarried or met someone else. Why had it taken her until now to give Douglas a chance?

'I don't know about anyone else but I'm starving. They do a very good Cornish pasty here. Clichéd, I know, but the tourists love them and they really are rather good.'

'I know,' I said, remembering Sam wolfing his down with great delight. 'I had one last time I was here with … with Sam.'

'That's your boyfriend?' asked Alicia and I could see my dad looking wary. 'Oh, Adrian, she's a young woman.' Typical dad response.

'Yes,' I said not wanting to talk about Sam. 'And how old are the boys?'

'Ben is ten and Toby is eight,' said Alicia. 'And they're dying to meet you. We just thought it might be easier without them the first time, although you have met them very briefly.'

'Yes,' I said with a smile. 'They were very cute.'

'Hmm,' said Alicia, darkly. 'Cute with a small c.'

Dad laughed. 'They're a pair of monkeys.'

'Why don't you come and have brunch with us tomorrow, then you can meet them?'

'I'd like that.'

'Right, well, I'll go and grab some menus for us,' said Alicia. 'And try and fend off Jason's questions. He's just about dying of curiosity behind that bar and still wondering if our appearance has stopped him putting another notch on his bedpost. He's a one, that one.'

'He'd better not,' said Dad bristling and shooting a glare towards the barman.

I laughed. 'I know the type. Local Lothario.'

'You've got him nailed,' said Alicia with a cheerful laugh. '"Mostly harmless" as Douglas Adams would have said.'

I shot her a startled glance. Sam would have got that. We'd have squeezed each other's hands and turned to smile in recognition. I almost doubled over at the stab of pain. How could it hurt so much, just wishing he were here?

'Sorry, my favourite author. Your dad doesn't get it. He prefers non-fiction.'

'I love Douglas Adams,' I said before adding more softly, 'so does Sam.' My heart ached remembering some of our early conversations about books and films and music when we were still in that eager-to-learn-about-each-other phase. Oh God, I missed him.

And like, a mirror image of that first time I met Sam, the conversation with Dad and Alicia gently flowed into our likes and dislikes, those basic dance steps of people getting to know each other.

Chapter Thirty-One

Despite the evening having gone so well, thanks to Alicia's irresistible warmth and good cheer, I didn't sleep well. I woke not long after midnight and stared up at the ceiling for several hours. Talking to my dad had stirred up so many memories and emotions. Although it had been amicable, I felt as twisted up as the sheets around my waist. I couldn't keep things straight in my head; I'd start following one thread and lose it, taking up another. My brain felt like a candy floss machine and I was desperately trying to capture the fly-away wisps of thoughts.

It's difficult when ingrained perceptions, held for so long that they're a part of you, are ripped open, and instead of the smooth skin you've always had, you're now looking into an open wound. The story – Mum as a victim, Dad as the villain – had been one of the building blocks of my life, defining so much of me. I hadn't expected Dad's side of the story to make me question so many of my entrenched beliefs. I'd always thought my mum was strong and independent. A survivor. I was proud that we were both survivors. Proud that I'd survived a father who hadn't wanted me. But now I realised that Mum hadn't survived. She'd existed. It was a revelation that, in the small dark hours, I couldn't let go of.

Mum could have made so much more of her life if she'd moved on. She blamed Dad for our financial situation, always saying that he'd refused to support us. And yet it was clear he'd been willing and able. Mum had let me believe that Dad had left her in a callous, heartless way, walking out without looking back. I'd believed her to be the victim. Now I wondered if, in fact, Dad had been the victim. He had tried to do the right thing. Marriages broke up. It was a fact of life. It was how you handled that break-up that defined you. Had Mum chosen to be a victim in not accepting that their marriage was over? In refusing him a relationship with me? In turning down his financial support? Her depression couldn't have been prevented, but was it all down to the break-up? Certainly it had exacerbated the situation but it sounded like, from what Dad said, she'd suffered from depression for many years before they broke up.

I was still ruminating when I became aware of the dawn chorus. Oh God. I had to be at Dad and Alicia's in five hours' time. I rolled over and set my alarm, just in case I did fall asleep, and plumped my pillows up in yet another desperate bid to persuade my body into sleep.

My alarm went off what felt like five minutes later. It was half past nine, which gave me half an hour to get ready. Clumsily, I lurched out of bed, numbed by grogginess, fighting my way through the heaviness of sleep to the en suite bathroom. My bleary face stared back at me in the mirror and when self-pitying tears threatened, I filled the sink with cold water and splashed my face. Today I was going to meet my brothers. That was cause for celebration. They were the innocents in all this. Unblemished by any fault in the situation.

Make-up did a little to hide the ravages of the night and when I set out, my mind started racing again and this time my thoughts turned to Sam. Why I chose to torture myself I don't know, but as I walked, I pulled out my phone and scrolled through my pictures. It was like a tapestry of our history together. I stopped on one in which I'd captured Sam looking up at me, with an intimate knowing smile that looked right into the heart of me, as if he knew all my secrets and my very soul. I bit my lip to stop an involuntary sob and closed my eyes. Swallowing hard, I shoved the phone back in my pocket and strode quickly along the green towards the house.

When I lifted the heavy door knocker, I heard squeals from inside floating through the open windows.

'She's here! She's here!'

I waited a moment and then beyond the door I could hear, 'No, let me. Let meeee.'

The door opened and two small bodies jostled for position on the doorstep, both peering up at me with three dogs pushing through their legs, sniffing at my legs.

'Hello, you must be Ben and Toby.'

'Yes. I'm Ben. I'm ten.' His eyes narrowed. 'You're the lady at the fence.'

'Yes, I was visiting a couple of weeks ago.' I patted the nearest dog which I suspected, by the insistent way he nudged at my hand, was probably the much-maligned Hugo, his tail going like the clappers against my leg. Another small white dog wove in and out of the boys' legs, its stubby tail wagging with excitement, while the third dog, a dark-grey velvety whippet, watched me with a mournfully sad little face.

'I'm Toby. I'm eight-and-a half and I can ride a bike and play Minecraft.'

'Are you Jessica?'

'Yes, although my friends call me Jess.'

'We're your brothers, what shall we call you?'

'Jess would be just fine.'

'Good. Now we can have the pancakes,' said Ben with feeling. 'I'm starving. We've been waiting for ever.'

'I want sausages,' added Toby. 'We're having brunch today. I like breakfast better because you don't have to wait so long.'

With that, the two of them turned tail, the dogs darting after them, disappearing in the direction of where the delicious breakfast smells were coming from, almost knocking over Alicia who appeared, wiping her hands on a tea towel. 'And do come in,' she said with a sarcastic roll of her eyes at the sight of me abandoned on the threshold. 'Honestly, pair of heathens. I'm sorry. Welcome. Come on in. You'd think I'd starved them the way they carry on. They've both had a bowl of cereal.'

I looked around the hall as I stepped through the low doorway. The narrow, dark hallway had been brightened up by the careful positioning of a big gilt mirror and a vase of bright cottage flowers on a wrought-iron semi-circular table. 'This is lovely,' I said. 'Have you been here long?'

'Thank you.' She moved off, expecting me to follow her along the uneven flagstone floor. 'We moved in not long after Toby was born. We were in Exeter, but Adrian sold the business, staying on as a consultant, so he works from home and doesn't need to go to the office more than once a week.'

'Music publishing,' I said, plucking the knowledge from last evening's conversation.

'That's right. Sheet music. Still something people need to buy. Thank goodness. It keeps the boys in shoes and ponies.' She paused and, looking back over her shoulder, said, 'Sorry, that sounds very flippant. I do appreciate that we're very lucky.'

'I think you've worked hard, too.' From what she said the night before, she ran her own successful online haberdashery business, supplying buttons, ribbons and all sorts of interesting bits and bobs to crafters. I'd taken a look on my phone while we were at dinner and been both impressed and inspired. 'I wish I could knit, or sew, or something.'

'So do I.' She laughed. 'That's how I got started. I'd see all the lovely bits – buy them with the best of intentions to make something amazing – and then never get around to doing it. Or I started and it didn't look anything like the pattern. I amassed a huge collection and became more interested in the trimmings.'

I followed her into the kitchen, which was a complete contrast to the front of the house. Several sets of bi-fold doors on two walls opened out onto a cottage garden, overflowing with colour and shape, bringing a flood of light into the unexpectedly contemporary room. 'Wow. It's like the Tardis.'

'I know.' She gave me a gleeful grin. 'It's beyond my wildest dreams. The only thing I didn't like about the house when we looked at it was the kitchen. Too small, dark and poky.'

'Not anymore.'

'I know.' She hugged herself. 'I love it. Sorry, I'm sure I should be more modest or something, but it's just transformed the house and I love it in here.'

I could see why. The kitchen had smart cream units with walnut-topped counters and an array of top-of-the-range appliances. In the centre of the room was a walnut table with three overhead copper-shaded lights, and beyond that a comfy area with two sofas around a big rug with a small wood-burning stove on the back wall.

'We tend to live in here, all year round.'

'I can see why.'

My dad rose from the table, where he had something in pieces on a sheet of newspaper. 'Morning, Jess.'

'Now you can tidy that lot up and lay the table for breakfast.'

'Yes, dear,' said Dad, coming over to give me a shy hug.

'What are you doing?' I asked intrigued.

'I like to buy and repair old radios. Most of them still work, although they don't pick up digital stations. They'll soon be obsolete but some people still swear by the old Roberts radios. Not much inside has changed.'

'And he makes a right old mess.' The warm smile she sent his way belied the words. 'I'm about to dish up. Oh God, you're not a veggie or anything are you? I forgot to ask, only I've got a ton of bacon and sausage. Local farm shop.'

'If I was, I think I'd be doing a hasty conversion. That bacon smells divine. Although I don't think Ben and Toby would mind. More for them.'

'And the dogs. If you catch either of them feeding the dogs at the table, shout at them. Little toads.'

'Uh-oh, no. I'm planning to be the nice big sister. I hope this is all right.' I pulled two bags of Maltesers out of my handbag.

'Bribery. I see you plan to start as you mean to go on,' said Alicia with a cheerful shake of her head.

'Absolutely,' I agreed.

'Do you want to round them up for me while I start dishing up and *Adrian*,' she said his name meaningfully as he was pottering with his radio again, 'lays the table. They're in the lounge. And make sure Ben switches the television off.'

The two boys were sprawled among a tangle of dogs on one of two enormous sofas watching some cartoon action adventure thing and I vaguely recognised a couple of Marvel characters. 'Brunch is nearly ready,' I said. They both leapt off the sofa, the dogs all jumping up with them and careered away to the kitchen leaving me to study the big room. It was expensively furnished and I realised the velvet sofas were both covered in throws to protect them from the dog hair. I was drawn to the low mahogany occasional table between the double sets of French windows filled with family photographs in silver frames. The biggest was a matt-finished photograph in a frame of Dad and Alicia on what was clearly their wedding day. I smiled at the sight of it, so typically Alicia. It was totally informal; she was holding Dad's hand, laughing her head off at something while he looked down with that fond tender gaze that I'd quickly realised was pretty habitual. Tears pricked my eyes. I was used to Lynn and Richard's happy marriage; there was a lot of banter and happiness there, and I knew they loved each other to bits, but they certainly weren't sentimental or lovey-dovey. Dad and Alicia's affection for each other was utterly heart-warming.

There were lots of pictures of the boys in the expected stages of development, babies, toddlers and the ubiquitous school shot with the hideous standard blueish-purple background. Mum had one like that—

I froze as if I'd conjured it up, but there it was, next to the ones of Ben and Toby. As I looked more closely, I realised there was also a picture of me at my graduation, one of my eighteenth birthday and a recent one.

I swallowed, noticing there were a couple more of me, as if I'd always been part of this family.

To me, it seemed an extraordinarily generous gesture. To be included when they'd been shut out. To be remembered when they'd been forgotten. I knew without even being told that I had a home here.

I scanned the rest of the photographs and my heart faltered at the sight of one tucked at the back. This one was recent, taken this summer. In Aunty Lynn's back garden.

My vision blurred as I stared at the picture. It was me talking to Sam. My head thrown back laughing. I picked up the picture, my thumb rubbing over Sam's face. Sam. My heart replicated that same quick jolt of recognition. The day we met. It brought with it that flare of awareness, the remembrance of clicking with someone. Like Lego. My fingers burrowed into the pocket of my dress, feeling the familiar piece of brick that for some reason I still carried around. I hugged the picture to my chest, overcome by the feelings welling up.

'Jess, are you...?' I turned and my father gave me the most brilliant smile as his gaze fell on the table of photos.

'We always hoped you'd find your way here one day. We were just waiting. You know you'll always have a home here and you'll always be welcome.' The words tumbled out as if he'd been saving them up for a long time.

I nodded, unable to say a word.

'You OK?'

I shook my head. 'No, not really.' I looked down at the picture in my hand and my lip wobbled. 'I've made a terrible mistake.' And I began to cry.

'Terrible mistakes are only the ones that can't be undone. Are you sure it's that terrible?' he asked putting an arm around me and leading me to one of the sofas, somehow snagging a handy box of tissues on the way. He sat down next to me, the tissues on his lap.

Could it be undone? Could Sam forgive me?

I narrowed my eyes at my father. He might even know. I could do with a male perspective.

'I… boyfriend Sam. I finished with him, the day we got back from here.'

'Ah.'

'For stupid reasons.' I turned the picture towards Dad. 'This is Sam. The first day I met him. He had a girlfriend. I don't normally believe in love at first sight but … there was something. A month and a half later he phoned me. He didn't have a girlfriend anymore. We started going out together.' I gave a mirthless laugh. 'We practically moved in together straightaway. It should have been perfect. It almost was.' I laid the photo in my lap and gave my dad a sad smile. 'Except now I was the other woman. Like the one that had supposedly wrecked my mother's life. And it wasn't a nice feeling. His girlfriend was genuinely heartbroken and I felt terrible.'

Dad nodded.

'I thought after a while she would get over him, get used to it. But she didn't. Oh God, she really didn't. She still hasn't.' I looked at him. 'Does this sound familiar?'

He nodded and reached for my hand. 'It does.'

'I kept blaming myself for their break-up and her continued unhappiness. It drove her to do some … stupid, annoying things. She wouldn't, *hasn't*, let go. It's made life difficult for Sam, with his mother, his friends, and it's caused problems for me at work.

'And now I realise … that she is at the root of her own unhappiness. I'm not to blame. And that Sam and I deserve to be happy. I've seen what you and Alicia have. You've built a life together, and that's what's most important.'

Dad nodded. 'It doesn't stop the guilt, but we've built a

good life for ourselves, and I love her very much. You have to make your own happiness, seize it and nurture it. Like gardening, things will grow if you give them the basic nutrients.'

'I bailed on Sam. But I don't know if he'll forgive me.'

Dad laughed and handed me a tissue. 'Alicia is better at this stuff than I am, but even I can tell you, we men are simple souls. It sounds like you and Sam had something special. That's not going to die in a few days. If you're hurting, he's probably hurting too.'

'I think I need to go and see him, but it doesn't change things.' I explained what I'd overheard at Sam's parents' house.

'That's interesting,' said Dad. 'Funnily enough, I have a few friends in the cricketing world. Used to play myself. That's how I met your mum. She was always cricket-mad. Would you like me to make a few enquiries?'

'That would be amazing, although I don't know how it will help.'

'Cricketing men pride themselves on playing the game. Doing the right thing. You've heard the phrase "it just isn't cricket". Well, this definitely doesn't sound like cricket. Leave it with me.'

'Daaad, are you coming? We're starving!' yelled a voice from next door.

'On our way,' he called back, putting a hand under my elbow and drawing me to my feet. 'You can bring him with you, next time you come.'

Chapter Thirty-Two

The heatwave had returned but I'd abandoned my shorts and T-shirt for a simple flowered dress, with pockets, that showed off my legs and the tan I'd built up lying in Dad and Alicia's garden.

I'd spent a lovely couple of days with them and had come back to Tring feeling so much more robust. I hadn't realised how much the situation with Victoria had worn me down. I felt like I was back to my usual optimistic self – although that might have been Alicia's force-of-nature personality rubbing off. We'd become firm friends and I'd completely fallen in love with my naughty brothers, who'd discovered I had a loathing for worms – the less said, the better. My dad was more reserved, but we'd built a quiet friendship over those few days and I treasured his calm wisdom. He was a very lovely man, and I did feel sorry that Mum had missed out on that.

I wasn't sure how I was going to broach it with her that I'd been to see Dad and had accepted Alicia and the boys into my life. I realised that I needed to reassure her that despite everything that had happened, I loved her and she was my mum. Spending a little more time with her was definitely one way of moving forward. Hopefully lunch with Douglas was the start of something for her. I really hoped so.

I also realised that I had to do something about Victoria. Spending the time with Dad and Alicia had further helped me realise that I wasn't responsible for her unhappiness and that she had to take responsibility for her own grief, and not blame me. Today I was going into battle, and although I'd dressed to impress, that was only for one particular person. Everyone else could think what they liked.

Slowly I took the stairs up to the first floor of the cricket club, to the bar area, girding my loins and every other bit of me. Sam's team were out on the pitch at the moment, but I knew that they had to come in for tea at some stage. I could wait, but it was Victoria I wanted to see first.

It didn't take me long to spot her. She was dressed in a navy spotted coat dress with a flowing skirt and matching navy heels; the ensemble would have taken her straight into one of the Queen's garden parties. She was holding court with a couple of other girls, some of whom I recognised from the pub that night, and photos. I think she caught sight of me quite early but she didn't let on for a moment, and then milked it for all she was worth. Like some 1940s starlet, she suddenly looked up and gripped her throat.

Everything about her seemed so fake and artificial, but I knew she must be hurting, and this was a confrontation I didn't relish.

'I don't believe it.' Her clear, cultured tones carried to where I stood. 'Just look what the cat dragged in.'

I smiled even though inside I didn't feel the least bit like smiling. I was here to deliver some cold hard truths, and it looked as if I was going to have to do it front of an audience, which seemed even worse.

'Hello, Victoria,' I said, nodding at the other girls with a friendly smile. I wasn't here to make enemies or trouble. 'Do you think we could have a word?'

Although her smile was patronising, I did catch a glimpse of unease in her eyes. 'You want to talk to me?'

Beneath the bravado there was a touch of anxiety and I realised that perhaps she wasn't as tough as she liked to appear.

'Yes.'

'I can't imagine what you have to say to me.'

I glanced at the other women avidly watching. 'I'd rather do it in private.'

With a toss of her long brown hair she laughed. 'I have no secrets.'

'I do. One of which you put out there. Where I work. Have you any idea the damage you could have done?'

'You do know that my vlog has been taken down.'

'Good,' I said. Holly had texted me on my first day away to say that George's shit-hot lawyer had managed to get it removed, and as no one had identified the house in the comments, the fuss had died down. My job, thankfully, was still mine.

'I don't know what the fuss was about, but somebody's

lawyers got very aggressive.' She eyed me suspiciously. 'I'll find out what you're up to.'

'It's not my secret,' I said levelly, biting back my fury at her shallow curiosity, pricked by sheer vanity. She was used to being Queen Bee and knowing what she wanted to know. I looked deliberately at Victoria's gang. 'I work in a women's refuge,' I paused, letting the words sink in, 'helping women who have nowhere else to go when their partners have turned on them.' Raising my voice, I met the gaze of each of them as I carefully enunciated each word. 'Women who turn up in their slippers, in their nightwear, usually with nothing but their tired, frightened children.' Turning back to Victoria I saw that she was listening with horrified fascination. 'Women with broken hands, black eyes and nothing to their names.' I paused again to allow them to absorb the full horror of what these women had been through. 'Women who've been abused, humiliated and terrified. They have nowhere else to go. We provide a place of safety, where they can start to build their lives again away from the men that terrorised them.' I stopped, to gather myself, to tamp down my anger. 'Their safety relies on the refuge being anonymous.' Taking two steps I stood in front of Victoria. 'And yet you, with your fancy clothes, designer handbags, posh car, put these women, who have nothing, at risk, all for the sake of your desire to get one over on me because I wouldn't tell you what my job was. You put those women in danger and I'll never forgive you for that.'

She gaped and a couple of the other women shuffled uncomfortably.

'But … I didn't—'

'You didn't know. That doesn't excuse it. Why was it so important for you to know? Ask yourself that?'

She stared at me and I could see her trying to justify it.

'You're obsessed. You're not making rational decisions. Following me to work. Puncturing my tyres. Stalking Sam on your phone. And worst of all, wrecking his cricket career. If you really loved him as much as you say you do, why would you do that? Take away something that he loves?'

I focused on Paige. 'Do you know why Sam hasn't been picked this season to play for the county team?'

Her eyes widened at the sudden attention and a group of older men at the bar paused and I could see them tuning in to the conversation.

'Er, no.'

'Haven't you wondered? Mike not said anything?'

Her face sharpened and she gave Victoria a quick, sharp glance. 'Just bad luck,' she suggested, but I could see that my words had made an impression.

Victoria tossed her hair again and shot me a terse, quick smile.

'You don't know anything about it.'

'What, that you've been telling someone not to pick him?'

'Nonsense. Where on earth did you hear that rubbish?'

'Sam's mum, actually.'

I saw her throat dip. *Gotcha*, I thought.

'As if I have any influence.'

'Again, that's not what I heard. I hear you have

considerable influence, as you know someone on the selection committee. I believe it's the chairman.'

She pursed her lips and there it was again, that quick sidelong glance to the bar.

'So you haven't been telling anyone that Sam isn't as committed anymore? Not telling people that he's missed lots of games?' I deliberately projected my voice so it rose above the low-level chatter in the room.

Once again, Victoria slipped another look towards the men and one of them detached himself and came over to stand next to Victoria. I saw the family resemblance immediately.

'Is there a problem, darling?'

'No, Daddy. This is Sam's *ex*-girlfriend.'

He gave me a sour look.

'She's just leaving.'

'I wasn't, actually. It was you I wanted to talk to, Mr Langley-Jones. I understood that cricket was a game played by gentleman of honour and integrity.' My eyes bored into him. 'So I was surprised to hear that you've been vetoing Sam's inclusion in the county side.'

'I don't know where you got that information.'

'That doesn't really matter, because you and I both know it's true, and I heard it from another committee member, if you want to know.' Dad's mate had been extremely informative and checked back through his meeting minutes for me. 'I have copies of the minutes of those meetings.' I didn't, it was a bluff, but I could get them if I had to.

'If the boy's not prepared to play, keeps missing

matches, and isn't showing the necessary commitment, I'm fully justified.'

'Not if the information you're basing that decision on is incorrect. I believe that cricket clubs keep very detailed records of every match. Scores, runs, team names.' Thanks, Dad. I wouldn't have known any of that stuff.

Under his bushy grey eyebrows, Mr Langley-Jones' eyes narrowed. 'So?'

'I think if you were to check, you'd find that Sam's batting averages are higher this year. He's missed two games this season.'

'I'm sure that's not the case,' he blustered, looking at his daughter. 'I'm aware that Sam has missed lots of matches this year.'

I raised an eyebrow. 'And how were you made aware of this?' I was rather proud of myself. I sounded every inch the representative for the defence.

'I don't have to answer to you,' he said, his cheeks turning pink.

'No, you don't. Just your conscience. Which, if I were you, I would check. And I'd check your facts. I'll tell you what I know. You've vetoed Sam's inclusion in the side a total of eleven times this season.'

Paige and another one of Victoria's cronies shared a scandalised stare and I saw Paige mouth a horrified 'Eleven'.

'Because he's missed so many matches.'

'He's missed two,' I repeated, 'one to attend a wedding, which he was supposed to go to with your daughter, and the second to attend a wedding after it had been made clear he was unlikely to be selected until he resumed his relationship with Victoria. You can check the scorebooks.'

'Is this true, Victoria?' asked Mr Langley-Jones.

Victoria turned scarlet under her father's bullfrog outrage.

'You bitch,' said Victoria, her eyes narrowing into squinty little lines as she turned to me. 'Everything was fine until you came along.'

'But I did come along, and I'm not going to apologise for that. At that stage, neither Sam nor I did anything wrong.'

'He was mine, not yours.' Her mouth tightened and she tapped her glossy fingernails on her wine glass. 'You should have left him alone.'

I winced but stood firm against the familiar guilt which was trying to creep back in. 'We don't own people,' I said gently.

Her mouth moved as if there was a lot she wanted to say but couldn't frame the words.

'I can forgive you for being heartbroken. It's not nice to be rejected, but Sam tried to do the right thing.'

'The right thing would have been to stay with me,' she spat.

'Not for him, it wasn't. Would you want him to be miserable?'

'He was perfectly happy until you came along. You ruined everything.'

I sighed. She had a point and now I had to be brutally honest with her.

'Victoria,' I said, more kindly. 'This is real life, not a soap opera or a Victorian melodrama. Sam's a grown man who can make his own choices. The harsh truth is … he didn't love you anymore, and you have to get over that. I'm sorry for that.'

She gasped, still in an actor fashion, looking to her friends for support, but Paige had subtly put a few steps of distance between them, along with the other girls.

'Why do you want Sam? Because you love him? If that were the case you'd want him to be happy, wouldn't you?'

'You need to leave,' she suddenly snapped, looking round, noting the space that had opened up between her and her friends.

'As long as you maintain this myth that Sam is yours, you'll never be happy. I felt sorry for you at first but you need to move on. You can't force someone to love you. My mother did that when my dad left. She's been miserable for years because she couldn't let go. I promise you, you're going to turn into a bitter and unhappy person, if you keep this up.'

'I don't think so.' Her smirk was suddenly triumphant. 'I heard from Sally that you've split up.'

'And has he come running back to you?' I asked the question quietly without any sense of victory because I knew that Sam would never go back to her. It wasn't vanity on my part, but just that sure knowledge of the depth of love that we shared. I knew that the question would cause her more pain than anything else.

For a moment, she lifted her head like a defiant Boudicca, determined to battle on but then her face crumpled, her eyes filling with tears. 'He will.'

I shook my head, feeling a punch of sadness for her. 'That's not going to happen.'

'How do you know?'

'I know Sam. He didn't break up with you lightly. He won't change that decision, and you know him as well as I do. He's a decent, honourable man.'

Her mouth quivered, the full lips oddly loose and shapeless as she tried to form words, but at last the defeat registered. Suddenly she looked smaller as if she'd shrunk into herself. 'What am I going to do?' she whispered, and I felt desperately sorry for her, but without the guilt and sympathy that I'd originally felt. For her own sake she had to move on. I'd seen first-hand what could happen if she didn't.

I caught Paige's eye and we exchanged a brief wordless message. She nodded at me and crossed to Victoria, putting her arm around the weeping woman's shoulders and led her away to the ladies.

There was a sudden hush in the immediate vicinity and the other women all lifted their heads, like a row of wide-eyed meerkats, and looked beyond me. In the same moment, I realised that the pitch below the balcony was now empty.

'Jess?'

I whirled around at the sound of Sam's voice.

'What are you doing here?' he demanded, already striding through the tables towards me, ripping off his gloves.

As soon as my eyes locked on his furious blue ones, my

heart which was beating furiously still managed to give a little sigh of relief.

Even so, my knees decided to play silly buggers and were threatening to give way. He was gorgeous. I was an idiot. I loved him. Drinking in every familiar feature of his face, I heaved in a breath, wondering how I'd ever seriously thought I could leave him.

'I came to put things right,' I said, my eyes never leaving his.

'About bloody time.' Sam scowled and, throwing down his helmet on a nearby table, strode over to me to stand in front of me, completely heedless of the bright-eyed interest of all around us.

'I don't give a toss about playing cricket, Jess.' He reached forward and took one of my hands, linking his fingers through mine and bringing it up between us. 'We fit, remember.' Lowering his head, he kissed my knuckles one by one. Inside, a little part of me melted. I loved him so much. 'Lego, Jess, Lego.'

I gave him a watery smile, looking up into his earnest blue eyes.

'Lego, Sam, Lego.'

I reached up and kissed him on the corner of the mouth and whispered, 'I love you.'

'I should bloody well hope so,' he said before kissing me back a lot more thoroughly.

When he let go, I realised we had quite an audience, and most of the women were looking positively misty-eyed, while the men were looking stunned, awkward or impressed.

'And I can tell you for nothing,' he said glaring around at his friends, 'I'm not going back out on that pitch until you agree to marry me.'

There was a collective gasp, not just from the women.

I grinned at the appalled expression on Mike's face as I realised that the whole clubhouse had gone silent.

Well, they could all go and stuff themselves because I certainly wasn't about to provide them with any further entertainment. With that lightning turn of mind that demonstrated so many times how in tune with each other we were, Sam glared at everyone before saying, 'I'm done with the emotional blackmail. The threats, the intimidation, the petty acts of vandalism. We'll move away if need be and start again. I love Jess and I want to spend the rest of my life with her and nothing is changing that.'

He snatched my hand and pulled me out of the room, tugging me down the stairs and out of the front door. Then, with a masterful move that had my heart melting even more, he pinned me against the wall. His hands were on either side of my head, his blue eyes boring into me with furious passion.

'Jess Harper. I love you, and you aren't bloody pulling that trick again. Where've you been all week?' I ran my hands up and down his back, savouring the bumps and curves of his spine, pressing against the broad muscle beneath his shoulder blades, my fingers inventorying the familiar geography of his body, and my whole system humming with sheer pleasure. I was back where I belonged. 'I've been sitting outside your flat every night waiting for you to come home.'

My heart almost burst at the sudden anguish in his eyes.

'I'm sorry. I went to see my dad,' I said, breathing in deeply. 'Realised that I'd got everything wrong.'

'Well, I could have told you that,' he said indignantly, before lowering his head to kiss me with so much tenderness that I thought I might faint from the erratic pace of my heart.

When we both came up for air, he stroked the hair from my face. 'I'm not sure I can let you out of my sight again.'

'Don't you have a game to play?'

His thumb rubbed along my jawline. 'I was serious back there. I'm not going back out until you agree to marry me. We had plans, remember?'

'I do remember. I don't remember the marrying part.'

'I want it to be official. For everyone to know that this is for keeps,' he paused, stroking my face, his eyes locked on mine, 'till death do us part.'

'Oh, Sam.' My throat closed and I could barely breathe. I loved him so much. The words weren't enough but they'd have to do for now. 'I love you.'

From his pocket he produced the familiar piece of red Lego.

With a smile I dug in my pocket and pulled out my piece of blue Lego. Taking his, I snapped the two together and held them up.

He grinned. 'I knew we clicked the minute I met you. That instant spark. You felt it too.'

'I did. Now before I get lynched, you'd better go back to the game.'

'Will you stay?'

'For a while,' I looked at my watch, 'but then I'm going to the estate agents to change the brief. We're staying in Tring. We've got a future to start building.'

THE END

Don't miss *The Saturday Morning Park Run*, a joyously uplifting and romantic novel full of fresh starts, friendship and the unexpected places we find happiness...

Get your copy today!

Acknowledgments

Normally I have lots of people to thank but this book is a little different from my others. It was one of those ideas that appeared from nowhere and wouldn't leave me alone. It was my secret project and I wrote it in my spare time, even though I was supposed to be working on other books. The words simply flowed out and it was a joy to write. I completely fell in love with both my characters, Jess and Sam, and I'm hoping that readers will too.

I guess I'm a little possessive of this one, it is all mine! However, I must thank my brilliant editor, Charlotte Ledger, who had the faith in me to let me go off on a tangent and as she says made me 'dig deeper' to make this book even better.

Despite considering this book as my baby, I would be remiss in not acknowledging that there are in fact lots of people behind the scenes who do all the work once the book is written and I'd like to thank my super agent, Broo, the whole brilliant team at One More Chapter and the fantastic Rachel Gilbey and her amazing team of bloggers. I make no apology for all the superlatives there, I am incredibly lucky to have such a wonderful professional team around me. They all rock!

YOUR NUMBER ONE STOP

ONE MORE CHAPTER

FOR PAGETURNING BOOKS

One More Chapter is an
award-winning global
division of HarperCollins.

Sign up to our newsletter to get our
latest eBook deals and stay up to date
with our weekly Book Club!
<u>Subscribe here.</u>

Meet the team at
<u>www.onemorechapter.com</u>

Follow us!

 @OneMoreChapter_
 @OneMoreChapter
 @onemorechapterhc

Do you write unputdownable fiction?
We love to hear from new voices.
Find out how to submit your novel at
<u>www.onemorechapter.com/submissions</u>